Josie watched w into chairs offstage while she was stuck sitting on the desk next to Robert. She hadn't even been this close to him when they sat by the lake in Yosemite. She kept her eyes pointed straight ahead, but she could still hear his soft breathing and the occasional rustle as he shifted position.

"Josie, I'm sorry."

He spoke so softly she wasn't sure she heard him at first. Her eyes went wide, and she turned to look at him. He cast his gaze down as soon as her eyes met his and he opened his mouth again.

"I—"

"All right, I think we've got it," the director said. Robert clapped his mouth shut, and Josie looked straight ahead again.

Good gravy, she hadn't expected an apology. But did he mean it? He *was* an actor. Her heart thumped. She wanted to forgive him, to go back to that easygoing companionship they'd started to form, but would he get the wrong impression again? She couldn't bear going through this twice.

"Josie?"

She looked at him again. His eyebrows rode high on his forehead, and his eyes darted back and forth, studying hers. He was waiting for her to say something. She could accept his apology, but they couldn't be friends, only coworkers. She hardened her expression.

"Okay," she said. A pang of guilt ripped through her when his face fell, but it was for the best.

Praise for Sarah Hendess

SECOND CHANCES IN HOLLYWOOD has been a finalist in the Florida Writers Association's Royal Palm Literary Awards competition.

Second Chances in Hollywood

by

Sarah Hendess

Second Chances in Hollywood

Cover Art by *Diana Carlile.*

The Wild Rose Press, Inc.
PO Box 708
Adams Basin, NY 14410-0708
Visit us at www.thewildrosepress.com

Publishing History
First Edition, 2023
Trade Paperback ISBN 978-1-5092-4740-0
Digital ISBN 978-1-5092-4741-7

Published in the United States of America

Dedication

For my sister,
who didn't put up with that garbage either

Acknowledgements

Thank you to my amazing husband, Dan, for his love and support and for giving me the most incredible little boy. Thank you to Mom for raising me on the Westerns that inspired this book, and to Dad for making me learn to type so I could actually write it. Thank you to my sister and the cousins squad for picking me up after each rejection and being just as excited as I was when my little project found a home with The Wild Rose Press.

Thanks to Jane Linnegar for being my first reader and making several early suggestions that helped bring this book to life. To my friends who sent encouraging, funny, and sometimes sarcastic memes, thank you for not letting me take myself too seriously. And thanks as well to my amazing beta readers, Kristin, Dee, Jennifer, and Leslie. Ladies, this book wouldn't be half as good without you. To the Seminole County Writers group, thanks for teaching me so much about the art of writing.

Thank you to my editor, Nan Swanson, for being such a great cheerleader for this book and for walking me through the process of publishing my debut.

To my teachers, Jan Bretz-Hughes, Theresa Corcoran, Kristine Leonardo, the late Martha Piontek, and the late David Dixon: The skills you taught me were valuable, but your unwavering belief in me was priceless.

Finally, to the good people of Hays, Kansas: Your town is lovely. Please don't send me hate mail.

Chapter One

March 1959

Josie prayed she wouldn't have to dodge another flying bedpan. Or, if she did, that this patient's aim wasn't as good as the last one. Taking a deep breath, she tucked a lock of dark hair back under her white nurse's cap and checked the chart to make sure she had the right room. Merrill Reynolds, male, age forty-two, cholecystectomy. Bingo.

He wasn't her patient, but Cassie had asked her to check on him.

"Dr. Greene took him off the morphine this morning," she'd said. "But when I went in there, he shook his head and said, 'You're not right either,' like he was still loopy. But otherwise, he made perfect sense. It was strange."

Josie agreed to go in. Cassie was her best friend and looking in on Mr. Reynolds would give her an excuse to put off going back into Mrs. Katz's room. She knew the old woman was in pain, but Mrs. Katz must have played baseball in another life, because she had one heck of an arm.

Josie smiled and shook her head as she turned the knob to Mr. Reynolds's room. Her brothers insisted that California was a different world from their home in Kansas, but patients here in Hollywood were the same as they were back in Hays, only with private rooms.

"Mr. Reynolds?" she said as she stepped into the room. "I'm Nurse Donovan. Nurse Felix is tied up with another patient right now. How's your pain?"

The man in the bed was looking out the window. There wasn't much to see, just a couple of tall palm trees bordering the parking lot. He turned his face toward her, a cigarette jutting from between his lips. With his balding head and heavy glasses, he looked older than forty-two, but patients usually looked rough the day after a gallbladder removal.

He stubbed his cigarette out in an ashtray next to his bed. "Tolerable," he said, his voice raspy. His eyes were wide and his gaze never left her face, but he could respond appropriately to a question, so that was good.

Josie smiled and pressed two fingers to the underside of his wrist. She looked at the second hand on her wristwatch and counted the little thumps against her fingertips.

The hair on the back of her neck prickled, and she flicked her eyes to him. He was still studying her intensely, his mouth slightly agape.

"Mr. Reynolds, are you all right?"

"You, my dear, are perfect," he said. He beamed up at her, eyes slightly unfocused, like she was the Madonna.

Cassie was right about his confusion. Time to call for Dr. Greene.

"Thank you," she said, tucking the blankets around him. "If you need anything, just ring." She turned to go.

"Wait." Mr. Reynolds's voice was urgent. She turned back. "This is an odd question, but have you ever done any acting?"

She stopped herself just before she rolled her eyes. Apparently, she'd spent two years in nursing school only for everyone to assume she was a struggling actress just because she'd moved to Hollywood. But this fellow didn't seem to be wrapped real tight.

Play along, Josie Girl. See what happens.

"A few school plays and one disastrous church Christmas pageant when I was ten. I was playing Mary, and I tripped and crashed into the manger. Squashed the baby Jesus flat." She chuckled. "Thank goodness we were using a doll and not a real baby."

Mr. Reynolds's eyes brightened, and he laughed. He almost immediately winced and clutched his right side, just under his rib cage.

Josie cringed. "I'm sorry," she said, laying a hand on his shoulder while he panted through his pain. "I shouldn't have made you laugh so soon after surgery."

He waved his other hand dismissively. "That was exquisite delivery," he said when he finally relaxed against his pillows, his face a shade paler than before. "My dear, do you know what I do for a living?"

Josie shook her head.

He smiled. "I produce a television show on WBC called *Gunslingers*. Perhaps you've heard of it?"

Good gravy. Had she *heard* of it? She and Cassie never missed an episode of the exploits of Sheriff Samuel Anderson of Folsom, California, and his two young deputies. They met up every Saturday night to watch the show together. Always at Cassie's apartment, though. Josie didn't have a television set. Too expensive.

"I certainly have," she said when she found her voice again. "My best friend is madly in love with every man on the show."

He grinned. "And how about you? Do you have a favorite, or do you love them all too?"

Oh, dear. Was he looking for a particular answer? The young men who played the deputies were both handsome, but unlike Cassie, Josie made a point of not paying much mind to handsome young men. She'd made that mistake before and didn't plan to repeat it. And based on what she'd heard from other fans of the show, women seemed to be squarely in either the Judah Mitchell or the Deacon Bell camp, and the rivalry between the two was fierce. She thought fast.

"Sheriff Anderson. He reminds me of my father."

Mr. Reynolds cocked his head. Clearly, he hadn't expected this response. But then he smiled.

"That's interesting." He studied her for another few moments. Heat crept up the back of her neck. She was usually the one doing the scrutinizing, not the other way around. What did this man want with her?

"How old are you?" he said.

"Twenty-two." She didn't usually answer patients' personal questions, but she was so flummoxed she'd spoken without thinking.

Mr. Reynolds took his wallet off the bedside table and flipped it open. Josie groaned inwardly. Wealthy patients—and there were a lot of those in Hollywood—were always trying to tip her like she

4

was the waitstaff. She plastered on her best fake smile, ready to politely refuse the money, no matter how much it was. But he pulled out a small white rectangle and handed it to her.

She took it and flipped it over to see the printing on the other side. It was his business card, complete with his phone number at the network studios.

"We're adding a character to the show next season," he said. "Sheriff Anderson's grown daughter. I'd like you to audition."

Josie couldn't clap her hand over her mouth fast enough to stop her laughter. The man frowned.

"I'm sorry, Mr. Reynolds," she said, swallowing the last of her snickers. "But I'm a nurse. A nurse from *Kansas*, of all places. Wouldn't you rather have a professional actress?"

He lifted one eyebrow. "My dear, I've been auditioning professional actresses for months, and I haven't found what I'm looking for." Mr. Reynolds paused. "But I think you just might fit the bill."

This was absurd. Something was clearly wrong with him. She should call for Dr. Greene.

"I'm flattered," she said, handing the card back, "but I can't imagine I'm your girl."

He pressed the card into her hand. "I'll be the judge of that. Come audition."

Josie sighed. He wasn't going to let up on this, and it wouldn't do to agitate him so soon after his surgery. "I'll think about it. But I'm not sure I can even act."

He scoffed. "Half the Oscar winners in Hollywood couldn't act their way out of an empty room when they started out. We can teach acting, but we can't teach a personality. Come audition." He glanced down at his hospital gown. "But maybe give me a couple weeks to recover first."

****

"You have to go," Cassie said.

Josie rolled her eyes. She never should have told Cassie about her conversation with Mr. Reynolds. "You just want me to get autographs from whatever-their-names-are."

"You know they're Beau Fraser and Robert Coolidge, but that's not the point," Cassie said. She reached across the cafeteria table and took Josie's hand. "You came to California to start over and have an adventure. Here it is! It's landed right in your lap, and you don't want to go?"

"He can't possibly want me. I'm not...special."

"You said he used the word 'personality.' " Cassie let go of Josie's hand and leaned back in her chair.

"Which he couldn't possibly have figured out in the five minutes I was in his room."

Cassie flashed a quick smile at a young resident walking past with his lunch tray, then turned back to Josie. "He's a Hollywood producer. It's his job to figure people out fast. Call him. Go for the audition. What do you have to lose?"

Cassie made an annoying amount of sense sometimes. What *did* she have to lose? The worst that could happen would be Mr. Reynolds sending her home when he discovered that no amount of personality could ever cover up her bad acting. At least she'd get a great story to tell.

"All right," she said, breaking into a grin. "I'll go."

Second Chances in Hollywood

Chapter Two

Robert *hated* being late.

Reliability wasn't always an easy trait to find in this town, and he enjoyed his reputation as one of the few actors who never missed a call time.

He checked his wristwatch: 10:22. He had eight minutes.

The traffic light turned green, he stomped the gas pedal, and the Corvette roared forward. Please, God, let him make it.

He couldn't even think of a good story to spin if he were late, and the truth probably wouldn't get him much sympathy. The part where he put his six-year-old son, Matthew, on a plane yesterday back to his ex-wife in South Carolina and spent the rest of the afternoon steeping in loneliness, sure. But probably not the part where he'd distracted himself that night with a redheaded waitress he'd met a couple weeks ago. He'd woken up at her place only twenty minutes before he needed to be at the studio.

In his defense, *Gunslingers* was on hiatus. He shouldn't have to be at the studio at all for another six weeks.

He tore onto the studio lot, gave a cursory wave to the security guard at the gate, and swung into a parking spot next to the main *Gunslingers* soundstage. Thank goodness it was near the front of the lot.

"Coolidge!" Merrill Reynolds's voice rang out when Robert burst through the door. Both men checked their wristwatches. "On the nose." Merrill tapped the face of his watch. "Impressive."

Robert shrugged and tried to look nonchalant, but that was tough given that he was out of breath and wearing yesterday's rumpled clothes. He ran a hand through his thick, dark hair, hoping it wasn't obvious he'd just rolled out of bed. A lumpy bed, at that. Next to a redhead who was awfully cute at the diner but who snored like a trucker and kept him up half the night. He probably hadn't fallen asleep until 3:00 or 4:00 a.m.

A heavy sadness washed over him. Geez, he was a mess. Seemed every time he met a woman, she turned out to be interested only in being seen with a TV star. They were never interested in *him*. And he wasn't even that famous. But his house felt so empty sometimes with just him in it that, like a fool, he kept trying anyway. He sighed. Maybe he should just get a dog.

Merrill stared hard at him, eyes narrowed in that squinting expression he always made right before he criticized him for something. Robert scowled. The producer had set his teeth on edge the first time they'd met, early last year at his *Gunslingers* audition. Robert asked some questions about the direction Merrill expected the character of Deputy Deacon Bell to take, and Merrill laughed in his face and told him this was a Western, not Shakespeare. He should have listened to his gut and walked out right then. How could he not be serious about his character? It was *his* name people read on the opening credits. *His* face on the screen. *His* reputation. Merrill could go on to produce other programs, but this was Robert's breakout role, the one that would affect all the other roles he'd ever get. But Merrill didn't care about any career except his own. He was shaped like an ice cube and had a personality to match.

Before the producer could say anything, Charlie Lyon lumbered over and greeted Robert with a warm handshake. Some of the tension in Robert's neck and shoulders loosened. It was hard not to relax around Charlie. He was well cast as the fatherly Sheriff Anderson of 1865 Folsom, California.

"Matthew get home all right?" Charlie's rich, deep voice could soothe an angry tiger. Robert relaxed another degree and nodded. He'd only mentioned his son's visit one time, but Charlie always remembered stuff like that.

"Merrill," Charlie said, "why don't you go get the young lady? I'll bring our friend here up to speed." He draped an arm around Robert's shoulders.

Robert wasn't chummy with his castmates, but right now, he was so grateful for Charlie's intervention that he wouldn't have complained if the older man had dipped him backward and kissed him. He didn't have the energy to deal with Merrill this morning.

This audition was pointless anyway. Merrill was being so picky with this new role that he'd likely send the girl packing after ten minutes, just like he had all the others. Certainly not worth dragging the whole cast in when they were supposed to be on vacation. But Merrill insisted he wanted a love interest for Beau Fraser's character, Judah Mitchell, which didn't make any sense. The ages of Beau's and Robert's characters were never given on the show, but Robert was clearly older by several years. Six, to be exact. Wouldn't the older deputy pair off first? But unlike him, Beau stood in Merrill's good favor, so Beau's character got depth and Robert's remained the comedy relief.

Besides, what was a female character going to *do* on the show? *Gunslingers* was about a sheriff in the Wild West. The only Western that pulled off having a woman in the regular cast was *Gunsmoke*, and Miss Kitty's occupation as a "saloonkeeper" was questionable at best. This had to be a desperate attempt to pull in viewers. Last season's ratings had been so terrible it was a miracle WBC even renewed them.

Charlie led him onto the stage and handed him a sheaf of papers.

"Here's the scene, in case you're rusty," Charlie said.

Robert flipped through the pages. It was the same scene they'd used for the three-dozen-or-so auditions they'd held since January for the part of Mary Anderson. And it was full of Deacon Bell's usual banality: *Yes, Sheriff; No, Sheriff; Do you think that's a good idea, Sheriff?*

He sighed. He was so sick of Westerns. When he moved to Los Angeles four years ago, his first few roles had been in Western films, and then he'd landed this show. Not that he would have been better off on any other television program. Seemed all anyone was making these days were Westerns. *The Life and Legend of Wyatt Earp*, *Gunsmoke*, *Rawhide*, *Wagon Train*, *The Rifleman*, *Have Gun—Will Travel*, the list went on and on. He rubbed his temples. What he'd give for someone to make a show set in outer space.

Think of Matthew, he reminded himself, picturing his little boy's huge smile. Those hazel eyes just like his, and that nose just like Mom's. *Gunslingers* may not be his dream role, but it paid well. He'd treated himself to a few niceties, like the Corvette, but he kept most of his expenses low so he could send more to his boy.

"I don't know about you, but I can't wait to meet this girl," Beau said, stubbing out a cigarette. Robert peered at him over the script pages. Only twenty-two years old, the skinny, curly-haired Beau Fraser was, as the girls would say, "gorgeous." It had to be his bright blue eyes. Girls always went for the guys with blue eyes.

"Why?" Robert said. They'd met dozens of girls the past few months. He didn't see why this one should be special.

"Merrill says she's different. He discovered her at the hospital. She's a *nurse*." Beau wiggled his eyebrows.

Robert rolled his eyes. This kid couldn't take anything seriously if it meant his life. "Hoping she'll wear her uniform for you?" he said.

"I'd rather she wear nothing at all, but hey, whatever the lady wants—"

Charlie cuffed Beau on the back of the head. "That's my on-screen daughter you're talking about."

"Touchy, touchy," Beau grumbled, rubbing his head.

"Touchy nothing," Charlie said, a growl in his voice. "You won't speak that way around any lady on this set, you understand?" He caught Robert's eye. "That goes for you too."

"He barely speaks to anyone anyway," Beau said, scowling.

Robert was about to retort, just to prove Beau wrong, when Merrill reentered the soundstage, a slender brunette trailing behind him.

"Gentlemen, may I introduce Miss Josephine

Donovan," Merrill said. He took the young lady's elbow and drew her up alongside him. Robert sucked in a breath.

Chapter Three

Suddenly, Robert was eight years old again, trying to get his wind back after falling out of the pin oak in the back yard.

If his mother had been there, she would have smacked him for staring while Charlie and Beau shook hands with Miss Donovan and introduced themselves. The young lady wore a sensible, calf-length blue shirtwaist dress with the sleeves rolled up above her elbows and a skinny black belt that cinched at her waist. She clutched a small handbag.

But it was her eyes that captivated him.

She had the greenest eyes he'd ever seen, bright and large like lily pads. With those eyes and her raven hair, she was what Mom would call "Black Irish." Even with her hair pinned up, he could tell it was long, probably falling to the middle of her back when it was loose. He imagined pulling out her bobby pins one by one, letting the long, dark tresses tumble over her shoulders.

Charlie cleared his throat.

Robert looked around and realized everyone was staring at him. They must be waiting for him to say something. He snapped into Deacon Bell's easy, relaxed persona and extended his hand.

"Robert Coolidge," he said, grinning. "A pleasure to meet you, Miss Donovan."

She clasped his hand, and a zap of electricity

traveled up his arm. He couldn't move. He just stood there, clutching Miss Donovan's hand like it was welded to his, and staring into those bright green eyes. She stared back, her lips slightly parted.

"Call me Josie," she said, her voice barely louder than a whisper.

"Josie," he whispered back.

Merrill clapped his hands once, and Robert jumped backward, letting go of Josie's hand.

"Let's get started," Merrill said. "Gentlemen, you know the drill for this scene. Miss Donovan, stand just offstage with Charlie. He'll bring you in to introduce you to Judah and Deacon."

Robert smiled, watching her eyes dart around as she tried to take in the enormous set for the sheriff's office. He remembered feeling overwhelmed the first time he stepped onto a soundstage. With all the boom microphones, lights, and cameras so close to the performers, it was more intimidating than a theater stage. And she probably didn't even have theater experience. Beau said she was a nurse. She must feel completely out of her depth.

Charlie led her to their position, Robert and Beau took places in the sheriff's office, and Merrill called "Action!"

Charlie, now as Sheriff Anderson, led Josie through a door onto the set, greeted his deputies, and introduced his daughter, Mary.

Robert was impressed. Gone was the nervousness Josie had worn on her face when she'd arrived. She looked every bit a confident young lady on her father's arm.

"You'll treat her with even more respect than you

treat me," Charlie boomed in his Sheriff Anderson voice. "She's a member of our little family now."

"You don't expect her to make arrests, do you?" Robert said as Deacon Bell.

Wearing his famous Judah Mitchell grin, Beau sidled up to Josie, winked at her, and said, "Sweetheart, you can arrest me *any* time."

Josie rolled her eyes. "Oh, Judah, you're *so* funny," she said, her voice drier than Death Valley.

All three men broke character and burst out laughing. Even Merrill joined in. All the other girls who'd auditioned had giggled through this line, batting their eyelashes and practically throwing themselves at Beau. Robert never saw Josie's dripping sarcasm coming.

This kid was a natural.

"Cut!" Merrill called when he finally quit laughing.

Josie crossed her arms over her stomach, Mary Anderson's confidence suddenly gone. "Did I mess up?"

"My dear, that was inspired," Charlie said. The tip of Josie's freckled button nose wrinkled when she smiled.

Damn, that was cute.

He got caught up staring at her again and didn't realize they were running more lines until Beau poked him and whispered a page number. He jumped and flipped pages so fast he gave himself a papercut down the side of his right index finger. Blood bloomed along the split skin. Grumbling, he whipped his handkerchief out of his pocket and wrapped up his finger.

They read two more scenes. Josie used that flawless deadpan when Mary was speaking to one of the deputies, but she struggled when Mary was talking to her father.

After a bit of prompting from Merrill, she found a warmth and devotion to use in scenes with the sheriff. Once she nailed it, Merrill asked her to take a seat in the hall outside the soundstage while the men had a quick chat.

"The decision is mine, but I'd like your thoughts," Merrill said when the stage door closed behind Josie.

Robert's spine went ramrod straight. Merrill hadn't asked them about any of the others. This had to be a good sign.

"I love her," Charlie said, sitting down on the edge of the stage. "She's how I imagine my daughter will be in a few years. You want no-nonsense, you've found her."

Merrill nodded. "Beau?"

"You heard how she delivered that first line. I think that speaks for itself."

"Coolidge?" Merrill said.

Robert's mind swirled with images of black hair and green eyes. He'd never wanted anyone to get a part so badly. He fiddled with the corner of the handkerchief still wrapped around his forefinger.

Say something in her favor without sounding like a fool, R.J. You can do it.

He took a deep breath and let it out slowly, like he always did before playing a scene. Right now he needed to play vintage Robert Coolidge, not this gobsmacked kid who had hijacked his brain when Josie walked in.

"She's obviously green," he said, his voice steady and disinterested. "She has no idea what to do with her hands. But Beau's right. She's got the instincts. If you're serious about adding this character, I think she's your girl."

17

He deserved an Emmy for that performance.

Merrill nodded, and one corner of his mouth twitched up. "I'll bring her back in. Let's talk to her. Pull up some chairs, would you?" He poked his head out the door, and a moment later, Josie returned, smiling shyly. Merrill motioned to the circle of five director's chairs the men had assembled, and she sat. Robert zipped into a chair next to her. She glanced at him, dug into her handbag, and handed him what appeared to be a slip of paper. He looked at it.

She'd handed him a Band-Aid.

Why had she given him a Band-Aid? He stared at her blankly.

"For your finger," she said, pointing to the makeshift bandage on his index finger.

He blinked several times. "You carry Band-Aids in your purse?"

She smiled, her nose wrinkling. "I'm a nurse."

His face flushed. "Right. Thank you." Feeling stupid, he unwrapped his handkerchief and stuck the Band-Aid on in its place.

"So, Miss Donovan," Merrill said, "we know you're a nurse, but we don't know much else. Are you from Los Angeles?"

Robert leaned toward her. He suddenly wanted to know everything about her.

She shook her head. "I've only been in California two years. I'm originally from Kansas."

There was no way to describe her accent except "flat"—like the landscape in Kansas, he supposed.

"Is your family still there?" Charlie said.

"Yes, we have a sunflower farm just outside of Hays."

18

A *sunflower* farm? Holy mackerel, this girl was interesting. A thousand questions came to mind, but he figured it was safest to go with the most obvious one. She probably already thought he was stupid for being confused by a Band-Aid.

"What brought you to California?" he said. He thought she flinched, but the movement was so quick he might have imagined it.

She shrugged and smiled. "What brings anybody to California? Adventure. I wanted a change of scenery, so I took the California nursing boards and got a job at Hollywood Presbyterian."

Robert grinned. He'd been a small-town kid once himself, spending his whole childhood dreaming of seeing the world. And it looked like he'd just met another kid who'd been lucky enough to pull it off too. He looked across their little circle at Merrill to see his reaction.

"Are you married?" the producer asked.

Damn. He hadn't thought about that. Josie looked to be in her early twenties. She could easily have a husband. He gripped the arms of his chair.

Josie swallowed. "No."

He let go of his chair.

"Boyfriend?" Merrill said.

Josie's eyes flicked upward before she shook her head, and Robert let his hands fall into his lap.

"Good," Merrill said, and for the first time ever, Robert agreed with him. Silently. "Mary Anderson is supposed to fall in love with Judah Mitchell," Merrill continued. "It would ruin the illusion for audiences if our actress was seen out and about with some other man."

Robert clenched his jaw to keep himself from saying something Merrill would make him regret. Merrill never

19

said a word to the men about not prowling around. He glanced at Josie and saw her eyes had narrowed, but she stayed quiet.

"And speaking of men," Merrill said, "Mary Anderson is our first recurring female character. Except for the makeup crew and a few extras now and again, we don't have many women on set. How do you think you'd handle working with just men?"

Josie didn't miss a beat.

"I have five older brothers, Mr. Reynolds. Believe me, these kittens will be no problem."

Robert laughed along with Merrill, Beau, and Charlie. This girl would keep them all on their toes.

Merrill caught the gaze of each cast member one by one, and Robert's heart quickened. Beau and Charlie each grinned and nodded. When Merrill caught his eye, he did the same.

"That's settled then," Merrill said. He stood, crossed the circle to Josie, and extended his hand. "Welcome to *Gunslingers*, Miss Donovan."

Season Two had just gotten a *lot* more interesting.

Chapter Four

Josie's head swam on the bus ride home from the WBC studios. In only about an hour and a half, she'd met and acted with the stars of one of her favorite television programs and been offered a part on the show.

It had been strange to meet the cast in color. Even if Cassie's television set were color—which it wasn't—*Gunslingers* shot in black-and-white. Color photos of Beau Fraser often ran in the celebrity magazines Cassie read, so Josie knew he had those bright blue eyes that most girls would kill for. And it was obvious even in black-and-white that Charlie Lyon's eyes were dark. But she'd never realized Robert Coolidge had such a pretty hazel. He was as tall as he looked on TV—probably a good inch or two over six feet. She rubbed her right hand, remembering his strong, warm grip when they shook hands. And that smile. She'd never noticed on television that he got a dimple in his left cheek when he smiled.

The bus hit a bump in the road, and she bounced out of her reverie.

Don't get so star-struck you forget why you moved here in the first place, Josie Girl.

She cut herself a break. A lot had happened this morning. Thank goodness Charlie, as Mr. Lyon had said to call him, had come along to Mr. Reynolds's—no, *Merrill's*—office to help hammer out the details. She never would have known what questions to ask. Charlie asked about publicity photos, and the two men started talking about taking her on location in June and setting her up with acting classes and then something about filing a Taft-Hartley report because she wasn't a member of the Screen Actors Guild... It was too much to take in. At the end of it all, Charlie gave her his home phone number and told her to please call any time she had a question. She tucked that precious slip of paper deep in her purse where she couldn't lose it.

"This isn't a full-time role," Merrill had said during the meeting. "We're going to bill you as a recurring guest star, at least for this season. "If the character is well received, we can consider making you permanent for Season Three."

She signed a contract to appear in fifteen of the season's thirty-four episodes. She nearly fainted when she saw she'd earn $1,000 per episode. She'd make three times as much working every second or third week on *Gunslingers* as she did in an entire year of full-time nursing.

Good gravy.

She looked around at the other people on the bus: a mother with two children, three teenaged boys Josie suspected were cutting school, and a handful of men in suits. How many of them would see her on television in a few months?

Did all actors and actresses feel like this when they landed their first part? Maybe. But then again, most of them planned on becoming actors and actresses. They worked for years to catch a break. All she'd done was check on a patient. Thank goodness the bus reached her stop just then. She needed fresh air.

"You should quit at the hospital," Cassie said late

that afternoon. As she and Josie had planned, she'd come straight to Josie's tiny apartment after work to hear about the audition. Josie's ears were still ringing from the scream Cassie let out when she announced she'd gotten the part. "Why deal with grouchy patients and doctors if you don't have to?"

"This role might not be permanent. I may need a job to go back to." Josie took a sip of her bourbon. Cassie had insisted they toast her big break, and a bottle of Jim Beam was the only alcohol Josie had. They were on their second round. "The hospital needs nurses badly enough I'm sure they'll let me stay on part time. I'll know well in advance what weeks I need to be on set, so scheduling shouldn't be a problem."

Lounging in a corner of Josie's ancient sofa, Cassie tucked her legs under her. The secondhand couch creaked loudly. "That's true. Nurse Fletcher will be relieved to have you at all." She sipped her drink. "How did the family react when you told them?"

Cassie *would* ask that. Josie tried to hide her face behind her lowball, and Cassie's jaw dropped.

"You haven't told them?"

Embarrassed, Josie shrank in her armchair. "Not yet." She paused. "I might not have even told them I was auditioning."

"Josephine!"

"I didn't expect anything to come of it. I figured we'd all get a good laugh over it after the fact."

"You have to say *something*. They're expecting you home next month."

Josie drained her bourbon and dropped her head back against her chair. "I know," she groaned. She'd requested the first two weeks of May off from the hospital for a visit home. She'd purchased her train ticket and everything. But Merrill had her in six weeks of acting classes during that same time. He wanted her ready to join the cast in mid-June when they traveled to Yosemite National Park for on-location filming. The acting coach would work around her hospital schedule, but he couldn't very well come to Kansas with her. She'd have to stay in town.

Josie squinted at the clock on the other side of the living room and struggled through her bourbon-induced haze to adjust for the time zones. It was 7:30 in Kansas. All her brothers were probably putting their kids to bed.

"I'll call them tomorrow," she said. She had no idea how she'd get them to believe she wasn't kidding, but she'd try. Maybe it would be easier to figure out once the Jim Beam wore off.

****

Josie twiddled the phone cord the next afternoon, debating which brother to call.

Ben might be a good option. He'd probably be downright delighted by her news. He loved anything bizarre, but he wasn't great with details. Josie frowned. By the time Ben finished telling the others, the story would probably include her marrying Marlon Brando or some such nonsense.

Better to go with Leighton. A general surgeon, he lived in Wichita, a few hours away from the old homestead in Hays. She loved all her brothers, but Leighton understood her the best. After things went bad, he'd been the first to realize she needed to get far away and helped her get to California. Not only would he take the news well, but he'd also pass it along correctly to the rest of the family.

Josie checked the clock—it was a quarter to six in Hays. Leighton should be home. She took a deep breath and dialed the phone.

"Josie Girl!" Leighton's voice rang out across the line. "To what do I owe the pleasure of a midweek phone call?" He paused, and when he spoke again, his tone was serious. "Is everything okay?"

She almost laughed. "Strange, but amazing," she said.

"You've got my attention."

Here went nothing.

She told him everything, starting with meeting Merrill at the hospital and on through accepting the part. When she finished, the other end of the line was dead silent.

"Leighton? You still there?"

Her brother chuckled. "Well done, Josie Girl. You really had me going there for a minute. Did Ben put you up to this?"

"I haven't spoken to Ben in a couple weeks. This is all true. I start acting classes next week."

Merrill had called yesterday evening, right after she and Cassie finished dinner, with the details about her acting classes with some teacher named Holliday…or was it Holloway? She'd had a third round of Jim Beam by then and wasn't clear on the name. Either way, he was supposed to be one of the best in the business, and he owed Merrill a favor.

Leighton was quiet again for a moment, and Josie knew he was stunned. She imagined him standing there in his kitchen in Wichita, eyes darting back and forth while he tried to take in everything she'd told him.

"Congratulations," he said at last, chuckling. "This

is incredible."

Thank goodness. Leighton would convince the rest of the family this wasn't a joke.

"You think Jimmy will finally buy a television set?" she said.

Oh, golly. *She* should consider buying a television set.

Leighton laughed again. "He just might."

"Listen, I hate to put this on you, but I'm going to be incredibly busy the next several weeks. Would you please tell everyone else about this? Tell them I'm sorry I won't be able to come home next month, but I'll be there for Christmas."

"Anything for you, Josie Girl. Just be careful, all right? From what I've read, those Hollywood men are real playboys."

Josie closed her eyes and took a deep breath, forcing the memories back down. "Don't worry. I won't let myself get hurt twice."

Chapter Five

Josie followed Charlie out of the airport terminal and into the bright morning sunshine. Her first day with the cast since her audition, and they were all boarding a plane bound for Yosemite National Park for two weeks of on-location filming.

"We'll be shooting bits for several episodes," Merrill had explained when she met with him a couple weeks ago for an update and to tell him how her acting classes were going. "That way we only have to go out there once for the entire season."

So, her first time acting on camera and her first time on an airplane, all at once.

If she thought about it too long, she got nauseated.

She'd spent all day yesterday packing, unpacking, and repacking her bag, trying to figure out what she should bring for two weeks in a cabin in Yosemite. She needed things to wear when she wasn't in costume, but what? She'd never been to a national park. She finally settled on blue jeans, blouses, and her old roper boots from Kansas. Merrill said they were trailering the horses out to Yosemite and there would be one for her. The boots might come in handy.

She could barely eat last night, and when the phone rang, it startled her so badly she yelped and almost fell out of her chair. It had been Charlie, calling to say he looked forward to seeing her tomorrow and that he was sending a cab to take her to the airport. That was awfully nice of him. She'd only met him the one time, but Charlie Lyon seemed as fatherly as the sheriff he played on the show.

But now she wondered if he was playing a trick on her. They couldn't actually be about to board the tiny plane sitting on the tarmac. The little turboprop didn't even look like a real plane, more like one of the models her nephews built. She turned to Charlie.

"Where's the jet?"

He glanced down at her, the June sunshine glinting off his Wayfarers, and smiled. "We don't need a jet to hop over to Yosemite. It's only an hour-long flight, even on a small plane. Besides, it's just the seven of us. Well, eight, if you count our new friend over there."

Josie followed his gaze across the tarmac to where Robert stood near the airplane steps with a brindle puppy prancing around on the end of a leash. She gasped and placed a hand over her heart.

"Oh, my goodness, he's adorable," she said with a little squeal.

"I *am* pretty darn cute, aren't I?" Beau said, sidling up to them, a large duffel bag in one hand.

Her stomach clenched. Charlie was clearly looking out for her—he really did remind her of Daddy—but she'd expected that either Beau or Robert or both might be another story. Best to put them in their places early.

"Sorry," she said, "but no man can hold a candle to a puppy. Take this for me, would you?" She shoved her tote bag at Beau and scampered toward the plane. Cassie would be horrified if she knew Josie had just shot down one of the most handsome men in Hollywood. The thought made Josie giggle, rinsing away her anxiety.

28

The morning was cool, bordering on chilly, and Robert wore a dark gray jacket over a blue button-down shirt and a pair of dark trousers. A black suitcase sat on the pavement next to his feet, and the puppy ran laps around both him and it, cinching his legs to the suitcase with the leash. Robert's arms windmilled, and Josie laughed. The side of people you never saw on television…

"Here, let me help you." She crouched, balancing on the balls of her feet, grabbed the puppy by the collar, and unclipped the leash so Robert could unwind it before he fell over.

"Thanks," he said when he was free. He knelt and fastened the leash back on the puppy's collar. Josie caught a whiff of bay rum aftershave, and the hair at the nape of her neck stood up. Robert lifted his head, and she found herself only inches from those hazel eyes. Golly, they were pretty. She swallowed hard.

"Good morning," she said.

He briefly looked surprised and then said, "Good morning." He chewed on his lower lip but didn't look away.

Josie swallowed again. "Cute dog."

The puppy strained against her hold on his collar, his little pink tongue reaching for her hand.

"Thanks. This is Sergeant. He's a boxer." Robert smiled, flashing that dimple in his left cheek. She released Sergeant's collar, and the puppy licked her hand. She laughed.

"How old is he?"

"About four months."

She scratched the puppy behind the ears. They'd always had a dog or two around the farm, usually a hound of some sort. She missed having one, but her landlord didn't allow pets. Maybe she should move, now that she could afford something nicer.

She was still squatting like the catcher on a baseball team when Sergeant tried to hop in her lap. She lost her balance and teetered backward, Robert grabbing her arm just before she fell onto her rear.

"Down, Sergeant! Sit!" he said. The puppy sat and hung his head like a guilty child. Robert looked back at Josie. "Sorry about that. He's a little excitable."

She grinned. "It's all right. I grew up around animals." She felt pressure on her arm and looked down to see Robert's hand still wrapped firmly around it. She could almost hear heavy panting behind her, a voice telling her to quit squirming. Stomach whirling, she yelped and jerked out of Robert's grasp.

"I'm sorry." Robert put his hands up like he was surrendering. His eyes were wide and shone with concern. "I didn't mean to hurt you."

Josie swallowed hard. "You didn't, I...just..." She needed to catch her breath before this got out of control.

Easy, Josie Girl, he was just trying to keep you from falling on your behind.

She inhaled deeply to stop her trembling. "You didn't. It's fine."

She stood and looked behind her, glad beyond glad that Charlie and Beau had caught up to her. They both set their bags down, dropped to their knees, and fussed over Sergeant.

"New girlfriend?" Beau said, grinning up at Robert.

Robert scowled. "Girlfriend? No, I thought this was your mother."

Josie laughed, some of her adrenaline draining

away. Until she realized she was the only one laughing. Robert glared at Beau, whose face fell, and the morning suddenly felt even chillier.

This was awkward.

"All right, let's get going," Merrill said, coming up behind them. Josie let out a relieved puff of breath. A harried-looking male assistant hovered behind the producer. "The equipment trucks and crew arrived last night, so time's a-wasting." He stopped short and pointed at Sergeant, who was wagging his stump of a tail so hard his whole back end wiggled. "What is that?"

"My dog," Robert said. "You said I could bring him."

Merrill goggled at him. "Good God, Coolidge, I didn't think you were serious." He and Robert stared each other down.

Gee whiz, didn't Robert get along with anyone?

Charlie stood, tapping the face of his wristwatch, and Josie felt everyone around her relax. Charlie was clearly a peacemaker. "Come on, gentlemen. As the man said, time's a-wasting," he said. He swept an arm toward the stairs leading into the plane. "Ladies first."

"Thank you," Josie said. She smiled, but her stomach still churned. This was it: Her first flight.

Breathe, Josie Girl. Breathe, breathe, breathe.

The plane was even tinier on the inside than she'd expected. There were only four rows of seats, with four seats per row, two on each side of the aisle. Where should she sit? Did everyone already have self-assigned seats like at church? If she took one all the way in the back, they might figure out she was terrified, but she'd look pompous sitting in the front. She chose an aisle seat in the second row. If she kept her face pointing straight ahead, she might not see anything out the windows on either side of the plane. She focused on relaxing her face and pretended she was riding the bus to the hospital.

Beau boarded next. He took the window seat in front of her and passed her tote bag over. She thanked him and placed it on the seat next to her without turning her head. Beau frowned.

"You all right?" he said, peering at her over the back of his seat.

"I'm fine." Her voice came out higher than usual, and she cringed.

Beau chuckled. "You've never been on a plane before, have you?"

Darn it. All those acting lessons must not have helped. She shook her head.

The mischief in Beau's eyes drained away, and his rakish grin turned into a kind smile. "Don't worry. I've flown hundreds of times, all the way to Ontario and back. And Robert there?" He pointed across the aisle to where Robert was trying to get Sergeant to lie down on the floor. "He's gone all the way to the east coast. Trust me, we'll be fine."

Beau's smile was a bright summer day. Even through her nerves, Josie couldn't help but smile back. He reminded her of her brother Ben. Goofy, full of himself, but with a soft heart. With any luck, he'd love pranks as much as Ben did too. She could have fun with this one.

Charlie settled into the window seat across the aisle from her, and Merrill and his assistant took places in the back. Soon, the pilot fired up the engine, and they taxied to the runway. Josie gripped the armrests so hard her knuckles went white as they shot down the runway and lifted into the sky.

Chapter Six

Sergeant whined and climbed into Robert's lap when the plane took off. Robert tried to move the puppy back onto the floor, but it was tough to do against the thrust from the climbing airplane. He gave up and let Sergeant curl up in a big ball in his lap.

He'd gotten the boxer shortly after Josie's audition. When he got home that day, he hopped in the shower, eager to wash away the night before. But the hot water stung his back like a million tiny needles, and he hopped right back out and inspected himself in the mirror. He hadn't realized the redheaded waitress had broken his skin in about three dozen places before he'd asked her to quit digging her fingernails into his back. He looked like he'd fallen backward into a thorn bush.

Something had to change. Clearly, bad sex wasn't going to help. But he didn't know how else to fight this gaping loneliness. He'd considered fighting for custody of Matthew, but he worked such long hours on set he'd barely see the boy. It didn't seem fair to rip a child from his mother, drag him clear across the continent, and then leave him in the care of a nanny. Better to have one parent than none at all.

This powerlessness was one of the worst things he'd ever felt. Not *the* worst, but close.

So, he got a dog. It was nice having someone to come home to, especially someone who was always happy to see him.

Now he wanted to read, but the book he'd left on the seat next to him had fallen onto the floor during takeoff, and he couldn't reach it with Sergeant in his lap. He glanced across the aisle at Beau, who was gazing out his window, then to Josie, who was clutching the armrests so tightly she was liable to snap them right off. She caught his eye, and he whipped his head back around to face forward.

He closed his eyes, remembering that moment when she'd helped him with Sergeant's leash. Those bright green eyes, only inches from his, the scent of her shampoo wafting up from her black hair...

He shook his head. He wasn't doing this. Especially not with a castmate, no matter how pretty she was. Besides, he wasn't lonely anymore. He had a dog.

A few minutes later, the plane leveled off, and he managed to shift Sergeant to the floor and grab his book. It was a new one his friend Ed had lent him called *The Manchurian Candidate*. Ed was a director and said he thought it would make a good film. Robert settled in and cracked it open.

He'd only gotten through the first chapter when he heard a groan. He looked across the aisle to see Beau leaning forward, head between his knees, and gulping air. Robert rolled his eyes.

"Geez, Beau, already?" Charlie said. "We've only been in the air thirty minutes."

Josie peeked around the back of Beau's seat. "I thought you said you've flown hundreds of times."

"I have," Beau moaned. "I'm fine on jets, but these little planes, sometimes they..." He burped, and everyone flinched. Charlie passed him an air sickness bag.

Robert shook his head. Beau could tear around a corner on two wheels in his Thunderbird, but put the kid in a plane, and he turned into a limp, sweaty mess.

"I can help," Josie said.

Robert watched her rummage in her large tote bag. She pulled out a tin about the size of a kid's lunchbox from which she dug out a pillbox. She fished out a small pill and, clutching the seat in front of her, slowly stood and slipped into the seat next to Beau.

"Take this," she said. "It's Dramamine. It'll help." She smiled and patted his shoulder as he popped the tablet in his mouth and chewed.

Robert rubbed his thumb along the side of his index finger, his papercut long healed. Josie caught him staring, and his face flushed.

"What?" she said.

"You brought a first aid kit?"

Josie placed the tip of her index finger on her chin. "Well, I thought, I'm going into the woods for two weeks with a bunch of men. What am I gonna need? And a shotgun wouldn't fit in my bag."

Robert laughed. There was that spunk again. Josie was well suited for this motley crew. And damn, she was making that nose-wrinkling smile again. She stood and leaned across the aisle to him. He smelled her shampoo again, and his breath caught.

"You missed a trick, by the way," she said, softly enough that the others wouldn't hear.

He knit his brow. "What's that?"

"When Merrill asked you what that was," she pointed to Sergeant, now asleep on the floor, "you should have told him it was Beau's mother."

Chapter Seven

Josie settled back in her seat, glad she'd been able to help Beau. After the chaos of the last several weeks—and now being trapped on this terrifying little airplane—it had been nice to just be a nurse for a minute.

Because tomorrow she'd be an actress again, shooting with the cast for the first time. Starting the week after her audition, she'd attended acting classes every weekday evening for six straight weeks. She'd go right from the hospital after work to Alan Holloway's—not Holliday's—studio for lessons on diction and camera presence and gestures and on and on. She'd learned so much, but she'd run herself ragged. If she hadn't had those two weeks off from the hospital in the middle of it, she would have collapsed. But now, at last, she only had to do one job at a time.

Just one little job of starring in a television show. No big deal.

Her palms started to sweat.

At least her castmates were friendly. Well, two of them were. Robert Coolidge had been nice enough to her, but what was his problem with everyone else? He sure did smell good, though. Musky. Kind of woodsy. A good man-smell. She shook her head. She must need more sleep or something.

But she snapped right to attention when the pilot said they were about to land.

She looked out the window to see the plane nearly skimming the tops of the trees. Oh, Lord, they were going to crash. She squeezed her eyes shut and clutched the armrests, bracing for impact. A big bump nearly popped her out of her seat as the wheels touched down, and her eyes shot open. She flew forward as the plane braked hard, and she had to press her hands against the seat in front of her. No one else seemed bothered except Sergeant, who whined and jumped into Robert's lap. She let out a long breath and prayed no one would see her trembling as she gathered up her bag and got off the plane.

A ninety-minute bus ride later, they pulled into Yosemite National Park. Josie gasped and nearly pressed her nose to the window as they drove into the Yosemite Valley.

There must have been more trees in this one section of the park than in the entire state of Kansas. She'd ridden through the Sierra Nevada on the train to Los Angeles, but the views hadn't been anything like this. Rocky cliffs jutted up sharply from each side of the valley floor like sentries. She knew her mouth was hanging open, but she didn't bother to close it.

Someone slid into the seat next to her, and she glanced over her shoulder to see Charlie. He smiled and pointed at an especially tall, sheer rock wall.

"That's El Capitan," he said.

"You've been here before?"

Charlie nodded. "Brought my two older kids here a couple years ago. We didn't go up in the High Sierra, though. That's where we'll be next week."

Josie gazed at the snow-capped mountains and shivered. "I should have brought a coat."

Charlie chuckled. "Don't worry, we won't be going up that high."

An hour later, Josie unpacked her suitcase in an adorable wood cabin at the base of an overlook Charlie said was called Glacier Point. She felt a little guilty that the crew were housed in pairs down the road in canvas-sided cabins with a communal bathroom while the cast each got their own wood cabin with a private bath. But those were the perks of stardom, she supposed. Charlie had said something about checking out the campground, so once she had her things put away, she changed into a pair of blue jeans, a black button-down shirt, and her boots.

She'd made a good call, bringing the boots. She hadn't worn them in the two years she'd been in California, but the leather remembered her, still perfectly formed around her feet. She wiggled her toes, remembering dozens of horseback rides with her brothers, grateful for something familiar in the middle of all this strangeness.

Suddenly exhausted, she flopped backward on the bed, booted feet dangling over the side.

She'd just closed her eyes when a sharp knock on her door was followed by Charlie's voice asking if she was ready to go.

"Coming!" she called back.

****

Josie was disappointed when Charlie said Robert had declined his invitation to come along. Having some bonding time with whole cast would have been nice, but at least Beau joined them.

Beau and Charlie were an absolute delight. Cassie had read up on the cast when Josie got the role, so Josie knew Beau was about the same age she was, and Charlie was forty-six—old enough to be father to them both. They clomped around the camp, checking out the canvas cabins, the swimming pool, and the dining pavilion, where a park ranger warned them that it was bear mating season.

"If you need to go anywhere after dark, go in pairs," he said.

Josie exchanged a wide-eyed glance with Beau, and they both stepped closer to Charlie.

Robert and Merrill joined them at the dining pavilion for dinner, probably because they had no other choice. The cabins didn't have kitchens, and they weren't allowed to have food inside anyway because of the bears. But neither of them sat with Josie, Charlie, and Beau. Merrill and his assistant sat with the crew, and Robert took a seat apart from everyone and cracked open a book. He didn't even glance over at them.

That was rude.

Josie nudged Charlie. "What's his issue?" She tilted her head in Robert's direction.

Charlie sighed and sawed his knife through the steak on his plate. He opened his mouth, but Beau cut in.

"He's got a stick up his ass, is his issue."

Charlie glared at Beau, who shrank back.

"Sorry," Beau mumbled. "He just doesn't ever talk to us." Beau looked hurt, and Josie got the impression that he wasn't used to someone shutting him out. Her brother Ben was the same way. He'd never met a stranger, and he couldn't understand it when someone treated him like one.

"He might if you didn't poke fun at him every thirty seconds," Charlie said. He turned to Josie. "He prefers to keep to himself. He's had a tough time the past year or so. Probably not my story to tell, but his wife divorced him right around the time we all got cast last spring. Hit him pretty hard, I think."

"That was over a year ago," Beau said. "You'd think he'd have gotten over it by now."

"Spoken like someone who's never been through a divorce," Charlie said. Beau opened his mouth again, but Charlie shot him a stern look, and Beau played with his food instead.

From Cassie's research, Josie knew Charlie was on his second marriage and Beau hadn't been married at all yet. The news about Robert was interesting, though. Cassie hadn't been able to find much about him. Apparently, he didn't do many interviews.

"Do you think he's upset that I'm here?" she said. Maybe he didn't like her intruding on his show.

Charlie turned to her. "Not at all. In fact, he spoke in your favor after your audition. He's a good fellow. Just aloof. Don't let him make you feel unwelcome." He put an arm around Josie's shoulders and gave her a squeeze. "We're happy you've joined our little family."

****

That evening the cast sat around a campfire, set in a clearing apart from the cabins to prevent a catastrophe. A thin line of pine trees separated their patch of bare earth from the cabins, whose lights winked dimly through the branches. To Josie's surprise, Robert joined them. Maybe he'd been drawn by the case of Schlitz that Beau had scared up. Whatever his reason, he sat on the opposite side of the fire with Sergeant at his feet, and the full cast lounged in chairs around the fire, drinking beers and kibitzing.

More correctly, Josie, Beau, and Charlie kibitzed while Robert listened quietly. But at least he'd joined the group. Josie hated seeing anyone left out. And Charlie and Beau were peppering her with so many questions, he wouldn't have had a chance to say anything anyway.

"So, a sunflower farm with five older brothers, was it?" Charlie said, leaning back in his chair and popping open another beer.

Josie grinned. "Yes, sir."

"Sunflowers are pretty, but I never knew enough people wanted 'em to need a whole farm," Beau said.

She giggled. Non-Kansans were always baffled by her family's business. "We don't sell many whole blooms. We used to raise them just for the seeds, but with all the rationing during the war, Daddy figured we could make more money producing sunflower oil. He was right. Now we do both."

"That was smart," Charlie said. "How did your parents feel about you coming all the way to California by yourself?"

Josie's chest tightened into an old, familiar ache. This was the worst part of meeting new people. She swallowed hard. "My folks are gone." She swirled the dirt at her feet with the toe of one boot. "Mom died when I was twelve. Cancer. Daddy had a heart attack two years later."

Silence settled over the group—the same uncomfortable silence she always made when she answered an innocent question about her parents. This time, at least, the popping of the campfire punctuated the stillness.

"Oh, sweetheart, I'm so sorry," Charlie said. He reached over and squeezed her hand.

Golly, that was refreshing. Too many people said something dumb, like, "They're in a better place," which always made her want to scream. Tears blurring her vision, she looked up at Charlie and smiled.

"Thank you. At least I still have all those brothers. They did a good job raising me."

"I can't imagine having a family that big," Beau said. "Can you even remember all their names?"

Josie laughed, her tears drying up. "I'll only do this once, so pay attention. In order from oldest to youngest, they're Jimmy, Leighton, Steve, Peter, and Ben."

"How many years between you and the oldest?" Charlie said.

"Thirteen. But only fifteen months between Ben and me."

"Are they all still on the farm?"

"Jimmy, Peter, and Ben are. Jimmy and his family are in the old farmhouse we all grew up in. Peter and Ben have houses on other parts of the property."

"How about—dang it, I already forgot their names," Beau said. "The other two?"

"Leighton's a surgeon in Wichita, and Steve teaches history at Fort Hays State College."

Beau flashed a mischievous grin that was already familiar. "Which one's your favorite?"

She laughed. "I don't have a favorite! I love them all equally."

Beau raised an eyebrow.

"All right, it's Leighton."

They all laughed. Robert had a great laugh. A bright sound that contained more joy than Josie would have expected.

"I wouldn't say he's my favorite, though." She

looked at her lap and thought for a second. "More like the one who understands me best. He convinced the others I'd be all right in California. He used a connection from medical school to help me get the job at Hollywood Presbyterian. But I don't know what I'd do if I lost a single one of them."

A strange little squeak came from Robert's direction, and she glanced at him. He coughed and looked down at Sergeant. She shrugged. Maybe he'd inhaled some beer.

"You are, by far, the most interesting of all of us," Charlie said, chuckling.

Not by a mile, Josie thought, but it was kind of them to take an interest.

"Where are *you* from?" she asked Charlie. Cassie had only researched the men's love lives, completely forgetting any details that might help Josie make small talk.

"Cleveland." He cast his eyes skyward.

Josie chuckled and turned to Beau. "What about you? You said you're from Ontario?"

Beau nodded. "Ottawa, to be exact."

Her face lit up. "I'd love to see Canada! I've never even met a Canadian before."

Beau straightened and puffed out his narrow chest. "That's a shame. We're a noble, handsome people."

Robert snorted, catching Josie's notice again. And since he kept drawing attention to himself, it was high time someone dragged him into the conversation. She cracked open another beer and leaned back in her chair.

"Where are you from, Robert?" she said.

His eyes widened and he shifted in his chair. Sergeant huffed when Robert's foot bumped him in the ribs.

"Me?"

She sipped her beer and kept her eyes fixed on him. "You."

He let out a long breath and settled back in his chair, studying her. The skin on her arms prickled. "Hell Hole," he said at last, his eyes boring straight back into hers.

"I beg your pardon?"

Beau and Charlie snickered. Robert may not talk to them much, but they'd obviously heard this one before. One corner of Robert's mouth turned up in a half smile.

"Hell Hole, South Carolina," he said.

Was he serious? She'd just told him she had five older brothers, and he thought he could pull this over on her? She set down her beer and crossed her arms over her chest.

"You're putting me on."

Robert placed his right hand over his heart. "I assure you, madam, I am not," he said in a commanding stage voice. "I hail from a tiny hamlet called Jamestown, right on the edge of Hell Hole Swamp. Population about a hundred and eighty. During Prohibition, we were the corn-liquor capital of the nation. You can still find moonshine stills all over the swamp."

Josie stared at him, eyes blinking. The longest speech she'd heard him deliver off camera, and it was...*this*? She looked at Charlie, who nodded.

"He's not kidding. I looked it up."

"Why didn't you say you were from Jamestown, then?" she said.

Both corners of Robert's mouth turned up this time, and he leaned forward, resting his forearms on his knees. "Two reasons. Number one, if I say I'm from

Jamestown, everyone assumes I mean Virginia." He shuddered theatrically, making Josie smile. "And two, everyone in the county calls the entire area Hell Hole. Jamestown, Moncks Corner, Awendaw, Saint Stephen, doesn't matter. It's all Hell Hole."

"So you grew up in a swamp."

Robert nodded, and Josie grinned. Finally, someone from a place funnier than Kansas.

"Best friend was an alligator?" she said.

Robert dropped his head and chuckled. He looked back up at her with just his eyes and smiled.

"Something like that."

Her stomach fluttered at the sight of that dimple in his cheek. She held his gaze and smiled back.

Chapter Eight

Josie's palms were so sweaty the next afternoon she was surprised they weren't dripping. She wished she could wipe them off, but she didn't dare dry them on her dress. She'd ruin the silk with damp patches that would surely show up on camera, especially in this bright sunshine.

The high-topped button-up shoes the ladies from Wardrobe had squeezed her feet into had only a kitten heel, but they still sank into the soft ground. Her heavy hoop skirt, petticoats, and crinoline threatened to drag her down, and she leaned against the wagon they were about to use for filming to keep from toppling over.

Good gravy. She'd been so worried about forgetting her lines or doing something awkward with her hands on this first day of shooting that she'd never stopped to think about her costume. For the scene they were about to film, Mary Anderson had just arrived in California from Boston where she'd been living with her aunt since her mother died and her father, now the sheriff of Folsom, moved west. Coming from Boston, of course she'd be dressed in high fashion. Unfortunately, high fashion for 1865 meant a skirt almost as wide as Josie was tall.

She looked down at the miles of sky-blue silk and laughed. She needn't worry about forgetting her lines. There was no way she would ever get up into this wagon to film the scene in the first place.

"You ready?" Beau said.

Josie looked up, surprised. She hadn't heard him walk up. He and Robert had the afternoon off because this scene was just her and Charlie.

"What are you doing here?"

Beau smiled, one hand tucked behind his back. "I remembered how nervous I was the first time I got in front of a camera, and I thought I'd come by and offer moral support."

Fondness for her curly-haired costar washed over her. In just the past two days, they'd found such an easygoing rapport. Being with Beau was like being with a brother again. Or a partner in crime. Though now that she thought about it, the two were often the same thing. She smiled back. "That was so thoughtful, thank you."

Beau's grin took a mischievous turn. "Besides, I heard they were dressing you up like Scarlett O'Hara, and I just couldn't miss it. Smile!" He whipped a camera out from behind his back and snapped a photo.

"You twit!" she said and dissolved into laughter.

"This scoundrel's not disturbing you, is he, ma'am?" Robert said. He ambled across the grass toward them, Sergeant prancing alongside him on a leash. Josie broke into a wide smile as she watched them approach. Robert wore dark jeans, a black button-down shirt, and a pair of black boots. Josie felt a twinge of envy. Her gown was magnificent, but these high-topped shoes were killing her. She'd give anything to be back in her own boots.

"Always," she said, laughing again. "And why are *you* here? Come to take pictures too?"

He grinned, flashing that dimple. "Sergeant was antsy. Since we were going for a walk anyway, I thought we'd swing by and see how things were going."

Beau looked askance at him, and Josie could tell he was thinking the same thing she was: Robert was mingling when he didn't have to? But he *had* joined them at the campfire both nights they'd been here. Maybe he was thawing. She hoped he was. She loved the brotherly relationship she was forming with Beau, but having only one brother around felt strange.

"Hard to say," she said. "Makeup dragged Charlie away because his forehead was shiny, so we haven't started yet. And I'm not sure how I'm ever going to get into this wagon."

"We can help with that, can't we, Beau?" Robert said.

Beau's face lit up like a puppy who'd just been invited along for a car ride. "Sure can," he said. He set his camera in the wagon bed while Robert told Sergeant to stay and clambered onto the seat. Beau took her hand. "Put your foot on the hub here next to the wheel and step up," he said.

She reached up with her other hand and took Robert's, and a line of goosebumps prickled up her arm as she stepped up and he helped lift her into the wagon. Her breath hitched as she settled onto the seat next to him. Goodness. It wasn't hot today, but the weight of this hoopskirt must be getting to her. Just climbing into the wagon left her breathless. No wonder women in the nineteenth century fainted all the time.

"Don't worry," Robert said. He was so close his breath fell warm on her cheek, and she felt her whole face flush. "They never dress the townswomen up this fancy. I'm sure it's only for this scene. You'll be in clothes you can move in once Mary's settled in Folsom."

"And just ignore the camera," Beau said. Josie jumped. She'd almost forgotten he was still here. She turned her head and saw him leaning on the wagon wheel. "Pretend you can see straight through it to the trees on the other side," he said.

Josie was sure he meant well, but his comment only made her acutely aware of the camera and the forest of lights and other equipment surrounding the wagon. She couldn't believe it hadn't spooked the horses. It sure as heck spooked *her*. Bolting for the trees sounded pretty good right about now.

"All right, I think we're finally ready," Charlie said, striding over from the shade of a large oak tree where he'd gotten a fresh layer of powder. Sergeant abandoned his post next to the wagon and bounded over to him. Charlie scratched the puppy and looked at Beau and Robert, his brow furrowed. "What are you two doing here?"

"Irritating Josie," Beau said.

"Beau is irritating Josie. *I* am being helpful," Robert said.

"Whatever you're doing, get out of here," Charlie said. "This is a father-daughter scene, and you're not invited."

Beau chuckled, patted Josie's knee, and strode away. Robert leaned toward her, and she breathed him in. Good gravy, she liked his aftershave.

"Just trust your training and have fun," he said. "You're gonna be great." He showed off his dimple one last time, jumped from the wagon, and walked away, whistling for Sergeant.

Josie watched him go, wishing she could follow him. But Charlie climbed into the wagon next to her, the crew swarmed around, and before she knew it, Charlie slapped the horses with the reins, and the wagon lurched forward.

They followed a camera truck so the cameraman could get a wide shot of the two of them as they rode side-by-side in the wagon. Josie cringed when a sound tech leaned way over the tailgate to hold the boom mic above them. Good thing she'd left her first-aid kit with Betty at makeup rather than all the way back in her cabin. They might need it.

"Ready?" the director called from the back of the truck.

Charlie nodded. Josie sucked in a breath and did the same. No turning back now.

"Action!"

"Welcome to California, my dear," Charlie, now Sheriff Anderson, said.

Josie—now Mary—looked around at the landscape and smiled. "It's beautiful, Papa."

She hoped she was getting her tone right. She and Charlie had run their lines for this scene a dozen times, but she still struggled with it. She tried to follow her acting coach's advice and imagine she was speaking with her own father again, but Daddy had been gone eight years. She'd still been a child the last time she talked to him. If he'd lived, would the way she spoke to him have changed by now?

Charlie cleared his throat and shifted in his seat. "I put together a room for you. It's not as nice as you had at your Aunt Poppy's, but—"

Josie laid a hand on his arm and smiled. Charlie's forearm was thick and solid, like Daddy's had been. She'd sat next to Charlie plenty of times the past couple days, but now that they were together in this wagon as father and daughter, she realized how much his presence reminded her of Daddy. The relaxed posture, the easy smile, the overall sense of safety she felt when she was around him. The corners of her eyes burned.

"I'm sure I'll love it. Thank you for bringing me out here." She paused to swallow a hard knot that had suddenly risen in her throat. "I've really missed you, Papa." Her voice trembled on this last line, and on impulse, she laid her head on Charlie's broad shoulder.

He turned toward her and kissed the crown of her head. "I've missed you, too, sweetheart. So much."

Chapter Nine

Even in the flickering firelight, Robert could see that Josie was wrinkling her nose again. He grinned. She deserved all the smiles in the world tonight. Charlie said she'd blown everyone away with her debut this afternoon, and they'd toasted her with their first beers this evening.

He hadn't wanted to join everyone at the campfire the first night, but Charlie had pulled him aside and told him Josie's feelings were hurt when he didn't sit with them at dinner. The guilt almost killed him. He was keeping his distance so he wouldn't do something stupid and embarrass them both. Hurting her feelings was exactly the opposite of what he was trying to do. So, against his better judgment, he sat with them by the campfire. He planned to just sit quietly, have a beer, and go to bed early, but Josie somehow hooked him into the conversation.

He usually clammed up when people started asking personal questions. Why anyone thought they had a right to know about his private life was beyond him. But he answered every single question Josie posed to the three of them: favorite books, sports they'd played as kids, why they became actors. She was curious about everything, and he answered nearly every question without hesitation.

The only one that hung him up was when she asked

if they had any siblings.

Charlie did. A younger brother back in Cleveland who worked at a steel mill. Beau did too. An older sister who was married to a dentist and had twin girls.

But him? He'd been trying to figure out how to answer that question for fifteen years.

He shifted in his chair as the image of a lopsided grin swam in front of his eyes. He had to swallow hard before answering. "It's just me," he said. Then he changed the subject.

The moment hadn't been uncomfortable enough for him to avoid what became the cast's evening ritual. As exhausted as he usually was after a day of filming, he actually looked forward to these couple hours where they'd drink beer and shoot the breeze around a campfire before bed. Even if he had to keep her at arm's length, he didn't want to miss a single second with Josie. She drew him in like a magnet.

A few days later, they packed up, got back on the bus, and drove about thirty miles into the High Sierra. It was a lot cooler up here, and Robert was glad they got wood cabins again. A park ranger told him the temperatures would drop below forty degrees at night. But damn, it was gorgeous. They were so high up they were nearly to the tree line, and he liked the way the crisp, clean air made his lungs burn. Even after eight years in big cities, he still wasn't used to breathing in exhaust all the time.

It was lucky they weren't doing many closeups here because that meant the cameras were out of his way and he was able to enjoy the scenery more. They spent most of their time doing long shots of the men charging across country on their horses—bits they'd use as stock footage for the entire season. They only needed Josie for one day up here to film a scene for a mid-season episode where Mary Anderson was whisked away by kidnappers, but she tagged along every day anyway. She could have spent her time resting in her cabin, but she seemed so amazed by everything—her eyes always wide and mouth half open—that she insisted on coming along.

The horses probably had something to do with that. Merrill had found a cute little Appaloosa named Sugar for her, and Robert had never seen someone so happy to mount up. The crew brought the horse along with the men's mounts every day, and Josie would trot around out of frame while they filmed. They always had some downtime between shots, and she'd lounge in the grass with them and chat or play cards. Her acting had improved—dare he say it?—*dramatically* since her audition, but someone needed to teach this poor girl a poker face. If they'd been playing for real money, she would have been in debt to Beau for the rest of her life. Beau probably would have let her off the hook, though. Those two had hit it off so fast Robert was surprised they hadn't already planned a heist of some sort. They were forever pulling little tricks on each other and sometimes on Charlie.

Thank goodness Josie seemed comfortable around him too. He'd worried after she yanked her arm out of his grip that first morning by the airplane. He'd replayed the scene in his head a hundred times and couldn't figure out what he'd done wrong. Maybe he'd misread her, because everything seemed fine now. Better than fine. Even when neither Charlie nor Beau was around, he and Josie would fall into easy conversation. And he usually hated conversation. It was odd, but he sure wasn't going to complain.

"Couldn't you just stay up here forever?" Josie said on their second to last full day. They'd wrap up filming tomorrow and fly home the next morning.

Robert looked over at her, stretched out on the other end of a large blanket in the grass. She lay back, upper half propped up on her elbows, eyes closed, and her freckled face tipped toward the sun. She wore her long hair in a single braid that lay coiled on the blanket next to her like a lariat. Like she had every day she wasn't filming, she wore boots, blue jeans, and a button-down shirt. That *Gone With The Wind* getup they'd put her in the first day had been funny, but he liked her better like this. It suited her more. Sergeant lolled on the blanket between them, and Josie idly scratched the dog's belly. Robert smiled.

"You know? I think I could," he said. He meant it too. These past two weeks had finally brought a break from the loneliness of the past couple years. The thought of going back to his usual routine and losing these moments with Josie brought the ache back all over again. They'd see each other on set, sure, but it wouldn't be the same as it was out here.

Josie turned her head toward him and opened one eye. "I just wish we could explore more. I asked Merrill if I could take Sugar out on the trail yesterday, but he said no." She tilted her head back and closed the eye. "I think he's worried I'll get eaten by a bear."

"This *is* wild country," Robert said.

Yuck. He'd just agreed with Merrill. He'd have to find something to be contrary about later. His eyebrows jumped. Unless…

"Do you think he'd let you go if one of us went with

you?"

Josie turned her head toward him again and opened both eyes as big as they could probably go. "He might. But none of you have time. These shots are taking all day."

Robert grinned. "I have time tomorrow. I'm only in two shots, and they're both scheduled for the morning."

Please say yes, Josie, he begged silently. *Please, please, please.*

Josie sat all the way up, her eyes shining with hope. "You'd take me for a ride?"

He almost swallowed his tongue.

Steady, R.J. You know that's not what she meant. Get back into character.

"Of course," he said casually. "I've never been up here either. Wouldn't mind seeing some more of it."

She grinned and leapt to her feet, agile as a cat. Sergeant jumped. "I'm gonna go ask Merrill!" She tore off to the copse of trees where the producer sat in the shade with his assistant.

Chapter Ten

Merrill hedged at first, but Josie buttered him up by thanking him for bringing Sugar for her, and he gave in. He probably would have been an easier sell if she'd asked to go with Beau or Charlie, but with a trail ride around Yosemite on the line, she would have begged on her knees if that's what it took. Fortunately, it didn't.

When she ran back to their blanket on the grass to tell Robert the good news, she found him stretched out on his back, long legs fully extended, Stetson over his face. She admired his strong, tall form for a moment. He certainly hadn't meant to frighten her when he'd grabbed her arm in front of the plane a couple weeks ago. She remembered the way he jumped back and raised his hands when she jerked out of his grip. He'd clearly felt awful. And he'd been a perfect gentleman this whole trip.

She laughed. Three months ago, she'd only been watching these men on television with Cassie, and now here she was worrying about the intentions of one of them—who was completely innocent, as it turned out. She did find herself in the oddest situations sometimes.

Robert must have heard her laugh because he pulled his hat off his face and sat up. She smiled and gave him a thumbs-up.

They pored over a trail map that evening next to the fire. The night air was chilly, but Robert radiated warmth, and for one crazy second, she considered huddling up against him. She wrapped her jacket tighter around herself instead. Eventually, they chose a seven-mile roundtrip trail that would take them from Tuolumne Meadows where they'd been filming up to Cathedral Lakes. She wished they could ride farther, but they only had the afternoon.

Miraculously, Robert's filming wrapped up right on time the next morning, and after a quick picnic lunch with Beau and Charlie, they mounted up and set off for the trailhead. Robert was still in costume except for his Stetson, which he'd swapped for a pair of aviator sunglasses. But considering his costume was a red button-down shirt, black pants, and boots, he was well dressed for a trail ride.

"Think we'll get lucky and come across one of these bears we keep hearing about but never see?" he said as they let the horses plod across the meadow.

Josie laughed. Despite the rangers' frequent warnings, the closest thing she'd seen to a bear was yesterday morning when Charlie got mad at Beau for hiding his hat for the third time. She'd been calling Charlie "Papa Bear" since.

Once they reached the trail, the horses had to walk single file, and Josie let Robert go first. That way if they got lost, it would be his fault, not hers.

They passed into the woods, the lodgepole pines sticking up tall and straight like syringes. Josie took a deep breath of the clear, cool mountain air. No one could have convinced her two years ago that today she'd be riding a cute little Appaloosa through the gorgeous Sierra Nevada with a new friend.

She stared at Robert's back and smiled. He was slow

to warm up to new people—probably why outgoing Beau didn't understand him—but he was a friend, all right. All three of her costars were. She smiled a little bigger.

Chapter Eleven

Holy smoke, it was gorgeous up here. Robert decided he'd have to bring Matthew camping when he got a little bigger. He looked up, straining to see the tops of the lodgepole pines they were ambling past. They must be almost a hundred feet tall. The sunlight threading its way through the branches cast patchwork quilts on the ground. He wished he'd brought a camera.

He checked behind him every so often to make sure Josie was all right. She looked so happy, gazing around in all directions, like she was trying to commit every little detail to memory. Her long, dark hair shimmered in the dappled sunlight.

God, she was beautiful. Beautiful and bright and funny.

He shook his head. Making a pass, even a chaste one, at a coworker was probably a bad idea. Definitely a bad idea. A terrible idea, in fact. But Josie was so different from any of the women he'd met in Hollywood. She was interested in *him*, not in his rising star, not in Deacon Bell. Maybe there was a chance.

About an hour later, they reached an unmarked spur trail their map had said would take them to the lakes. Robert nudged his horse, Abby, that direction. She tossed her head and snorted. He tightened up on the reins and directed her again, pressing hard with his opposite leg. Behind him, Josie giggled. He swiveled his head, one corner of his mouth turned up.

"Sassy thing, isn't she?" Josie said.

He chuckled. "Yeah, but she's so pretty I put up with it." He patted the buckskin's neck. Merrill had offered to replace her, but Robert liked her spunk.

He sucked in a breath a few minutes later when they came out of the trees and stepped onto a grassy expanse leading to a huge, sparkling blue lake mirroring the snow-capped peak towering behind it. Josie reined up alongside him.

"Look at that," she said, her voice breathy. He tore his gaze from the mountain and watched Josie take in the scenery. Her eyes were wide, and her heart-shaped lips were slightly parted. Damn, even her mouth was beautiful. He licked his lips. She turned to him. Right. She'd said something. She was probably waiting for a response.

"It's stunning," he said.

"Should we get closer?"

She means to the lake, R.J. Closer to the LAKE.

"Let's tie the horses up. I don't trust Abby not to toss me in the water."

Josie laughed and slid out of the saddle. Robert did, too, and they led the horses to a tree and wrapped their reins around a branch.

A few other hikers lounged at the water's edge. Robert picked a spot apart from them and sat down. The water was probably really cold, but the ground was warm from the sun. Josie sat beside him, and they stared in silence across the glittering lake to the mountain beyond. Her hand rested on the grass only inches from his. He ached to touch her. He slid his hand a fraction closer to hers.

This was undoubtedly a bad idea. If she rejected him, things would be awkward on set between them for the entire season.

But he slid his hand another fraction closer anyway.

"Thank you for coming with me," Josie said.

At the sound of her voice, he chickened out, and his hand flew away from hers. He reached up and scratched the back of his head, praying it looked like that's what he'd intended to do all along.

"Thanks for talking Merrill into it," he said, more coolly than he felt. "I hate knowing how close I was to missing this."

They fell into a comfortable silence. He liked silence and didn't see why most people felt the need to fill it. Josie clearly wasn't most people. She seemed as happy as he was to just enjoy the view.

He smiled, closed his eyes, and tipped his face toward the sun like Josie did. It was nice, the sun warming his skin like this. After a minute or two, he opened his eyes and turned his attention back to the lake. The water was a deeper blue than he'd seen anywhere else. And so clear. Growing up in a swamp, he wasn't used to being able to see through water, but he bet if he swam out to the middle of this lake, he'd be able to see straight to the bottom.

As he watched, a family with two teenaged boys ventured right to the water's edge. The boys were laughing and shoving, clearly trying to knock each other into the chilly water. He chuckled. It was exactly something he and Jack would have done.

Jack had been one of the few other people who understood how to sit in silence. Ed wasn't bad at it, but even he started talking after a while. Robert glanced at his wristwatch. Josie hadn't made a peep in nearly twenty minutes. He scooted his hand an inch closer to hers again. She yawned and stretched, and he snatched the hand back. She checked her own wristwatch and stuck out her lower lip.

"We should probably head back," she said. "It took us, what? Two hours to get up here?"

He nodded, reluctant to agree with her. "It'll be faster going back since we'll be heading downhill, but you're right. If we're going to be back for supper, we should get moving."

They strolled back to the horses, Josie clearly in no more hurry than he was for the afternoon to end. She pivoted at the waist to take one more look at the lake. Shielding her eyes with one hand and resting the other hand on her hip, she looked like a perfect, youthful, dazzling statue. She looked at him and smiled her pure, incredible smile.

He *really* should have brought a camera.

Chapter Twelve

At dinner that evening, Josie could hardly believe that Robert didn't just join the conversation, he initiated it. He went on for several minutes about the trail and the lake. Maybe a quiet ride with gorgeous scenery was all he needed to loosen him up. Or he was entertained by Beau and Charlie's disappointed groans over everything they'd missed.

He was so handsome when his face lit up. It was a shame he didn't do it more often. Maybe he would now that he'd come out of his shell a bit. He was even getting along with Beau. His relationship with Merrill was probably a lost cause, but at least the cast could be a family. She hoped it would last when they were back at the studio, that the magic of Yosemite wouldn't wear off.

Sitting between Robert and Beau by the campfire that night, she was sad this was their last evening of the trip. The past two weeks had been amazing. The filming with costumes and makeup and all those blinding lights, the scenery, everything. Even Sergeant, she thought, leaning down to scratch the dog behind the ears. Robert had left him with a production assistant that afternoon, and judging by the way he'd tried to leap into Robert's arms when they returned, he hadn't been too happy about it.

A hand bumped hers, and she looked down. Robert had reached down to scratch Sergeant too.

"Sorry," he said and started to pull his hand away.

Josie smiled and gave his hand a quick squeeze. He'd been so kind giving up his free afternoon to take her on that long ride. She missed the rides she used to take with a brother or two. She flicked her eyes to Robert. Good gravy, he was doing that cute half-smile thing again. A shiver zipped up her spine, and she turned her eyes to Charlie, who was telling a story about the time he and his little brother tried to run away to Pittsburgh when they were kids.

Charlie's stories were great, but the ride must have worn her out, because by only 9:30, her eyes were heavy. Seemed a shame to go to bed so early on their last night, but she couldn't stop yawning.

"I'm sorry, fellas, but I need to hit the hay," she said. She stood and stretched.

"Let me walk you back," Charlie said, standing as well. "Ranger told me they spotted a bear prowling around earlier. Reminded me we shouldn't walk around alone after dark." He turned to Beau and Robert. "I'll be right back. Save me a beer."

Josie held up a hand. "But if you leave me at my cabin, you'll be walking back here alone."

Charlie's brows met. "Oh. Right."

Beau stood. "I'll go with you too. We can walk back together."

"Then we've left Robert by himself," Charlie said.

"He's got Sergeant." Beau pointed to the dog. "Does that count?"

"Sergeant can't call for help," Charlie countered.

"I suppose we could all go," Josie said. "Then the three of you can come back."

"But we're not supposed to leave a fire unattended,"

Beau said.

Josie groaned and rubbed her temples. She was too tired to figure out anything this complicated.

"I can solve this," Robert said and stood. "I wouldn't mind getting to bed early either. You two stay with the fire until it burns down, and Josie and I will go back to the cabins."

"Thank God that's settled," Charlie said, sitting back down. "That was making my head hurt."

Josie and Robert said their goodnights, Robert clucked to Sergeant, and the trio headed toward the cabins. The cold air bit into Josie as they stepped away from the warmth of the fire, and she gathered her jacket around her.

"Stay close," Robert said as they passed through the thin line of trees separating the fire ring from the cabins. "Those phantom bears could be anywhere."

Josie laughed. "I think I repel them. It's a shame too. I've never seen one in person."

"I have. They live in the swamp, but you don't see them much. It's the alligators you have to watch out for."

"Never seen one of those either. I'd love to, though."

Robert chuckled. "As long as you see it before it sees you, you're usually okay."

As they crossed the last few yards to the cabins, they fell into the same comfortable silence they'd had that afternoon. Josie smiled. With five boys, the house had always been chaotic growing up. She missed the noise sometimes, but it sure was pleasant to enjoy some peace and quiet with a friend. Beau was a lot of fun, but Robert's quieter ways were a nice break. Strange being around a man who didn't demand a thing from her, not even conversation. She could get used to that.

Robert and Sergeant walked her to the door of her cabin and stood with her in the little yellow halo from the porchlight while she fished her key out of her pocket and unlocked the door.

"Thank you again for talking Merrill into that ride," he said when she turned back to say goodnight. He'd stepped in awfully close. She'd never noticed how long his eyelashes were. "That was the most fun I've had in a long time."

She smiled. "Me too." She was startled to realize that was true. When *was* the last time she'd enjoyed such a carefree afternoon?

Robert took another step closer, and her heart started pounding. She looked down, hoping to see Sergeant trying to push past him into her cabin.

Please just let him be trying to block the dog. Please don't let him be about to—

He leaned in lips-first, and her stomach clenched. Oh, God, it was happening again. Someone she thought she knew… She had to get away. She scrabbled her hand around behind her but couldn't find the doorknob. She was trapped between Robert and the cabin door, so she had nowhere to go. Desperate, she put her hands on his chest and shoved. He stumbled backward, tripped over Sergeant, and landed hard on his rear in the dirt.

"How dare you," she said, pointing a shaking finger at him. Her nostrils flared. "How *dare* you!"

Robert blinked up at her. Sergeant sniffed his face, and he nudged him away. "Josie, I'm sorry, I…I just thought…"

"You didn't think at all, you presumed." She had to fight to keep from shouting. Every muscle in her body twitched, and her eyes stung. She couldn't keep the tears at bay much longer, and she would *not* let him see her cry. She shook her head hard. "I trusted you!"

He opened his mouth again, but she didn't hear what he said because she darted into her cabin and slammed the door. She fumbled with the lock several times before her shaking fingers secured it. She looked down at her trembling hands.

Please, not again.

The all-too-familiar tornado swept her up, and she collapsed onto her bed, thinking she might pass out or vomit or both. She curled into a ball on top of the quilt and took deep, gulping breaths, trying to block out the memory of rough hands and ripping fabric.

You're safe, Josie Girl. You're safe, you're safe, you're safe.

Then she burst into tears.

Chapter Thirteen

Where had he gone wrong?

Robert knew better than to read too much into all the smiles they'd shared that afternoon, but when Josie squeezed his hand by the fire, he thought she was telling him something.

Apparently not.

He groaned and rolled over in bed. It had been so long since a woman had touched him affectionately and not greedily or lustfully. Not like they were only interested in what he could do for them. And he'd ruined it by charging in like a linebacker.

The worst part was he'd clearly scared her out of her wits.

Some man somewhere must have hurt that poor kid, and he'd just made it worse. Her half-sobbed "I trusted you" bounced around in his head. That was going to haunt him forever.

To top it all off, he couldn't even avoid her. They'd be filming together every couple of weeks from now until March. For the first time, he was glad his character wasn't the one getting the love interest. At least he and Josie wouldn't have to kiss on camera.

He had to apologize. He didn't expect her to forgive him, but he still had to apologize. Oh, God, Merrill was going to read him the riot act when he heard about this. If Charlie and Beau didn't kill him first. He rubbed his eyes with his fists and rolled over again, his weight settling briefly on his backside mid-roll. He winced. He'd hurt the first girl in years who truly saw him, *and* he'd bruised his tailbone.

That flight home tomorrow was going to be hell.

****

The flight home the next day was hell.

Robert tried to pull Josie aside before they got on the bus to the airport and again while they waited to board the plane, but he couldn't get her away from Charlie. She stuck to him like a magnet, and when Charlie ducked into the men's room at the airport, she darted into the ladies' room and didn't come out for much longer than even a woman should have needed to be in there. As they got on board, she made a show of sitting next to Beau in case he got sick again and needed a nurse.

Robert slunk to the back row with Sergeant, hunkered down in the window seat, and pretended to sleep so no one would talk to him. Pain shot up his spine from his bruised tailbone, but it was better than having to talk to anyone. Takeoff wasn't too bad, but the bump on the landing nearly made him cry out. He bit his lower lip so hard to stay quiet it was a miracle he didn't draw blood.

When the plane door opened and the stairs were rolled up, Merrill waved a quick goodbye to everyone.

"We'll see you in a week," he said to Josie, then bounded off the plane, his assistant in tow.

Robert tried to speak to Josie as they deplaned, but she stuck to Charlie again. Charlie's wife, Nancy, met them just inside the terminal, and Robert looked away while they embraced. At least Nancy would be driving Charlie home, leaving Josie to catch a cab out front like him and Beau. Maybe he could talk to her then.

"Josie, would you like a ride home?" Nancy said when Charlie introduced the ladies. Robert's heart sank as Josie's face lit up and she nodded.

Dammit, Nancy.

There was nothing he could do but wave goodbye.

"Nice of them to adopt her like that," Beau said, sidling up to him. "You can tell she misses her family."

Robert just grunted in reply.

Beau studied him. "You all right?"

Robert stiffened with annoyance and stayed silent. Beau *would* choose right now to be serious about something.

"I'll take that as a no," Beau said. "Well, see you Monday. Bye, Sergeant. Take care of this old grouch, you hear?" He reached down and ruffled the puppy's ears, then strode away, leaving Robert alone in the terminal.

Chapter Fourteen

"You should have given him a knuckle sandwich," Cassie said, taking a sip of her beer.

She and Josie lay stretched out in side-by-side chaise lounges next to the swimming pool at Cassie's cute garden apartment complex. Josie sure envied this pool. Her own apartment was in a boxy two-story building with parking spaces tucked underneath and nothing in the back but a small weedy lot. Maybe she should use some of her *Gunslingers* money to move in here.

"He got the point anyway," she said. "You should have seen him on the bus out of Yosemite yesterday. He kept squirming around like he couldn't get comfortable. I think he bruised his tailbone when I pushed him."

"I hope he broke it." Cassie paused, then laughed out loud.

"What's so funny?"

"The men are back on set tomorrow?"

Josie nodded.

"He's gonna have to ride a horse like that."

They both cringed, then giggled.

Cassie held out her beer bottle. "To putting men in their place."

"I'll drink to that." Josie clinked bottles with her and took a swig.

The whole experience was kind of funny here in the

sunshine with her best friend, but Friday night in her cabin had been awful. Once her tears dried up and she changed for bed, she burrowed under the covers and shook for the next hour. She wouldn't have thought that after two years a man could still terrify her like that, but when Robert leaned in to kiss her, she was a defenseless twenty-year-old all over again, this time with no older brothers around to rescue her.

"Ain't that a bite, though," Cassie said. "He's a handsome one."

"It's the handsome ones you have to look out for." Josie paused. "Except Beau. Beau's safe."

Sitting with Beau on the plane ride home had been a ball. She'd given him Dramamine before they boarded, so he'd been his usual silly self the whole flight. He'd taught her a card game that seemed to be some form of War but with rules that changed whenever he started to lose. They laughed the whole way back to LA.

"Stick close to him and Charlie then," Cassie said. "They're the ones who matter anyway."

****

Going back to work at the hospital two days later was a relief. Josie couldn't believe she'd missed the smell of antiseptic, but the familiarity was soothing after two busy, unusual weeks in Yosemite. She and Cassie took their lunches together and often met up after work to watch television at Cassie's apartment. They had Thursday off, and Cassie dragged Josie to Sears and made her buy a TV.

"You're about to be *on* television, Josephine," she said. "You have to *own* a television."

Cassie tried to prod her into buying a color set, but Josie nearly fainted when she saw the price—$500!—

and chose a small black-and-white set instead. The television was far too heavy for them to carry back to her apartment on the bus, so she arranged for delivery, and by Saturday evening she and Cassie were watching television at her place for the first time.

Sunday night, she could hardly sleep. She'd be back on set tomorrow, shooting in the studio for the first time…and seeing Robert for the first time since Yosemite. Lying in bed, she shivered under her covers. She hadn't breathed a word to Charlie, Beau, or Merrill about his trying to kiss her. That would have just made things even more tense between Robert and Beau than they already were, and she didn't want Merrill to think she was a troublemaker. She balled the sheets up in her fists. She'd just have to do what Cassie said and stick close to Charlie and Beau.

If only they weren't shooting the worst possible scene first thing tomorrow.

They were going to film the episode where Charlie's Sheriff Anderson brings his daughter Mary home to Folsom. Both deputies would vie for her attention in this first episode, and there was one scene where Robert's character, Deacon Bell, would make a pass at her. Thank heavens the script didn't call for him to try to kiss her, but he was still going to put his arm around her. She felt her heartrate tick up, and she breathed deeply to try to slow it down.

There will be more than a dozen other people there, Josie Girl. And this time, at least, it will be just an act.

Josie tried not to yawn the next morning as Betty caked foundation under her eyes to hide her dark circles. The poor woman already had her work cut out for her without Josie's face becoming a moving target. When

Betty finished, Josie looked in a mirror and nearly fell over with surprise. Good gravy, no wonder Charlie had told her Betty was a miracle worker. Even Josie's own mother wouldn't have been able to tell she hadn't slept well last night. Forget Merrill and the cast. Betty was the real genius on this show.

The director cut her marveling short by calling the cast to the stage. Sweat pooled at the base of her spine. Here went nothing. She joined Charlie and Beau on the set of the interior of the sheriff's office.

"Where's Robert?" the director said.

Josie looked around. She'd been relieved when she hadn't seen him first thing, but it wasn't like him to be late.

"I'm right here," Robert said, stepping out of a shadow near the stage. He was in costume, and unless he wore eyeliner in his private life, he'd already visited Betty too. He must have gotten here early. He tossed a book onto the floor back in the shadow and walked onto the stage.

"There's not much blocking here, so we'll just run it once before we shoot," the director said. He gave instructions for the beginning of the scene where Sheriff Anderson introduces Mary to his deputies. After the introduction, the sheriff and Beau's Judah Mitchell run outside to investigate some commotion in the street, and the sheriff tells Deacon Bell to stay with Mary.

"Then, Josie, sit on the edge of the desk, and Robert will sit next to you," the director said. "Robert, when you say your line 'Don't worry, sweetheart, I'll keep you out of trouble,' put your arm around her. Then Josie, you just duck out from under him, say your line, and leave. Got it?"

Everyone nodded and took their places. The director called "Action!" and Josie's first scene at the studio was underway.

Things started out smoothly. Josie shook hands with Beau and Robert as their characters were introduced, but right when Beau and Charlie ran off stage and her nerves ramped up, the director called "Cut!"

"I don't like this lighting," he said. "Josie looks washed out." He looked up at Robert and Josie. "Stay there a minute while we fix this."

Josie watched with envy as Beau and Charlie settled into chairs offstage while she was stuck sitting on the desk next to Robert. She hadn't even been this close to him when they sat by the lake in Yosemite. She kept her eyes pointed straight ahead, but she could still hear his soft breathing and the occasional rustle as he shifted position.

"Josie, I'm sorry."

He spoke so softly she wasn't sure she heard him at first. Her eyes went wide, and she turned to look at him. He cast his gaze down as soon as her eyes met his and he opened his mouth again.

"I—"

"All right, I think we've got it," the director said. Robert clapped his mouth shut, and Josie looked straight ahead again.

Good gravy, she hadn't expected an apology. But did he mean it? He *was* an actor. Her heart thumped. She wanted to forgive him, to go back to that easygoing companionship they'd started to form, but would he get the wrong impression again? She couldn't bear going through this twice.

"Josie?"

She looked at him again. His eyebrows rode high on his forehead, and his eyes darted back and forth, studying hers. He was waiting for her to say something. She could accept his apology, but they couldn't be friends, only coworkers. She hardened her expression.

"Okay," she said. A pang of guilt ripped through her when his face fell, but it was for the best.

They got the scene shot, and as soon as the director yelled "Cut!" Robert tore off the stage, plopped down on the floor in a corner, and buried his nose in his book.

Thank goodness that was the only time the two of them would have to shoot a scene like that. By the end of the episode, it was clear Mary preferred Judah. Beau would be so much easier to shoot with.

To her relief, Robert didn't try to talk to her again, either on or offstage. Apart from "Good morning" and "See you tomorrow," most days he didn't say anything to anyone apart from his lines. Between scenes, when she, Charlie, and Beau would chat or play cards, he sat by himself and read.

She actually felt a little sorry for him.

But with him out of the way, she enjoyed every second at the studio.

The whole process of making a television program was fascinating to watch and took so many more people than she'd realized. Watching television with Cassie, she only ever saw the actors, but there was the producer, of course, a director, and more crew than she could count. Lighting, sound, cameras, wardrobe, makeup, craft services, just trying to name them all made her head spin.

And the sets! The WBC studio had an entire Western town built on the backlot. If she turned her back to the cameras and crew, she could almost imagine she really was back in 1865. Charlie told her the network used the set for several shows, and she couldn't believe she'd never noticed.

"Most people don't," Charlie said, chuckling. "Use a different camera angle, change a few storefront signs. It's amazing how they can make it look different without doing much at all."

One week in early August, it was just her and Charlie filming an episode where Sheriff Anderson takes Mary on a trip to Sacramento. That was one of the best weeks so far. She missed Beau and his pranks between takes, but filming with just Charlie, she could almost pretend she had her father back.

The only downside was how much less time she got to spend with Cassie. They worked the daylight shift at the hospital, so during the weeks Josie was nursing, they still spent most evenings together, but days on set usually ran close to twelve hours. By the time Josie got home from a day of shooting, she didn't have time for much but a simple supper and a shower before bed.

"It's all right," Cassie said at the hospital one day as they finished up a shift. "I know filming wipes you out."

Cassie smiled, but Josie detected a sadness in her friend's voice that she'd never heard before. Her heart sank. She'd have to find some way to make it up to her.

But otherwise? She'd never had so much in her life.

Wait until the people of Hays see you on television, Josie Girl. Just wait.

Chapter Fifteen

"Sergeant, no!" Robert called.

The dog ignored him and took a flying leap into Ed's swimming pool.

Robert started to get up from his lounger to drag the animal out of the pool, but Ed put a hand on his arm.

"Let him enjoy it," his friend said, waving his beer. "It's hot."

It wasn't that hot. Hot would be if they had the same temperature but with eighty percent humidity, like in Hell Hole this time of year. But Robert never had any luck explaining that to Californians.

He sat back down. In the pool, Matthew laughed as Sergeant paddled over to him and licked his face. Robert grinned. As soon as he'd gotten the production schedule for August and saw he had this whole week off, he'd called up his ex-wife, Laura, and asked to have Matthew for the week. She'd suggested he come out to South Carolina and see his parents, too, but he hated going back. Seeing Laura face-to-face reminded him of his failure, and he hated being badgered by the folks in town about life in Hollywood. He *really* hated feeling obligated to visit the cemetery. Apart from Matthew and his parents, there was nothing he liked about going back to Hell Hole.

Besides, he could spoil Matthew better here. The boy had only been in town two days, and they'd already gone to Marineland of the Pacific and seen the pilot whale. Matthew begged to go to the studio to watch *Gunslingers* being made, but Robert didn't want to disrupt Charlie and Josie's filming. He'd hoped that his apology to Josie would have mended the fences between them, but even when they were standing next to each other on stage, he felt like they were miles apart. Not getting her friendship back broke his heart and looking like he was coming to gawk at her on his week off would only make it all worse.

He promised Matthew a trip to Knott's Berry Farm and Ghost Town instead. Matthew would love the mine train. Robert wanted to take him to Disneyland, but that park had just opened a bunch of new rides and was probably mobbed. They could go when Matthew came back for his birthday in October.

Throwing himself into this time with his son worked wonders on that old, lonely ache. He took Matthew on some sort of adventure every day, and every night around midnight, when he probably thought Robert was asleep, Matthew crept into his room and slipped into bed next to him.

He knew he should make the child sleep in his own room. Laura had insisted on it when Matthew was a baby, leaving him to cry himself to sleep in his crib. The sound of his wailing infant had brought Robert to tears, but even Mom had assured him it was for the best. But Laura and Mom weren't here. And since he only got his little guy for a few short weeks each year, he couldn't bear to waste a single second. So, when he heard his bedroom door creak open each night, he smiled and waited for his son's warm little body to snuggle up against him.

Two nights before the end of the visit, he saved them both some trouble and let Matthew go to sleep in his bed. He settled into an armchair in the living room and was three chapters into *Dr. No* when the telephone rang. He frowned. Who would be calling at nine o'clock on a Friday night?

He almost ignored it but got up, leaped over Sergeant, and darted for the kitchen anyway. What if something had happened to one of his parents and the other was trying to reach him? If nothing else, the ringing might wake Matthew. He snatched up the receiver and said hello.

"Hey, Robert!" Beau's voice rang out.

He nearly dropped the phone. Why the hell was Beau calling him? The cast had each other's telephone numbers, but they never used them. At least, *he* never used them.

"Robert, you there?"

Robert shook his head, trying to clear it, and leaned against the wall. "Yeah, I'm here. What...why... Beau, it's nine o'clock on a Friday."

"I know. I tried you this afternoon, but you didn't pick up."

"I was out." He and Matthew had gone to Knott's Berry Farm, where Matthew had loved the mine train very much.

"I figured. Listen, some friends and I are going bowling tomorrow night. You want to come along?"

This was getting more bizarre every second. Beau should be out sparking some girl right now, not inviting him to go bowling. The only time he and Beau had interacted outside of work had been one day they came around different corners of the same aisle at the grocery store near the studio and crashed their shopping carts into each other.

He had to sit down. He stretched the phone cord to the table in the breakfast nook and dropped into a chair.

"Did Charlie put you up to this?" he said.

"Of course not. I put me up to this. Believe it or not, I'd actually like you to come bowling with me and my friends. Now are you coming or not?"

He racked his brain, trying to think of a reason—any reason—why Beau would invite him out. He supposed they'd thawed toward each other in Yosemite. All those evenings by the campfire shooting the breeze and drinking beer with Charlie and Josie. But it would still make a lot more sense if he invited Josie. Those two had become such fast friends. It was pretty annoying, when he thought about it.

"Wouldn't you rather invite Josie?" he said.

"Josie's great, but this is a boys' night. Beer and cigarettes and dirty jokes. So how about you drag yourself out of your cave and come bowling with me and the boys?"

Robert suddenly remembered Beau asking him at the airport if he was all right. He softened. It had taken Beau a year and a half to show it, but the kid wasn't just an obnoxious pain in the neck.

He smiled when he spoke again. Maybe Beau would be able to hear it in his voice. "That sounds like fun, but I've got my son this week. Tomorrow's his last night in town. Thank you for the offer, though. Unexpected, but not unappreciated."

"You're welcome. Enjoy your last day with your boy. Maybe we'll get you next time."

"Yeah, maybe."

He rose from the chair and hung up the phone, then stood there, staring at it. He never would have expected Beau to reach out to him like that—not after his falling-out with Josie. *He* certainly wouldn't have reached out to someone who hurt one of his friends.

Unless Beau didn't know.

Come to think of it, he'd never gotten the ear-blistering he'd expected from Merrill or Charlie either.

Josie must not have told anyone.

Had she been afraid to speak up, or was she protecting him? Seemed more likely she'd been afraid to say anything, being the new kid on the block and all. He massaged his tailbone. She'd handled it herself anyway.

Chapter Sixteen

Saturday night, September 12, 1959
Josie's stomach flip-flopped around her liver when the *Gunslingers* theme blared from Charlie's television set. Here it was: Her big debut.

Everyone cheered when, at the tail end of the opening credits, Josie's picture popped on screen with the words "Special Guest Star Josephine Donovan." Sitting next to her on the giant sofa, Charlie gave her a one-armed hug around the shoulders. Cassie hugged her from the other side.

Charlie had been awfully nice to invite her and Cassie over. She'd talked so much about Cassie on set that Charlie said he just had to meet her. And Josie was delighted to meet his children: his and Nancy's five-year-old boy, and Charlie's daughter and son from his first marriage. He'd invited Beau and Robert, too, but Beau's parents were visiting from Ottawa, and Robert, to no one's surprise, declined without explanation.

She and Charlie rolled onto the screen in a wagon, driving down the main street of the Western town set that viewers would recognize as the fictional Folsom, California. They stopped outside the façade of the sheriff's office, and Charlie helped her down from the wagon. He opened the office door for her, and they stepped inside.

Seeing the scene move from the exterior of the

office to the interior so seamlessly was surreal because they'd spent almost an entire afternoon shooting it in two parts. The soundstage with the interior office set was a golf-cart-ride across the studio lot from the Western town set where they'd shot the exterior. But from the viewers' perspective, she and Charlie had simply walked through a door. Josie shook her head. Television was magic.

They moved into the scene she'd auditioned with, where Sheriff Anderson introduces Mary to Judah and Deacon. Her palm tingled as she watched herself shake hands with Robert on-screen. She'd been reluctant to touch him when they shot the scene, but now her fingers curled as if they were gripping his warm, strong hand again. When they reached the part of the episode where Deacon makes his pass at Mary, she remembered Robert tearing off stage as soon as the director yelled "cut." He always hid behind a book between scenes, but he only shot away like that when he and Josie interacted in a scene, like being around her was repulsive.

No, not repulsive, Josie Girl. Painful.

He hid it while the cameras were rolling, but offstage his whole body went rigid if she came too near him. His shoulders would roll forward, and his jaw would clench, exactly like a patient in pain. She'd never seen him do that around anyone else.

Good gravy. He really must feel bad for scaring her at Yosemite. And he *had* apologized. Though another man had apologized to her a few times before, too, and never meant it. He'd always done the same thing all over again. But Robert hadn't. He'd kept his distance. He didn't even try to talk to her.

Was she punishing him unfairly?

"Well done, Josie," Charlie said, hugging her again.

She jumped. She'd gotten so lost in her own thoughts she quit paying attention to the show. A commercial was on now.

"That was a dynamite opener if I ever saw one," Cassie said, grinning. Cassie hadn't stopped smiling since she and Josie stepped off the bus near Charlie's house earlier that evening. Josie was excited to be able to bring her into her TV world, at least this little bit. Being invited to a celebrity's home was a dream come true for Cassie, even if *Gunslingers*' two handsome young deputies weren't there. And if Cassie were starstruck, she hid it well. As soon as they'd arrived, she started chatting Charlie up about the history of his neighborhood. Sometimes Josie forgot that Cassie was Hollywood born and bred, and she knew a lot about the area that transplants like Josie—and nearly everyone else in town—would never have guessed.

Nancy passed around a plate of cookies and Josie took one, determined to stay focused for the rest of the show. Seeing herself on screen was strange. Was that *really* what her voice sounded like? And she cringed at the way she delivered a couple of her lines, but overall, she didn't think she'd done half bad. When the end credits rolled, everyone jumped up and applauded.

"Cut it out," she said, blushing. Happiness welled up inside her even as she hid her face in embarrassment.

An hour or so later, Charlie drove them to Cassie's apartment. They'd planned to take the bus back, but Papa Bear wouldn't hear of it. Josie and Cassie both had to be at the hospital at seven the next morning, so they'd decided to have a sleepover after the premiere and go in to work together. They lay awake giggling in Cassie's bed far later than they should have.

"I see why you love Charlie," Cassie said. "He's wonderful. Nancy's lovely too." She giggled. "Josephine Donovan: Television star."

Josie snorted. "A single guest appearance hardly makes me a star."

"You've got fourteen more guest appearances ahead of you. You'll be a star by the time this is over." She sighed. "Just don't forget your poor old friend Cassie."

The sadness in Cassie's voice stabbed Josie like a dagger. She groped around under the covers until her hand found her best friend's. The first true friend she'd ever had and the one person she'd always been able to tell everything. She twined her fingers around Cassie's and squeezed. "I could never."

Chapter Seventeen

Once the season premiered, Josie was inundated with requests for interviews. Apparently, a woman appearing regularly on a Western was a big deal. Thank goodness the requests went through Merrill, and he passed along only the best ones. She was already busy enough balancing work at the hospital and work on the show.

The interviews had all been with Hollywood-based magazines, but toward the end of September, her brother Jimmy called to say a reporter from the *Hays Daily News* had asked if he could put him in touch with her.

"He wants a story about the local girl who's made it big in Hollywood," Jimmy said.

Anger burbled in her chest, and she growled. "Sure, *now* everyone's interested in *my* story."

Jimmy sighed. "I know it. And you can say no. I just promised the fellow I'd ask you, so I'm asking you."

She thought for a moment. This could be her chance to set the record straight about why she'd left Hays. But did she really want to dredge up those memories? Not especially. Though there was a third option.

"Tell him I'll do it, but I won't answer any questions about you-know-who. One word, and I hang up."

Three days later, Josie called up the *Hays Daily News* office and asked for David Lowry.

"Miss Donovan," the reporter said. "Thank you so

much for calling. Everyone here in Hays is eager to hear your story."

Josie held back a snort. The people of Hays already thought they knew her story. This was the first time anyone had asked *her* anything. Her life in Kansas had been ruined by rumors and assumptions.

"I can't say how proud we all are of you," Lowry went on. "To have a local girl—"

"Mr. Lowry, I appreciate this very much, but I've had a long, busy day. Could we please get to your questions?"

"Yes, of course. So, tell me, what's it like to go from being a farmgirl to being a star?"

She rolled her eyes. She'd appeared in exactly two episodes so far. That was hardly stardom. She gave a blasé answer about how mind-boggling it all was, and Lowry lapped it up. She checked the clock, then chastised herself. She was turning into a downright diva. She should be more gracious, more appreciative. How many girls were blessed with this opportunity? She gave more enthusiastic answers to the next several questions about what activities she'd done in high school—just glee club—and what she missed most about Kansas—her family.

Then Lowry blindsided her.

"Do you ever speak with Ethan Winchester?"

Her mouth went dry. Lowry had promised Jimmy he wouldn't bring that up. He'd *promised*. She'd given him answers to all these questions so he could get his big story, and then he'd stabbed her in the back.

"Miss Donovan?"

Josie cleared her throat to tamp down an unladylike string of words she desperately wanted to let loose. "This interview is over," she said and slammed the receiver down. Hands shaking, she picked it right back up and dialed Jimmy.

"You said he promised." Her voice shook as badly as her hands. "You said."

Her brother's breath came hard and fast through the phone line. "That no-good son of a bitch *did* promise," he said, his voice dangerously low. "Don't you worry, Josie Girl. I'll take care of this."

He called her back the next evening to let her know Lowry wasn't going to run a story at all—not even one with Ethan left out of it.

"Did you threaten him?" she said.

"There won't be a story," Jimmy said again.

Chapter Eighteen

The first Saturday in October, Robert looked at his calendar and grinned. Only three more weeks until Matthew's birthday. Laura always sent the boy to California for his birthday, and he couldn't wait to see his son again. He grabbed the phone and dialed Laura's number to run some flight times by her.

"I've been meanin' to tell you," Laura said, and Robert's heart dropped. This was going to be bad news. "Matthew's got a school play that week. He's real excited about it, and I don't want him to miss it."

She might as well have punched him in the stomach. Robert stretched the phone cord to the table in the breakfast nook, dropped into a chair, and rubbed the back of his head. "But I've been looking forward to this since I sent him home in August."

"It's not about you, R.J. Matthew's in school now. You need to think about him."

"He's damn near all I ever think about." His voice almost broke. "I bought a bunch of new books for his room. I was gonna take him to Disneyland." He picked up a plastic stegosaurus Matthew had forgotten on his last visit. It had sat on the kitchen table for the past two months. Robert ran a finger down the spines and bit his lower lip. "What about the week after?"

"I still don't like him missin' so much school." Laura paused. "You could come here to see the play, you know. You haven't been back for what? Three years?"

How could she forget that? On his last trip, they'd made one last attempt to rekindle their relationship, and the sex had been so awkward the date should be seared into her mind for life. It was sure as hell seared into *his*. He shuddered. They should have filed for divorce right then and there.

"Two. And I can't. I'm working that week."

"Oh, that's just great. What were you plannin' to do with my child all day while you worked? Leave him at home with the dog?"

Robert's fist closed around the dinosaur, the spines digging into his hand. "For your information, I was planning to take him with me. He's been begging to see the studio. I thought he'd like watching us film. And I figured we'd scare up a kid-sized costume and let him be in the background of a scene or two. He'd love it."

Laura sighed. "He would. But it'll have to wait for another time. I'm sorry."

Robert's hand unclenched. A line of angry red dents ran the length of his palm. He'd proven he was thinking of Matthew, but he'd still lost. He dropped his head and closed his eyes.

When Laura spoke again, her voice was gentle. "How much time do you get off for Christmas?"

"Two weeks."

"How about you take him then? He'll be off school."

He raised his head. He'd only gotten Matthew for Christmas once, and that was three years ago. They could go to Disneyland then. Maybe the park would be decorated for the holiday. But that was more than two months away.

It's better than nothing, R.J.

"I'd like that. Thank you."

****

Asking for time off with only a couple weeks' notice had been a long shot, but as soon as Robert stepped off the plane in Charleston and Matthew jumped into his arms, he was so glad he'd taken it. For the first time in almost two years, he'd made something happen *for* him rather than *to* him. And he'd had a civil conversation with Merrill, to boot. The producer had grumbled about having to tweak this week's script to write Robert out, but he'd actually smiled and told him to have a nice trip.

But good Lord, why was it still so humid in mid-October? Maybe California was making him soft, but this sort of weather just shouldn't be allowed.

"What did you do with Sergeant?" Dad asked as they drove toward Hell Hole, the tall, plumed palm trees of Charleston slowly giving way to the scraggly pines and scrub brush of the swamp.

"Charlie took him. He found out I was leaving town and said he couldn't bear the thought of me boarding him." Robert chuckled. "I think he's hoping his wife will let him get a dog of his own."

"Mommy won't let me have a dog," Matthew said. He crossed his skinny arms over his chest and stuck out his lower lip.

Robert ruffled his son's hair. "That's probably because she already has her hands full with you."

Laura had agreed to let Matthew stay with Robert at his parents' house for the week. Having his son in the house would make Hell Hole a lot more tolerable.

"Y'all didn't tell anybody I was comin', didja?" He blinked. Geez, they'd barely reached the outskirts of the swamp, and he was already slipping back into the accent.

He'd have to break himself of it all over again when he got home.

"Of course not, sweetheart," Mom said. Robert smiled. His last visit had been so embarrassing with everyone in town poking in to ask about life in Hollywood. He should have known Mom would look out for him.

"I did," Matthew said. "Told everybody at school they better practice hard for that play 'cause we got a real actor comin' to watch."

Robert swallowed a groan. He liked being on display when he was playing a character but not when he was just himself. And telling even one person in Hell Hole something was as good as telling the whole county. Ladies would be coming over with casseroles by tomorrow morning.

He was wrong.

There was a tightly wrapped casserole already waiting on the front porch of his parents' house when they arrived. He plucked the note from the top.

"Welcome home, R.J.! Love, Mrs. Wilson."

His third-grade teacher. He sighed. This week wasn't going to be mortifying at all.

Chapter Nineteen

The Coolidges ate Mrs. Wilson's chicken and rice casserole for dinner that night. Mrs. Wilson might not have been great at teaching penmanship, but she was an excellent cook. Sitting around the table with his parents and Matthew, Robert felt part of a family again. Matthew sat in Jack's old seat, and Robert was struck by how much Matthew was like Jack. Same skinny body, same quick sense of humor. Maybe coming back to Hell Hole once in a while wasn't so bad.

Halfway through dinner, the doorbell rang. Mom started to get up, but Robert waved her back down.

"Probably someone hoping to catch a glimpse of me anyway," he said. Better to just face the music than make Mom come up with excuses for him to whoever was at the door.

He crossed the house to the front door. A dizzy sense of déjà vu swept over him as soon as he grabbed the doorknob, and he leaned against the doorframe. He closed his eyes, suddenly fourteen-year-old R.J. again.

They'd been eating dinner, him and Mom and Dad, when the doorbell rang. It was a Wednesday in mid-July, and he'd spent the day stocking shelves at Dad's grocery store. They'd all been on edge the past month since the D-Day invasion. Jack's unit was there, and they hadn't heard anything from him. The Allies were busy moving through France, they told each other. Jack hadn't had time to write. And even if he had, there was probably nowhere to post a letter from. Trying to break the tension at supper, R.J. cracked a few jokes, and Dad chuckled, but Mom didn't even seem to notice.

He could tell by the drawn look on her face that Mom was all worn out. She had been for weeks. She spent her days tending their victory garden, knitting socks and scarves for soldiers, and collecting scraps of everything from nylon to tin foil for the war effort—all in this awful mid-summer heat. So, when the bell rang, R.J. jumped up and answered the door.

His blood ran cold as soon as he saw Mr. Morris standing on the front porch in his Western Union uniform. He clutched a yellow telegram in his hand. R.J. gripped the doorframe.

Mr. Morris shifted his weight, his face somber. "Hey there, R.J." He cleared his throat. "Is your father home?" His eyes flicked to the left, and R.J. followed his gaze to the blue star in the front window. Hot, burning bile rose in his throat.

"Son?"

"Please, no." His voice cracked. "You can't do this to us."

Mr. Morris laid a hand on his shoulder. "Go get your father, R.J."

He shook his head and blocked the door with his lanky teenage frame.

"Will," Mr. Morris called into the house. "You home?"

"No!" R.J. shouted. He slammed the door, but his father came up behind him at the same time.

"Who is it, son?"

"No one." Tears streaming down his face, he tried

to herd his father back to the dining room. Dad pushed past him and opened the door, revealing Mr. Morris on the porch, that damned telegram still in his hand.

"Ralph?" Dad said. His face went white. "Oh, God, no." He took the telegram with a shaking hand. "Please, God, not my boy."

Mom came into the living room then. "What is going on in h—" Dad turned to her, his face stricken. She took one glance at the yellow paper in his hand and let out a scream that pierced R.J. like a bullet to the gut.

"My baby! My baby!" Her knees buckled, and Dad dropped the telegram and caught her just before she hit the floor.

"My deepest condolences," Mr. Morris said and scurried away, leaving the front door hanging open.

R.J. picked up the telegram and read it.

"The Secretary of War desires me to express his deepest regret that your son Private Jackson M. Coolidge was killed in action on 6 June in France. Letter follows. UL10 The Adjutant General."

He balled the telegram in his fist, flung it to the floor, and turned toward his parents. Mom and Dad clung to each other in a wailing heap on the floor, and his throat cinched. He couldn't breathe. The little house that had always seemed so happy and snug was suffocating him. His feet twitched, and he took off out the gaping front door. Dad called after him, but he didn't stop running until he'd reached a spot at the edge of the swamp where he and Jack used to play as kids. He climbed up high in their favorite cypress tree, clung to the trunk, and sobbed.

Now, fifteen years later, Robert had to close his eyes and take two big, gulping breaths before he answered the door.

"Deacon Bell, Deacon Bell, Deacon Bell," he muttered, plastered on a big smile, and opened the door.

"R.J.!" A woman ten or fifteen years older than Mom, with gray hair piled up in curls on her head, beamed at him, her horn-rimmed glasses winking in the light shining from behind him. He knew her instantly.

"Mrs. Hawkins, so good to see you," Robert lied. "How are you?"

"I'm fine, darlin', just fine. A little birdy told me you were in town, and I just had to stop by and see you for myself. I brought you this." She thrust a foil-covered plate into his hands. Whatever was under the tall, tin dome wobbled.

"Thank you so much, I—"

"I was so sorry to hear about you and Laura," she continued. "I was hopin' the two of you would work things out."

"Yes, thank you, ma'am, I—"

"Will you be at church tomorrow? My granddaughter, Shelly, you remember Shelly, don't you? She'll be there with me tomorrow, and I'm sure she'd be thrilled to see you too. She's all grown up now, you know. Beautiful girl of twenty and not seeing anyone." Mrs. Hawkins gave him a wink.

Oh, Lord, he needed to wrap this up quick. "I hadn't thought about church tomorrow. I've only been in town a couple hours. I need to get back inside. We're still eating dinner. But thank you so much for the dish."

He smiled, stepped into the house, and closed the door. With the slab of solid oak separating him from Mrs. Hawkins, he exhaled.

"Who was it?" Mom said, coming into the living room.

"Mrs. Hawkins." He held up the plate in his hands. "I think we got a Jell-O salad."

"Oh, goodness, well, stick it in the refrigerator." She headed back toward the dining room, muttering something about having enough food to feed the entire state.

Chapter Twenty

Robert woke the next morning to an earthquake.

Wait. They didn't have earthquakes in Hell Hole. He dragged his eyes open. Mom loomed over him, hands reaching for his shoulders to give him another good shake.

"I always said you could sleep through the Second Comin'," she said. "Get on up now. Church is in half an hour."

He looked at his bedside clock, groaned, and pulled the quilt over his head.

"It feels like 5:30 to me, Mom."

She yanked the quilt back down and stared hard at him like he was twelve years old and trying to get out of going to school. She frowned.

"I suppose it does. But I was hoping we could go to church as a family this mornin'."

Mom did love going to church together on those rare occasions when he came back to Hell Hole. But then he remembered Mrs. Hawkins winking at him and he groaned again.

"I'm really tired, Mom. I didn't get to sleep until two."

Mom's face fell, breaking his heart. He was about to drag himself out of bed when he thought of a better idea—one that would keep him out of the clutches of Mrs. Hawkins and her granddaughter while still giving

Mom a chance to show him off.

"How about I take everybody out for lunch after?" he said. "The four of us together as a family."

She beamed, and he cheered inwardly.

"All right," Mom said. "You rest up, but don't sleep too late, or you'll never adjust to the time zone." She brushed the hair off his forehead. "I've missed you, baby." She leaned down and kissed his cheek. "I love you."

He closed his eyes and breathed her in, the scents of Blue Grass perfume and Drene shampoo taking him back to his childhood.

"I love you too."

She left the room, and her high heels clicked down the hall toward the staircase. The smell of her perfume lingered in his bedroom. Smiling, Robert nestled under the quilt made for him by a woman he knew would always love him and fell back to sleep.

The family was still out when he woke, and he lumbered downstairs and put some coffee on the stove to reheat. While it warmed up, he wandered around the house. Before he left for New York City eight years ago, this was the only home he'd ever known. His parents had bought it the year before Jack was born. He knew every nook, cranny, and sticky drawer by heart. Even the furniture was the same.

He ambled through the living room and ran a finger over the burn mark on one arm of the sofa. He chuckled. When Jack was thirteen, he swiped one of Dad's cigarettes. He waited until their parents went out for an afternoon and then whipped it out of his pocket with a flourish.

"Wanna smoke?" he said.

Jack said he liked it, but looking back, the way his eyes watered should have been a warning. When R.J. tried it, he took one drag and barfed all over the living room rug. In the process, he dropped the lit cigarette. It landed on the arm of the sofa, but he and Jack were so worried about the vomit on Mom's rug they didn't notice right away that the sofa was smoldering. Jack saw it when he turned around to get the mop bucket. He ripped off his shirt and beat it out while R.J., sweaty and trembling from throwing up, watched in horror.

Robert chuckled again, looking at the scorched spot. After that, he never had taken up smoking, even when he moved to New York. Mom and Dad had to have noticed the burn, but they'd never said a word. He glanced up and saw Jack's Army photo smiling down at him from the mantel. Jack's dog tags and a framed, folded American flag sat beside the photo.

"We had some fun, didn't we?" he said to the picture. Jack stared back, his face frozen in time, forever eighteen. Guilt gnawed at Robert. He should visit the cemetery, but it always felt so fake because Jack wasn't really there. His body was, but that wasn't Jack. Robert felt closer to his brother here in the living room than he ever could at his grave. He sat on the sofa and stared at the photo.

"I'm a mess," he said. He dropped his head and scrubbed his hands through his hair. "My marriage failed, I hate my job, but I can't leave it because I need the exposure, and I screwed everything up with the first girl who seemed to understand me. She actually saw *me*, not my paycheck." He rubbed his eyes with his sleeve. "Sometimes I think I should just quit everything, come back to Hell Hole, and take over the store from Dad."

His eyes traveled from his lap along the floor to the spot on the rug where he'd thrown up from the cigarette. If he squinted, he could just make out the faint line of a stain. One corner of his mouth turned up. He and Jack had scrubbed that rug for an hour to get all the vomit out. His skinny nine-year-old arms burned for the next two days from the effort.

"Don't give up, R.J.," Jack had said when R.J. started to cry from frustration. "You can do it. Just don't give up."

Robert looked up at Jack's photo and sighed.

"All right," he said. "I won't give up."

Chapter Twenty-One

Josie leaned back in her chair and tilted her face to the sun. They'd been on the Western town set all day, which was fine with her. Last week had been so nuts that spending a day outside was a relief. She'd never seen flu season hit so hard by Halloween, and her shifts at the hospital had been insane. She'd had a dozen influenza patients, three of whom got moved to ICU with pneumonia. And this week on set hadn't been any slower. Merrill was trying to get ahead on filming so they wouldn't have to come in the week of Thanksgiving, so this week's production schedule was jam-packed. They'd been hopping since 6:30 this morning.

Next to her, Beau stubbed out a cigarette, stood, and stretched.

"I think we've got some time before they're ready for us again," he said, nodding toward the crew setting up for the next scene. "Thought I'd get a Coke. You want one?"

"Yes, please."

Robert walked past and Beau called to him. He ambled over, black Stetson pulled low over his brow. He looked good in a cowboy hat, Josie had to give him that.

"Bowling this Saturday," Beau said. "You wanna go?"

Robert opened his mouth and immediately closed it again. He jammed his hands in his pockets and studied

Beau for a moment. "Yeah," he said. "I think I do."

Josie almost fell out of her chair. She stared, open-mouthed, while Beau told Robert the place and time.

"Did he just accept an invitation?" she said when Robert said goodbye and walked away.

"He did." Beau looked every bit as amazed as Josie felt. "I've been trying to get him to come along with me and the boys for months."

"Do you think he'll show up?"

Beau laughed. "Guess we'll find out."

Robert had seemed different in the week or so since he'd come back from South Carolina. He still sat alone with a book between scenes, but he'd been eating lunch at the commissary with the rest of the cast. He rarely said anything, but he sat with them. And this week, they were all so worn out that even Beau didn't have much to say at lunch.

By Friday, Josie was ready to drop. This week, they'd been outside on the Western town set, inside on the soundstage, and outside again at the Iverson Ranch. They'd been called in at 6:00 a.m. every morning and some nights didn't finish until eight. She was used to long shifts on her feet at the hospital, but this was a different sort of exhaustion. Being another person wore out her brain as well as her body. The only bright spot was Merrill handing her an invitation to the network Christmas party next month. Cassie would be over the moon when she asked her to be her date. She and Cassie could use a fun night out together.

Josie couldn't wait for next week. She wasn't needed on set, and she'd asked Nurse Fletcher not to schedule her at the hospital either. She was taking a hard-earned rest.

The only thing making the 6:00 a.m. call tolerable this morning was knowing she'd be done by lunchtime today. She could go home, take a long nap, and call Cassie. Her friend had phoned Wednesday night to chat, but Josie had been too exhausted even to talk. She told her she'd call tonight since she didn't have to be up early again tomorrow.

Josie dragged herself into the studio and dropped into a seat at the makeup table. She looked in a mirror on the table and frowned. Betty was going to need a lot of rouge to keep her from looking like a ghost.

Judging by the way Robert trudged in and plunked into the chair next to her, she guessed the early call wasn't agreeing with him either. He was even paler than she was. He mumbled a "Good morning," leaned his head against the back of his chair, and closed his eyes while Betty set to work on Josie.

She was only in two scenes today, and the whole cast was thrilled when they got the first done in a single take. This was the episode where Josie's character had been kidnapped, and the second scene was a fight in the saloon where some men who robbed a stagecoach were holding her hostage. The crew needed to set up the saloon, so craft services set out a carafe of coffee and a fresh tray of doughnuts.

Josie caught Beau's eye, and the pair of them darted for the doughnuts. She bumped him out of the way with her hip and reached the table a step ahead of him. She needed the sugar.

"You're in luck," she said. "There are two chocolate ones, and I'm feeling generous today."

Beau laughed and took the proffered doughnut. They munched their treats and chatted about their weekend plans for a few minutes. Charlie joined them, but Robert sat on the floor on the other side of the soundstage. He leaned against the wall, his head tilted back and his eyes closed.

That was strange. Why wasn't he reading? Something niggled her. Josie didn't especially want to investigate, but Nurse Donovan had to.

She poured a small cup of coffee and carried it across the soundstage. Robert sat in a shadow, but even in the dim light, she could see a flush in his cheeks.

"Hey." She nudged his arm with her toe. He looked up at her with glassy eyes. "Thought you could use perking up."

His face brightened, and he sat up a little straighter and took the coffee. His hand was too warm when it brushed hers. "Thanks," he said. He took a small sip of coffee and grimaced when he swallowed.

Yep.

"How long have you been sick?"

He ducked his head. "I'm all right. Just tired."

He was lying, but she couldn't ask any more questions because the director called them over. Good gravy, the crew had set up fast. They must be eager to finish up too. She studied Robert for one more second, then scurried onto the stage. The best thing she could do for him right now was to help get this scene shot quickly so he could go home.

Chapter Twenty-Two

Robert had woken up that morning feeling like he hadn't slept at all. This week's schedule had been rough, and he hadn't done himself any favors having Ed over for beers a couple nights ago instead of going to bed early. His stomach was a little unsettled—probably from being so tired—so all he had for breakfast before leaving the house was a cup of coffee.

His head felt fuzzy on the drive in to work, and when he sat down at makeup, he didn't even realize until his ass hit the chair that Josie was sitting right next to him. He should have been thrilled to have an excuse to be close to her, but he was so damn tired all he wanted was to go home.

When he finished at makeup, he trudged to the soundstage. Craft services had set out a tray of pastries, but he still wasn't hungry. He poured himself a glass of water and took a sip. The water prickled on its way down, and he frowned. A scratchy throat could mean only one thing. But with as hectic as the schedule had been since he got back from South Carolina, he probably shouldn't be surprised he was getting a cold.

Just get through this morning, R.J. Then you can spend the whole weekend in bed with a book and your dog.

The first scene they shot was an easy one—the interior of the sheriff's office after the men had rescued

Mary from the kidnappers. A few minutes of them congratulating each other and cracking a couple jokes, and that was that. But in just that half hour or so, he started feeling a lot worse awfully fast. His head throbbed, and despite the blazingly hot stage lights and the heavy jacket Wardrobe had put him in this morning, he couldn't stop shivering.

Josie was an angel bringing him that coffee between scenes. That was the first time she'd approached him since Yosemite, and her nose had scrunched when she smiled. He should have said something nice to her to try to break some of the tension between them. A compliment on her acting, a cute joke at Beau's expense... something. But it took all his brainpower right then just to thank her for the coffee. And even if he'd managed to come up with something witty to say, talking was starting to hurt too. Drinking that coffee was like swallowing razorblades. At least the warm cup had felt good on his hands. Even his fingers ached.

Now, this scene with the fight in the saloon was taking longer to shoot than it should have. First, Charlie flubbed his lines, then none of the kidnappers could find their marks, and then Beau tripped over a chair and crashed to the floor. Each time the director yelled "Cut" and made them do it over, Robert felt a little piece of himself die. He'd stopped shivering and started sweating buckets. His handkerchief was soaked with sweat, so he started mopping his brow on his jacket sleeve. Hopefully the growing damp spot wouldn't show up on camera, but he couldn't tell how obvious it was. He had to blink a lot to keep things in focus.

On the fourth try, they finally got the scene's intro right and set up for the big fight between the lawmen and the kidnappers. They'd been practicing the blocking for the fight all week. Please, God, let them get this right the first time. This was going to take everything he had left.

At least the cast wasn't filming the entire fight. They only had to do the opening and closing shots, and the stuntmen would fill in the rest. After Charlie accidentally gave Beau a shiner last season, Merrill quit letting them do their own stunts. So, after thirty minutes of shots of the men getting angry and rushing the robbers from various angles, they were finished. But it was an intense thirty minutes. He, Beau, and Charlie had to do a lot of running around. All Josie had to do was stand there and look scared. He would have given anything to trade roles with her right then, even if it meant wearing a skirt.

He righted an overturned saloon chair and sat while the director went over his list to make sure he got all the shots he wanted. Couldn't they at least shut off the stage lights while they waited? Sweat poured down his face. He rested his elbows on his knees and dropped his head into his hands, knocking off his hat. He didn't pick it up.

"That's a wrap," the director called. Josie and Beau whooped, and Charlie muttered something that sounded like, "Thank you, Jesus."

Robert could second that.

He lifted his head, put his hands on his knees, and shoved himself up. His vision narrowed to a slim tunnel, and the floor rushed toward him.

That was strange. Why was the floor coming up? Floors didn't do that. Must be an earthquake. He hoped Sergeant was okay at home.

"Grab him!" Beau hollered from somewhere far away.

Grab who? He tried to look around, but everything

had gone dark.

Something hooked around his chest, and he fell backward, landing hard on his backside.

"Easy there, Robert, easy there," Charlie said from nearby.

That must be Charlie's arm around his chest. The floor hadn't been rushing toward him. He'd been falling. Charlie caught him, or at least pushed him back into his chair. He wanted to say thank you, but he couldn't force out the words. Someone pulled off his jacket. He shivered as the air hit his sweat-soaked shirt.

"He's burning up," Charlie said. "And I mean bad."

A soft, blessedly cool hand landed on Robert's cheek. He opened his eyes, and a freckled face framed by black hair swam into view.

Good God, Josie was touching him.

His guts did a somersault, and he drew in a deep breath.

Do not throw up on Josie, R.J. Don't you dare.

Her eyes grew to the size of dinner plates.

"Get him out from under these lights," she said, her voice tight. "Now."

Chapter Twenty-Three

Josie had snapped out of her Mary Anderson persona the instant Robert went down. Now she hovered around Charlie and Beau as they each swung one of Robert's arms around their shoulders and heaved him from his chair. Young, strong men like him didn't go down easily. Whatever was wrong, it was bad. He needed Nurse Donovan.

Robert growled, "I can walk."

"Sure you can," Charlie said while he and Beau half-dragged Robert into the dim light offstage. They eased him to the floor and propped him against the wall.

Josie whipped her handkerchief from her skirt pocket and knelt next to him. "Get me a first-aid kit and a glass of water," she said. She reached to wipe the sweat from his face, but Robert drew his knees up to his chest, crossed his arms over them, and dropped his forehead onto his arms, hiding his face.

She looked behind her. The entire cast and crew were gathered around, staring down at them. "And maybe a little privacy?" she said, letting irritation creep into her voice. The last thing Robert needed right now was an audience. "Good gravy, don't you all have work to do?"

With muttered apologies and flushed cheeks, the crowd dispersed. Robert raised his head.

"Thanks," he said, his voice raw. He dropped his

head again and coughed.

"Don't mention it," she said. At least he was talking normally. The fever wasn't high enough to make him delirious, but it still had to be pretty high to make him pass out. He must be dehydrated. Charlie knelt next to her and handed her a small tin first-aid box. She flipped the latches open. *Please let this kit be properly stocked.*

"You want me to go?" Charlie asked Robert, who shook his head. He reached for the glass of water Charlie held, but Josie put a hand on Charlie's arm.

"Let's get your temperature first," she said. She dug into the first-aid box and found a thermometer and a couple packets of aspirin. She gave the thermometer a good shake and popped it into Robert's mouth. His face screwed up, but he clamped the thermometer between his lips and sat quietly. She frowned. He must be really bad off if he couldn't muster the energy to be contrary.

When she took the thermometer from him a few minutes later, her heart sank.

"One-oh-*five*," Charlie said, reading over her shoulder. Josie looked at him and saw his face go pale. "We should call an ambulance."

Robert's head snapped up, and he locked eyes with Josie. The pupils of his sunken eyes were wide, and she could hear his breath coming quick and shallow. She'd seen that look before from hundreds of patients.

He was scared.

She couldn't blame him. Being this sick was frightening. She opened her mouth to tell Charlie to make the phone call, but Robert's face crumpled, taking her heart with it. She closed her mouth and put herself in his shoes. All his family was on the other side of the country, and apart from someone named Ed who he'd mentioned once or twice, he didn't seem to have many friends. He was sick as a dog and all alone.

In the same situation, Josie Girl, you'd be clinging to any familiar face too.

She sighed. He most likely had the flu. So long as he didn't get pneumonia, all they could do for him at the hospital that she couldn't do right here was administer intravenous fluids. The high fever was probably just from the hot stage lights anyway. She looked at the clock on the wall. 11:30. She'd give herself two hours to bring his fever down. If she couldn't get him below 104 by then or if he worsened, she'd call for that ambulance. She told Charlie and Robert the plan.

"But you have to drink all the water I give you," she said to Robert. "All right?"

He nodded. "Thank you," he rasped.

She smiled, and without thinking, she reached to brush the sweaty hair off his forehead. She stopped her hand halfway and let it hover in the air for a moment until she patted his shoulder instead.

"All right, Charlie," she said. "Help me get him to the dressing room?"

All three men shared a dressing room. *Gunslingers* wasn't a big enough moneymaker for the studio to give them each their own, and Josie didn't get one at all. She changed in and out of her costume in the ladies' restroom near the set. Charlie waved to Beau, who was flitting around the coffeepot. He skittered over, slung one of Robert's arms over his shoulders again, and said "Where to?"

Beau and Charlie hauled him to a golf cart, and they all rode across the lot to the dressing rooms building, where they settled their burden onto the sofa in the men's dressing room. Beau pulled off Robert's boots while Josie handed her patient three aspirin and a glass of water.

"You need anything?" Charlie asked.

She shook her head. "I'll call the stage if I need you."

"All right," Charlie said. "I'll check on you when I'm finished." He and Beau had one last scene to shoot, just the pair of them.

"I guess this means you're not coming bowling tomorrow?" Beau said. Charlie rolled his eyes, grabbed Beau's arm, and dragged him out.

When the door clicked shut behind them, Josie looked down at the pale, sweaty man laid out on the sofa and shook her head. "You are a mess. When did this start?"

He looked at her for a moment as if considering something, then rubbed his temples. "Felt okay this morning when I got up. Just tired. Figured I hadn't slept well." He took a swallow of water and grimaced. "But it kept getting worse."

"Your throat hurts and you're dizzy. What else?"

"My head's pounding, and I hurt all over." He coughed twice. "And that's starting." His hand shook as he tried to take another sip of water, and a few droplets splattered on his shirt. He cursed and immediately apologized.

She knelt next to the sofa and laid a hand on his shoulder.

"It's all right. All this is common with influenza."

He glanced at her hand on his shoulder and lifted his gaze back to her face. His pupils were a normal size now, but his eyes still radiated anxiety. His irises were flecked with gold like they'd been sprinkled with glitter. She'd never noticed that before. She stared into them.

"You think that's what it is?" he said.

His voice snapped her back like a rubber band, and she snatched her hand off his shoulder, crossing both arms over her stomach.

"I'm certain of it," she said. "If there's one thing I know, it's the flu. Now let's get this fever down."

She went to the dressing room's small bathroom and rolled up her sleeves. Thank goodness Wardrobe had put her in a practical shirtwaist and skirt today instead of a frilly dress. She opened the cabinets under the sink and smiled when she saw a stack of plush towels. She grabbed a washcloth, dampened it, and headed back to the sofa.

Robert's eyes were closed, and his breathing was slow and even. Lucky stiff. She'd give anything to take a nap right now. She'd gotten a nice shot of adrenaline when he collapsed, but now that she knew he wasn't going to die on her in the next ten minutes, her exhaustion crashed back down. She shook her head to wake herself up. Her patient needed her.

She sponged his hot face and neck with the washcloth. An uneven row of little red nicks dotted his jawline like a rash. His hands must have already been shaky when he shaved this morning. She traced the angry line with a finger, and he sighed.

Don't wake him, Josie Girl. Let the man sleep.

She pulled her finger away and waited to make sure he was still settled. Then she draped the washcloth over her arm and reached for the top buttons of his shirt.

She froze up.

That was strange. What was the problem? She'd

undressed hundreds of male patients over the years, beginning with her brother Ben that time he accidentally set his pants on fire when they were kids. Then her stomach rumbled. That was it. All she'd eaten today was a piece of toast before she came to work and that doughnut a couple hours ago. She glanced at the wall clock. A few minutes past noon. She'd finish sponging Robert off and then call the stage to ask a production assistant to please grab her some lunch from the commissary.

She reached for Robert's buttons again and caught a whiff of his bay rum aftershave. The woody, masculine scent made her lightheaded. She *really* needed to eat. Before she could freeze up again, she undid the top three buttons of his shirt and mopped his chest. He didn't even stir, his eyes still closed, long, dark lashes nearly brushing his cheekbones. She blinked furiously.

"Keep it together, Josie Girl," she muttered.

Chapter Twenty-Four

Before Josie could call about lunch, someone knocked on the dressing-room door. She opened it and saw an assistant standing in the hallway. He held a tray with two covered bowls, two sets of silverware, and two bottles of Coke.

"Mr. Lyon asked me to bring you lunch."

God bless Charlie.

"I could kiss you," she said, taking the tray from him. The young man blushed and stuttered an offer to fetch anything else she might need, but she thanked him and closed the door.

She set the tray on a small table near the door and danced in a little circle when she uncovered the first bowl and found her favorite macaroni and cheese from the commissary. The second bowl was full of hot vegetable soup.

"Charlie, you are getting a nice Christmas present," she said. She grabbed a fork off the tray and shoveled macaroni and cheese into her mouth. Robert could sleep a few more minutes while she ate. She wouldn't be any good to him if she fainted from hunger, and that soup looked too hot anyway. Between bites, she used a butterknife from the tray to pry the cap off a Coke bottle. She smiled when the first biting, fizzy drops hit her tongue. This would perk her up. She polished off her lunch in no time and let out a satisfied sigh.

Waking Robert seemed cruel, but she needed to take his temperature again to see if the aspirin had helped. She walked to the sofa and shook his shoulder. He groaned, and his eyes fluttered open slowly. He blinked several times and looked around the room, clearly confused. His gaze finally settled on Josie, and he smiled just big enough to dimple his cheek.

"Oh, hey." He covered his mouth with his elbow and coughed.

"Sorry to wake you. I need to get your temperature again, and Charlie had lunch sent up."

He nodded, and Josie poked the thermometer in his mouth. When she read the numbers a couple minutes later, she closed her eyes and let out a puff of breath. Progress.

"A hundred and three point six," she said. "Still pretty high, but better."

He didn't want to eat, but she coaxed him into having a little soup and Coke. The carbonated soda probably burned his throat, but the sugar would help because—good gravy!—he was still so weak and dizzy. He got up to use the bathroom and had to hang onto various bits of furniture just to cross the short distance from the sofa. Fevers must hit him hard.

When he came back, as slowly and cautiously as he'd left, he dropped onto the sofa and immediately closed his eyes. She checked his pulse and frowned. Just that short walk had sent his heartrate skyrocketing. She dampened a fresh washcloth and wiped down his face again. He smiled.

"Thank you, that feels nice," he said, his eyes still closed.

At least he didn't seem so scared any more, but he

looked awfully helpless and miserable, lying there on the sofa. Poor guy. She reached for him and, this time, didn't resist brushing a damp lock of dark hair off his forehead. "Go back to sleep. I'll be right here."

He nodded, but she wasn't sure he'd heard her. He was asleep within seconds.

She'd had the good sense to bring along the bag with her regular clothes, so she ducked into the bathroom and changed. Then she sank into a chair and picked up a James Bond novel that was sitting on an end table. She tried to read it, but she was so tired, and her attention kept drifting to Robert, still sound asleep on the sofa.

The aspirin was doing the trick with his fever, but it couldn't make him steadier on his feet. If Charlie hadn't caught him when he fainted, he would have cracked his head on the corner of the saloon bar. What if he fell when he was home alone? Even if he stayed upright, there was no way he could stand long enough to make himself a decent meal. Maybe this nap would help.

She woke him thirty minutes later and took his temperature again. His fever was down to 103 on the nose.

"Good," he said, "I can go home." He closed his eyes and smiled.

"First I want to see you walk across this room."

He opened his eyes. "I'm sorry?"

"I need to know you're not going to collapse again. If you can walk across the room and back with no trouble, we'll send you home."

He scowled. "That wasn't the bargain."

"I know. I'm sorry. I thought the dizziness would clear up as your fever went down."

He propped himself up on his elbows, heaved, and

sat up. It clearly took some effort, but he could do it.

So far, so good.

He swung his legs over the side of the sofa, inhaled, and stood. He wavered for a moment and sank right back onto the sofa and dropped his head into his hands. Josie sat next to him and spoke softly. He wasn't going to like this.

"We need to take you in."

He bristled. "I'm not going to the hospital."

"It's not that bad. You get to lie in bed all weekend and have beautiful young women tend to your every need." Surely that would appeal to him.

"You can take me in, but I'll check myself out as soon as you leave."

She sighed. "Robert, listen to me. I've seen hundreds of flu cases, and I'm here to tell you that you're too sick to be on your own. If your fever spikes again or you fall and there's no one around, you're gonna be in big trouble."

"I'll be fine. I'll keep some aspirin next to my bed, and I won't get up."

She growled deep in her throat.

"You're infuriating, you know that?" She clapped a hand over her mouth as soon as the words were out. She knew better than to snap at a patient. People this sick didn't act rationally. Still, it had felt good to say.

Robert's face crumpled like it had on set when she'd read out his first temperature. He tucked his lower lip under his front teeth and looked up at her, his eyes red and watery.

"I'm sorry," he said, nearly whispering.

Why did he have to look so sad when he apologized? It made it really hard to stay mad at him. She sighed.

"Do you have any friends you could stay with?" she said.

He shook his head. "Ed and his kids are sick. Found out last night." He groaned. "Dammit, Ed! We had beers a couple nights ago." He coughed, and she gave him the water glass.

"At least we know where you got the flu."

He took a sip of water. "And who to blame when everyone else gets sick too."

"Not me," Josie said. "I got a flu shot." If she was still around next season, she was going to make sure every cast and crew member got one, even if she had to administer them herself.

The corner of Robert's mouth turned up in a half-smile, and he took another sip of water. "Still leaves me without a friend to stay with."

Josie frowned. The hospital was the obvious answer, but for someone so private, having a parade of strangers poking at him all weekend would be torture. Would he get much rest like that? And rest was what he needed most. Besides, the set look on his face told her he wasn't bluffing when he said he'd check himself right out. He could leave the hospital and end up home alone anyway. She had a patient once who died after doing that. There had to be another solution. *Think, Josie, think.*

Her scalp jumped.

Oh, no. No, no, no, Josie Girl, bad idea. Don't do it.

But she'd become a nurse to help people, and if anyone needed that compassion right now, it was him.

"What if a friend stayed with you instead?" she said.

Robert's eyebrows met. "Ed's the only friend I'm close enough to for that sort of a favor, and I just told you he's sick."

"But I'm not. I could sleep on your couch for a weekend."

Robert's mouth gaped, and he started coughing. He drank some more water.

"I have guestrooms," he said, wiping his mouth with his sleeve. "You don't have to sleep on the couch." They stared at each other.

Too late to turn back now.

"That's settled, then," she said at last, breaking their eye contact. "I'll go find Beau and Charlie. We'll need help getting you home."

Chapter Twenty-Five

Robert would have given almost anything to curl up on the back seat of Charlie's Skyliner and go back to sleep, but thanks to his habit of keeping to himself, Charlie had no idea where he lived. Instead, he sat up in the front passenger seat, trying to stay awake enough to give directions.

There was no way he could have driven himself home. He'd had to stop twice to catch his breath and wait for the floor to stop rolling under him just on the walk from the dressing room to Charlie's car.

Good God, he'd never felt so horrible in his life. Everything hurt: his head, his throat, his joints. When Charlie and Beau dragged him off stage, he'd had a moment where he honestly thought he was dying. And if Josie hadn't been there, he'd be settling into a hospital room right now rather than on his way home.

He wished he hadn't slept through most of their time together in the dressing room. It was largely a haze of soft hands and cool rags. He vaguely remembered her unbuttoning his shirt. He *really* wished he'd been fully awake for that.

And now she was coming to stay with him this weekend.

His stomach rolled, and he wasn't sure whether it was from the flu or nerves. Maybe this was a second chance. Even if he could stand up right now, he wouldn't dare make another move on her. But maybe they could at least mend the friendship he'd ruined.

He couldn't believe she'd offered to stay. They'd barely spoken since Yosemite, even after he started eating lunch with the cast. Now she was going to be sleeping in the bedroom across the hall from his. He didn't deserve this sort of compassion. He shook his head and was immediately punished with a sharp stab of pain like someone had shot him in the temple. He winced.

"Hang in there," Charlie said, downshifting for a traffic light. "We close?"

"Yeah." Robert gave him directions for the last two turns. Thank God he'd bought a house near the studio and not all the way out in Santa Monica or Inglewood. He definitely would have had to lie down on the back seat if they were going that far.

When they reached his house, he unlocked the door and sent Charlie in first. Sergeant was always so excited when he came home, and he didn't want to get knocked over and end up with a concussion. Josie would send him to the hospital then for sure.

He told Charlie where to find the dog food and shuffled to his bedroom. Another wave of dizziness hit him, and he gripped the edge of his dresser.

God, this was awful.

When the spell passed and he straightened up, his hand bumped a photo frame, knocking it askew. He straightened it. Jack's eighteen-year-old face smiled up at him, and he smiled back. When he came home from South Carolina, he'd set it out for the first time. He'd never been able to bear displaying it before. But it looked nice on his dresser next to a picture of Matthew, and he drew a sense of comfort knowing that his big brother was still there, in some form, watching out for him. He fingered the gold star pin that sat next to the photo and chuckled.

"You will not believe who's coming over."

Chapter Twenty-Six

Josie took Robert's car to her place so she could pack a bag and hit the grocery store while Charlie drove Robert home. Staying the weekend with Robert was probably the dumbest idea she'd ever had, but at least she got to drive his car. All the guys had flashy cars, but his was the sweetest chariot she'd ever seen: A sleek, black Chevrolet Corvette flip-top with white swoops on the side panels, black interior, and four on the floor. In a big city with public transportation, owning a car seemed unnecessary, but she sure wouldn't mind having a Corvette. She couldn't wait to get behind the wheel and put it through its paces.

But as soon as she slid into the driver's seat and took the shiny black steering wheel in her hands, she broke into a cold sweat.

"Do not crash the five-thousand-dollar car, Josie," she muttered. She hadn't driven anything for nearly a year, and something told her the Corvette's clutch would be very different from the clutch in Daddy's old pickup. She turned the key, and the engine roared to life, sending tingles up both arms. She said a silent prayer to the manual transmission gods to not let her stall the car too many times and slid it into gear.

She stalled twice on the ten-minute drive to her apartment but not at all between her apartment and the grocery store. There was no telling what Robert might have in his refrigerator, so she loaded up on just about everything, especially aspirin and cough drops. She smiled as the cashier rang her up. She had so many groceries it almost looked like she was shopping for her family again.

When she reached the address Robert had written down, she double-checked his note to make sure that she had the right place. The house was a three-gabled bungalow, the style that was so popular in LA. Covered in dark-red siding with a gray-brick chimney, the two-story home was larger than she'd expected a bachelor to have. A swing hung from the rafters of the covered front porch, and a large bow window popped out from one side. This couldn't be it, but there was Charlie's car, parked out front.

"How charming," she said, pulling into the driveway. She never would have expected Robert's house to be so cute. A dank cave seemed more likely.

Charlie stepped outside, greeted her, and took the groceries. Her nerves jangled as she approached the front door. No turning back now. She was spending the weekend at Robert's house.

Oh, Lord, please let this have been a good decision.

Sergeant bounded up as soon as she stepped over the threshold into the living room. The floppy-eared brindle puppy had grown a lot since she'd last seen him. He was probably about his adult height, but he hadn't filled out yet, giving him the lanky, big-headed look of a teenage boy. She set her bag on the floor and scratched him behind the ears. His tongue lolled out the side of his mouth, and she grinned, her nervousness melting away. How could she possibly feel anxious in this adorable house with this goofy dog?

Almost everything inside the house spoke to simplicity and orderliness, and the furniture looked new. Josie snickered. She bet Robert's sofa didn't complain every time someone sat on it. Apart from a clock, nothing hung on the living-room walls. Daylight poured through numerous windows, giving the whole space a much friendlier, more outgoing feeling than she would have expected. Definitely not a cave.

The one material thing Robert had in abundance was books. Three large bookcases took up one wall of the living room. Every inch of space was filled, but the books were neatly arranged, without a speck of dust on them. Josie was instantly jealous. She didn't have room for many books at her place. She had to make do with borrowing a few at a time from the library, and she'd love to have a stockpile like this. She ached to run her fingers across the spines, read the titles, open a few and smell the pages, but Charlie was moving on without her. With Sergeant trotting along, she scurried through a set of French doors, crossed the dining room, and met Charlie in the kitchen.

Charlie gave her Sergeant's feeding instructions while they put the groceries away. There wasn't a single drip on the counters or speck of dirt on the linoleum floor. Robert must have a housekeeper.

With the groceries squared away, Charlie led Josie down a small hallway and pointed to the guestroom. The room sported only a double bed, a small chest of drawers, another bookshelf, and a nightstand with a reading lamp and an alarm clock. She liked it instantly.

"Robert's just across the hall," Charlie said, dropping her bag onto the bed. "He changed into some pajamas and fell asleep as soon as I got him home." He pulled his car keys out of his pocket. "I'll call you tomorrow to see how you're getting on. I expect Beau will too."

"Thank you."

Charlie studied her hard and fiddled with his keys. "You sure you don't want me or Beau to stay with you?"

Josie smiled. They'd both offered, but she didn't want this flu to spread. Charlie had already played with fire by driving Robert home. "I'll be fine."

"This is awfully good of you, Josie. I'm sure Robert appreciates it."

He better, she thought. She was ready to drop from exhaustion and was giving up the first weekend of her long-awaited vacation, to boot.

She and Sergeant saw Charlie to the door and then went past a set of stairs and back down the hall to her room. She'd set the medications she'd bought on her nightstand, so she stuck a few cough drops in her jeans pocket and grabbed a bottle of aspirin. Taking her stethoscope and thermometer from her valise, she went across the hall and paused outside Robert's door.

She was about to go into his bedroom, where he was lying in his bed. This wasn't like going into a patient's room. This was much more familiar than that. Her stomach fluttered.

Just get it over with, Josie Girl.

She took a deep breath and knocked softly on the door.

No answer. He was probably sleeping soundly now that he was home. She cracked the door open and poked her head in. Sergeant pushed past her. The room was dim, but even in the low light, she could see it was as simply furnished as the guestroom and as clean as the rest of the house. The bed was bigger, and the dresser held a couple framed photographs, but otherwise, it was pretty spartan. Except for another bookshelf, of course. This one a bit smaller, only chest high, and filled to the brim with neat rows of books. On one side of the bed, Robert lay flat on his back under a patchwork quilt, one arm thrown up over his head. Sergeant ran to his side, sniffed him, then came back to Josie and whined. She smiled and scratched his head.

"Don't worry, boy, I'll fix him up for you," she whispered.

With Sergeant at her heels, she crossed the room and looked down at Robert. People always looked so much younger when they were asleep. Sick people, especially. Younger and vulnerable. Maybe that's what drew her to nursing, protecting vulnerable people. She shook her head. She never would have imagined Robert Coolidge of all people as vulnerable, but here they were.

A light sheen of sweat glistened at his hairline and along his jaw, and his face was pinched, his brows meeting in a "v." He coughed a few times and groaned without opening his eyes. Good thing she bought those cough drops. She laid a hand on his forehead and frowned. His fever burned nearly as hot and angry as it had when he blacked out, but—she checked the bedside clock—he hadn't had any aspirin in over four hours. She turned on the bedside lamp and shook his shoulder gently.

Robert's eyes blinked open, and a smile bloomed across his face. "You actually came over," he said. He lowered his arm to his side.

He seemed so relieved. Why would he think she wouldn't come?

"Of course. I said I would."

He cast his eyes to the quilt and traced a finger along a red floral starburst block on the quilt, which Josie recognized as a scrap from an old flour sack. Her mother had a skirt in the same sack fabric when Josie was small.

"I thought you hated me," he mumbled.

Did she? Josie considered this. Four or five months ago, she might have agreed. But apart from that single moment at Yosemite, he'd been a gentleman since they met. She should give him some grace.

"'Hate' is a strong word." She put a finger under his chin and tilted his face up to look at her. "Besides, if anything happened to you, they'd have to recast the part. And the next guy could be an even bigger pain in the neck."

He chuckled, which made him cough a couple times. She'd have to be careful about making him laugh until he was feeling better. But the cheek-dimpling grin that spread across his face was worth it, at least this once.

"That's better," she said, smiling. "Now don't worry. Nurse Donovan is here to pull you through. Let me get your temperature."

She popped the thermometer in his mouth before he could reply. The mercury shot to 104.2. She shook three aspirin out of the bottle and pushed them into his hand. He swallowed the pills, chasing them with a swig of water from a glass that Charlie must have set on the nightstand.

"I want to listen to your lungs," she said, sticking the earpieces of her stethoscope into her ears. Something shifted inside her as soon as she wielded her stethoscope. She wasn't an exhausted, bewildered girl trying to figure out this man she found herself alone with. She was Nurse

Donovan again, treating a patient. And Nurse Donovan didn't hesitate to tell the patient to unbutton his shirt.

Robert's eyebrows nearly hit his hairline, but he unfastened the buttons of his striped pajama top.

She was suddenly that bewildered girl again.

She'd seen Beau shirtless at least a dozen times already—he enjoyed showing off his body on camera—but not Robert. Barrel-chested and chiseled, he looked like he could snap Beau in half. She bit hard on her tongue and pressed the diaphragm of the stethoscope to his chest, being careful not to brush his skin with her hand. No good getting *that* familiar. She closed her eyes and focused on the sound of the air whooshing in and out of his lungs. He sounded clear, thank goodness.

"No signs of pneumonia," she said, stepping back and pulling the stethoscope from her ears. "I'll keep an eye on it, but so far, so good."

He nodded, buttoned his shirt, and fell back onto his pillows. He looked so pitiful, lying there pale and sweaty. She didn't have anything to worry about. She was in complete control of this situation. She smiled and patted his arm.

"I'll go make supper."

She thought Sergeant might stay with Robert, but the dog must have sensed there was food involved and followed her to the kitchen.

Robert's kitchen was amazing. She'd been surprised how well stocked the pantry and refrigerator were when she'd put the groceries away, but the appliances were the best part. The counters sported a toaster and a shiny electric mixer—both spotless, of course. In a little closet off the kitchen, Josie found an automatic washing machine and a dryer. A dryer! Jimmy wouldn't buy their family an electric dryer. He said with all the wind in Kansas, they didn't need one. She hadn't gotten to use one until she moved to Hollywood and went to the laundromat for the first time.

The automatic dishwasher was her favorite, though. She swore she'd spent half her life washing and drying dishes, and here was a machine that would do it for her. Her fingers hovered over the buttons, but she pulled back. The last thing she needed was to break Robert's dishwasher. Maybe he could show her how it worked once he felt better. She could wash dishes by hand until then.

Twenty minutes later, after opening just about every kitchen cabinet and drawer to find what she needed, she carried a tray with a steaming bowl of chicken noodle soup, a few saltine crackers, and another glass of water into the bedroom. Robert heaved himself to sitting, and she placed the tray on his lap.

"You didn't have to go to all this trouble," he said.

She chuckled. "It's just Campbell's soup. But I bought the ingredients to make you the real thing tomorrow."

Robert looked up and caught her eye. "Let me know what I owe you for the groceries."

Josie wrapped her arms around her middle. "I need to eat too."

Robert didn't break eye contact. "I'll repay you for the groceries."

There was no use arguing with him, so she nodded. "If you're all right here, I've got a sandwich waiting for myself in the kitchen." He nodded, and she left the room.

Chapter Twenty-Seven

Robert wasn't hungry, but he forced down the soup
and crackers anyway because it would make Josie happy.
As it turned out, the hot soup felt good on his throat, but
eating wore him out. When Josie collected his tray, he
was barely able to thank her before he dozed off.

Sometime later, he woke to his shoulder jiggling. He
opened his eyes and saw Josie looming over him, the
light from his bedside lamp casting a halo around her
head. Sergeant sat next to her, leaning against her legs.
Traitor. Apparently, dog was only man's best friend until
woman came over. His throat had dried out while he
slept, making it hurt worse than ever. He swallowed
some saliva, but it wasn't enough. It felt like a thousand
fingernails raking down his throat. He reached for his
water, but Josie laid her hand on his arm and stopped
him. Even through his pajama sleeve, her touch prickled
his skin.

"Let me get your temperature first," she said. Her
voice was soft and soothing, and he let her stick the
thermometer under his tongue.

While they waited for the mercury to climb, she took
hold of his wrist and pressed two fingers to the underside
to take his pulse. While she stared down at her
wristwatch and counted, he studied her.

He still couldn't believe she was in his house. She
could have sent him off to the hospital in an ambulance

and gone home to enjoy her weekend without a backward glance. She owed him nothing. If anything, tonight was costing her. Her face was pale, and the thin skin under her eyes was smudged purple. This week had taken its toll on her too.

"Seventy-three," she said, letting go of his wrist.

"What?" The delicate skin on the underside of his wrist tingled as if it were trying to hold onto the memory of her touch.

She smiled and readjusted the thermometer in his mouth.

"Your heart rate. Seventy-three beats per minute. A bit higher than I'd typically expect, but not bad given how sick you are."

A minute or so later, she took the thermometer and read it off. 103.4.

"That's not terrible, either, considering it's time for more aspirin," she said. She shook three tablets out of the bottle on the nightstand and handed them to him. He sat up and flinched as he swallowed them, those damn fingernails raking his throat again. He groaned as he lay back down.

"Hang in there. It'll get better eventually, I promise," Josie said, pulling the quilt up to his shoulders. She ran a finger along the edge of the fabric. "This is beautiful, by the way."

Warmth that had nothing to do with his fever flowed through him. "My mom made it for me when I was born." He sipped some water so he could croak out one more sentence. "Brought it home from my trip a couple weeks ago."

The quilt wasn't quite big enough for his bed— Mom had made it for a double, not a queen—but he didn't care. She had made it especially for him. And in the middle of the Depression, she probably spent months scrounging up enough fabric scraps and then months more sewing it while caring for two young boys and keeping house. He'd slept under it almost every night of his life until he moved to New York. Even on summer nights when it was too hot to burrow under a quilt, he'd at least stick his toes under it. When he packed his suitcase to come back to LA last month, he just couldn't stand to leave it behind.

Josie studied him for a moment, her gaze so intense she might have been reading his thoughts. She cocked her head. "That trip was good for you," she said at last. "You've been happier since you came back."

His felt his eyebrows lift. He thought she'd been flat-out ignoring him for months, but she couldn't have known that if she hadn't been paying attention to him.

Something in the back of his brain told him this should be a momentous revelation, but he was so damn tired he could barely think straight. He rubbed his eyes.

"Get some sleep," Josie said. "I'll be poking in on you every four hours with more aspirin, I'm afraid, but we need to keep that fever down."

He nodded. He wouldn't care if she woke him every forty-five minutes. He was just so glad to be at home in his own bed.

Josie turned to leave, then glanced back. "Do you mind if I use your phone? I promised a girlfriend I'd call her this evening. It's local."

"Please do." He held her gaze. "And thank you."

She stared back, then swallowed hard. "What for?"

He steeled himself. He was so sleepy, and talking hurt like hell, but he had to get this last bit out.

"Everything. Taking care of me at the studio. Staying here this weekend. Making dinner. Just… everything."

She crossed her arms across her stomach. She did that a lot, like she was trying to hug herself. She glanced down at her middle and dropped her arms. "Like I said. I don't want to take any chances with who might get recast in your part."

****

He slept fitfully, with hazy, bizarre dreams shuffling him in and out of wakefulness. He was shooting a film in the swamp. Matthew called for him, but he couldn't tell from which direction. Jack was there, saying something. Robert couldn't figure out what, but he basked in the sound of his big brother's voice—that voice he'd known so well but had faded in his memory over the years. A hard knot rose in his angry throat. He tried to apologize for not remembering better, but Jack disappeared. Hot tears burned his scrunched eyes.

"Hey." A soft voice, not Jack's.

He dragged his eyes open and winced at the sudden blast of yellow light from the bedside lamp. Josie hovered over him, her long black hair falling loose over her shoulders.

He whispered her name like it was poetry, his throat burning in protest. He moaned. Good God, it shouldn't be possible, but he felt even worse than he had this afternoon. It was like his entire body was clenched in a vise.

"Your fever's going back up," she said. "We need to get more aspirin in you. Can you sit up?"

He wasn't sure, but he'd try anything if she asked him. He braced his elbows on the mattress and pushed, and Josie propped up his pillows behind him. He leaned against them and dropped his head back against the headboard. Josie stuck the thermometer in his mouth. A couple minutes later, she shook her head.

"One-oh-four point two." She scowled. "Oh, no, you don't." She handed him three aspirin and a glass of water. Throat screaming, he took the pills. "Fevers often get worse at night." She patted his arm. "You lie down. I'll be right back."

He shifted his pillows and settled back. The clock on his nightstand said 2:30 a.m.

Geez, had Josie been up with him all night? He groaned and rubbed his temples with aching fingers. Even if she hadn't, she must have been up a few times to check on him. Last evening swam back into his brain. She'd said she'd wake him every four hours for aspirin. She must have come in at least once already and he didn't remember.

She came back with a damp washcloth and mopped his face. He disintegrated when she brushed his hair off his brow. He closed his eyes, wishing he could hold onto the feeling of her hand on his skin forever. The familiar medicinal scent of Lifebuoy soap drifted down. She must have used his shower.

Oh, Lord. Don't think about that, R.J.

She unfastened the top button of his pajamas and sponged him off all the way down his throat and over the delicate notch where his collarbones met. His heart pounded, and he dug his fingernails into his palms to ground himself.

"Your hands hurting bad?" she said. "Viruses always make my joints ache."

She set the washcloth down and picked up his right hand. She rubbed his palm with her thumbs, moving in slow circles. She worked her way down his thumb, then up each finger, gently squeezing each fingernail. Finished with that hand, she set it down on the bed and picked up his left and repeated the process.

His heart shattered.

Her touch was like balm on a sunburn, soothing away the pain in his hands, but she wasn't doing it out of affection. She was Nurse Donovan tending a patient, not Josie helping a friend. A friend who loved her. No sense denying it. He loved her, and he'd ruined everything. Any chance they'd had at something more had imploded that night in Yosemite.

This was all he was ever going to get.

Chapter Twenty-Eight

All Josie wanted to do was go back to bed, but she had to make sure the aspirin she'd just given Robert was working before she left him alone. She sat on the floor, leaned against the bed, and glanced at the clock on the nightstand. 2:45. At 3:15 she'd take his temperature again and see where they stood.

"Come on, Robert," she whispered. "Don't make me drag you to the emergency room in the middle of the night."

The aspirin should bring down the fever, but she couldn't go back to bed until she was sure. She just had to stay awake long enough to check again. Robert had knocked right back off after she massaged his hands, and the sound of his soft, even breathing only inches behind her wasn't helping. She looked at Sergeant, who was curled up on the rug next to her.

"Don't let me fall asleep, okay?"

The boxer yawned and stretched, his back feet pressing into her thigh. He grunted and rolled onto his back, hindlegs splayed, testicles rolling on his belly.

She covered her eyes with one hand. "Thanks, Sergeant, that's really helpful."

She should have gone to bed right after cleaning up supper, but she'd desperately wanted a shower to wash away the grime and stress of the day. She didn't remember she'd promised to call Cassie until she got out, and by that time, she only had fifteen minutes left until Robert needed more aspirin. That was nowhere near enough time for a phone call with Cassie.

She didn't dial her friend's number until almost eight o'clock.

"Josie!" Cassie's voice was shrill. "I was so worried when you didn't call. I tried you three times. I was afraid you'd had an accident or something."

"I'm sorry," Josie said. She stretched the long phone cord to the breakfast nook in the corner of the kitchen and sat down at the small table. "I'm not at home. I'm staying with a...patient this weekend." She paused briefly. "And probably into the first part of next week." With the shape he was in, Robert would likely be flat on his back for several days.

"With a patient? Are you at the hospital? I thought you were on set today."

Josie sighed. There was no way around explaining. "Someone came down with a bad case of the flu on set this morning. He refused to go to the hospital, but he couldn't possibly be left by himself all weekend."

She'd never known it was possible to hear someone's eyes widen over the phone.

"*He*?" Cassie said.

Josie's cheeks burned. She shouldn't have said "he." But she would have told Cassie eventually anyway. She was no good at keeping secrets from her.

"Yes, he. And someone needs to keep an eye on him in case he takes a bad turn. He gave us all a good scare."

"What happened?"

Being careful not to mention Robert's name—he probably wouldn't like her broadcasting his business—Josie told Cassie how she'd suspected all morning that he wasn't well and how he'd passed out and almost smacked his head.

"The hospital definitely would have admitted him," Cassie said. She paused. "Are you ever going to tell me who it is? I'm dying to know."

"Sorry. Patient privacy."

"If he's not paying you, he's not your patient. But maybe I can guess." Cassie's voice bubbled with enthusiasm. "Let's see..." Josie imagined her friend tapping her finger on her chin like she always did when she was thinking. "It's more likely that a member of the cast rather than the crew would have been close enough to the bar to hit his head if he fell. It's a man who lives alone, so that rules out Charlie, and if it were Beau, you'd just tell me." She gasped. "It's Robert Coolidge, isn't it? Isn't it?" Her voice was at least an octave higher by the second "it."

Cassie should have been a detective. But since Josie was found out, no point in continuing to be coy.

"It is," she said.

Cassie gasped. "Are you alone with him?"

Josie scratched Sergeant's head. "His dog is here."

Apparently, it was also possible to hear someone roll their eyes over the phone.

"I can't believe you agreed to be alone with him at his house," Cassie said.

"That makes two of us," Josie said with a little chuckle. "But he's so sick I couldn't *not* be here. My conscience never would have let me live with it. I'm certain he would have checked himself out of the hospital, and he needs supervision."

"Do you feel safe?"

Josie's chest ached with love for her friend. Cassie

always knew exactly how to get to the heart of the matter. Josie considered her response for a moment. "I don't feel *un*safe, but it's awkward between him and me."

"That's understandable," Cassie said. "You did knock him on his ass pretty hard."

Josie laughed, relieved to let go of some of the tension she'd carried since Robert collapsed. Then she hesitated, uncertain she wanted to voice her next thought aloud. But this was Cassie. If she could ask anyone this, it was her best friend. "Do you think I've been too hard on him?"

Cassie was silent for several beats. "I can't blame you for reacting the way you did, not with everything you've been through." She paused again. "But he doesn't know about all that. From his perspective, all he did was try to give a pretty girl he'd had a fun day with a goodnight kiss. And it sounds like he realized he scared you. You said he apologized."

Josie groaned and rubbed her eyes. She was so tired they were probably bloodshot. "I hate that you're always right."

Cassie laughed. "One of my many gifts. And you don't have to marry him, you know. But maybe at least be his friend. If nothing else, it'll make being on set together a lot less awkward."

Josie thought of Beau and how much fun they had joking around and playing cards between scenes. Charlie joined them sometimes, and it would be nice to include Robert too. Maybe he'd even start talking at lunch. "Again, you're right," she said. "I'm sorry I won't be able to come over tomorrow." It was bad enough that she and Cassie didn't see each other during the week much anymore. Canceling on a weekend made her feel plum awful.

"I'll let it go this once," Cassie said with a light laugh. "You relax and take care of your patient. Try talking to him. I have an inkling you'll feel better once you get to know him more. And Josie?"

"Yes?"

"*Please* let me know what he looks like with his shirt off."

Josie said goodbye, hung up the phone, and, laughing softly, leaned against the kitchen counter. Cassie never failed to make her feel better after a long, and in this case, frightening, day.

Now sitting on the floor of Robert's bedroom hours later, she giggled at the memory.

Behind her, Robert coughed, and she glanced at the clock. 3:13. Close enough. She stood, rubbed the life back into her backside, and grabbed the thermometer. She nudged Robert's shoulder, waking him just enough to hold the thermometer in his mouth. 103.6. Good. She could go back to bed.

As she reached for the switch to turn off the bedside lamp, Robert murmured something. She leaned in closer.

"What was that?"

"Thank you," he mumbled. His eyes flickered open. "My hands feel better." He closed his eyes and was asleep again.

Chapter Twenty-Nine

Robert relaxed his lips' grip on the thermometer so Josie could pull it out of his mouth. She smiled when she read it.

"102," she said, her nose wrinkling. "Well done." She patted the top of his head, and his scalp tingled.

The dark circles under her eyes broke his heart, though. She couldn't have gotten much sleep last night, not with as restless as he'd been. His body still ached this morning, but at least it wasn't as bad.

"Sorry if I kept you up," he said.

She shrugged. "I knew what I was getting into when I came over. Besides, I plan to take a nice, long nap after breakfast. Your guest bed is really comfortable."

He smiled. "That's Matthew's room." When he'd moved in, he spent more time picking out furniture and a mattress for Matthew's room than he did for his own.

"That explains the books in there," Josie said. "I didn't figure you still read *The Hardy Boys.*"

"No, but sometimes I pull the building blocks out of the closet to make a fort."

Her bright laughter surprised him so much he fell into a coughing fit. She handed him a glass of water. When he settled, she handed him two aspirin as well.

"Let's see if we can get away with a lower dose," she said. "You take those. I'll get you some breakfast."

He smiled despite his exhaustion as he watched her

slip out of the room.

She'd laughed at his joke. A genuine laugh, like before everything fell to pieces.

Damn, he hadn't realized how much he'd missed that sound. Hope sparked in his chest.

****

He wasn't dizzy anymore, but after eating breakfast and making a trip to the bathroom, Robert was so exhausted he fell right back to sleep. He woke just after noon when the phone rang in the kitchen. A few minutes later, Josie came in with lunch. She must have slept, too, because the dark circles under her eyes were gone.

She gave him more Campbell's soup, promising she'd have a pot of the real stuff for dinner tonight.

"Charlie and Beau both called to check on you," she said. "They hope you're feeling better."

Robert smiled. Beau and Charlie had probably been calling more to check on Josie than him, but he was still touched by their concern. He supposed it wouldn't kill him to talk to his costars a bit more. They didn't have to be bosom buddies, but he could at least make small talk at lunch.

"Merrill called a few minutes ago too," Josie said.

His warm feelings turned to ice, and he scowled and stirred his soup. "What did he want?"

Josie furrowed her brow. "To see how you are, obviously. He heard what happened yesterday."

Thank God Merrill hadn't been on set yesterday when he'd passed out. The whole thing had been mortifying enough without him.

"Anyway," Josie said, "he said to tell you not to worry about coming in next week. They'll write you out of the episode, and he'll even pay you."

He cringed. He'd rather Merrill docked his pay. Now he'd have to kiss his boots when he went back.

"Is it all right that I answered the phone?"

He looked up. Josie's expression was pinched, and she had her arms wrapped around her middle. She looked so cowed he wanted to hug her. He smiled instead.

"Of course. That was the right thing to do. Merrill just annoys me."

Josie smirked. "I've noticed. Enjoy your soup."

After lunch, he slept the entire afternoon, not waking until Josie came in with a bowl of homemade chicken soup and more aspirin. Sometime during the day, his nose had started running, and now his eyes were watering too. He felt like he was melting, like the Wicked Witch in *The Wizard of Oz*. The soup was amazing, but he could barely manage to eat half the bowlful. He'd never felt so drained in his life.

"It's delicious," he said, dropping his head back onto his pillow. "I'm just so…"

"I know," Josie said, patting his shoulder. "There's plenty left over for when your appetite comes back. It reheats real nice."

He loved the way she said "nice," like it had a y instead of an i.

"Thanks," he muttered.

Just before he drifted off to sleep, he felt her brush the hair off his forehead. He loved that too.

Chapter Thirty

Josie called Cassie that evening to let her know everything was still okay. Still feeling guilty about canceling their plans for today, she invited her to come along to the network Christmas party. Once Cassie stopped screaming, they made plans to go dress-shopping right after Thanksgiving.

That night, Josie took a gamble and woke Robert only once, and come Sunday morning, he was still at 102. That was pretty good for less aspirin on day three of the flu. And his lungs still sounded clear. She listened to them first thing in the morning, trying not to stare at the way his pectorals expanded with each inhalation or how his trapezius muscles angled sharply from his shoulders to his neck.

The smell helped distract her, though. After two sweaty, feverish days in the same pajamas, Robert needed a shower.

He wasn't dizzy anymore, thank goodness, but he was still so tired. Just walking to the bathroom and back left him needing a nap. He couldn't possibly shower yet. And no way was she giving him a full sponge bath in bed like she would a patient in the hospital. She didn't ever see most of her patients again. She and Robert would be seeing each other every time she came on set for the rest of the season. Longer, if Merrill renewed her contract for next year. And Robert was much younger and more...*virile* than her typical male patient. Where they were usually withered and wrinkled, Robert would not be.

Sweat trickled down her back.

She'd just have to draw him a bath and hope he didn't slip and crack his head getting in or out.

"Think you could manage a bath?" she said after breakfast. "I'm sure it would feel good."

One corner of Robert's mouth lifted. "Is that your polite way of telling me I stink?"

She bit back a smile. "I would never say that." She paused. "Directly, anyway."

Robert chuckled, then coughed and grabbed a handkerchief from his nightstand and blew his nose. "A bath does sound nice."

"Great. I'll give you one."

His eyebrows shot up, and Josie's face and ears caught fire.

"I mean I'll *draw* you one," she said. "You can, you know, you can bathe yourself. I'll, um, I'll get that going." She fled the room.

She grumbled while she filled the tub. "Nice work, Josie Girl. That wasn't embarrassing for anyone." She groaned and sat on the bathroom floor, back against the tub, while the faucet ran. "Admit it," she muttered, "you're attracted to him. And you have been since your audition."

And why shouldn't she be? She was an unmarried young woman, and he was a handsome, unmarried man. The same could be said of Beau, but Beau was different. Goofy. Brotherly. He reminded her so much of Ben. Robert didn't remind her of anyone she'd ever known.

He had that night at her cabin when he presumed he

could kiss her, but everything since then was nothing like old what's-his-name.

Ethan, Josie Girl, Ethan. Don't be afraid of his name.

Ethan, who never would have gotten a big, nutty dog. Who never would have asked for time off work for his child's birthday. Who had never thanked her for anything she'd done for him.

Robert thanked her for everything. Even half asleep and fighting a high fever, he thanked her for every aspirin tablet, every bowl of canned soup, every glass of water. He didn't expect or demand the attention. He was grateful for it.

He thanked her for the hand massage the other night too. That hadn't even been a conscious decision. She just picked up one of his hands and got to work. She rubbed the pads of her thumb and index finger together, remembering the gravel road of his calluses. How would it feel to have his hands run down skin?

She slapped her cheeks lightly.

A romantic relationship, especially with a coworker, couldn't be anything but bad news, but she wasn't exactly drowning in friends. Beau and Charlie had increased her friend group threefold. She certainly had space for one more. Especially one with such a cute dog.

****

Josie went into Robert's room to let him know the bath was ready, only to find the bed empty, the quilt pulled up and straightened like no one had ever been there. Odd. She wandered into the living room and heard Robert's deep voice drifting from the direction of the kitchen. She crossed through the dining room and spotted him sitting at the kitchen table, talking into the telephone. He rested one elbow on the table, head leaned forward into his hand, his eyes closed. Sergeant sat next to him, leaning against his leg.

"I will, Mom, I promise," he said. He coughed twice. "Say hi to Dad for me." He paused. "I love you too. Bye."

She darted back to the living room so he wouldn't see her when he hung up the phone. Getting caught eavesdropping probably wasn't the best way to start rebuilding a friendship.

But good gravy, he'd called his mother. His first time walking farther than the bathroom in two days, and he called his mother. She giggled. That was so sweet it was almost gross. Comforting, though. Mom had always said you could tell a lot about a man by the way he treated his mother.

She arranged her face into her best "bewildered" expression and called out.

"Where'd you go?"

Robert shuffled into the living room, leaned against the door jamb, and gave her a tired smile.

"Sorry. Just remembered what day it was. I always call my folks on Sunday. Didn't want them to worry."

All the pieces fell into place, and guilt settled heavily on Josie's shoulders for thinking he was just being stubborn the other day. "That's why you wouldn't go to the hospital."

He looked down at the tufted carpet. "I didn't think they'd let me make a long-distance call."

She pressed a hand to her heart. "One of us could have called for you."

Robert looked back up. "And told them what? That I was in the hospital?" He shook his head. "They would have been frantic. I couldn't do that to them. Mom and Dad... They've been through enough."

There was a big piece of something right here that he wasn't telling her. She wanted to ask about it so badly her throat ached, but his bath was getting cold. She nodded and waved him toward the bathroom.

Chapter Thirty-One

The bath saved his life.

Not literally, but it sure felt like it. Robert had to fold up a bit to get all six-feet-two-inches of himself into the tub, but as soon as he settled into the hot water, the achiness in his joints eased. Even if he didn't reek, this bath would have been a good idea. The steam opened his sinuses, too, and he could breathe clearly through at least one nostril for the first time in two days. He rested his head against the wall, closed his eyes, and sighed. He'd never realized how far the walk was from his bedroom to the telephone in the kitchen. He could fall asleep right here in the tub. Alarmed at the thought, he lifted his head and opened his eyes so he wouldn't drift off. With his luck, if he fell asleep, he'd slip underwater and drown.

He washed up and then sat and soaked until the water went tepid. He thought about heating it back up, but if he lingered any longer Josie would probably start banging on the door to make sure he hadn't died. He pulled the bathplug and heaved himself out of the tub. Josie had set a fresh towel out for him on the small table next to the bathtub. That girl thought of everything.

He spritzed on some deodorant, put on fresh pajamas, and dragged a comb through the tangled mess of his hair. He traced the stubble on his jaw with his hand. Only two days of not shaving, and he was starting to look like a Gold Rush prospector. But there was no way he could stand long enough to shave right now. He left the bathroom, and by the time he made it back to his bedroom, he felt like he could sleep for days.

Josie came in just as he slipped beneath the covers. Geez, she'd even changed the sheets. She shouldn't have gone to all that trouble, but the crisp, cool sheets felt amazing on his feverish skin. He smiled at her.

"You didn't have to change the sheets, but thank you."

She smiled back, her nose wrinkling. "Don't mention it." She turned to leave, and a desperate, almost frantic urge surged through him.

Fix this, R.J. Completely.

"Josie." He spoke her name as a statement, not a question. She turned back, face quizzical, clearly expecting a request. Those bright green eyes, like new grass in the spring, focused on his face. Much as he craved her attention, right now he wanted to hide under his quilt.

His stomach clenched, and he swallowed. At least the razor-sharp prickles in his throat were letting up. "I need to apologize again. Properly."

Her eyebrows, dark as her hair, met in a chevron. "Whatever for? Getting the flu?"

He shook his head and chewed his lower lip for a moment. "That last night in Yosemite outside your cabin... I read too much into our ride that afternoon, and I tried something I shouldn't have. I scared you, and I am so sorry."

Josie stared. And stared. And stared.

Oh, God, maybe he shouldn't have brought it up. Maybe they'd moved past it already and he was just reopening old wounds. Where was Sergeant? Couldn't he come in right now and cause a ruckus? Anything to stop those eyes from boring straight through him like this. He squirmed.

"Josie?"

She blinked several times. "Sorry. I mean, thank you. I appreciate that." But she didn't stop staring. Then all at once, she said she should wash the dishes from breakfast and whirled toward the door.

As she spun, her elbow knocked into Jack's photograph on the dresser. Robert sat up when it clattered to the floor.

"Yikes! I'm so sorry!" Josie said. She knelt and picked it up, frantically turning it around in her hands. "No harm done, thank goodness."

He worried the edge of the quilt between his fingers as she studied Jack's photo.

Just set it back down, Josie, please, he thought. He yawned, hoping she'd notice and leave him to sleep. No one outside Hell Hole knew about Jack—not even Ed—and he didn't have the energy to explain right now. Or ever.

But then why did you leave his photo out, R.J., when you knew she was coming over? His Army photo, of all things?

Josie smiled and looked back and forth between the photo and Robert, clearly noticing the family resemblance. He and Jack were hardly identical, but strangers looking at the pair of them side-by-side had never doubted they were brothers. Something about the shape of their noses.

"Who's this?" she asked.

He took a deep breath. "That's my brother, Jack," he said softly. The name tasted rusty in his mouth.

Holy smoke. He'd just spoken Jack's name aloud. He hadn't said it for years, and probably no more than twice since Jack died. But he couldn't have stopped himself answering Josie. She was a truth serum.

Josie tapped her lips with her knuckles. "But you said that—oh." She looked at the dresser again, clearly spotting the gold star pin still sitting there. Her shoulders slumped and she turned back to him, her hands gripping the picture frame so tightly her knuckles went white. "Oh, Robert, I'm so sorry. Where?"

His stomach lurched, but he managed to say another word he'd avoided for fifteen years. "Normandy."

Josie closed her eyes. "I'm so sorry," she repeated. She set the photo back on the dresser and straightened the pin next to it. "Did they send him home?"

He supposed he should be relieved she was talking to him so much. He just wished it was any other topic but this one.

He nodded. "Eventually. We didn't get the choice until two years later. I don't think Dad wanted to disturb him at that point, but Mom wanted him home." He squeezed his eyes shut, willing away the image of soldiers carrying a flag-draped coffin off the train in Jamestown. His chest tightened and his nose ran, and neither had anything to do with the flu. He grabbed a handkerchief from his nightstand.

Bless her heart, Josie must have understood. She picked up the other photo from the dresser and grinned at it. "Is this your son?"

Now here was a topic he could talk about all day. He grinned back. "Yeah, that's Matthew. He turned seven last month. I'm getting him for Christmas, and I can't wait."

Josie looked up. "He's the same age as one of my nephews. He looks so sweet."

His sadness washed away on the warm tide of her words, and he sat up straighter. "He is. I have no idea where he got it from."

Josie laughed harder than Robert thought was necessary for that little joke, but he couldn't be insulted. Josie's joy was too infectious.

Chapter Thirty-Two

"I have to run home for a few minutes," Josie said the next morning when she took Robert's breakfast tray away. "You'll need me a couple more days, so I want to grab more clothes."

"You're welcome to use the washer and dryer," he said.

And skip the trip to the laundromat this week? Yes, please. She smiled.

"Even more reason for me to run home." She winked. "Gotta pick up the rest of my laundry."

He chuckled, and for once didn't start coughing. "Take the car." He jerked his chin toward the dresser, where his keys lay next to his brother's photograph.

Oh, golly. She shouldn't. She felt like she'd been tempting fate driving his car the other day, and there was nothing wrong with the bus. But then she pictured that gorgeous black Corvette. Sure would be a shame to leave it sitting in the garage on a beautiful fall day in southern California.

She grinned. "How do you put the top down?"

Fifteen minutes later, she popped on the Wayfarers she'd treated herself to with her first *Gunslingers* paycheck and slid behind the wheel of Robert's Corvette, top now down. She giggled as she cruised down the palm-tree-lined road toward her apartment, sunshine on her face, and Elvis Presley blaring "A Big Hunk O'

Love" from the radio.

Twenty minutes later, she parked at her apartment building and dashed up the stairs to her second-floor unit. She headed straight for the phone and dialed Leighton's house. When his wife, Dottie, answered, Josie told her that she'd been staying with a friend and no one should worry if they couldn't reach her at home. Dottie thanked her and promised to let Jimmy and the rest know as well.

Josie stuffed a couple more outfits and various underthings in her valise and gazed around her bedroom. Funny. When she'd packed her bag three days ago, she dreaded leaving home and going to Robert's. Now she was eager to get out of here and return to his house.

You don't miss him, Josie Girl. You miss the company, especially since he gave you such a nice apology yesterday. And you want to drive that Corvette some more.

She ducked into the bathroom to get another tube of toothpaste, and when she stuck her hand into the back of the drawer she thought it was in, her hand bumped cold metal. Her fingers closed around a little tin.

Oh, dear Lord, she'd just grabbed her diaphragm.

Why hadn't she thrown the silly thing away? She hadn't even wanted another diaphragm in the first place, but last winter Cassie announced she was tired of being a virgin and asked Josie to come with her to the gynecologist for a fitting. Josie had almost thrown up just at the thought, but Cassie did so much for her without ever asking for anything in return that turning her down felt ungrateful. And Josie had to admit that a gynecological exam was probably a good idea. She hadn't had one since...well, since *before*.

She'd meant to just get the exam and get out of there,

but when the doctor asked if she needed anything else, Josie lost her mind and asked for a diaphragm. Cassie had worried aloud that Josie might think her immoral, and getting one herself would put her friend more at ease. And her last one had kept her out of a situation that would have been *really* hard to get out of. She wouldn't be able to insert it in a hurry if someone surprised her, but it was better than nothing. And maybe someday, decades from now, she might want to use one again.

She pulled it out of the drawer and dropped it in her bag.

Good gravy, Josie Girl, what are you doing?

She was headed back to a patient's house. She didn't need a diaphragm for that. Cheeks burning, she ripped it out of her bag and shoved it back into the depths of the drawer.

When she got back to Robert's, she greeted Sergeant, turned down the hallway toward Matthew's room, and nearly smacked into Robert as he came out of the bathroom. She yelped and dropped her valise. He jumped, too, and nearly lost the towel wrapped around his waist—the only thing he wore. He gripped the towel with one hand and rested the other against the frame of the bathroom door.

"Geez, Josie, you startled me," he said, his laugh turning to a cough.

Josie stared at the towel, settled low below his belly button and barely big enough to wrap all the way around him. Heat shot through every part of her body.

Look at his face, Josie Girl, look at his face, look at his face, look at his face.

She lifted her eyes, paused at his broad chest, still hopping from his cough, and forced her eyes the rest of the way up.

"I'm- I'm so sorry," she said, bending over to pick up her bag. "I thought you'd be in bed."

Robert leaned his whole body against the bathroom doorframe. "The phone rang, so I had to get up." He chuckled. "It was my mom calling to check on me. And that bath yesterday felt so good, I decided since I was up I might as well shower."

She noticed now the wet hair plastered to his forehead and a few stray droplets of water cutting rivulets through the dark curls on his chest. He'd shaved too. The dark stubble dotting his jaw and upper lip was gone. What she'd give for him to drop that towel.

She clapped a hand over her mouth, alarmed by her own thought.

"What's wrong?" he said.

Either he wasn't fazed by her stumbling across him nearly naked or he should be nominated for an Academy Award.

She stared.

Say something, Josie Girl, say something.

"I forgot my laundry." She'd been so flustered after nearly packing her diaphragm that she'd completely forgotten to grab her hamper.

He smiled, and she nearly turned to liquid. Curse that dimple of his.

"Did you remember more clothes?" he said, clearly not noticing that her entire body was Jell-O.

She nodded.

"No problem, then." He shoved away from the doorframe and grunted. He was really pale. The phone call and shower must have worn him out. She should send him to bed. Alone, of course.

She stepped forward and laid a hand on his cheek to check his fever. He radiated steam from his shower, intoxicating her with the scents of soap and aftershave. He leaned into her touch and sweat broke out along her hairline.

"You're so warm," she said. Energy surged through her pelvis, and she leapt backward. She couldn't let herself get swept away just because he was handsome and naked. Besides, a naked man was a dangerous man. She wrapped her arms around her stomach and squeezed to keep herself from breathing too hard. "Probably from the shower." She cast her gaze to her loafers. The left toe was scuffed. She swallowed. "You must be wiped out. Go back to bed. I'll come take your temperature in a couple minutes."

"As you wish," Robert said. He turned and headed down the hall to his room.

"Leave your shirt off," she called after him and cringed. Dear Lord, she wasn't making this any better. She wanted to sink straight through the floor and disappear forever.

He stopped but didn't turn around.

"I should listen to your lungs again."

"Right." He coughed twice and disappeared into his bedroom.

Chapter Thirty-Three

Robert lay in bed with the covers pulled up to his shoulders. When the door creaked open, he sat up. The blankets fell to his waist, and he arranged the quilt carefully over his lap in case his body reacted to Josie and his pajama bottoms weren't enough to hide it. She'd nearly gotten a show a few minutes ago when she caught him in the hallway. He was okay until she laid her hand on his cheek and he had to use every ounce of his self-control to keep his towel from poking straight out in front of him.

Fortunately, the business end of Josie's stethoscope was so cold it shocked all the arousal right out of him when she pressed it to his bare skin.

"You still sound good," Josie said, patting his shoulder when she finished listening. "And you haven't been above 101 today, either. I think we're turning a corner."

God, he wanted to kiss the tip of that little button nose. But they were just friends, and he was lucky he'd gotten that back. He had to stop thinking stuff like this, no matter how much it made him ache. To give his hands something to do, he shrugged into his pajama top and started fastening the buttons.

"When does Matthew arrive for Christmas?" she said.

His head snapped up. More questions? And about

Matthew too. Maybe she'd like to meet him. He blew his nose to hide the dopey grin trying to spread across his face.

"Sunday, the twentieth," he said when his nose wasn't dripping anymore. "Laura's sending him for those whole two weeks we're off."

Josie stiffened. "And Laura is your," she swallowed hard, "ex-wife?"

He tilted his head. Why was she asking about Laura? Oh, no, was his divorce a mark against him? Surely it wouldn't matter since they were just friends, though. Josie was friends with Charlie, and he was divorced. Robert studied her face. Her pupils were wide, and she clutched herself around her middle, her breathing rapid. She was scared. But of what? Was it possible she was afraid he still had feelings for Laura? "Yes," he said. He dragged the word out, hearing the old South Carolina drawl creep into the single syllable. He cringed.

Josie took a deep breath and loosened her hold on herself. She smiled tightly and folded down one corner of his pajama collar that was sticking up. "That's nice of her to send him for so long. I bet he's excited too."

He grinned in what he hoped was a reassuring way. "I promised to take him to Disneyland."

Josie's eyes lit up, the last of the fear draining from her expression. "He'll love that, I'm sure. I've heard Disneyland is great fun."

He lifted his eyebrows. "You've never been?"

Josie shook her head.

"You've been in Los Angeles for two years, and you've never been to Disneyland?"

She shook her head again. "I take it you have."

"Yeah, last year. My friend Ed has four kids, and his

wife was worried they'd lose one, so I went along to help herd the flock." He ran a hand through his hair, remembering how much fun they'd all had, even the adults. "They added a lot of new rides this summer. They have something called a…" he snapped his fingers a few times, "monorail! That's the word. It's this train that rides up high on a single rail." He paused. "Not sure what it's for, but it looks like fun."

Josie laughed, that beautiful bright sound he loved so much. God as his witness, he'd do everything he could to keep her in his life at least as a friend, even if it killed him. He couldn't live without that laugh.

"It sounds delightful," she said. "Matthew will love it."

"You should go sometime," he said.

"I certainly want to. I'll have to see if Cassie would like to go."

A spark ignited in his brain.

No, R.J. Bad idea.

But then again, if he delivered the invitation just right, maybe she'd accept. She'd relaxed so much these past few days, acting like she had before that one bad night. It was worth a shot.

He scooted down a few inches so he wasn't sitting up quite so tall. He looked down and picked at a loose thread on the hem of the bedsheet. This line would best be delivered without eye contact.

"This is probably a long shot, but would you consider going with Matthew and me?"

He looked up to see Josie's eyes wide and her mouth agape.

"Oh," she said, her hands worrying the hem of her blouse. "I, uh, won't be in town. I'm going home to

Kansas those two weeks we're off."

Damn.

Robert's shoulders slumped. He fiddled with sheet again. What if…?

You're crazy, R.J.

But crazy or not, he wanted to try. He cleared his throat.

"Would you consider going with just me before then?"

Josie was silent for so long, he looked back up to make sure she was still in the room. She'd wrapped her arms around her middle again and was staring at him.

"As repayment for this weekend," he said, the words racing from his mouth at a full gallop.

Josie took a step back. "You don't owe me anything for this weekend. This was nothing any decent person wouldn't have done." She looked away, but at least she didn't run screaming out of the room. Still, he needed to set her at ease. He'd never survive it if he ruined things with her again.

"Josie." He said her name gently. She kept staring at the floor, and he said her name again. Slowly, she raised her eyes to his, her arms still tight across her stomach. A knot rose in his throat when he realized she wasn't trying to hug herself. She was trying to hold herself together.

What had happened to the poor kid?

"I promise, I'm not trying to get anything from you," he said. "Except your friendship."

Her shoulders relaxed, and she dropped her arms to her sides.

Thank God.

"So what do you say?" he said, breaking into a smile. "Let a grateful friend take you to Disneyland?"

168

She gnawed on her lip. "I really would like to see Disneyland," she said in a small voice.

Chapter Thirty-Four

Tuesday morning, Josie woke early and peeked into Robert's room. He was still asleep, and she tiptoed to the side of the bed and laid her hand on his forehead. Nice and cool. She smiled. His eyes fluttered open, and he smiled back.

"Good morning," he said sleepily.

"Good morning. I think your fever broke."

He shivered. "I think so too. I'm drenched."

He wasn't kidding. His pajama top, dark with sweat, clung to his body. His bedding was damp too. Josie sent him off to the shower and changed the sheets again. This was the last set of clean sheets in the linen closet. Robert was probably running low on pajamas too. He needed to have laundry done.

"What day does your housekeeper come?" she said when he came back from the shower.

He blinked. "I don't have a housekeeper."

She blinked back in surprise. "Oh. I just assumed."

Robert chuckled. "Didn't think a bachelor could keep a clean place on his own, did you?"

She smiled. "None of my brothers could. Probably why they're all married. Don't worry, I'll get some laundry going."

"You don't have—" He smiled and cast his eyes to the floor for a second, giving Josie a view of his long eyelashes. "Thank you."

Robert sat up in bed and read all morning, but he took a long nap after lunch. His fever might be gone, but Josie knew it would be several days still before he shook off the fatigue. She spent the time doing their laundry. She pretended she was at the hospital handling patients' clothing while dealing with his unmentionables. She'd been washing her brothers' underwear for most of her life, but she'd never known a man to wear boxer shorts before. She wouldn't let herself imagine what he looked like in them. Or out of them.

Keep it friendly, Josie Girl. Remember what happened with Ethan.

She was already nuts for accepting the invitation to Disneyland. She didn't need to get swept up in another school-girl crush to boot.

Robert's fever hadn't returned, so if he had a good night, she could go home tomorrow. There were leftovers in the refrigerator, so he wouldn't have to cook for a couple more days while he got his strength back. It would be good to get home. She could rest up the next five days until she was due back at the hospital. Five glorious days all to herself.

All by herself.

She suddenly felt hollow, like if she looked in a mirror, she'd be able to see straight through her body to the room behind her.

She'd been taking care of people her whole life. First her brothers—at only twelve years old, she'd taken over for Mom when she died—then her patients at the hospital. She felt unmoored if she wasn't needed, like she'd just drift away.

Maybe she should rest tomorrow and pick up a shift at the hospital either Thursday or Friday. That should scratch her itch.

But patients weren't the same as someone you cared about.

The thought didn't surprise her as much as it should have, which *did* surprise her. Good gravy, this man was a roller coaster. First he was her friend, then her enemy, and now…this. But it was all right to care about him, wasn't it? Didn't mean anything. She cared about Beau and Charlie too.

She didn't ache for missing Beau, though. And already, just thinking about going home tomorrow made her feel sluggish and heavy. But Robert was probably looking forward to having the house back to himself and Sergeant. She'd be fine once she got home.

"I'll probably get out of your hair tomorrow," she said that evening over pork chops.

Robert raised his eyebrows, two dark slashes on his pallid face. He'd insisted on coming out to the breakfast nook for dinner, but the effort was clearly taking a toll. She wanted to tuck him back into bed and sit with him until he fell asleep.

"Unless your fever comes back, you don't need me to supervise you anymore."

He gazed down at his plate. "I'm sure you'll be glad to get home," he said quietly. "Thank you for everything."

"You're welcome."

They ate in silence for a few minutes, both staring at their plates. She couldn't leave it like this. She needed to say something more, to let him know she forgave him.

They both started talking at once.

"It's been great—"

"Robert, you know—"

172

They stopped, eyes meeting, and laughed.

"You go first," Robert said.

"No, please."

He smiled, flashing his dimple. "It's been great having you here. I don't mind being on my own. Often prefer it, to be honest. But it gets lonely sometimes, even with this goofball." He reached down and scratched Sergeant's head. The boxer never drifted far from the table during a meal. "So it's been real nice having some company." He chuckled. "Even if I slept through most of it."

"You're still not recovered, you know. You need to take it easy the rest of the week."

"I will." He let the silence hang for a moment. "What were you going to say?"

She couldn't meet his eyes. Those beautiful, gold-flecked eyes would completely undo her. She stared at her plate and chased a stray green bean with her fork.

Be brave, Josie Girl. You're safe here.

"Just that I've enjoyed the company too," she said. "When you grow up with a family as big as mine, being alone feels strange."

She blushed and glanced into the kitchen to find some excuse to get up from the table but couldn't see one. When Robert spoke, she could barely hear him.

"You don't have to go."

Her head snapped up. Was he suggesting she stay the rest of the week? Her mouth popped open to say "yes," but she clamped it shut again. She couldn't possibly, no matter how appealing the idea was. She'd already accepted the invitation to Disneyland. If she said yes now, he'd certainly get the wrong idea again. She wasn't willing to sacrifice the tenuous friendship they'd carved out these past couple days. The thought of another estrangement from him broke her heart.

"I'm sorry," Robert said, shrinking in his seat, his dimple vanishing. "I didn't mean to sound forward. Please don't think I'm pressuring you into anything. I'm not trying to..." He dropped his fork on the table, closed his eyes, and rubbed his temples with one hand.

Josie's heart swelled. He was so tired. And he'd be tired for several more days. He could still use her help. If she stayed, he could rest up a lot more before he had to be back on set next week. There wouldn't be anything improper about it. And deep down, she knew she'd accepted that invitation to Disneyland so she'd get to spend more time with him.

She reached across the table and took his free hand. "I'd love to stay."

He looked up. The dimple was back.

Chapter Thirty-Five

Robert wandered out of his bedroom the next morning feeling twitchy. Josie had left a bit ago to meet her friend Cassie for lunch and pick up more groceries, and the house felt too empty. He decided to call Matthew. Laura answered, and they chatted for a few minutes.

He didn't hate Laura, not by a long shot. Matthew was the product of a genuine love they'd once shared. But Robert was still so tired, he didn't want to spend what little energy he had talking to anyone but his boy. Fortunately, Laura had heard from Mom that he was sick—news traveled fast in Hell Hole—and she kept her part of the conversation short.

Talking to Matthew usually left him cheerful the rest of the day, but after he hung up the phone, he felt sad. Maybe it was the exhaustion. Just sitting at the table and talking on the phone for twenty minutes had worn him out. He trudged to the living room, clicked on the television, and stretched out on the couch.

Josie bustled in a few minutes later, arms full of grocery bags, and smiled at him. Her cheeks were slightly flushed, and the pink tinge made her freckles stand out more than usual, like sprinkles on an ice cream sundae.

A man could lose himself in that face. He wanted to cup her cheeks with his hands and kiss every single freckle. Instead, he got up, took the bags from her, and carried them to the kitchen. He was out of breath by the time he set them down, and he leaned against the counter.

Josie scurried over and laid her hand on his forehead. Tension he hadn't even realized he was carrying flowed out of him at her touch. He couldn't believe she'd agreed to stay. He'd regretted the words as soon as they had flown out of his mouth last night. The request was too forward, too presumptuous, too much of everything that frightened her. But she'd said yes. She'd taken his hand and said yes.

He'd remember that perfect moment as long as he lived.

"Still nice and cool," she said. "Just sit. I can put the groceries away."

"I'm all right." He moved to help, but the phone rang, so he answered it instead.

"Hey, R.J.," Laura said. "Sorry to bother you again. I forgot to tell you that Matthew's got a dentist appointment next week."

Hearing his ex-wife's voice while watching Josie in her cute, swingy dress put away groceries in his kitchen sent his head spinning like he'd been launched on a rocket. This must be that fifth dimension the narrator of *The Twilight Zone* talked about at the beginning of the show.

"Just send me the bill," he said.

He hung up and pinched the bridge of his nose. God, that was weird.

"Wasn't bad news, was it?"

He jumped. "No, just Laura telling me Matthew has a dentist appointment." His eyes popped wide. Why in the world had he explained? Normal Robert would have just said "no" and left it at that.

This fifth dimension really was a strange place.

Josie blinked. "Oh." She clutched her arms so tight around her stomach he worried she was about to squeeze all the air out of her body. "I'm sorry, it's none of my business." She whirled around and finished putting away the last few groceries.

Curiouser and curiouser.

That was twice now the mention of Laura upset Josie, but he didn't think it was his divorce that was bothering her. He'd seen her hold onto herself like that enough times to figure out she did it when she was feeling insecure, not when she was upset with someone else. He remembered his tailbone and bit back a chuckle. Josie had no problem lashing out at whoever she was upset with. And given all the information she'd dragged out of him lately, maybe it was time he interrogated her back just a little bit.

He stretched out on the sofa while she made meatloaf, mashed potatoes, and broccoli for supper. His mouth watered as the enticing smells reached him in the living room. He felt like he hadn't eaten for days. And he nearly hadn't. Except for the pork chops he'd only picked at last night, he'd been living off soup and toast since Friday. When they sat down at the table, he inhaled two helpings of everything, finishing it off with a bowl of strawberry ice cream. He leaned back in his chair, eyelids drooping.

Josie giggled. "Good to see your appetite's back. That'll bring your energy back faster."

He drew in a deep breath, gave his head a little shake to wake himself up, and helped her clear the table. She started piling the dishes in the sink and let out an excited "ooh!" when he opened the dishwasher. She watched with rapt attention while he loaded the dishes and added the detergent. He couldn't hold back his chuckle when she leaned over his shoulder as he pressed the "start" button.

"Never seen a dishwasher before?" he said.

"Only in stores." Her breath fell warm on the back of his neck, making all the little hairs stand up. "I've never seen one running."

The machine came to life with a loud hum.

"Nothing else to see until it's done, I'm afraid."

He wished he hadn't said it. As soon as he told her the show was over, Josie stepped away, the space where she'd stood feeling like a vacuum. He was exhausted, but now was the time. He leaned against the counter and hoped he could keep his still-ragged voice gentle. "What is it?"

Josie cocked her head. "What is what?"

She wasn't going to make this easy. He almost chuckled. He could respect that.

"Something's bothering you." He ducked his head and looked up at her with just his eyes. May as well go straight for it. "Was it my ex-wife calling?"

That pinched expression from earlier squeezed her face again. She took a step backward and bumped into the counter. A flash of fear sparked in her eyes. There were several feet between them, but she clearly felt cornered. Something told him her reaction had nothing to do with him, and his heart splintered into a million shards. Josie's face should never have to do anything but smile. He wanted to wrap her in his arms and promise her that no one would ever hurt her again, but that would only make things worse. Right now, he needed to calm her down fast. He guessed he had about three seconds to defuse this bomb. He coughed twice and slowly straightened.

"Would you like a cup of tea?" he said.

She blinked. "What?"

How did she manage to look cute even when she was confused?

He smiled. "Tea. Thought I'd have some for my throat. Would you like some?"

Her arms relaxed, thank God. "Um, sure."

"Go sit down while I make it. You've been on your feet all day." He stepped to the side, away from the door into the dining room, so it was clear he wasn't blocking her exit. She looked at him, obviously still puzzled, but left the kitchen.

He put the kettle on and sank into a chair like he might never rise again. That was the longest he'd stood at once since he passed out last week. But Josie had done so much for him. It was time to do something for her.

When the tea was ready, he sent Sergeant outside and carried the two mugs on a tray with some lemon slices and honey. Josie sat on the sofa in the living room, bunching up the pleats of her skirt in her fists. The slack, dull expression on her face nearly destroyed him. She didn't look at him when he set the tray on the coffee table where she could reach it.

"Thank you," she said softly. She squeezed a single slice of lemon into one of the mugs and picked it up.

He picked up the other and added some honey and a slice of lemon—he'd need them to keep his voice going a bit longer. Josie was sitting far to one side of the couch, so he sat down all the way at the other end. They both stared straight ahead for several moments while they sipped their tea and Robert racked his brain, trying to think of a clever way to start the conversation.

Face it, R.J. You've never been that smooth. Just jump in.

"You're not okay," he said, still staring straight ahead.

Josie's head snapped around so fast he couldn't believe she didn't fling tea all over the living room. "What makes you say that?" Her voice was tight and high.

He turned and caught her eye. Her pupils were so large he could see only a thin ring of green. "You've been upset ever since Laura called."

She gated her lower lip with her teeth and looked down. He couldn't hold her, so he shifted, turning his body toward her and tucking his left leg up on the sofa between them.

"Does my divorce bother you?" he said.

Josie's breath hitched. "Why would it bother me? This is Hollywood. Isn't everyone divorced?" She set her tea on the coffee table.

Robert watched her wage a battle to keep her face neutral that she almost won. Her acting was getting better every day, but this was a tough scene for her. He traced the swirl in the rug with his big toe. "But you're not Hollywood." He looked up and smiled. "You're so much better than Hollywood."

The only other time he'd seen someone turn as gray as Josie did just then was a couple years ago when Matthew came down with a horrible stomach bug on one of his visits. He'd turned that color just before he started vomiting all over the place. Robert considered running for a bucket, but Josie caught his eyes and stared hard at him, like she was struggling to make a decision.

You can trust me, he thought, hoping that somehow she'd pick up on the message. *Please trust me.* He set his mug on the coffee table and slid one hand, palm up, toward her. She stared down at it and then slowly, so, so slowly, slid her hand into his.

An electric thrill zipped up his arm and shot through his body as his hand closed lightly around hers. Her skin was warm and oh, so soft. He wished he still had a fever so he could feel her touch his cheek again.

Focus, R.J. You might still need to run for that bucket.

A little color was returning to Josie's face, but he wasn't convinced they were out of the woods yet. They sat quietly, hand-in-hand, for several moments, at long last comfortable again in their silence.

Please, God, don't let him mess this up again.

Finally, Josie swallowed hard and spoke, her voice barely above a whisper.

"Your divorce doesn't bother me because I'm divorced too."

Holy shit. He hadn't expected *that*.

Josie cast her eyes down, but not quickly enough for him to miss seeing the tears slide down her cheeks. He wanted to reach over and wipe them away, but he couldn't risk startling her. He ran a hand through his hair instead.

"But you're only twenty-three," he said. They'd celebrated her birthday on set just a couple weeks ago. Charlie had surprised her with a cake. Robert did the math in his head. If she was twenty-three and she'd been in Los Angeles for a bit over two years... Good God, she couldn't have been more than twenty when she and her husband split up. For the second time that evening, he wished he could hug her. He squeezed her hand instead. "You've never told anyone, have you?"

"Just Cassie." She didn't look up. "Out here, anyway. Everyone in Kansas knows."

He leaned forward. "Is that why you moved to LA?"

She nodded. "I fled in disgrace." She chomped down on her lower lip, but not hard enough to stop her chin from quivering and another tear from sliding down her cheek.

"It's not disgraceful," he said. "Sometimes it just doesn't work out. Two people realize they want different things."

"We wanted different things all right." Josie made a sound that was probably supposed to be a laugh but came out somewhere between a bark and a sob. She bit her lip again.

He wanted to know everything, to somehow set it right for her so she'd never cry again.

"You don't have to tell me about it if you don't want to," he said instead. "I know how private that sort of thing can be."

She nodded, and they sat quietly again for several moments. Her hand was warm in his, and he hoped she'd never let go. He'd happily sit like this for the rest of his life. But then Josie let go of him and reached for her tea, wrapping both hands around the mug.

"Thank you," she said, taking a sip.

"For what?"

The corners of her mouth lifted ever so slightly as she turned her head toward him. "For listening." She blinked her wet eyes. "For not judging me."

"I would never."

She held his gaze forever, then tilted her head, looking slightly surprised, like she'd had a revelation. "No, you wouldn't, would you?"

There it was. That same recognition he'd seen in her face in Yosemite. She was seeing *him* again. A hard knot rose in his throat.

Josie swallowed and set her mug on the coffee table. "You must be exhausted. I should let you get to bed."

Like hell he was going to bed now.

"I'm all right," he said.

Josie shook her head. "You still need your rest." She smiled. "If you don't get better, you can't take me to Disneyland."

He laughed, and she smiled a little bigger, making her nose wrinkle. He let out a long breath.

They were friends again.

Chapter Thirty-Six

Josie lay awake that night, staring up into the darkness, replaying the evening in her head. Something in her had snapped when Laura called. She felt silly now because of course Robert still talked to her. They were raising the same child. But when he'd mentioned her a couple days ago and again this afternoon, all she could hear in her head was that awful reporter asking her, "Do you ever talk to Ethan Winchester?"

Then she'd almost thrown up when Robert said "divorce." She didn't care that he'd been divorced, but the word brought back all the shame heaped on her when she'd left Ethan. People were so quick to throw stones at a divorced woman.

Except Robert.

Sure, he'd been surprised, but that was a reasonable reaction. Twenty-three *was* awfully young to have already been divorced at all, let alone for more than two years. But once he got over the shock, his first instinct had been to comfort her. He'd done it before, too, when she'd felt so trapped and frightened in the kitchen.

Golly, how long had it been since someone had fixed her a cup of tea? Probably not since Mom died. Robert had made her tea and held her hand and hadn't pressed her for more than she was ready to tell him. Ethan had never cared about her comfort like that.

She rubbed her palm with her hand, remembering

the feeling of Robert's skin against hers. That warm, strong hand had kept her grounded while she spoke, a physical reminder that she was safe in California, far away from Ethan.

Yikes.

She'd thought Ethan's name more in the past couple hours than she had in the last two years. Even Cassie referred to Ethan as "*him*."

What Josie would give to go back in time and tell her eighteen-year-old self not to be swept away by the banker's son's sandy hair, bright blue eyes, and cocky charm.

She was in her second semester of nursing school and shadowing an RN at the hospital in Hays when Ethan stepped into the patient room she was in and introduced himself as the patient's son. Of course she knew who Ethan Winchester was. Everyone in Hays did. Roy Winchester's handsome and intelligent twenty-three-year-old son would take his father's place as president of the bank someday. The Winchesters were old money, and they let everyone know it. Rumor was that Ethan had broken things off with his longtime sweetheart, Margie Dayton, a few months earlier because his parents considered the Daytons poor white trash.

Josie didn't think that was fair. The Daytons were decent people, just down on their luck. But she supposed that if Ethan wanted to inherit the bank, he had to do as his father asked. And she'd never put much stock in rumors to begin with. Maybe Margie had been the one who broke things off.

In any event, that day, Ethan was just another young man, come to visit his mother while she recovered from a hysterectomy.

"Miss Donovan has been a wonderful help to me," Mrs. Winchester said to Ethan. "Isn't she lovely?"

Ethan turned those sparkling blue eyes on Josie and agreed. Butterflies collided in her stomach. She hadn't dated much in high school because between her schoolwork and her chores at home, she didn't have much time. She also guessed that a lot of boys were scared off by all her brothers. And she'd never been noticed by someone as dashing as Ethan Winchester.

He returned every day to see his mother, and at the end of the week, when he managed to talk to her away from the reproachful gaze of her supervisor and asked her on a date, she accepted immediately. She would have been crazy not to.

He took her to see *Bride of the Monster* at the drive-in and pulled her close on the bench front seat of his car and put his arm around her. When he dropped her off at home afterward, he kissed her, right under the porchlight where any brothers who might be watching out the front window could see. His brazenness both shocked and thrilled her.

"I'm gonna take you out again next weekend," he said. Josie gazed at him, admiring everything from his strong chin to the bare slash through his left eyebrow.

They went out nearly every weekend after, and by the end of that summer, they were engaged.

Ethan wanted to marry right away, but Josie insisted on finishing nursing school first. She wanted to complete her degree and work for a year or two before starting a family. Ethan scowled when she told him.

"I just turned twenty-four, Josie," he said. The hour was late, and they were parked one small sunflower field away from Josie's house. Lights from the house winked at them like stars. Ethan shifted in his seat. "My father had two children by the time he was my age."

"I'm not even nineteen for two more months," Josie said. "We have plenty of time."

He leaned in close and fingered a tendril of hair near her ear. "At least let's play a little backseat bingo." The soft purr of his voice and the scent of his Aqua Velva aftershave nearly drove her wild. She wasn't crazy about her first time happening in the backseat of a car, but they weren't likely to get a better opportunity. She almost said yes, but then the nurse in her prompted her to ask one very important question.

"Do you have any rubbers?"

Ethan laughed. "Of course not. I don't carry those around. Come on, Josie, we're engaged."

She stared at him. Was he serious?

"Ethan. I told you less than a minute ago that I don't want children for a few years."

He scoffed. "You're not going to get pregnant from one time."

"I most certainly could."

He scowled. "Are you frigid? Because if you are, I need to know right now."

A surge of adrenaline shot through her.

"Not wanting to get pregnant tonight does *not* make me frigid," she said through gritted teeth. "And you're being insulting. Good night, Ethan."

She got out of the car and trudged through the field toward home. Ethan didn't follow her. She heard him drive off before she was halfway across the field.

He showed up the next afternoon with a bouquet of flowers and a contrite expression. Josie stood in the doorway, Peter and Ben glowering over her shoulder.

"I was rude last night, and I apologize," he said, handing her the flowers. He smiled his charming, dazzling smile. Josie smiled back and forgave him.

But he kept pressuring her for sex while refusing to wear a condom.

"I won't be able to feel anything," he whined.

Josie asked her doctor for a diaphragm, but he wouldn't give her one.

"We can't have you spoiling yourself before your wedding night," he said, wagging a finger in her face. "Come back a day or two before, and you can have one then. With your fiancé's permission, of course."

When she told Ethan they'd just have to wait, all he said was, "Fine."

They still necked in his car, but something felt off. He was distant, less passionate. She told herself they were both just nervous about the wedding. They'd be fine once they could settle into their lives together.

Her wedding day dawned clear and bright, and Josie's sisters-in-law spent the day helping her get ready. At 4:00 p.m., as Jimmy escorted her down the aisle, Josie saw Ethan waiting for her at the altar. He stood there in a new black suit, his sandy hair neatly combed, and that dazzling smile pointed right at her.

She relaxed. Everything was going to be okay.

The ceremony went by in a blink, and before she knew it, the minister was presenting Mr. and Mrs. Ethan Winchester. She looked out across the assembled guests: her brothers, her sisters-in-law, her nieces and nephews, friends from school. Everyone applauded, and Josie gave them a huge smile.

Ethan's mother had insisted on a large reception, including a catered dinner, so it was past ten o'clock by the time Ethan and Josie pulled up to their new house: a large, modern ranch-style home with three bedrooms and an attached garage. Ethan's parents had purchased it for them as a wedding gift.

And now, at long last, they were home as husband and wife with nothing to stop them from exploring all the pleasures their married life had to offer. By the time Ethan stopped the car in the driveway, the blood was pulsing through Josie's pelvis.

"Go on inside," Ethan said. "I'll be back later."

He might as well have shoved her into the duck pond in January. What did he mean he'd be back later? This was their wedding night. He must be playing a joke. She laughed.

"What's so funny?" Ethan said.

Josie stared at him. "We just got married. Aren't you going to carry me across the threshold? I've got my diaphragm ready." She wiggled her eyebrows.

He rolled his eyes. "I told a couple of the guys I'd meet them at the Pig Pen."

He was going to a bar? Tonight?

"But…we just got married." She blinked back tears.

"Which is why they wanted to take me out. To celebrate."

"What about *our* celebration?"

Ethan reached into his pocket and pulled out a key that he handed to her. "Let yourself in and get comfortable. I won't be out long." He kissed her, and, not knowing what else to do, Josie got out of the car.

"I love you," she said, but he was already backing out of the driveway.

Josie let herself into the house, walked alone to the master bedroom, and changed into the silky negligee

Jimmy's wife had made her for tonight. She pulled back the brand-new quilt and sheets on the bed, climbed in, and cried herself to sleep.

****

Remembering the crushing loneliness of that night, Josie wrapped her arms around herself and shivered under the blankets of Matthew's bed. She'd never felt so alone as she had that night, not even after her parents' deaths. At least then she'd always had a brother or two nearby.

Hot tears welled up, and she ground her knuckles into her eyes to push them back.

No more tears over him, Josie Girl, no more tears.

Across the hall, Robert broke out coughing. She waited, breath held, listening for him to settle. When he didn't, she threw back the covers and padded softly across the hall and into his room. Enough light from the street slipped in around the blinds that she didn't have to turn on the lamp next to his bed. Eyes still closed, probably not fully awake, he felt around on the nightstand. Josie picked up his water glass and placed it in his hand. He took a couple swigs, put it back on the nightstand, and, cough finally calmed, nuzzled back into his pillows without ever opening his eyes. She felt his forehead to make sure he was still cool. It would probably be another day or two before that cough went away. Some more tea tomorrow would help.

Tomorrow. She'd get to spend tomorrow with him. And Friday, and the weekend too.

She smiled again and fingered that lock of dark hair that fell over his brow. When he didn't stir, she ran her hand slowly through his hair, surprised by its flower-petal softness. He sighed but didn't wake, so she bent down and kissed his forehead, letting her lips linger on his skin.

"Thanks for the company," she whispered.

Chapter Thirty-Seven

Josie expected more questions about her divorce the next day, but Robert didn't bring it up. It would have been natural for him to pry a bit deeper, try to get all the sordid details, but he didn't ask.

He didn't pressure her for anything, come to think of it. Not information, not attention, not conversation, nothing. He waited for her to offer.

All he wanted was her company.

They spent Thursday and Friday watching television and playing board games. The only games Robert had were for Matthew, and they laughed themselves silly over Candyland and Chutes and Ladders. By Friday evening, he'd regained enough energy to help cook dinner. He was surprisingly good at breading chicken-fried steak, despite not being from Kansas.

And he was so easy to be around. On Saturday evening, she felt mopey, knowing she'd have to go home tomorrow. They sat together on the sofa with the evening tea that had become their ritual, Sergeant snoring on the rug in front of them. She tried to burn the moment into her memory so she could hang onto it forever.

"I'd invite you to stay another week, but I have to be back on set Monday morning," Robert said, taking a sip of tea. He hadn't coughed more than once or twice today, and the rosiness was slowly returning to his cheeks.

"I'm on the schedule at the hospital seven to three

every day next week anyway," she said, then chuckled. "And I should probably spend some time with Cassie before she reports me missing to the police." She delivered her next question while staring down into her teacup. "But maybe you could call some evening? At least talk for a bit?" She looked up in time to see his dimply grin.

"I'd like that." He cocked his head. "We should pressure Merrill to pay you more so you don't have to keep nursing."

Josie smiled. "He pays me more than enough now, but there's no guarantee he'll keep me on next season. I need to keep my skills sharp in case I need to go back full time."

"Would you quit nursing if he offered you a longer contract?"

"In a heartbeat." She grinned. "I love nursing, truly I do, but hospitals will always be there. If Merrill gave me an opportunity to stay on long-term, I'd take it."

Robert's face twitched, and she guessed he was holding back a question.

"Go ahead and ask," she said.

He smiled bashfully. "But you weren't planning to go into acting when you moved here, were you?"

She shook her head. "Merrill offering me that audition was a complete surprise. But I like new experiences, and I get to ride a horse."

"The horseback riding *is* fun," Robert said. "There are a lot of things about the show I dislike, but the horses are great."

That piqued her interest. She'd picked up that he and Merrill knocked skulls over the direction Robert felt his character should take, but she'd never asked either of them about it. Didn't seem like any of her business. And taking a cue from Robert, she decided to let him tell her when he was ready. They sat quietly for a few minutes until Robert finished his tea.

"When do you want to go to Disneyland?" he said.

Josie's mopiness dried up in a flash. She might be going home tomorrow, but she had a whole day with him at Disneyland to look forward to. They compared schedules and decided on the first Saturday in December, exactly three weeks away.

"I'll be on set that whole week prior," Josie said with a grin. "Sure you won't be sick of me by then?"

He met her eyes. "Never," he said, his voice husky.

Josie shrank back a few inches but didn't break their gaze. She didn't want to turn away from those warm, golden eyes. So much prettier than Ethan's plain, cold blue. Ethan who *had* gotten sick of her. Everything about Robert was better than Ethan, that ridiculous golden boy of Hays with his dirty-blond hair, his father's money, and his undeserved sense of superiority.

Yuck. Why was she thinking about Ethan so much these past few days? Here she was with a friend she'd never expected to make—a male friend who happened to have beautiful eyes—and all she kept thinking about was her ex-husband. She shuddered.

"Josie?"

She blinked and shook her head. "Sorry. Miles away."

"You all right?"

He was still studying her, concern etched on his face.

He genuinely cared about *her*. Not what she could do for him, but just...*her*. She wanted to tell him

194

everything. Somehow, she knew it was safe to tell him. He'd understand, and he wouldn't judge.

"His name is Ethan," she said.

God bless him, Robert betrayed no surprise or shock at the sudden change of subject. He reached over and took her teacup.

"Hold that thought," he said. "Let me get you more tea."

He carried their cups to the kitchen and returned a few minutes later with both cups steaming again, Josie's already sporting a single lemon slice. She smiled. Ever since that first night he made her tea, he always put in the lemon slice she liked. She patted the spot on the sofa right next to her, and his eyebrows went up. They usually sat at opposite ends. She appreciated that he didn't corner her, but tonight, she wanted him close. Feeling him next to her would remind her that she'd escaped, that she wasn't trapped anymore.

He sat where she told him to but faced forward, stared across the living room, and sipped his tea. That was nice. He was so close their hips nearly brushed, but he wasn't ogling her, which made it easier to launch into her story.

She told him about everything from the day she met Ethan until their disastrous wedding night when she went to bed alone.

"He finally did come home around three a.m.," she said. "Drunk as a skunk. But I was asleep." Her next words caught in her throat, and she took a sip of tea, hoping Robert wouldn't notice she was skipping ahead in the story. She'd woken up when Ethan got home, but she wasn't ready to share the details of *that* experience.

"When I woke up the next morning, I saw he'd left

his jacket on the floor, so I picked it up, and there on the collar were two long, wavy red hairs."

Robert turned toward her, his eyes wide. "He was fooling around on you?"

She nodded. "The girl he'd broken up with, Margie, had long red hair. I didn't say anything then. I told myself it was just a coincidence. But we got married in early June, and on Halloween, she showed up on our doorstep with a baby in her arms."

Robert squeezed his eyes shut. "Oh, no."

"Oh, yes," Josie said. "I was stunned. No one had seen her around town for months. Now we knew why. She demanded to talk to Ethan, but he was out with his friends at the bar, as usual. Left me to hand out candy by myself. Margie got real upset when I told her he wasn't home. She started hollering about how she was pregnant again already and he wasn't taking care of this first one like he'd promised."

"She could prove the babies were his?"

"I never saw the younger one, but the older one had that same bare patch in his eyebrow that Ethan has. The baby was three months old when she came to the house, so that means he got her pregnant while we were engaged and then again after we were married." Josie's hands shook so hard with anger at the memories that she had to set her tea on the coffee table.

Robert's jaw clenched. "I'm guessing you used the adultery to sue for the divorce?"

Josie nodded again, focusing her gaze on her hands knotted in her lap, her fingernails digging into her palms. "He had the nerve to be angry at *me* when we served him the papers. Right in front of all my brothers he said if I'd been easier stuff, he wouldn't have had to stray."

"All your brothers went with you to serve him the papers?"

She looked up and saw him smirking. The corners of her mouth turned up too.

"All five. Leighton drove in from Wichita just for the occasion. And I can't say for certain, but I think Peter was carrying his service pistol from Korea."

"Good." Robert set his empty teacup on the coffee table. Josie picked hers back up and drained it. She felt his eyes on her and flushed.

"What?" she said.

"He never should have said that to you," Robert said, his eyes flinty and his voice hard. "Not in front of your brothers or in private. He should have been honest and controlled himself. His cheating wasn't your fault."

She barely held back a rush of tears. She'd waited so long to hear someone besides her family say that. Someone who didn't have an obligation to defend her. Her chin quivered, and when she spoke, her voice shook.

"Wish you had been there to tell the good people of Hays that. The Winchesters ruined my reputation. They spread it all over town that I abandoned my wifely duties. I had patients in the hospital lecturing me on how to better satisfy my husband. It was so humiliating I couldn't stay. People I'd known for years, who I thought were friends, turned on me. Finally, Leighton called up a med school buddy of his here in Hollywood, and he got me my job." She ground her teeth. "Ethan had two babies with another woman, but *I* abandoned *him*."

"That's a bullshit accusation," Robert said, sniffing. His shoulders slumped, and he looked down at his lap.

Uh oh. She'd hit a nerve.

Say something, Josie Girl. Something supportive.

Something helpful.

"Is that what happened with you and Laura?"

Not great, but it could have been worse.

Robert nodded and dug at a hangnail on his thumb.

"'Bout a year and a half ago, she sued on the grounds that I abandoned her and Matthew." He tore off the hangnail, and blood bloomed along the edge of his thumbnail. He pressed his index finger against the spot and looked up at her, his eyes wet. "I didn't abandon them, Josie. I never could have done that. As much as we argued, I would never have just abandoned Laura. And Matthew... I could never... Not my little guy." He rested his elbows on his knees and dropped his face into his hands. Sergeant trotted over, sat next to him, and nudged his arm.

If only she could have seen this side of him months ago. Not the moody persona he had on set. Here was the real Robert Coolidge: The man who loved his son more than anything in the world, who ached being apart from him. Who was devastated by the implication that he had deliberately hurt someone. She laid a hand on his shoulder.

He looked up at her, his eyes red and puffy. Seeing him so unraveled made her chest ache.

"I'm sure you wouldn't," she said.

He reached up and squeezed the hand on his shoulder.

"For what it's worth, she left me," he said.

His story tumbled out. He and Laura were high school sweethearts. He went off to the College of Charleston, but he'd come home every school break and they'd pick right back up.

"I wasn't a very good student," he said. "Once I

discovered theater there, that was all I wanted to do. I dropped out so I could work and save up money to move to New York City."

He moved to New York right after he turned twenty-one and found stage work quickly. Nothing huge, but it paid the bills and whet his appetite for more. But a month or two after a visit home to Hell Hole—Josie bit her tongue to keep from laughing at the name—he got a phone call from Laura saying she was pregnant. So he did what he'd always believed was the right thing to do in that situation: He went home, married her, and took her back to New York City, where Matthew was born that fall.

"She hated New York," he said. "Absolutely hated it. Everything was too big, too loud, too crowded, too expensive. Growing up in a place like Hell Hole, I can understand that. But I thought she'd get used to it. I thought being together with our little family would be enough."

"But it wasn't," Josie said.

Robert shook his head. "I was getting good work in New York, and I really wanted to come out to Los Angeles to try my hand at film or television. I knew I could make a lot more money. The Depression hit Hell Hole hard, and I wanted Matthew to have more than I did." He rubbed his eyes with the heels of his hands. "But Laura refused to come to LA. She took Matthew—he was about two by then—and went back to her parents in Jamestown. I thought she was bluffing. I thought once I got here, she'd change her mind. After the first year, I knew she wouldn't come back, but I never thought she'd accuse me of abandonment."

A tear finally escaped one eye and rolled down his

cheek. He scrubbed it away.

Josie's eyes burned. No wonder he'd been so miserable after the divorce was finalized. He'd had to admit to something he hadn't done. She slid her hand from his shoulder to the middle of his back and rubbed small circles. He exhaled and leaned toward her.

"You didn't fight it?" she said.

He shook his head again. "Wouldn't have done any good. Even if she'd come back to me, we never would have been happy. We weren't a good match, and all I really wanted was Matthew. Laura deserved to move on with her life." He sighed. "I was just trying to provide for them, Josie. I *do* provide for them. I send Laura money every month. I pay every bill she sends me. I know she had to accuse me of *something* to get the divorce, and abandonment was the easiest way to go, but it still…" He slumped against the sofa cushions, looking drained. Josie scooted even closer, so their hips touched.

"I'm so sorry," she said, her voice gentle. She cringed, realizing she was using the bedside voice she used with agitated patients, but it seemed to work. His shoulders lowered an inch or two. She took his right hand with her left and interlaced her fingers with his. He looked at her, clearly surprised, but smiled and gave her hand a little squeeze.

"You haven't told anyone else all this, have you?" she said, echoing his question from earlier in the week.

He chuckled, obviously remembering too. "Just Ed. Out here, anyway. Everyone back in good old Hell Hole knows." He cast his eyes skyward and waggled his head with each syllable as he said "Hell Hole." Josie laughed, and he smiled. Golly, she loved that dimple. And the way his eyes crinkled at the corners when he smiled. And his aftershave…

Stop it, Josie Girl. Don't ruin this moment. He's your friend.

She looked down and focused on Sergeant instead. The dog had lain back down and was snoring again.

"I'm sorry," Robert said. "You were confessing everything, and I turned the conversation around to myself."

She almost laughed. This was probably the first time in his life that Robert Coolidge had *ever* turned a conversation around to himself.

"It feels good to have said it, doesn't it?" She felt lighter than she had all week.

"It does," he said. He squeezed her hand again and shifted in his seat. "Would it be all right if I put my arm around you? Strictly as friends."

Her breath caught. Would he get the wrong idea if she let him? She didn't dare. But then she glanced up at his face. He was looking away, chewing on his lower lip, his eyes red-rimmed, and realization hit her. He wasn't looking for a cheap thrill. He was asking for comfort but coming right out and saying he needed a hug wasn't very manly. She smiled and said yes.

He grinned, unlaced his fingers from hers, and draped his arm across her shoulders. Josie took a deep breath and relaxed.

So this was contentment. She'd nearly forgotten what it felt like. She tucked her feet up on the sofa, rested her head on his solid chest, and lost herself in his heartbeat.

Chapter Thirty-Eight

Josie's stomach fluttered with excitement a couple weeks later when Robert called midweek and told her he'd pick her up at 8:30 Saturday morning for their trip to Disneyland. She'd been thrilled to be back on set with him this week, but it wasn't the same as having him to herself. Now they'd have an entire day together.

The closest thing to an amusement park Josie had been to was the Kansas State Fair, and that couldn't possibly compare. What in the world should she wear? She called Cassie in a panic Friday evening, and her friend was at her door within twenty minutes.

"I'm staying the night so I can help you in the morning too," Cassie said, holding up a small carpetbag. "Don't worry, I'll leave before Robert gets here. He never needs to know." Josie hugged her and dragged her inside.

Josie and Cassie woke at 6:30 the next morning so Cassie had time to eat a little breakfast, fix Josie's hair, and get the heck out of there. Josie's hair was way too long to leave down for a day outdoors, so Cassie pinned it securely in a low chignon. Practical, but prettier than Josie's usual tight nurse's bun or a braid. Josie had thought about wearing a cute dress, but Cassie pointed out that she'd be climbing in and out of ride vehicles all day and put her in a pair of black cigarette pants and a red blouse instead.

Before she left, Cassie pressed a dime into Josie's palm.

"What's this for?" Josie said.

"So you can call me if you need me. I'll borrow Dad's car and come get you."

Josie bit back tears before they could spoil her mascara. She threw her arms around Cassie and held her tight. Cassie hugged her back.

"Thank you," Josie said. "I'm sure I'll be all right, though."

"I am, too, but a safety net never hurt anyone."

Josie stepped back and smiled at her best friend. Cassie had been pleased when she told her how she talked to Robert about Ethan and her divorce and how he'd asked before putting his arm around her. Josie knew Cassie wasn't worried about Robert misbehaving today. Cassie was giving her the dime to remind her she'd never be trapped again.

"Have fun. I expect a full report tomorrow." Cassie hugged her again and headed out the door.

Her nerves singing, Josie watched out the living room window for Robert's Corvette to pull up. As soon as she spotted it, she dashed across the room and threw herself into the armchair. It groaned under her, and she frowned. Maybe she should use some of her *Gunslingers* money to get new furniture. This secondhand outfit was going to dump her onto the floor someday, probably sooner than later.

His knock took forever to come. Next apartment she got, she wanted to be on the first floor so her guests didn't have to climb a flight of stairs to reach her. She strode to the door, took a deep breath, and opened it.

She smelled Robert's aftershave before she could

see him. When the door was open all the way, there he stood, in gray trousers and a blue polo shirt with two thin brown stripes down the right breast. She stared at his forearms, the tendons and veins bulging under the tanned skin. He'd slicked back his hair, securing that unruly forelock. His lips parted, but a long moment passed before he spoke. In the empty space, they stared at each other. Josie's mouth watered.

"You look nice," he said at last.

Josie swallowed. "You too."

They stared a bit longer.

"Ready to go?" he said.

Josie smiled, forcing her attention back to their plans for the day. "Mickey Mouse is waiting."

When they reached the parking spaces tucked underneath the building, he opened the Corvette's passenger door and took her hand to help her in. A thrill prickled up her spine. She hadn't touched him in more than two weeks, and the feel of his skin against hers brought her to life. She would have held his hand the whole way if he hadn't needed it to shift gears.

The drive to Anaheim lasted nearly an hour, and once Josie was done marveling at the freeway—nearly three years in LA and the wide, elevated highways still amazed her—they chatted most of the way. Robert got her laughing with tales of growing up in the swamp. Her favorite was his story about the time he and Jack had to chase an alligator off the back porch.

"Wasn't unusual to see one lurking around the edge of the yard, but we'd never had a gator come right up to the house like that," he said and laughed. "First and only time I've ever heard my mother curse."

"I'd love to see the swamp," Josie said, "but I'm

glad I don't live there. I'd get eaten in a second."

Robert grinned. "You learn to watch your step."

Before long, he pulled off the freeway and Josie spotted the huge marquee sign that read "Disneyland" in giant letters. She squealed and clapped her hands. Robert chuckled.

"Sorry," she said. "Little excited."

They rode a tram from the parking lot to the front entrance, where Josie clapped her hands again. In front of them loomed the huge train station, decorated in wreaths and garland for Christmas. A loud "Whoo-whoo!" rang out as, on the other side of the ticket booths, an old-fashioned steam engine puffed past the station. Josie bounced in place.

When they reached the front of the ticket-booth line, Robert bought two jumbo ticket books, which he slipped into his pocket.

"These should last us a while. And if we run out, I'll get more. Today, you get to ride everything you want as many times as you want." He grinned.

She followed Robert around to the left of a giant floral portrait of Mickey Mouse and through a little tunnel, where an employee in a vest, bow tie, and straw hat handed Robert a park map. He passed it to Josie, and she immediately unfolded it and pored over the list of attractions while she walked. When they emerged from the other side of the tunnel back into the bright sunshine, Robert tapped her shoulder.

She looked up and gasped as she caught her first glimpse of Main Street U.S.A.

"Good gravy," she said.

Lining both sides were shops and storefronts styled like the turn of the century. In the distance at the end of the street towered Sleeping Beauty's Castle, also done up in wreaths and garland for the season. Wafting through it all was the salty scent of hot, fresh popcorn. She could hardly believe she was still in southern California.

"Darn it, I should have brought my camera," she said.

"We'll get you a postcard," Robert said. He led her to the sidewalk, out of the way of other guests coming in. "Where do you want to start?"

Golly, where *should* they start? She studied the map, but there were so many choices she nearly went cross-eyed.

"Can we just go clockwise?" she said.

"The day is yours," Robert said. He offered her his arm, and she smiled and slipped her hand through it. The morning was chilly and having him close was nice. They approached the castle, made a left, and headed into Adventureland.

Chapter Thirty-Nine

Robert loved watching Josie's face light up when she saw the mechanical animals on the Rivers of the World Jungle Cruise. Afterward, he led her over a little bridge and through a stake wall into Frontierland, where he immediately burst out laughing.

"What's so funny?" Josie said.

"It looks like we're on set." He swept a hand to indicate the rows of mid-nineteenth-century-style buildings lining each side of the thoroughfare. They sported names like "Pendleton Woolen Mills" and "Frontier Trading Post."

Josie laughed too. "At least it feels familiar."

They skipped the pack mules, but they rode nearly everything else—the little mine train, the Indian war canoes, and the three-masted sailing ship *Columbia*, which Josie clearly loved. The way her eyes lit up made his heart swell with so much love he thought he might burst. There was no way he'd survive today, but there were worse ways to go.

After the ship, they relaxed in chairs under a green umbrella outside a restaurant and dug into heaping plates of fried chicken. He'd never seen a girl eat as fast as Josie did. Must be from competing with all those brothers at the dinner table.

About halfway through a drumstick, she dropped her chicken onto her plate and grabbed a fistful of napkins. She took a long time wiping her face and… Was she hiding?

"That guy's staring at me," she said.

Robert followed the tiny bit of her gaze that peeped over the napkins and saw a young man about Josie's age staring at her from a few yards away, completely ignoring the pretty young lady he was holding hands with.

Damn. He so rarely got recognized in public that it hadn't crossed his mind that Josie might. She'd only appeared in a handful of episodes so far, but this fellow sure seemed to recognize her. Robert caught the guy's eye and spread his hands in a "what do you want?" gesture, and the young man and his date moved on. Robert watched them go, making sure they didn't point Josie out to anyone else. He wasn't about to let some punk kid wreck their day by attracting a crowd.

"We should talk to Wardrobe about putting you in a hat," he said. "I almost never get recognized without one, especially if I'm wearing these." He tapped the rim of his aviators.

"If I'm around long enough to bother." Josie took a pull from her Coke bottle. "Merrill said he won't know about next season until spring."

"He's a fool if he doesn't keep you." He snorted. "Well, he's a fool anyway."

Josie studied him for a moment. "What is the problem between you two?"

He sighed and leaned back in his seat. It was a reasonable question. He was surprised she hadn't asked it before now. May as well answer it.

"It drives me crazy that he won't give Deacon Bell any depth," he said. "Sheriff Anderson's got his daughter now, and Judah Mitchell is getting a love affair, but Deacon Bell is still nothing but 'Yes, Sheriff, no, Sheriff, whatever you say, Sheriff.' First time I asked Merrill for a little more, a scene where Deacon goes on a date or talks about having family somewhere or...*anything*, you know what he did?" He felt his blood pressure rise, and he balled up a napkin in his fist. "In the very next episode, he changed the script to have the sheriff make a big production of handing Deacon the keys to the jail and crack a joke about not letting all the inmates escape again. It was humiliating."

Josie frowned. "That was a mean trick." She paused and tilted her head, clearly considering her next words. "He's actually quite a fragile person, you know. He's one of those men you have to butter up before they'll do anything for you."

"And that's why he doesn't like me. I won't stoop to stroking his ego." He *really* didn't want to talk about Merrill anymore. He smiled and squeezed Josie's hand. "But I don't want to dampen the day by complaining about work. You want some dessert?"

Josie laughed. "I couldn't possibly, right now. Let's find something to ride. Something gentle."

They spent some time in Fantasyland, enjoying the slow kids' rides, but Robert barely paid attention to any of them. Every time they boarded a vehicle his attention went straight to Josie. He drank her in: The blackness of her hair, the bright green of her eyes, and that beautiful laugh. If they never spent another minute together after this, he could live on today for the rest of his life.

But he sure hoped he wouldn't have to.

He desperately wanted to impress her. When they got off Mr. Toad's Wild Ride, he led her to the towering, snow-capped mountain at the edge of Fantasyland.

"Miss Donovan, may I present the Matterhorn," he said, sweeping a hand toward the peak.

Josie's eyes were the size of wagon wheels. "Are those men *rappelling* down it?"

"Oh, yeah." He grinned. She was impressed, all right. "I've been looking forward to seeing this. They were still building it when I was here last year."

They watched a few bobsleds zip down the track that wound in and out of the mountain, which echoed with the delighted shrieks of the passengers.

"I've never been on a rollercoaster," she said.

"Let's change that." He squeezed her hand, and they took off for the ride's entrance.

The line was long—nearly an hour—but with Josie's hand in his and her laughter filling his ears, he hardly noticed the time passing. Before he knew it, they'd reached the front of the line and an employee in lederhosen was directing them to a blue-and-white bobsled.

Oh, good God.

He hadn't even thought about the seating arrangements. Each bobsled had two seats, each seat meant for two, single-file riders. Mr. Lederhosen directed him into the back of their seat and Josie into the front.

Josie was nearly going to be sitting in his lap.

He swallowed hard, settled into the back of the bobsled, one leg on each side of the bench, and patted the seat in front of him.

"Come on," he said.

If they'd been in a Looney Tunes cartoon, he imagined Josie's eyes would have popped completely out of their sockets. As it stood, he wasn't sure she was still breathing.

His stomach dropped. Please don't let her think he did this on purpose.

He stretched out a hand and nearly fainted in relief when she took it and stepped wordlessly into the bobsled. She sat carefully on the seat between his knees, leaving several inches of space between them. Thank goodness. This would be okay.

Then he saw the seatbelt.

Damn.

"Scoot back a little," he said, surprised that his voice didn't crack. "We have to buckle this thing." She swiveled her head, looked at the seatbelt, and flushed crimson. But she did as instructed, leaving a sliver of daylight between their bodies. He wrapped the seatbelt around them, trying not to be consumed by the warmth of her body so close to his. Less than two inches of space and clothing between them...

Stop it, R.J.

"Enjoy your ride," Mr. Lederhosen said. Their bobsled lurched to life, and Josie fell backward against his chest.

Chapter Forty

As their bobsled clacked down a dark tunnel and picked up speed, Josie felt Robert's heart pounding against her back—that strong, steady thumping she'd come to know so well through her stethoscope and that one night at his house when she laid her head on his chest. When they turned a corner, his inner thigh brushed her right hip. His touch sent a shiver straight up her spine, and she gripped the handrails on the outside of the bobsled a little tighter.

Play it cool, Josie Girl.

But then they lurched again as their bobsled started up a hill, and Josie was pressed even harder against Robert. She hoped the loud clanking of the track's chain covered the sound of her ragged breath. They climbed forever, occasionally getting flashes of light from the gaps in the mountainside.

She wished he'd let go of the handrails and put his arms around her. What would it be like to face him and have him embrace her? She imagined Robert pressing her to him, the full length of their bodies touching. Her heart rate picked up.

Good gravy, she loved feeling him against her.

She didn't get to focus on it very long, though, because they reached the top of the mountain and started their downward journey, making wide loops around the mountain.

The ride was probably no faster than a running horse, but it felt like lightspeed. Behind her, Robert let out a whoop of glee, which Josie drowned out with a long scream, certain she was going to fly out of the bobsled at any moment. But as they continued to hurtle down the mountain, and she stayed put, the thrill caught up to her, and she laughed too. They shouted in surprise as their bobsled splashed through a pond toward the end of the ride, spritzing them with cold water.

When their car slowed to a stop back at the loading station, they were still laughing. Robert unbuckled their seatbelt, and Josie, breathless, tried to stand, but wobbled and fell. Robert jumped to his feet and caught her with an arm around her waist. Josie froze in place, and Robert snatched his arm away.

"Sorry," he said, swallowing hard. "Wasn't trying to be forward."

Even though it terrified her, Josie wished he *would* be forward. She longed for him to touch her again. She smiled. "That's the second time you've saved me from falling on my rear end."

A relieved grin brightened his face, and she took his hand and held onto him as they made their way to the ride exit. Terrified or not, she couldn't bring herself to let him go.

Chapter Forty-One

While they strolled through Fantasyland, Josie relished the feel of Robert's warm, strong hand wrapped around hers. An elderly couple smiled at them, and for a second, Josie worried they'd been recognized. But when the old man whispered something in his wife's ear that made her giggle, Josie realized they thought she and Robert were a young couple here on a date.

The thought almost stopped her cold.

But why not treat today as a date? She was safe with Robert. He'd proven that multiple times.

And holy smoke, did she love holding his hand.

Just flirt a little and see how it feels, Josie Girl. You don't have to tear his clothes off.

Though now that she'd spent several minutes leaning against him on the Matterhorn, she sure as heck wouldn't mind seeing that carved, bronzed chest again. She bit back a giggle.

Taking a deep breath, she shifted her hand in his so she could lace their fingers together. He stopped walking and turned to face her, the crowd flowing around them like they were a stone in a stream. He studied her, and he raised his free hand like he was about to caress her cheek. She closed her eyes, but his touch never came. She opened her eyes and saw him still staring at her, hand again at his side and a line of sweat beading along his hairline. He swallowed hard.

"Tomorrowland?" he said. His voice croaked.

She hoped her disappointment didn't show on her face. Maybe he needed a clearer signal. "Tomorrowland," she said.

Robert had to buy more tickets on the way, but soon they were waiting for the monorail in Tomorrowland. Josie couldn't believe how quietly the sleek, streamlined train rolled up to the platform on its single track. Moving from Kansas to California would have been even more exciting if she could have taken one of these rather than that bumpy old train.

Robert let her take the window seat, but as they pulled out of the station and started their elevated journey around Tomorrowland, he leaned over her shoulder to peer out the window. His mouth was inches from the right side of her neck. She took a deep breath, inhaling the last lingering scent of his aftershave, and closed her eyes, relishing the brush of his warm breath on her skin. His lips were right there, that perfect Cupid's bow mouth. All she had to do was turn her head.

"Look at that," Robert said.

Josie opened her eyes and let her gaze follow Robert's pointing finger to the Matterhorn. They were so close she could see the open-mouthed faces of the riders on the bobsleds.

"That was so much fun," she said and gave him a sly smile. "Maybe we should ride it again."

Robert grinned. "Don't have to ask me twice."

As soon as they got off the Monorail, they hoofed it back to the Matterhorn and got into a much shorter line than they'd stood in earlier. Dusk was falling, and lights were winking on all over the park. Josie checked her watch: 6:30. Lots of guests were probably getting dinner.

After only twenty minutes, they were stepping into a bobsled. This time, she didn't hesitate. She sat right down and leaned back against Robert's chest, leaving just a hairsbreadth of space between her rear end and his front. Nestling against his chest was nice, but she wasn't quite ready to feel how much he might be enjoying this arrangement. There were some things that even the nicest, most well-intentioned men couldn't control.

She thought she heard his breath catch as he leaned forward to fasten the seatbelt, and she felt his breath on her neck again. A strange mixture of peace and excitement flushed through her. Flirting was *definitely* the right idea.

Now that she knew she wasn't going to be flung out of the bobsled to her death, she enjoyed every second of the ride. Zipping down the mountain was even more exciting in the dark, and she whooped and laughed with Robert the whole way.

She was steady this time when she stood at the end of the ride, so he didn't put his arm around her waist again, but he still took her hand, and she didn't let go, even when she was safely back on the platform.

Chapter Forty-Two

Robert couldn't believe Josie was holding his hand in public. They'd only ever touched in the privacy of his house. Now, the feel of her hand in his sent a constant tingle up his arm. He should have worn long sleeves so she couldn't see his goosebumps.

Something had changed in her since they'd taken that first ride on the Matterhorn, like a switch had flipped in her brain. He'd almost passed out from shock when she'd nuzzled into his chest at the start of their second Matterhorn ride. Because that was definitely a deliberate nuzzle.

But was he reading her wrong again? Maybe she was just cold. Or tired. And she might be holding his hand so they didn't lose each other in the crowd. That had to be it. He couldn't jump to conclusions. If he messed up again, she'd never give him a third chance, and then he'd shrivel up and die.

At least for now, he got to hold her hand.

He bought them hamburgers and iced tea from a walk-up cart, and they sat on a bench to eat, watching young couples—and a few elderly ones—stroll past hand-in-hand and parents dragging sobbing children toward the exit.

"Hope Matthew doesn't end our day like that," he said, chuckling. "Maybe I'll bring Mom and Dad along to help."

"Are your parents coming for Christmas too?"

He finished the last bite of his burger and leaned back against the bench. "Yeah, I forgot to tell you. They called the other day, said we don't spend Christmas together nearly enough, and invited themselves to LA." He smiled and shook his head. He got no say in the matter. When Mom said she was coming, all he could do was get a guest room ready.

"Don't you usually go home for Christmas? I know Matthew's coming to you this year, but…"

His smile dropped, and an old, familiar ache pulsed deep in his chest. "LA is home now. I don't much like going back. I'll go if it's the only way to see Matthew, but I prefer to bring him here." He leaned forward and clasped his hands between his knees, his next words sticking in his throat.

Just say it, R.J. Josie of all people will understand.

"My folks' place…it hasn't been the same since we lost Jack." He looked away toward the castle, lit up brightly against the dark sky. It reminded him of Jack: A spark in the night. Put it out, and all you had was the darkness, so easy to get lost in.

He felt a slender arm wrap around his shoulders.

"There are some losses you don't get over," Josie said. "You just learn how to live around the pain."

Oh, Josie. His unexpected little beacon. He didn't realize until the words were out of her mouth that he'd been waiting fifteen years to hear someone say something like that. He wanted to burst into tears and propose to her at the same time, but either one would cause a scene. He scrubbed his hands through his hair, not caring that he was messing up his careful pomade job from this morning.

He looked up at her. His eyes were probably red-rimmed, but at least they were dry. "Thank you." He sat up straight, and her arm slid from his shoulders. He took her hand and wove their fingers together. He needed to feel her there, anchoring him in place. "Anyway, they all fly in on the twentieth." He brightened. "What day are you heading home?"

"The twenty-second. Why?"

A thread of joy embroidered its way back through him. "Would you like to come over for dinner on the twenty-first and meet everyone?"

He might as well have proposed for as shocked as Josie looked. Meeting his family was pretty significant, he supposed. Come to think of it, he'd never introduced a girl to his parents. The only girl he'd ever dated in Hell Hole was Laura, and they'd known her all her life. That's what happens when you live in a town with fewer than two hundred people in it. But they'd love Josie. She was impossible not to love. He smiled, hoping she could see that too.

"That sounds lovely," she said.

****

A few minutes later, they stood in front of the castle and watched fireworks explode in the sky. The evening had grown chilly, and Robert slipped his arm around Josie's shoulders. She seemed to be all right with that. Smiling, she snaked her arms around his waist, drew up close, and rested her head on his chest.

Okay, she was *definitely* all right with that.

She had to be able to hear his thumping heart, even over the pop of the fireworks and the oohs and ahs from the crowd around them. He'd misread her hand squeeze in Yosemite, but there could be no mistaking this.

Friends didn't hold each other like this. He wanted to wrap both arms around her, tilt that perfect face up to his, and kiss her until he couldn't breathe.

But not here in front of all these people. And not when it was too loud for him to ask her first. Because he was sure as hell asking her first.

This moment was perfect anyway. With the fireworks above him, the towering Christmas tree near the park entrance behind him, and Josie beside him, he was happier than he'd been in years. He gave her a gentle squeeze, and when she looked up at him, all he could do was smile. She smiled back, her adorable nose wrinkling, and held his gaze until shouts from the crowd drew her attention away. The fireworks display had reached its grand finale, and colorful bursts set the sky above the castle ablaze.

When the show ended, they followed the stream of guests out of the park. Robert couldn't remember the last time he'd felt this conflicted. He was overjoyed by their perfect day together, and so sad that it was nearly over. Please, God, let them get more days like this. He loved her so much. And, unlike when he was sick, now he thought there just might be a chance she could love him back.

When they reached the Corvette, Josie plunked into the seat like someone had dropped an anvil on her. She seemed too tired for conversation, but that was all right. Every now and again as they cruised back toward LA, he glanced over, and they shared a smile.

He'd ask her when they got to her door. It would be simple. Walk her there and say, "Would it be all right if I kissed you?" If she said no, he'd give her a goofy grin and make a show of shaking her hand, then get the hell out of there before she saw him shatter into a thousand pieces. But if she said yes…

He shook his head.

Focus on the road, R.J. You'll never get to ask her if you crash.

His nerves jangled when they pulled up to her apartment building, and he wiped his palms on his pants as he walked around the car to open her door. She held his hand as they climbed the stairs to her apartment. She unlocked the door and turned back to him.

"Thank you so much for today," she said. "I don't remember the last time I had this much fun." She paused. "I'm not sure I ever have."

He grinned. "Same here." He reached up and tucked a loose strand of silky hair behind her ear. "So thank *you*." He took both her hands in his and stared into her eyes, which sparkled like emeralds in the hall light. She smiled at him.

This was his moment. He opened his mouth to ask.

"There you are, Josie!" A dumpy, gray-haired lady popped out of the next apartment.

Robert jumped away from Josie, his hopes shriveling and dying in the empty space he opened between them.

"Mrs. Pullman," Josie said, clutching her chest. "Is everything all right?"

The lady smiled, shuffled over, and clasped Josie's hand in both of hers. "Everything's fine, my dear. I just wanted to tell you that your phone rang a lot this afternoon. I was worried someone was trying to reach you about something important."

"Thank you, Mrs. Pullman. I'm sorry if it bothered you."

"Not at all, dear." She turned and saw Robert, seemingly for the first time. "Oh, my! Well, I won't keep you from your young man." She ogled him like he was a pot roast at the grocery store. "Aren't you the handsome one?" She winked at Josie and patted her cheek. "Enjoy your evening." She scuffled to her door and disappeared into her apartment.

Josie turned to Robert, her cheeks scarlet. "I'm so sorry about that. The walls here are thin, and I'm not sure Mrs. Pullman still has it all together anyway." She shook her head. "It was probably the hospital calling to see if I could cover a shift."

Robert couldn't believe it. The interruption was like something out of a bad screenplay. But unlike a bad screenplay, he wasn't going to let his character be so rattled that he lost his nerve. Not when he'd spent the entire drive here from Anaheim working up his courage. He stepped close to Josie again, took her hands, and listened hard to make sure Mrs. Pullman wasn't about to jump out again.

Josie stared at the old lady's door for a moment, making a show of turning her head so her ear faced the door like she was listening too. He chuckled, and she grinned. "Anyhow," she said, "thank you again for today. It was perfect."

He smiled back. "It was. Well, almost." Josie cocked her head, and Robert drew a deep breath, praying his voice didn't shake. "Josie, at the risk of ruining everything, can I kiss you?"

For one eternal second, Josie didn't react. She stared at him, unblinking, face still. Then slowly, so slowly, her nose wrinkled as a huge smile spread across her face.

"At the risk of ruining everything," she said, "yes,

please."

He never knew the sun could rise at 11:30 at night.

Grinning like a fool, he stepped closer. His heart pounded so hard he was sure she could hear it. He slipped an arm around her waist and drew her close, pressing her body gently to his. He needed to feel her against him, but he didn't want to scare her. He must not have, because she wrapped her arms around him, resting her hands on his shoulder blades.

Oh, God, how long had he hoped to feel her hold him like this? He paused, memorizing the sensation in case it never happened again. Then he rested one hand on the back of her head, feeling that silky hair under his fingers, tilted his head down, and pressed his lips to hers.

Her lips were as soft and pillowy as they looked, and she tasted of the iced tea they'd had at dinner. All at once she was every good thing that had ever happened to him, and he pressed himself to her like she was the source of life itself. She pressed back, sighing ever so softly.

Sheer relief almost overwhelmed him, and if he didn't break this off now, he might go too far. He pulled his lips away from hers slowly, pausing for a second or two when they were only just brushing. Then he stepped back and cleared his throat.

"I should let you get to bed," he said, his voice raspy.

Josie's hands slid from his shoulders and dropped to her sides. Her cheeks were flushed, making her freckles stand out.

"See you on set Monday," she said, smiling coyly.

He grinned and planted a swift kiss on her forehead. "I'll look forward to it."

Chapter Forty-Three

As soon as she woke up the next morning, Josie dialed Cassie's number.

"Gee whiz, Josie, it's not even nine o'clock," Cassie said, yawning. She rarely woke before ten on a day off.

"Robert kissed me."

"And suddenly, I'm wide awake." Cassie's voice was eager. "Tell me everything."

Trying hard not to gush too much, Josie told her about the entire day, especially their first ride on the Matterhorn and their goodnight kiss at her door.

"I can't believe he asked first," Josie said. "It was so sweet. What man does that?"

Cassie snorted. "A man who got his tailbone bruised the last time he tried to kiss you."

Josie laughed. "Good point."

"When do you get to kiss him again?"

Golly. When *did* she get to kiss him again? She and Robert were on set together this week, but she sure couldn't kiss him there. If nothing else, Beau would tease her about it until kingdom come. And Merrill probably wouldn't be a fan of her planting a big one on his least-favorite cast member. Besides, she didn't want an audience.

Maybe next week? No, she was scheduled for four shifts at the hospital, and that weekend was the network Christmas party—another place she certainly couldn't kiss him. She'd be at his house the following Monday, but his family would be there, and then she'd be home in Kansas until New Year's.

She groaned.

Maybe 1960 would be more her year.

****

"Get cozy, you two," Merrill said to Josie and Beau on Monday. "When we come back in January, you're kissing."

Kissing.

Josie stopped herself just before she sighed aloud. She'd been replaying her kiss with Robert for the last thirty-six hours, remembering the warmth of his lips on hers, his hand on the small of her back.

Beau poked her in the ribs, snapping her out of her reverie. He wiggled his eyebrows suggestively. She knew he was trying to make her laugh, but her lip curled. Here she was hoping to ring in the new year kissing Robert, and now it looked like the first lips to touch hers in the new decade would be...*Beau's.* She tried not to shudder visibly.

"You knew it was going to happen eventually," Merrill said. "And you'll need to look like you're enjoying it." He looked from Josie to Beau and back again. "I guess we'll get to see how good an actress you really are."

Everyone laughed but Beau. He stuck out his tongue at the back of Merrill's head.

"Kissing someone on camera isn't as bad as you think," Robert said at lunch.

"He's right," Charlie said. "As long as both people are professionals, it's fine."

Robert smirked. "So it looks like you two have four

weeks to learn to be professionals."

Josie exchanged a look with Beau, who nodded, and they both threw balled-up napkins at Robert. He ducked and laughed. At least he didn't seem jealous that she'd be kissing Beau. But, oh, dear Lord, would he be on set that day? He probably would be. Terrific. The man she wanted to kiss would be standing there watching her kiss someone else.

She loved this job, but good gravy, did it get complicated sometimes.

They were filming outdoors a lot that week, and the days flew by. Through some unspoken understanding, she and Robert were friendly on set, but they didn't mention their Disneyland trip, and they never touched. She ached to feel his hand on the small of her back, his arm around her shoulders...*something*. But she sensed that kind of display wouldn't be welcome at the studio, so she held back.

On Tuesday, Charlie brought a Monopoly set, and the four of them played between scenes. Beau went bankrupt Wednesday afternoon, and Josie followed him on Thursday morning. Late Friday, Robert and Charlie were still battling it out. Josie loved watching Robert laugh with Charlie over the game, and she suspected that Charlie had brought it purposefully to get Robert to join the rest of them between scenes. Maybe he sensed the longing between her and Robert and wanted to give them an excuse to interact. That Charles Lyon was a sneaky one. Though not sneaky enough to beat Robert at Monopoly, as it turned out.

Robert surprised her with a phone call Friday evening. They hadn't spoken in private since he'd dropped her off after Disneyland, and she bit her lip to keep from squealing when she answered the phone and heard his voice.

"Just wanted to make sure you could still come over on Monday," he said.

As if she would have scheduled anything else.

"Of course! I'll bring a dessert. What time should I come over?"

"We usually eat around six, but let me pick you up. How about I come get you at five?"

There was a bus that could drop her a block from his house at 5:10, but arguing with him was probably useless. Besides, she'd gotten recognized on the bus home from work on Thursday. Fortunately, the fan was a polite little boy who only wanted to say hello, but it brought home how vulnerable she was in an enclosed space like that, even with fifty other commuters around her. She'd talked to Charlie, and he was taking her car-shopping when she got back from Kansas.

"Five sounds perfect," she said.

"Good." His voice rang with relief. "I made the mistake of telling Mom you were coming over for dinner. I told her I'd cook, but she's insisting on doing it herself, and she's been calling me every night to run ideas past me. Poor Dad's gonna have a stroke when he sees the phone bill next month."

Josie laughed. Her own mother had agonized over the menu every time one of her brothers brought a young lady home for dinner. So long as she approved of the girl, that was. If she didn't, she intentionally ruined the meal so the young lady wouldn't be so inclined to come back. More than once Mom had left a meatloaf in the oven until it was rock hard. Those girls hadn't stuck around long.

Oh, goodness. Did Mrs. Coolidge think she was

Robert's girlfriend? She pulled at a loose thread on the hem of her blouse. *Was* she Robert's girlfriend? Surely not. One kiss didn't mean you were going steady. But you didn't invite casual friends of the opposite sex over to meet your parents, either.

This was so complicated it made her head hurt.

"I won't keep you. We have a late night tomorrow, and I wanted to get to bed early. But I'll see you at the party," Robert said. "You shouldn't have any trouble finding me. I'll be the guy in the tuxedo."

Josie laughed again. "See you tomorrow night," she said, and they hung up.

Good gravy.

Not only was she meeting Robert's family on Monday, but tomorrow night she'd see him in a tuxedo.

She took two aspirin before she went to bed.

Chapter Forty-Four

Cassie showed up at Josie's at 11:00 the next morning. The party wasn't until 8:00 p.m., but Cassie claimed she couldn't possibly sit around her boring apartment all day long.

"I can't believe we're going to the Biltmore tonight," she said, sighing. "I've lived in Los Angeles my whole life and I've never seen the inside of it. And the Crystal Ballroom, no less!"

Josie shook her head. It *was* pretty surreal. Three years ago, she'd thought her life was ruined, and now she was on a television show and about to attend a fancy party in the fanciest ballroom of the fanciest hotel in Los Angeles. It was enough to make her head spin.

And Robert would be there in a tuxedo.

Her heart rate picked up just thinking about it.

They passed the day playing canasta and listening to records. At 5:30, Betty arrived, carrying a large valise in each hand.

"Who's ready to get gorgeous?" she said with a huge smile.

Josie was grateful the *Gunslingers* makeup artist had agreed to do their hair and makeup for the party. Josie had offered to pay her, but Betty said she wouldn't dream of charging her for her first big Hollywood party. Over the next two and half hours, Betty rouged, lined, shadowed, and lipsticked both women. She left Josie's long hair down and curled it into soft waves that cascaded over her shoulders, finishing it off with a generous amount of hairspray. Then she styled Cassie's chin-length blonde hair into a bouffant and secured it with even more hairspray than she'd used on Josie.

When Betty bid them farewell and it was time to put on their gowns, Josie suddenly envied Cassie. Her friend's simple strapless blue gown looked light as a feather compared to hers. She still couldn't believe she'd bought such an extravagant dress. It was a rich red with cap sleeves, a line of buttons down the back, and a full skirt. The extra material from the front of the skirt gathered in the back to create a bustle topped with a bow. There must be four yards of fabric back there. But when she'd tried it on at Saks Fifth Avenue, Cassie had gasped and declared it to be "the one."

It *was* gorgeous, if she did say so herself. Just heavy.

"One last thing," Cassie said, reaching into her pocketbook. "I had dinner with my parents last night, and Mother gave us a little"—she pulled a small glass atomizer out of her bag—"Chanel No. 5!"

Josie gasped and snatched the bottle, stuck it under her nose, and inhaled deeply.

"It's divine," she said with a sigh.

Cassie took the bottle back and spritzed some scent onto Josie's throat, then dabbed some on her own bosom. "Coco Chanel says a woman should always wear perfume wherever she hopes to be kissed," she said with a naughty giggle. Josie laughed. Cassie was the one who belonged at this party, not her, and Josie was thrilled to be able to bring her along. Cassie had never once complained, but Josie could hear the disappointment in her voice whenever she told her she'd be filming late and couldn't come over. But now she got to bring her along to rub elbows with some of her favorite television stars. Not a bad way to repay her best friend.

They were already outside when their cab pulled up to Josie's apartment building at 7:45. Cassie slid easily into the back seat and then had to slide right back out to help Josie bunch up her huge skirt enough to fit through the door.

Twenty minutes later, the cab pulled up to the curb outside the Los Angeles Biltmore Hotel. Josie gasped. Somehow, she'd never passed by it since coming to LA. She tended to avoid downtown and stick to Hollywood. She grabbed Cassie's hand, and Cassie leaned around her to stare too.

Occupying half a city block, the Biltmore rose eleven stories in the air—certainly not the tallest structure in town, but still impressive. Light twinkled through the windows like stars in the dark sky, and a long red carpet stretched from the front door to the curb.

She'd promised herself she'd never utter this line, but Josie couldn't help saying, "Toto, I've a feeling we're not in Kansas anymore."

Cassie laughed. "The architecture is a combination of styles, you know. It's meant to reflect the Castilian heritage of the city. You'll also see the 'Biltmore Angel' incorporated throughout the interior."

Josie turned her head and stared at her. Cassie knew a lot about Los Angeles, but this was a bit much, even for her.

Cassie shrugged. "I read a tourist brochure yesterday."

Before the driver could get out of the taxi and walk around to open their door, two tuxedoed doormen appeared. The one in the lead opened the door and offered Josie his hand.

"Good evening, Miss Donovan," he said.

Josie beamed. This was much better than being recognized on the bus. But when the second doorman extended his hand to Cassie and said, "Good evening, Miss Felix," her jaw dropped.

How did he know Cassie's name? Josie had listed her on the RSVP, but surely the doormen hadn't memorized those, had they?

The doormen escorted them into the hotel lobby, where Josie strained her neck looking up at the soaring ceiling, lit by large glass chandeliers.

"They say there's a ghost nurse on the second floor," Cassie said.

Josie snorted. "How? No nurse could afford to stay here."

"Maybe she died when she saw the bill."

They laughed as the doormen led them to the Crystal Ballroom. If Josie thought the exterior and the lobby were amazing, the ballroom took her breath away. Floor-to-ceiling marble columns circled the expansive, two-story room, separating individual little balconies with heavy drapes on the second floor. Sconces between the columns illuminated the room with a soft yellow glow, apart from the far end where a magnificent Christmas tree shined brightly in front of a string quartet.

Down the center of the room ran a wide dance floor emblazoned with the Biltmore logo in the center. It shone like marble, though it couldn't possibly be. The hotel staff would never be able to move a marble dance floor if they needed the space for something else. On the small stage, on the side of the room opposite the Christmas tree, another string quartet played, far enough away from the first group that their sounds never collided. Lining each side of the dance floor were dozens of round tables, draped with white linen and set with crystal goblets.

"Good evening, Miss Donovan, Miss Felix," a tuxedoed host said.

Josie felt her eyebrows shoot all the way up to her hairline. How did *he* know? The entire hotel staff must have memorized the RSVPs.

"*Gunslingers* is assigned to table nine," the host said. "Dinner is not for another hour, so please feel free to mingle and enjoy the hors d'oeurves."

Josie and Cassie thanked him, linked arms, and wandered, wide-eyed, farther into the enormous room, but not straying too far from the entrance. Josie wanted to be able to keep an eye out for the rest of the cast. Conversations buzzed around them, bouncing off the music from the nearest string quartet. There must have been two hundred people there already, and more were sure to arrive fashionably late. The room wasn't crowded—there was more than enough space to accommodate several hundred more people—but if Robert, Charlie, or Beau were already here, they had no hope of finding them before they met at their table for dinner.

Josie felt suddenly self-conscious. Apart from her castmates and Merrill, and Cassie, of course, she didn't know a soul here. What would they do for an hour until dinner?

"Have some champagne," Cassie said, poking a crystal flute into her hand.

Josie looked down at the ivory bubbles fizzing at the top of the slender glass. "Where did you get this?"

"Waiter." Cassie nodded in the direction of a man in tails carrying a tray of filled champagne flutes. She held hers up. "Cheers!"

They clinked glasses and sipped, the fizzy liquid making Josie's nostrils tingle. A few minutes later, they handed their empty flutes to another waiter and were looking around for more when Cassie grabbed Josie's arm.

"Holy smokes," she said, "that's Isaac Daniels!"

Josie followed Cassie's gaze and saw the tall, thin star of WBC's other Western, *Aces High*, standing at the entrance of the ballroom with an almost equally tall and even thinner blonde woman on his arm. Behind him was his co-star, Chris Andrews.

"They are just too handsome," Cassie said. She gasped and dug her fingernails into Josie's arm. Thank goodness they were both wearing gloves. "Josie! Do you think we'll see Michael Landon or Pernell Roberts tonight?"

Josie knit her brow, trying to place the names. "Wrong network, honey," she said, when they came to her. "*Bonanza*'s on NBC."

"Oh. Right." Cassie stuck out her lower lip, then brightened again. "How about Robert Fuller from *Laramie*?" Before Josie could reply, Cassie corrected herself. "Darn it, that's NBC too. Josie, you're working for the wrong network."

Josie laughed. "Sorry. I didn't get much choice."

"You know, NBC only cast Mike Landon because he looks so much like me," a familiar voice said from behind them.

Josie spun around to see Beau grinning at her. She was so relieved to see someone else she knew that she threw her arms around his neck and gave him a squeeze. He laughed and hugged her back.

"You clean up nice," she said. Beau had pomaded his unruly brown curls carefully into place, his face was flawlessly shaven, and his fitted tuxedo didn't have a single wrinkle. He'd used a healthy dose of Old Spice aftershave, but it wasn't overpowering. His blue eyes sparkled, crinkling a little at the corners when he smiled. He blushed at her compliment, which was so adorable she wanted to pinch his cheek. How had he managed to stay single so long?

He straightened his bow tie and looked from Josie to Cassie. His eyebrows shot up, and for an instant, he looked like he'd just had the wind knocked out of him.

Josie pretended not to notice. "Cassie, this is Beau Fraser," she said. "Beau, please meet Cassie Felix."

Beau blinked, bowed at the waist, and took the hand Cassie had extended, kissing the back of it. "Josie's told us a lot about you," he said. "All good things." Josie snorted. Beau was laying it on thick, but Cassie's giggle told her she didn't mind.

Beau straightened. "I haven't seen Robert yet, but I left Charlie and Nancy by our table." He crooked both arms. "Shall we, ladies?" Josie and Cassie each took an arm, and Beau escorted them through the growing throng toward table nine.

"Isn't this place incredible?" he said as they neared the entrance of the ballroom.

"The Academy Awards were held here eight times," Cassie said. "Not in this ballroom, though. In the Biltmore Bowl. It's even bigger."

Josie looked around, trying to picture that.

Then she spotted Robert, and her breath caught.

Chapter Forty-Five

Robert finished speaking with the host and scanned the ballroom, getting his bearings before venturing farther in. This place was huge. Were there *two* string quartets? He could wander around for forty days and forty nights and never find Josie. Probably best to head straight to the *Gunslingers* table.

He wove his way through the room, and when he was only a couple tables away from number nine, he saw her.

Long black hair cascading in waves over a ruby-red gown with a full skirt, her beautiful heart-shaped lips painted bright red.

Staring at her was like being frozen in a single moment in time. The music and the buzz of the crowd faded away. All that existed was Josie.

Her head was turned to the side toward Beau and a comely blonde—this must be the famous Cassie—but then Josie turned, and their eyes locked. Even from this distance he could see her chest heave. He boiled inside his wool tuxedo jacket.

A waiter with a tray of champagne passed in front of him, momentarily blocking his view. He snagged a flute and took a big gulp, then closed the distance to Josie. He couldn't have taken his eyes off her if his life depended on it. And now, close up, his nostrils filled with the floral scent of her perfume. She consumed him.

His mouth slowly rose into a smile, and he fought the urge to kiss her right there in front of everyone. "You look beautiful," he said.

"Thanks, you don't look so bad yourself," Beau said.

Robert would have kicked him, but he didn't want to scuff his oxfords.

The pretty blonde laughed, drawing everyone's attention.

"Oh," Josie said, "Cassie, please meet Robert Coolidge. Robert, this is my friend, Cassie Felix. You already know Beau." She rolled her eyes.

"Sadly, yes, we've met," Robert said. He extended his hand to Cassie. "But it's lovely to meet *you*, Cassie."

Cassie stared hard at him, and Robert knew he was being sized up. How much did she know about him and Josie? But she smiled and shook his hand, then laid her hand back on Beau's arm. Robert swallowed a laugh. Beau hadn't wasted any time charming Josie's best friend, it would seem. And convenient too. Beau had been complaining about having to come stag—seemed he had the same problem Robert did with most women being interested only in his stardom—but now Robert wouldn't have any guilt over monopolizing Josie. He grinned at Beau.

"You can't have them both, my friend," he said. "I'm taking the brunette."

Josie tucked her arm through his, the two of them fitting together so perfectly he was surprised he didn't hear a click. He kept them a few steps behind Beau and Cassie as they made their way to the table and leaned down so his mouth was closer to Josie's ear. "You look like a princess," he murmured. That perfume intoxicated him, and he brought his face a little closer still and inhaled.

Scarlet blotches rose on her cheeks. "You don't look too shabby yourself," she said, squeezing his arm. "I was starting to worry you'd gotten lost."

He chuckled. "I wanted to be here sooner, but Matthew called, and he was talking my ear off. He's so excited about flying in tomorrow I couldn't bring myself to hustle him off the phone."

"I can't wait to meet him."

His heart soared because Josie was excited to meet his little boy. "He's shy at first, but once he warms up to you, watch out. I hope you're interested in dinosaurs."

They reached table nine and greeted Charlie and his wife, Nancy. Merrill and his wife arrived, and Josie introduced Cassie to everyone.

Damn, he was glad Josie had brought Cassie. She was a font of interesting facts—apparently the Biltmore's Gold Room was a speakeasy during Prohibition—and with her on Beau's arm, not even Merrill raised an eye at Josie holding onto him.

A bell chimed, and they all took their seats for dinner, the men pulling out chairs for the ladies. Robert found himself tucked between Josie and Charlie—not at all a disagreeable situation. Beautiful girl on one side, anybody but Merrill on the other.

Cassie fascinated everyone at the table, including him. She was the only Los Angeles native among them, and while they ate their salads, they all took turns asking her questions about growing up in the area. All of them except Beau, that was. The younger man's usual bravado was gone, and he seemed to be preoccupied with cutting his salad into tiny pieces.

That was strange.

"So, what about you?" Cassie said to Beau as a waiter took their empty salad plates.

"What about me?" Beau said.

"You've been awfully quiet. Tell me about yourself."

Beau took a long swallow of champagne, and Robert stifled a chuckle. So that was the problem: Beau Fraser, tongue-tied by a pretty girl. Even if Josie weren't here, this would have been worth coming to the party for.

Beau fiddled with the napkin in his lap. "I spend a lot of time on set. At home, I'm usually busy learning my lines."

"I know about your job," Cassie said. "Josie tells me about life on the set, and I've watched the show. I'm not interested in Judah Mitchell. Tell me about Beau Fraser."

Robert almost choked on his champagne. Cassie couldn't possibly know it, but she'd just smacked this one right out of the ballpark. He squeezed Josie's knee under the table. She flicked her eyes to him and grinned.

Beau stammered something about Canada and looked relieved when the waiters arrived with the main course right then.

Dinner was delicious. Filet mignon, mashed potatoes, roasted vegetables, and a never-ending supply of a dry red, provided by waiters who always seemed to know exactly when to show up. Dessert was crème brûlée topped with sliced strawberries. Robert fancied himself a decent cook, but he hadn't eaten this well since Josie stayed with him. He had to remind himself to eat like a gentleman instead of inhaling everything.

After dinner, the WBC president gave a short speech saying how good 1959 had been for the network and that he hoped the new decade would be even more prosperous for all of them. Then he stepped aside so a band could set up. Five Black men took the stage, lugging equipment with them. A shiny black grand piano already sat on stage, but the men dragged in a drum set, several amplifiers, a saxophone, a guitar, and a tall bass.

While the band set up, Josie and Cassie excused themselves, and Robert nearly tripped over himself rising from his seat to stand while the ladies departed. He glanced at Beau, who wasn't any more graceful. When they sat back down, Beau scooted into Josie's empty chair and mopped his brow with a handkerchief.

"You all right there?" Robert said.

Beau looked at him, his pupils nearly dilated. "Cassie's something else, isn't she?"

Robert felt Charlie's eyes on him, but he knew if he looked over at the older man, they'd both start laughing, so he kept his gaze on Beau. "She seems like a real nice girl."

"Did you hear she asked about *me*?" Beau said. "She didn't care about the show. She wanted to know about *me*."

Robert had to chomp down on his lower lip. He completely understood where Beau was coming from, but seeing his costar come so unglued was hilarious. He snagged two flutes of champagne from a waiter and handed him one.

"Have some liquid courage."

Just as they finished their drinks, Josie and Cassie returned, and a photographer approached the table and asked everyone to pose for a few shots for the network. Robert sprang into place next to Josie and grinned when Josie grabbed Cassie's arm and tucked her in beside

Beau.

"Squeeze together," the photographer said.

Everyone shuffled a step or two closer. Robert's jacket brushed Josie's left shoulder, sending up a waft of that intoxicating perfume. She must have put more on in the ladies' room. She'd swept her hair over her right shoulder, leaving the side of her neck closest to him exposed. He stared at the delicate skin, barely resisting the urge to lean down and trail a line of kisses down the side of her throat.

He drew in a sharp breath.

Neither the time nor the place, R.J.

But he had to touch her. Their day at Disneyland, even with the goodnight kiss, hadn't been nearly enough. And with everyone facing the photographer, no one would see. He rested his hand on the small of her back, just above the bow on her dress. Her felt her lean into him ever so slightly, and goosebumps rose on his arms.

The photographer blinded them with several flashes, thanked them for their time, and hustled off to the next table. Everyone sat back down.

"Good evening, WBC," a voice boomed. Robert looked up to see a member of the band standing at a microphone on stage. An electric guitar was slung around his body on a black strap, contrasting sharply with his white tuxedo. "We are so pleased to be here with you this evening. You've had such a refined night so far, what do you say we shake things up?"

Everyone in the ballroom clapped, a few of them, Beau included, hooted and called out.

"Let's do it then," the band leader said. He counted off, and the band launched into Little Richard's "Good Golly Miss Molly."

The liquid courage must have done its work, because Beau launched to his feet and extended his hand to Cassie.

"Come on snake, let's rattle," he said.

Cassie flashed an excited grin, took Beau's hand, and tore off with him to the dance floor.

Robert could hardly believe his luck. He'd never expected to wind up with Josie all to himself tonight. He leaned toward her. "It would appear your date has abandoned you."

Josie snickered. "It would appear so."

"That's a shame. She seems like she'd be a great dancer."

Josie laughed. "She is."

Robert seized the opportunity.

"Would you settle for me?" He held out his hand.

Chapter Forty-Six

Josie figured no one at the party would think twice about her dancing with Robert. He and Beau had both come stag, and Beau had just run off with Cassie. Excitement singing through her veins, Josie took Robert's warm hand and let him lead her to the dance floor. They found space near Cassie and Beau and started shimmying to the music. Josie was no dancer, but, at least when it came to rock and roll, Robert didn't seem to be, either.

The song ended and the band launched immediately into "Jailhouse Rock." Beau and Cassie joined them, and the foursome formed a circle and danced around crazily like teenagers at a high school prom. Josie grabbed Cassie and spun her around and glanced over her shoulder just in time to see Robert spin Beau. All four of them laughed until they couldn't breathe.

The band slowed down after that, and Robert settled his right hand on her waist and took her right hand with his left. Her body tingled as she rested her other hand on his shoulder, and he led her around their little section of the dance floor. She breathed him in, not noticing for a minute or two that Beau and Cassie as well as Charlie and Nancy danced nearby. She watched each of them for a moment, burning the images of each person into her memory. What a strange little family she'd found here in California. Strange and unexpected and wonderful.

Warm contentment welled up inside her.

When the song ended, the band segued into another slow song, and Charlie tapped Robert on the shoulder.

"Mind if I cut in?" he said.

Robert chuckled and passed Josie to Charlie.

Josie didn't want to let Robert go, but dancing with Charlie turned out to be special too. She'd never gotten to dance with her father, but Charlie was as good a surrogate as a girl could hope for.

"Thanks, Papa Bear," she whispered in his ear when the song ended.

After that, she pried Beau away from Cassie for one song. She wasn't letting the evening pass without a dance with her honorary brother. She was a little worried about leaving Cassie by herself, but within seconds Chris Andrews from *Aces High* approached her and extended his hand. Josie couldn't believe Cassie didn't faint dead away. She'd loved Chris Andrews for years. Josie caught her friend's eye as the handsome young actor led Cassie to the dance floor.

"I can't believe this!" Cassie mouthed to her.

"I know!" Josie mouthed back, and they both giggled.

She wanted to go straight back to Robert after dancing with Beau, but having been in Hollywood a little while, Robert knew a lot of people on other shows and kept getting pulled away. He cast Josie an apologetic look each time. She hated to see him go, but she didn't lack for dance partners. She danced with young men from *Aces High* and *Scene of the Crime*, WBC's detective show. At some point, both Merrill and Charlie and their wives came by to bid them good evening, Charlie saying how old folks like him couldn't stay up so late. Josie hardly heard him, because yet another young actor was extending his hand to her. She was giddy, caught up in a whirl of music, handsome men, and champagne.

But when the band announced the final song of the evening, she shook the other men off, determined to get her hands back on Robert. He must have been searching for her, too, because they exchanged a look of relief when they found each other back at table nine. Silently, he extended his hand. Her heart pounded as she took it and returned with him to the dance floor. He rested his hand on her waist, and she took hold of his free hand and placed her other on his shoulder. The band played the song's introduction, and they began to sway.

"Earth angel, Earth angel," the bandleader sang, "Will you be mine? My darling dear, love you all the time."

Robert pulled her a little closer, not quite closing the gap between their bodies, but coming close.

"I'm just a fool," the singer continued, "a fool in love with you."

Heat radiated off Robert's body, and she didn't think it was just from the exertion of dancing. She looked up at him and smiled. He smiled back, and they held each other's gaze. The other couples on the dance floor seemed to fade away, and it was just the pair of them, eyes locked, hands clasped. He swept her around in large circles, his breath quickening, that intense stare never breaking, his perfect mouth parted ever so slightly and turned up at the corners. Josie clutched his shoulder, grateful that her gloves would keep her from leaving a sweaty mark on his jacket. His hand on her waist electrified her entire body. Her breath was ragged, and the blood pulsed between her legs. She wanted to bury her fingers in his hair, pull his face down to hers, and kiss him.

She wanted to do a lot more than just that.

He pulled her even closer, their bodies pressing together as the song reached its crescendo.

Golly, she loved him.

The realization should have terrified her. The last time she'd fallen in love she'd been hurt worse than she knew was possible. But Robert wasn't Ethan. And she suddenly understood that what she'd felt for Ethan had been nothing but a teenage crush on a pretty boy. This was real love. A deep, pulsing desire for a man who cared about her more than himself. Who was content just being in her company. Who gripped her a little tighter as the song reached its climax.

"Earth angel, Earth angel, please be mine," the singer belted out. "My darling dear, love you for all time. I'm just a fool, a fool in love…"

Robert dipped her backward, his hand sliding from her waist to the exposed skin between her shoulder blades. Josie's hand traveled from his shoulder to his hip. Her long, loose hair brushed the floor.

"…with you," the singer finished.

They held that position for a long moment, chests heaving, Robert's lips a hairsbreadth from her throat. His warm, moist breath nearly drove her crazy, and for one wild moment, she considered clawing at his shirt buttons.

Around them, people applauded, and Josie almost died on the spot. Robert helped her straighten up, and praise be, everyone was clapping for the band, who were taking their bows. No one was paying any attention to her and Robert.

No one except Cassie, who pulled her back to their table under the guise of collecting their pocketbooks.

"What was *that* all about?" Cassie said, a grin spreading across her face.

Josie smiled coyly. "What was what all about?"

"The two of you were practically making love on the dance floor."

Heat flushed through Josie's face at the word "love," and she tried not to imagine what making love to Robert might be like. "He's a good dancer," she said.

They laughed, Josie hopeful she could change the subject. She wasn't sure she could explain her feelings for Robert to anyone just yet. Fortunately, Cassie grew serious. Uncomfortable, even. She shifted her weight.

"What is it?" Josie said.

"Beau asked if he could take me home," Cassie said in a rush. "I told him I had to talk to you first since we came together." She bounced on the balls of her feet.

Josie clapped a hand over her mouth to stifle an excited shout of surprise. "Of course," she said, grinning. She couldn't believe she hadn't introduced the two of them ages ago. They made perfect sense together, now that she thought about it.

Cassie squealed and threw her arms around Josie's neck. But when she pulled away, she was serious again.

"Josie," she said, her voice quavering a little, "are you *sure* those diaphragms that we got work?"

Good gravy. *That's* what she meant by "take her home."

She should talk Cassie out of this. She and Beau had only just met a few hours ago. This was too fast.

But…

She trusted Beau. He'd take good care of Cassie.

And if he didn't, Josie knew where he worked.

"My first one never failed me," she said at last. "Just follow all the directions the doctor gave you, and you have nothing to worry about." She smiled. "And have fun."

Please, let it be fun for her, she thought.

Cassie squeezed Josie's hands. "I'm going to be like Marilyn Monroe and wear nothing but my Chanel No. 5 to bed." She laid a wet kiss on Josie's cheek and bounced away toward Beau, who offered his arm and escorted her from the ballroom.

"Are they leaving together?" Robert said, sidling up to Josie.

Josie's stomach fluttered at his sudden closeness. She nodded. "And I don't think he's gonna just drop her off at her apartment, either."

"Good for them," he said, chuckling. "They seem like a good pair."

"Looks like I'll be calling a cab for one," she said.

Robert's smile dropped. "At this hour? Josie, it's one a.m."

She shrugged. "I don't mind. I worked a night shift when I first moved here, and I took the bus home in the wee hours all the time. A cab will feel luxurious."

Robert shook his head. "All dressed up like you are, it doesn't feel safe. Let me drive you home."

He didn't have to ask her twice.

****

They didn't talk much on the drive to her apartment, but Robert reached over and squeezed her hand between gear shifts. She could have ridden around with him like that for days, but the traffic was light, and in only fifteen minutes, they pulled up outside her apartment.

After dancing all night in high heels, her feet were two blocks of lead. She stifled a groan when they reached the stairwell, the steps ascending endlessly into the flickering yellow light cast by a faulty bulb fixture the superintendent had promised to replace months ago. What she'd give to have an elevator in this building. She clutched Robert's arm the whole way up the stairs and tried not to hobble when they finally reached the second floor and made their way down the hall to her apartment. She unlocked the door and turned toward Robert. He slipped an arm around her waist, drew her close, and pressed his warm, soft lips to hers, sending heat coursing through her.

"Been wanting to do that all night," he said, when he pulled back, far too soon. "Sorry I kept getting dragged away. I wanted to spend the whole night with you."

"It's Hollywood. You've gotta keep up with those connections." She smiled. "Besides, it made me appreciate our time together even more."

Tell him you love him, Josie Girl.

She opened her mouth, but the words stuck in her throat.

What if she said "I love you," but he didn't say it back? No, she couldn't do it. Not tonight. She didn't want to ruin a perfect evening.

Robert smiled and cupped her chin. "See you at five on Monday?"

She smiled back. She'd have other chances to tell him. "I'll be ready."

He leaned down and kissed her again, soft and quick, and then whispered in her ear, "Goodnight, Princess."

Chapter Forty-Seven

Josie woke to the sound of her phone ringing. She rubbed her eyes and looked at the clock. Almost 1:00 p.m. Oh, goodness. She couldn't remember the last time she slept this late when she wasn't working night shifts. But it was nearly 3:00 a.m. by the time she'd figured out how to get out of her gown by herself and washed up. When she'd bought the gown, she thought Cassie would be there to help her out of it.

She zipped to the kitchen and grabbed the phone, expecting to hear Leighton on the other end. He often called on Sunday afternoons.

"Josie!"

She jumped at the piercing female voice on the other end of the line. This was clearly not her brother.

"Cassie?"

"Josie!" Cassie shrieked again.

This was an excited shriek, not a horrified one, and Josie grinned and stretched the phone cord to the table and sat down. This was going to be good.

"How did it go?" she said.

"Beau just left," Cassie said. She sounded breathless. "It's one o'clock in the afternoon, and he *just* left!"

Josie bounced in her seat. "And?"

"He was so sweet. I told him it was my very first time, and he was so gentle. It still hurt a little, but only at first. Once I relaxed, it was incredible."

Incredible sex. What must that be like? And for your first time too? A hard knot tightened in Josie's throat.

"Josie? You still there?"

She swallowed hard and forced a laugh. "Sorry, just trying not to picture Beau in the act."

Cassie giggled. "It's all right. But, oh, Josie, the second time was even better. I had no idea the woman could be on top."

All at once, the hard knot in her throat disappeared. Josie had never considered that position either. How exactly would it work? If Robert lay down on the bed...

"I came," Cassie said, her voice breathy. "I actually *came.*"

Josie shook her head to clear it.

Focus, Josie Girl, focus.

"That's wonderful!" she said.

"Isn't it?"

Josie tucked her legs up so she sat cross-legged in her chair. "Did you make plans to see each other again?"

"He invited me to go to a New Year's Eve party with him, but I won't see him until then." Cassie made a pouty sound. "He's flying home to Ottawa on Tuesday and won't be back until the thirtieth."

"Right, I knew that." Josie slapped her forehead. "He and I are sharing a cab to the airport on Tuesday." She paused, a bit of doubt niggling her. "If that's all right with you, of course."

"It's fine," Cassie said, giggling. "I wouldn't expect your friendship with him to change. I know he's like one of your brothers."

Josie relaxed, but only for a moment. "I suppose I should tell you I have to kiss him on set in a few weeks."

God bless Cassandra Felix because she didn't miss a beat.

"It's strange, but that's something you're doing for your job. I undress men at the hospital every single day, but that doesn't mean I want to make love to them. It's just part of what I do. So don't worry about it."

Josie sighed with relief. It was bad enough she hadn't been seeing much of Cassie since starting on *Gunslingers*. Kissing her friend's new boyfriend on top of that could have caused a *real* problem.

"Besides," Cassie said, "I think you need to worry more about Robert getting jealous than me."

Josie glanced at the clock. Just under twenty-eight hours until she saw Robert again. Not that she was counting.

"I love him," she said, sighing.

Cassie snickered. "It's about time you figured that out. I've known for weeks."

This was annoying, but Josie still had to laugh. Cassie was right, as always.

She told Cassie about Robert driving her home and the way he called her "Princess."

"It's like a fairy tale," Cassie said, sighing dreamily.

"A fairy tale where the princess falls in love and then leaves town for two weeks," Josie grumbled. Why had she booked such a long trip? What in the world was she going to do in Hays for ten days? It was about as different from Hollywood as she could get without leaving the planet.

"Just think how wonderful it will be to come home," Cassie said.

Josie smiled. Coming home to her strange, wonderful little California family. That *would* be something to look forward to.

Chapter Forty-Eight

Josie picked her cast-iron skillet up off the stove, took a deep breath, and inverted it over a platter.

"Please work, please work, please work," she said and slowly lifted the skillet, revealing an intact cake on the platter. The bright rings of pineapple glistened in the light from the overhead fixture.

She danced a little jig before setting the skillet on the stove and wiping her brow with her sleeve. That had been terrifying. The last time she'd tried to make her mother's pineapple upside-down cake she'd forgotten to let the cake rest after she took it out of the oven. Half of it stuck to the pan while the other half landed in an untidy heap on her cake plate. The time before that, she'd poured in too much pineapple juice from the can, and the cake was a soggy mess in the middle. Come to think of it, she'd *never* successfully made her mother's pineapple upside-down cake.

So naturally this was the recipe she'd chosen to make to take to dinner with Robert's parents. But this time, success.

She covered the cake loosely with foil and went to her bedroom to get dressed. She stared into her closet. She'd spent at least an hour last night debating what to wear, and she'd gotten no further than deciding on a dress instead of pants and a blouse. Surveying her wardrobe again now, she groaned. Cassie was working today, so she couldn't call for help. She was on her own.

She didn't have a lot of casual clothes. When she wasn't lounging at home, she was usually either in her nurse's uniform or a *Gunslingers* costume. Even so, it was amazing how her options had seemed to multiply when she had to decide what to wear to meet the parents of her...whatever he was.

She finally chose her favorite royal-blue broadcloth shirtwaist dress with sleeves that rolled up and buttoned just above the elbow, and a belt to accentuate her waist. She had to dig a slip and her black t-strap pumps out of the suitcase she had packed for her trip tomorrow, but within thirty minutes she was dressed and made up. She swept her hair up in a chignon not quite as perfect as the one Cassie had styled for Disneyland, but still good. She finished off her look with her mother's pearl earrings and smiled at her reflection in the bathroom mirror.

Not bad, Josie Girl. Not bad at all.

A shame she didn't have any scent. Maybe she should invest in a bottle of Chanel No. 5.

The clock read 4:40. She still had twenty minutes until Robert was due to arrive, so she settled onto the sofa to wait. She was delighted that Robert was bringing her into his inner circle—a place, she realized, that few people ever got to go—but the suspense was horrible.

At 4:45, she got tired of her jiggling right leg making the sofa creak, so she stood up and walked around her small living room, checking the sagging bookcase for dust, straightening photos.

At 4:52, she checked on the cake. Still there on the counter, still in one piece. Good.

At 4:55, she dug through her handbag for the second time, making sure she hadn't lost the little toy she'd bought yesterday, when she heard a sharp knock on the door. Startled, she dropped the handbag.

"Darn it," she said, scrabbling around on the floor to pick up the spilled contents and stuff them back in her bag. "Coming," she called out, feeling stupid that it had never occurred to her that Robert might be a little early.

Get it together, Josie Girl.

She stood, smoothed her dress and her hair, and strode to the front door. Taking a deep breath, she turned the knob and opened the door.

Robert stood in the hallway in a pair of dark jeans, a burgundy sport shirt with the top button open, and a lightweight gray jacket that he'd left unzipped. He hadn't pomaded his hair, and that unruly forelock drooped over his forehead. Without saying hello, she slipped her arms around him and pressed her lips to his. He laughed when she pulled away

"I missed you too," he said. He placed another quick kiss on the tip of her nose. "Ready?"

"Just let me grab the cake."

They were soon settled in the Corvette, its top up against the chilly December breeze, and on their way to Robert's house. Josie clutched the cake platter in her lap. She wasn't about to let anything happen to it now.

"Everyone's still adjusting to the time zone, but they're excited to meet you," he said.

"I'm excited too," she said. Her voice came out strained, and she cringed. Apparently, she could act just fine on camera but in real life, she had no hope of hiding her nerves.

Robert's eyes flicked to her, then back to the road. He patted her knee. "Don't worry. They're gonna love you. And if they don't, I'll send the whole lot of them straight back to Hell Hole."

Most of her tension flowed away on the wave of her laughter. She loved being in this car with Robert. The Corvette was smaller inside than most cars, forcing them closer together than they'd be in just about any other car. She liked being able to reach over and easily squeeze his hand. Sitting in the Corvette with Robert, she felt like maybe they actually were a couple.

Ten minutes later, he pulled into his driveway and cut the engine. He walked around, opened Josie's door, and helped her out of the car.

"Let me get that," he said, taking the cake from her and offering his other arm. Goosebumps prickled along her skin when she took it and he led her up the porch steps.

"We're back," he called into the house. He beckoned Josie to follow him inside.

She stepped into the living room, the space at once familiar and not. The last time she'd been in Robert's house, she'd been in charge. Now she returned as a guest. Her eyes flicked around, trying to see if anything had changed, but the house was exactly the same. It was her relationship to its owner that was different now.

No, there *was* something different about the house. She sniffed. A mild piney scent filled the room. She glanced around and saw an air freshener on top of the television console. She looked at Robert and raised an eyebrow. His eyes rolled skyward, and he shook his head.

A thin man in gray trousers and a crisp white shirt rose from one of the armchairs and stepped toward them, his hands extended. He was several inches shorter than his son, and his hair, threaded with gray, still showed proof that it was once as dark as Robert's. He wore glasses, and behind them sparkled a set of hazel eyes exactly like his son's.

"Well, of course, you're Miss Josephine," he said.

Good gravy, his Southern accent was thick. But the Coolidges were from rural South Carolina. Naturally, they'd have an accent. Though Robert didn't. That was odd. An acting coach somewhere must have trained it out of him.

Robert grinned. "Dad, meet Josie Donovan. Josie, this is my father, Will."

"A pleasure to meet you, Mr. Coolidge." Josie extended her hand, which the older man clasped in both of his.

"The pleasure is all mine. We've enjoyed watching you on the show."

She heard the back door creak open and Sergeant's excited toenails scrabble across the kitchen floor. A moment later, the dog burst into the living room and darted to Josie, his bobbed tail wagging so hard his entire back end wiggled. She laughed and ruffled his ears.

"So sorry," a female voice came from the dining room. Josie straightened. Seconds later, a woman wearing an apron bustled into the living room. She paused by the television and pulled the air freshener a little farther out of the bottle. Josie beamed. Mrs. Coolidge was a sunflower—a beautiful, radiant face atop an impossibly thin stalk, albeit a short one. Robert's mother couldn't be more than five feet tall on a lucky day. A gold star pin identical to the one on Robert's dresser winked from her dress collar.

"I was checkin' on the roast and didn't hear you come in the door," Mrs. Coolidge said in an accent as thick as her husband's.

"Mom, this is Josie Donovan. Josie, my mother, Helen."

Mrs. Coolidge smiled broadly, getting that same dimple in her left cheek as Robert. She grabbed Josie's hand and pumped it.

"It's so wonderful to meet you, my dear," she said, her graying curls bobbing in time with the handshake. Still gripping Josie's hand, she turned to Robert. "Oh, R.J., she's beautiful. You didn't tell me she was so pretty. The television doesn't do her justice. I hope you're taking her out."

Large scarlet patches rose on Robert's cheeks. "She can hear you, Mom."

Josie wished Mrs. Coolidge would let go of her now-aching hand, but the older woman didn't subside. "I keep saying it's high time you got back out there. You can't let one bad relationship ruin you for life."

Robert's face was now the same shade of burgundy as his shirt. "She can still hear you, Mom."

Mrs. Coolidge released Josie and narrowed her eyes at Robert. "Yes, Robert Jeremy, I know."

Robert hunched his shoulders, and Josie bit back another burst of laughter. Her own mother had never taken any guff from her boys either, no matter how big they got.

"Here, son," Mr. Coolidge said, taking the foil-covered plate from Robert. "Let me take that to the kitchen." He darted out of the room.

"Where's Matthew?" Robert said.

"I'm not sure," Mrs. Coolidge said. "I've been in the kitchen. Last I saw him, he was playing in here." She strode into the dining room and hollered down the hallway. "Jackson Matthew Coolidge the Second! Your father's home. You come on out now."

Matthew's first name was Jackson? And "the Second"? Good heavens, Robert had named the child after his brother. He'd never mentioned that. The family probably called the boy Matthew to keep from mixing anyone up.

Mrs. Coolidge returned a moment later, nudging a little boy in a Roy Rogers outfit in front of her. She pulled the red cowboy hat off his head and smoothed his dark hair. He was bigger than in the photograph on Robert's dresser, but his face still held its roundness. When he saw Josie, he leaned back against his grandmother's legs. Mrs. Coolidge prodded him forward.

"Go say hello to Daddy's friend," she said.

Robert squatted and held out a hand. "Come here, buddy."

Matthew ran to Robert, who gathered him in his arms, stood, and turned to Josie. The lanky little boy was going to be tall like his father. Even at only seven years old, his feet dangled down by Robert's knees. He was almost a carbon copy of Robert, and in that cowboy outfit, he looked like Deacon Bell in miniature.

A rush of love coursed through her, watching Robert hold his beautiful little boy. She wanted to wrap her arms around them both, but she didn't want to scare Matthew. She took just a small step forward.

"Hi, Matthew," she said, smiling. "I'm Josie."

Matthew only waved.

"I heard you like dinosaurs." She dug into her handbag, pulled out the small plastic brontosaurus she'd purchased yesterday, and held it out.

His hazel eyes widened, and he reached forward and took it.

"Thank you," he said, his accent apparent even in his breathy whisper.

"You're very welcome." She shifted her gaze to Robert, who stared at her, a wide smile on his face.

"How about that, buddy? Isn't that nice?" he said.

Matthew nodded and grinned.

Good gravy, the child had that dimple too.

Mr. Coolidge wandered back into the living room and invited everyone to sit down, and Robert's mother excused herself to kitchen.

In the time-honored tradition of women, Josie asked Mrs. Coolidge, "Can I help you?"

Josie expected Mrs. Coolidge would follow tradition, too, and assure her guest that she had everything well under control. Mrs. Coolidge, however, clearly didn't give a hoot about tradition.

"That would be wonderful, Josie, thank you." She took Josie by the arm and led her into the kitchen, Josie's heart pounding the whole way.

Chapter Forty-Nine

"It's a relief to have another woman around, even if it's just for the evening," Mrs. Coolidge said when they reached the kitchen. "There's only three men in this house, but I declare, it feels like at least a dozen."

Josie laughed. "I know that feeling well."

"That's right, R.J. said you had a big family. All brothers?"

"Yes, ma'am. Five of them. All older." She tried not to laugh at Mrs. Coolidge referring to Robert as "R.J." again. Must be a pet name.

The older lady patted her cheek. "You poor dear." She laughed and peeked under the foil on Josie's cake plate. "Oh, how wonderful. Will loves pineapple upside-down cake, but I can never seem to get it quite right. You'll have to tell me your secret."

"Luck, I'm afraid."

Mrs. Coolidge laughed again and turned to Josie, who knew immediately that she was being sized up. She prayed she didn't start sweating visibly. Several seconds passed before Robert's mother spoke again.

"I wanted to thank you in private for taking care of R.J. while he was sick. I think I embarrassed him enough already for one evening."

Josie ducked her head. She didn't know he'd told his parents about her nursing him.

"He scared me that weekend," Mrs. Coolidge went

on. "I hadn't heard him that sick since he had scarlet fever when he was six. And no amount of acting could have covered it up. A mother knows. I was about to get on the next plane to Los Angeles, but then he told me you were here, so thank you."

"You're welcome." Golly, Robert sure didn't inherit his reticence from his mother. "I'm glad I had the time and skills to be able to help."

Robert's mother put Josie to work slicing a loaf of crusty bread next to another air freshener on the kitchen counter. Mrs. Coolidge chattered the whole time about the traffic in Los Angeles, the dry air, the traffic again, and the "funny smell" that hung over the whole city.

That would explain the air fresheners, Josie thought.

"It sounds like I'm complaining, but Will and I have thought about moving out here to be with R.J.," she said, stirring a pot of boiling potatoes. "But there's Matthew to consider. We like being only five minutes from him. And, of course, it would mean leaving Jack behind." She paused her stirring and fingered the gold star pin on her collar. Her eyes reflected the same pain Josie had seen in Robert's when he talked about his brother's body coming home.

"I was so sorry to hear about your loss," Josie said.

Mrs. Coolidge spun and faced her, head cocked. "He told you about Jack?"

Uh-oh. Was this a family secret she wasn't supposed to know? If so, why was Mrs. Coolidge wearing her gold star pin so openly? Sweat trickled down Josie's spine.

"Yes, ma'am." She took a small step backward.

Mrs. Coolidge raised one eyebrow. "Really?"

Josie hunched her shoulders and reduced her voice nearly to a whisper. "Yes, ma'am. He speaks of him often."

"That's remarkable." The older woman exhaled and turned back to the potatoes, and Josie relaxed. "R.J. doesn't talk about his brother, even to his father and me. He wouldn't even speak Jack's name after he was killed. Not for eight years until he named his son after him. And then we don't even call the boy 'Jack,' do we? Call him Matthew." She looked over her shoulder at Josie. "But he tells you about him."

"Yes, ma'am." Josie felt like a skipping record player, repeating the same phrase over and over, but she was so stunned it was the best she could do. She was the only person he talked to about his brother? Though she supposed she'd forced his hand the first time.

She told Mrs. Coolidge about knocking Jack's photograph off Robert's dresser and how Robert told her about bringing Jack's body home. Mrs. Coolidge's eyes grew red around the rims, and she studied Josie for a moment.

"You know," she said, "when we first got word that Jack had been killed, R.J. quit talking completely for two weeks. Such a heartbreaking thing to see a fourteen-year-old boy do. Wouldn't talk to me or his father or any of his friends, nobody."

Josie thought of her brother Peter after he came home from Korea when he was twenty-one. He didn't speak for three straight months. Even now, six years later, he didn't talk much, and sometimes he'd get up in the middle of a family gathering and go off by himself. His wife said he still woke up screaming in the middle of the night every once in a while. The doctors called it "operational exhaustion," but that was just a fancy term for "pain." And pain did funny things to people.

"But I'd hear him at night," Mrs. Coolidge said. "When he thought his dad and I were asleep, I'd tiptoe past his bedroom and hear him sobbing." She shook her head. "He was always reserved and a little moody. Jack was the only one who could really draw him out. I think he felt lost without him. I think he still does." She wiped her eyes. "I'm sorry. Here we just met, and I'm laying all this on you." She paused. "But I suppose you understand, don't you?"

Good gravy, it was like the woman could read her thoughts.

"I do," Josie said. "I lost my mother when I was twelve. Daddy died two years later. I still feel lost sometimes."

Mrs. Coolidge nodded. "I'm so sorry, darlin'. R.J. told me. He asked me not to bring it up."

Their eyes met, and they laughed.

"As you can see, I'm not very good at holding back," Mrs. Coolidge said. "Come on, let's get these men fed before they start chewing on the furniture."

Dinner was phenomenal. Pot roast, mashed potatoes and gravy, green beans, corn, and fresh bread. Mrs. Coolidge kept up a steady stream of chatter during the meal, with the three men popping in with quips now and again. It was like the family dinners the Donovans enjoyed before Mom and Daddy died. Josie sat next to Robert, who periodically squeezed her knee under the table. She couldn't remember the last time she'd been so at ease—even with yet another air freshener spitting out its fake pine scent from the buffet behind her.

She held her breath when Robert's mother brought out the cake and sliced into it.

Please, please, please be good.

Mrs. Coolidge lifted the first slice on a cake server and slid it neatly onto a dessert plate.

It was perfect.

Josie exhaled and sent a silent thank-you up to her mother in Heaven, because only divine intervention could have made the cake turn out so well.

She wished she weren't leaving town tomorrow. She wanted to come back here every night to be with this beautiful little family that had been shattered but survived. She reached under the table and squeezed Robert's hand. He smiled at her and squeezed back.

She'd just have to relish tonight.

Chapter Fifty

Robert wasn't a big fan of pineapple, but Josie's cake was so good that when Matthew asked for a second piece, he had one too.

This was going so well. Josie seemed at ease with the whole family, and her bringing that toy dinosaur for Matthew was incredibly thoughtful. She must be a good aunt to all those nieces and nephews back in Kansas. When she squeezed his hand under the table, he wanted to take her in his arms and kiss her right there in front of everybody.

After dessert, Dad suggested the two of them give Mom a break and do the cleaning up. It was the right thing to do, but oh, God, it meant giving Mom more time alone with Josie. He was already worried about what she might have said while they were cooking. But then Matthew grabbed Josie's hand and dragged her away toward the living room, prattling on about every dinosaur toy he'd ever owned. Josie flashed Robert a grin before she disappeared through the French doors leading out of the dining room, and he relaxed. Once Matthew started in on dinosaurs, even Mom couldn't get a word in edgewise.

He started sliding silverware into the dishwasher, and Dad soon came in carrying a stack of plates. He set them on the counter in front of Robert.

"Dessert was excellent," Dad said.

"Sure was."

Dad went silent, and the hair on the back of Robert's neck prickled. Even staring down into the dishwasher, he knew his father was studying him hard. Questions were coming. He braced himself. Dad didn't often pry, but when he did, watch out. Robert grabbed the empty mashed-potato pot and rinsed it out.

"Josie's a real sweetheart," Dad said. He handed Robert the empty meat platter. "Is it serious?"

Geez, he had no idea how to even begin answering that question. If it were solely up to him, they would have been serious months ago. He'd loved her practically since they met, but they'd only been out once since they mended their friendship. Twice, if you counted the Christmas party, but they both had to be there anyway, so he didn't think it should count. They'd shared secrets, but they'd only had their first kiss a couple weeks ago. And with Josie leaving town tomorrow, they wouldn't be doing more anytime soon. Not that he could move fast with her anyway. She needed time and care.

"Tough one to answer, I see," Dad said. "It's like that sometimes. But Josie's a gem, R.J. Doesn't take a detective to spot that. I can see why you love her."

Robert's cheeks caught fire, and he hung his head. He never could get one past Dad. "Is it that obvious?"

Dad chuckled and squeezed his shoulder. "Plain as the nose on my face, son. Have you told her?"

Robert shook his head.

"You should."

He sighed. "It's complicated."

Dad handed him a serving spoon. "No, it isn't. You love her, you tell her."

"I have to be careful with Josie, Dad. She's…" He

paused, trying to figure out how to explain without spilling secrets that weren't his to share. "She's been hurt. Bad."

The amusement drained from his father's face. "Poor little thing. But all the more reason to tell her. Seems to me the more someone's hurtin', the more they need to hear they're loved."

****

Once the dishwasher was running, Robert followed Dad to the living room, where he discovered Josie sitting on the floor with Matthew and Sergeant. He laughed as she and Matthew brandished toy dinosaurs at each other and roared at the top of their lungs. Every now and again, Sergeant would chime in with a bark. Smiling, Robert settled onto the sofa and watched them play for a few minutes. Josie was a natural with the little guy. And Matthew seemed head over heels for her, in his own seven-year-old way. He usually warmed up all right to strangers, but he'd taken a real shine to Josie. When she glanced over her shoulder at him and beamed, Robert thought he might burst. God, he loved her so much. Dad was right. He needed to tell her.

After another minute or two, Josie handed Matthew the dinosaur she'd been playing with.

"I'm gonna sit on the sofa and chat with the grownups for a little while, okay?" she said.

Matthew stuck out his lower lip. "Grownups are boring."

Josie laughed and ruffled the boy's hair. "And don't I know it. But they also get grumpy real easily, so I better give them a little attention too."

"Yeah," Matthew said, "Daddy can be awful particular like that."

From one of the armchairs, Mom barked out a laugh that she tried unsuccessfully to disguise as a cough. Just to spite her, Robert got up and made a show of pushing the air freshener on the television console all the way back into its bottle. He sat back down, caught Josie's eye, and patted the sofa next to him. She sat close, her thigh brushing his, and her touch sent a shiver straight through him.

Smiling, he took her hand and massaged the back of it with his thumb while they chatted with his parents. Dad, especially, was fascinated by the Donovans' sunflower farm and asked all sorts of questions about planting, harvesting, and processing the crops. Matthew played on the floor for a bit longer, then wedged himself and several dinosaurs behind the sofa. A few minutes later, the sounds of great dinosaur battles ceased. Robert let go of Josie's hand and looked behind the sofa. He chuckled.

"He's sound asleep back there."

"Poor little fellow's still on South Carolina time," Mom said.

Robert got up and gently pulled his son out from behind the couch. The boy squirmed and whimpered, but Robert leaned in close to his ear.

"It's all right, buddy. Daddy's got you."

Matthew snuggled against his chest and went still.

"I'll be right back," he said, and turned toward the hallway to put his boy to bed. When he reached his son's room, he paused next to the bed, closed his eyes, and lost himself for a moment in the feeling of Matthew's warm little body pressed up against his. He laid him on the bed, pulled off his cowboy boots, and tucked him in. He could change him into his pajamas when he got back from taking Josie home. He kissed Matthew's forehead and returned to the living room.

Mom smirked as soon as he stepped back into the living room, and he cut his eyes to the television console. She'd pulled the air freshener back out while he was gone.

He rolled his eyes and was about to go push it back down, but as if on cue, the clock struck 9:30. He turned to Josie.

"What time is your flight tomorrow?"

"Nine o'clock. Earlier than I'd like to be up on a day off, but not bad."

"Do you need a ride to the airport?"

Josie shook her head. "Beau flies out at nine forty-five. We're sharing a cab."

Damn. He should have asked her sooner. He trusted that Beau and Josie were nothing more than friends, but he was still annoyed that Beau got to her first.

"I suppose I should take you home so you can get to bed."

Josie rose and bid goodbye to his parents, who both invited her out to Hell Hole, and with a smile, she followed him to the door, scratching Sergeant's head on the way out.

"Your folks are lovely," she said as he wound the Corvette through Hollywood toward her apartment. "And I am completely smitten with your son."

Warmth surged through him. She liked Mom and Dad. She adored Matthew. There had to be warm feelings in there for him too. He should tell her tonight that he loved her. The thought made his palms sweat.

"Thank you. I like him too." He chuckled at his own cleverness.

"You bought the house for him, didn't you?"

Geez, she was perceptive. He ran one hand through his hair.

"Yeah. I wanted a nice place for him to come to when he visits. And Mom and Dad like to visit, too, so the extra space is handy." He cleared his throat as he made a right-hand turn past soaring palm trees, their trunks impossibly skinny, and onto Santa Monica Boulevard. "I hope Mom wasn't too overbearing."

Josie giggled. "She's incredible. She's got the same no-nonsense way about her that my mother had."

He was afraid to ask, but he had to. "What were you two talking about in the kitchen?"

She waved a hand dismissively. "Just this and that. Why does she call you by your initials?"

Robert chuckled. The girl had no poker face, but she sure as hell could dodge a question. Might as well let it go. Ignorance was likely bliss in this case anyway. "Everyone back in Hell Hole calls me 'R.J.' Jack started calling me that when I was born. No one knows why he did, but it stuck."

"R.J. Coolidge," she said. Robert had to keep his eyes on the road, but he swore he could hear her nose wrinkling. His name was music on her voice. "Got a nice ring to it. Why'd you switch to Robert?"

As always around Josie, the truth tumbled out, even if he didn't want it to. "I told Mom and Dad I did it to sound more professional, but..." He sighed. "But that nickname is one of the few things I have from Jack. And I didn't want the whole world feeling like they had a right to it."

It seemed silly now, especially when he said it out loud. But at the time, he'd worried that if too many people used the name Jack gave him, it would stretch so thin it would snap, like when Matthew drew his Silly Putty out too far. Though even after eight years, hearing people call him "Robert" still sounded strange. It was the hard stop at the end of the name that did it. The "T" was too crisp, too sharp. It didn't fade away like the "Jay" in "R.J."

Josie reached over and squeezed his hand that was resting on the gearshift, anchoring him again. "All my brothers call me 'Josie Girl,'" she said. "They say it like it's all one word. Leighton started it."

"Older brothers, huh?" he said. Josie squeezed his hand again and left hers resting atop his all the way back to her apartment.

His heart started pounding as soon as they pulled into a parking space under her building. What was wrong with him? He'd never been so nervous over a girl. He'd been all of fifteen when he'd said "I love you" to Laura the first time, and he hadn't broken a sweat. Nothing about that relationship had ever made him nervous.

Geez, maybe that was the problem.

Falling into that relationship with Laura as kids had been easy—expected, even. He'd never worried what his family thought about her or even what *she* thought about *him* because in the end, the relationship just hadn't meant that much to him. Not that he'd never loved her. He did. But in that way you love someone simply because you've known them your whole life, because they know so much about you. And he would always love her for giving him Matthew.

But Josie was different.

If his parents hadn't liked her or, worse, if she rejected him, he wasn't sure how he'd ever recover. And he was about to give her one big old opportunity to reject him.

He wished he hadn't eaten that second slice of cake.

He wiped his right palm on his pants and took her hand while they made their way slowly up the stairs and down the hall to her apartment door. When they reached it, he pulled her into a hug.

"I'll miss you, Princess."

She nuzzled her face into his chest and inhaled deeply. "I'll miss you too."

Do it now, R.J.

He listened hard for sounds from Mrs. Pullman's apartment. When he didn't hear any, he caressed Josie's silk-smooth cheek and spoke again, words he now realized he'd been desperate to say to her for a long time.

"I love you, Josie."

She snapped her head up and stared at him. Oh, God. Why was she staring? She didn't seem mad or scared, but her face didn't drop that deer-in-the-headlights look.

His breathing sped up, and his eyes searched hers. "Is that okay?" He chewed his lower lip.

She let out a breath and traced his jawline with one finger, leaving a tingling trail along his skin. Her chin quivered.

"It's more than okay. Because I love you too. So much."

His eyes burned. "Really?"

She smiled. "Really."

Something deep inside him knit itself back together, and he wrapped his arms around her and pressed his lips to hers, desperate to absorb more of her healing force. He skated his hands down to her hips and tightened his clutch. She sighed into his mouth, her warm breath shooting heat straight down to his belly. He'd give anything for her to invite him inside right now.

Cool it, R.J. Remember what you told Dad about needing to be careful with Josie.

He loosened his hold on her hips and stepped back, drawing in a shaky breath as he caressed her cheek again. He wanted her more than he wanted his next breath, but if experience with Josie had taught him anything, it was that he had to let the next move be her idea. Besides, it was getting late, and she had an early start tomorrow. God, he was going to miss her.

He wanted to say something romantic to leave her with, but his blood was still swirling around his lower half, leaving none for his brain. All he could came up with was, "Can I call you in Kansas?"

She beamed, either not noticing or choosing to ignore that he wasn't on the stick just then. Probably the latter, which just made him love her even more.

"I'd love that," she said. She pulled a slip of paper and a pen from her handbag and jotted down the number. He folded it and tucked it into his wallet.

"What day do you come home?" he said.

"The second. My plane gets in about noon."

He swore he heard an angel choir burst into song. "Can I pick you up? Mom, Dad, and Matthew fly home that morning, so I'll be free the rest of the day."

She beamed. "Yes, please."

This must be what it feels like to win an Oscar, he thought. Only better. He'd take a day alone with Josie over a gold statue any day.

"It's a date," he said. He kissed her forehead. "I love you, Princess."

She scrunched her nose. "I love you, too, Robert."

He grinned. "You know something? Call me R.J."

Chapter Fifty-One

On the way to the airport the next morning, Josie desperately wanted to ask Beau about Cassie, but she didn't dare with the taxi driver listening in. He'd already recognized them and said how much he enjoyed the show. She didn't need to give him any gossip.

But she did replay last night's scene with Robert— no, *R.J.*—in her mind. He loved her. She repeated the sentence over and over in her head, emphasizing a different word each time. And he seemed just as nervous about a relationship as she was. For different reasons, and maybe in a different way, but he was nervous. He wouldn't ever hurt her because he understood. Warm love flooded through her. She never wanted to be without him again.

But here she was, leaving town for two weeks. She sighed. Beau must have mistaken her sigh for a yawn because he offered to buy her coffee when they got to the airport.

"So, you and Robert, eh?" Beau murmured in her ear while they stood in line to check their luggage.

"Who said anything about Robert and me?"

"Your dancing at the party said a lot."

Josie blushed and checked to make sure no one was listening in.

"It's none of your business."

Beau chuckled and bumped her hip with his. "Just

looking out for my buddy. Besides, I don't think he's as big a grouch as he pretends to be. And my lips are sealed."

Their gates were near each other, so Beau bought her that coffee and they sat together at Josie's gate while they waited for her to board. She glanced around. No one seemed to be paying them any mind. She opened her mouth to ask about Cassie when a shrill squeal erupted a few feet away.

"Oh my gosh! It's Judah and Mary!"

A gaggle of teenage girls flocked over from the other side of the gate. Josie pressed back against her seat and grabbed Beau's hand. No one who'd recognized her had ever rushed her before.

Beau chuckled and stubbed out the cigarette he'd been smoking. "It's all right. It's just girls." He grinned mischievously. "Should we give them a little preview of coming attractions?"

"I am not kissing you in the middle of this airport." The last lips to touch hers had been R.J.'s. She sure as heck wasn't going to leave town with *Beau* as her last kiss.

"Just on the cheek. They'll love it."

She sighed. Beau did love pleasing his fans. He always said that Merrill might write the checks, but he wouldn't have any money to write them with if not for the fans. And the girls had already spotted her gripping his hand.

"Are you dating for real?" the girl at the head of the pack said when she reached them. She nearly shouted, her voice half an octave higher than Josie imagined was typical.

She marveled at the group. There were six girls, and

they all looked the same. Different facial features, but the same bouncy bobbed hair, fluttering eyelashes, and saddle shoes. Not one of them looked older than fifteen. Beau stood, and since she was still holding his hand, so did she. People from all over the gate were now staring and pointing at her and Beau. A few pulled cameras out of their handbags.

They wanted to take pictures of her. *Her*. Josephine Frances Donovan, late of Hays, Kansas. The girl who Ethan Winchester said would never amount to anything and was now a star on a television show.

All right, *part-time* star, but still. She could have fun with this.

She beamed and stepped closer to Beau, who slipped an arm around her waist.

"Now, ladies," he said, "a gentleman never kisses and tells."

The girls shrieked with giggles.

"But I might," Josie said, and she planted a big kiss on Beau's cheek.

The girls shrieked again, and flashbulbs went off all around them, including one from the girl who'd led the charge.

They signed autographs and posed for photos until Josie's flight got called for boarding.

Beau cleared the way for her to get to the door, where they hugged, illuminated by more flashbulbs.

"Have a safe trip," Josie said.

"You too."

"And enjoy New Year's with Cassie," she whispered in his ear.

Beau made a funny little squeak and Josie giggled. She stepped back and straightened his tie. "See you on set."

He pecked her on the cheek. "See you on set."

Josie laughed all the way across the tarmac. That had been too much fun.

****

When she stepped out of the plane and onto the tarmac in Wichita, a snap of cold wind blew her loose scarf over her face, blinding her for a moment until she pulled it away. The icy wind cut right through her jacket. Thank goodness she still had her heavy winter coat in a closet at Jimmy's, otherwise she'd freeze to death on this visit.

"There's no place like home," she muttered to herself with a laugh. She walked as quickly as she could in her high heels across the tarmac and into the warmth of the little airport. Funny. This airport used to feel so big, but now that she'd been through LAX a couple times, it seemed tiny.

Just inside the door, Leighton, his wife, Dottie, and their two boys stood in a cluster. Ten-year-old Thomas held a hand-lettered sign that said "Welcome Home, Aunt Josie. Our Star."

She suddenly felt ashamed for grumbling about making this trip. How could she have been reluctant to come home? She'd miss her strange, wonderful California family, but she needed her normal, beautiful Kansas family too.

Leighton saw her then and broke into a wide smile, so much like their mother's, and she rushed to him and threw herself into his arms. He clutched her tightly and buried his face in her hair.

"Hey, there, Josie Girl," he said, his voice muffled by her long tresses.

A lump rose in her throat, and before she could stop them, tears poured onto her brother's coat.

"What's all this?" Leighton pulled her back and peered into her face. "Has something happened?" He gave her a once-over with his eyes like he was examining a patient.

Something had happened, all right, but nothing bad, like he obviously thought.

She shook her head. "Everything's fine. Wonderful, actually." She smiled and hugged him again. "I've just really missed you."

She felt pressure on her back and knew that her nephews had joined the embrace. Soon, Dottie wrapped her arms around the whole group, and the Donovans held onto each other for several long moments.

Dottie gamely offered to sit in the back seat of the station wagon with the boys so Josie could ride up front and chat with Leighton. They talked and laughed the whole way. He was especially interested to hear about Disneyland, though Josie was careful to say only that she had gone with "a friend." If Leighton assumed she meant Cassie, well, that was his mistake. She'd tell him about R.J. later, out of earshot of her nephews. She didn't need them bursting into Jimmy's house yelling, "Aunt Josie's going steady!" before she'd even had a chance to say hello to everyone.

They stopped for dinner in Hutchinson and pulled up to Jimmy's house after dark. Josie gazed fondly upon the old house her father had built and sighed. Daddy wasn't gone so long as they had his house.

She'd barely stepped out of the car when a dozen people tumbled out of the house, down the steps of the wraparound porch, and into the yard. In the yellow light spilling from inside the house, she could see that four of her favorite faces led the pack. She yelped when they reached her and she was swept away on the gust of older brothers. If Leighton hadn't been standing behind her, Jimmy, Steve, Peter, and Ben would have bowled her over.

Jimmy hugged her and passed her to Ben who passed her to Peter who passed her to Steve, and then she was caught in a whirlwind of sisters-in-law and the nieces and nephews who were old enough to still be up. After she hugged everyone, they stood in a group, chattering and laughing. A rush of wind kicked up, and she shivered.

"Let's get you inside before you freeze," Jimmy said, putting an arm around her shoulders.

They hustled her into the house, where she kicked off her high heels and sank into her favorite corner of the familiar sofa in the living room. The rest of the family found perches on armchairs, the rest of the sofa, and the floor. Jimmy's wife, Alice, disappeared into the kitchen, soon reappearing with two steaming mugs of hot chocolate. She handed one to Josie, nudged her twelve-year-old daughter off the sofa, and sat down with the other mug of hot chocolate. The rest of the family stared at her.

"You all know where the kitchen is," she said.

The kids took off for the kitchen, leaving the adults alone in the living room. As alone as nine people could be, anyway.

"Josie, you've had quite the year," Alice said, poking her in the hip. "Tell us all about it."

Josie thought of Charlie, her "Papa Bear," of Beau, her sixth brother, and of R.J. *Oh, R.J.*

She shook her head and laughed.
"I don't even know where to begin."

Chapter Fifty-Two

The grandfather clock in the living room struck 11:00 before Steve, Peter, and Ben gathered up their families and headed home. Steve and his family lived in town near the college where he taught, and Ben and Peter had houses elsewhere on the farm. There certainly wasn't enough space in the old farmhouse for the entire clan. They were crammed as it was with ten people in four bedrooms. Josie shared her old bedroom with Jimmy's two girls. Typically, she would have stayed up into the wee hours giggling with her nieces, but tonight she was so worn out from her trip that she dropped right off to sleep.

And good thing, because Alice didn't let her sleep in the next morning. She barged into the bedroom right at 7:00 a.m.

"Time for Christmas shopping!"

She, Josie, and Dottie, along with Peter's wife, Peggy, and Ben's wife, Shirley, left their collective seven children with Jimmy and Leighton, wished them luck, and piled into Leighton and Dottie's station wagon for the ride to town. Dottie drove, and Josie squeezed into the back seat with Peggy and Alice, letting Shirley, who was seven months' pregnant, have the front passenger seat.

They peppered her with questions the whole way to town. Was it still hot in Los Angeles? What was the television studio like? Did she have a fancy dressing room like Lucille Ball's? What did she wear to the Christmas party? Who did she dance with? Did Beau Fraser smell as good as he looked?

"What?" Josie said to the last question.

Shirley shrugged. "He looks like he'd smell real nice," she said.

"That's because you're pregnant," Dottie said. "You're smelling everything."

"He wears Old Spice," Josie said.

Shirley let out a dreamy, "Oooooooooo."

"Have you been close enough to Robert Coolidge to smell him too?" Peggy said, nudging Josie in the ribs.

Josie swallowed hard. She hadn't planned to keep R.J. a secret, but now that the moment to tell her family about him was here, she clammed up. It was one thing to tell Cassie. Telling her sisters-in-law was *serious*.

"She's blushing!" Alice said, giggling.

Shirley twisted in her seat, and Dottie glanced at her in the rearview mirror. Darn it, why did she offer to sit in the middle? She was completely on display.

"She knows what he smells like, all right," Peggy said.

"I think she knows a bit more than that," Shirley said, winking.

Josie shrank in her coat, trying to hide her face in her collar, but she only got as far as her lower lip.

"Shirley!" Alice said.

"Sorry," Shirley said, fanning herself with one hand. "It's these pregnancy hormones. They get me all riled up."

"You're our prisoner right now, Josie," Dottie said, her eyes back on the road. "May as well tell us what we want to know."

Good gravy, where to even start? If she told them about Yosemite, they'd hate him immediately. If he ever met her family, the poor guy would never have a chance. These ladies were far more formidable than her brothers.

Start with the best day, Josie Girl. They'll love it.

"He took me to Disneyland," she said in a small voice.

Her sisters-in-law screamed, and Josie spent the next ten minutes explaining how she helped him when he was sick and that he took her to Disneyland as a thank-you. The other women exchanged winks and nudges through the whole story.

"That's so sweet," Alice said. "Reminds me of the time Jim took me to the state fair when we were courting. This was right after he came home from the war, and we weren't even sure they were going to hold the fair that year…"

Alice launched into the story she'd told at least a hundred times, and Josie settled back in her seat, relieved to be off the hook.

She cringed when they passed the drive-in theater where Ethan had taken her on their first date, but as they rolled into town, excitement took over. Golly, she was actually looking forward to being in town. She'd avoided it since her divorce. The first year she came home for Christmas, she'd stayed at the farmhouse, outright refusing to leave the family property. Last year, her sisters-in-law had dragged her out for some shopping, but she insisted on going home before lunch. She didn't want to sit in the middle of a restaurant where all of Hays could see her. Even worse was the possibility that she might run into one of the Winchesters.

But this year, why should she be ashamed to hide her face? She was on a television show. Complete strangers knew who she was and wanted to take photos with her. And she was making more money than she'd ever dreamed of. The Winchesters could all take a long walk off a short pier.

Everyone in the county must have been Christmas shopping that day, because Dottie had to park a block away from Wiesner's Department Store, where Steve's wife, Irene, met them outside. They spent the next couple hours selecting gifts for the men and the children. Remembering how much she owed Charlie, Josie grabbed a copy of James Michener's new book, *Hawaii.* Charlie had mentioned that he'd love to see the new state.

As they browsed the children's department, a display of boys' cowboy costumes caught her eye. She stopped and gazed at one with a red hat that looked just like the outfit Matthew had worn the other night. She checked her wristwatch and adjusted for the time zones. The Coolidges were probably getting to Disneyland about now. Did R.J.'s parents go along? Little Matthew would love Frontierland.

She fingered one of the cap guns on display next to the outfits and smiled, imagining Matthew stalking R.J. around the house with it. A shame she didn't have time to mail one to Los Angeles before Matthew flew home. She'd have to give him one the next time he visited. When R.J. called, she'd ask him when that would be.

When R.J. called.

She'd seen him less than two days ago, and she was already anxious to hear his voice.

"You ready to ring up, Josie?"

Josie jumped, startled to see Irene right next to her.

"Oh, yes, I am," she said and followed Irene to the counter. The young woman behind the register let out a squeal.

"Oh, my goodness, Josie!" the lady said. It was amazing how just one woman could be nearly as shrill as the entire gaggle of teenage girls at LAX.

Josie squinted. The lady was familiar, but she couldn't quite place her.

"It's me! Phyllis Walker! Well, Phyllis Carson now." She held up her left hand and flashed a gold band on her third finger.

"Oh, Phyllis," Josie said, finally recognizing her. They were in the same grade in school. Phyllis had sat behind her in trigonometry in eleventh grade. She'd bobbed her hair since then and was wearing a good bit of makeup. "How are you?"

"Absolutely thrilled to see you is how I am," Phyllis said. "Congratulations on your big break! I love the show. I've been telling everyone how we're old school friends."

Josie's head snapped back. She and Phyllis certainly hadn't been enemies, but they'd never said much more in school to each other than, "Can I borrow a pencil?" She remembered something Charlie had told her not long after she joined *Gunslingers*.

"Once you get a little bit of fame, you'll be amazed how many old friends you didn't know you had," he'd said.

Phyllis was apparently one of those.

"Lovely to see you, Phyllis," Josie said. "I'm glad you're well."

"This is fancy," Phyllis said, picking up the bottle of

Chanel No. 5 Josie had grabbed in the ladies' department. "Enjoying that Hollywood money, are we?" She wiggled her eyebrows.

Josie smiled and paid for her purchases as fast as she could. Then she hustled outside to wait for her sisters-in-law.

The icy wind cut through her, and she shivered. Golly, it couldn't be much above freezing, and an unbroken sheet of gray clouds blanketed the sky. There wouldn't be any sunshine today. How had she survived living here for twenty years? It was probably thirty degrees warmer back home.

Yikes. She'd just thought of LA as "home." She gazed up and down Main Street, taking in the familiar buildings. She knew every single one of them. The grocery, the hardware store, the public library, the Presbyterian church. Nothing had changed but everything had.

You just stumbled upon the meaning of "perspective," Josie Girl.

"You all right?" Irene asked when she stepped out of the store.

"I'm fine," Josie said. "Just annoyed. Phyllis hardly said two words to me in school and suddenly we're best friends."

"Those Walkers always were opportunists," Irene said. "I went to school with a couple of them too. Come on, let's get in my car before we freeze to death. The others got caught up in the baby department. They can meet us at the diner."

Josie smiled and climbed into the passenger seat of Irene's car. Miraculously, Irene had managed to find a parking spot right outside the store. Five minutes later, the ladies claimed an enormous corner booth at the Roller Derby Diner. Usually, Josie would order a chocolate milkshake, but it was too dang cold for that. She'd ask for hot chocolate instead. Maybe the steam would thaw her nose.

Irene excused herself to the ladies' room, and Josie scanned the menu, though she didn't need to. One of the best things about the Roller Derby was that the offerings hadn't changed in her lifetime. She'd been thinking about the open-faced pot roast sandwich since yesterday.

A shadow fell over her, and she looked up, expecting to see the waitress. Instead, she took in sandy hair, bright blue eyes, and a distinctive slash through one eyebrow.

Oh, God.

A chill coursed through her, and her heart pounded so fast someone probably needed to call an ambulance. Her chest tightened until she could barely breathe, and her vision went spotty. Please, no. She couldn't do this now. She clutched her arms across her stomach and pressed hard.

Don't let him see you scared, Josie Girl. He doesn't get to see that ever again.

She forced in a deep breath and narrowed her eyes.

"What do *you* want?" she said.

Ethan Winchester's eyes widened. He looked hurt. The son of a bitch had the gall to look hurt. Josie's fear turned to white-hot anger. Ethan started to slide into the seat across from her, and she sprang to her feet.

"I didn't say you could sit down. I asked you what you wanted." Her voice was rising, and she didn't care. The last time she'd seen Ethan was when the judge finalized their divorce almost three years ago. That day, she'd sat trembling in the courtroom between Jimmy and Leighton, flinching every time Ethan looked her way. But she wasn't trapped any longer. There was nothing he could do to her.

How had she never seen before what a small, pathetic person he was? He was nothing without his father's money. And even with his father's money, he wasn't such a much. No one outside of Hays had ever heard of Ethan Winchester, and likely no one ever would. She'd feel sorry for him if he wasn't such a miserable excuse for a human being.

Ethan raised his hands, a gold wedding band flashing on his left ring finger. "I just wanted to say hello."

He was trying to be charming. Exactly like he always did to win her trust before he turned around and stabbed her in the back. Adrenaline flooded her veins, and every muscle in her body twitched.

"What for? Old times' sake?"

"Can I just sit down for a minute?"

"You can stand."

Ethan lowered his hands and stuffed them awkwardly in his pants pockets. "I just wanted to tell you how proud we are of you, my parents and me." He smiled. "We always said you were something special."

Her anger burned so hot it was a miracle she didn't melt.

"Did you now?" she said through gritted teeth.

"I'm sorry?"

Josie tensed, a revolver with the hammer cocked. "Did you always say I was special? Because the last thing I remember you and your parents saying about me was that I was a prude who couldn't satisfy you."

She hadn't meant to say this loudly enough for half the crowded restaurant to hear, but too late to do anything about that now. The diners at the tables around them turned and stared.

Let them stare, Josie Girl. Let them take a good, long look.

She pulled the trigger. "You spread nasty, vile rumors about me. You, with your money and holier-than-thou attitude. But now that I've found a tiny crumb of fame, you're sucking up to me. You don't get to trail along on my success, Winchester. You want to give your family something to spread around town? They can tell everyone that Josephine Donovan is through putting up with your shit."

A few customers, factory workers from the looks of their jumpsuits, burst into applause.

Ethan's dangling lower jaw swung up and down a few times before his face hardened like it did just before he tore into her when they were married. But Josie wasn't backing down this time. She narrowed her eyes and glared right back. His face turned red, then purple, and Josie nearly choked holding back her laughter. She was probably the first person to ever challenge him.

When he spun on his heel and stalked off, she let her laughter ring out through the diner before she called after him.

"Tell Margie I said hello!"

Chapter Fifty-Three

R.J.'s heart kicked up when he spotted Josie through the airport window as she stepped out of the plane. He'd seen Mom, Dad, and Matthew off early this morning and had spent the last three hours killing time in the airport. But he'd brought a book along and nursed a couple cups of coffee and a sandwich at the lunch counter.

He smiled when Josie paused at the top of the airplane's stairs and tilted her head toward the sunshine. When he'd called her on Christmas Eve, she said she'd been freezing cold the entire trip and couldn't believe she'd survived her childhood. He chuckled, remembering how he'd felt about the humidity on his last trip to Hell Hole. That was about all they'd gotten to say to each other, though. With about a thousand nieces, nephews, brothers, and sisters-in-law behind her, Josie's house had been too chaotic for them to have an actual conversation.

God, she was beautiful. She wore a bright blue scarf on her head, a few tendrils of dark hair cascading from under it. He wanted to bury his hands in that hair and get lost forever. Josie dug into her bag, pulled out her sunglasses, and popped them on. Good. She was unlikely to get recognized. This reunion would be just the two of them. And then they'd go back to her place and have the whole day together. Alone. His palms started sweating.

He locked eyes with her as soon as she stepped

through the gate door. She rushed at him, flinging her arms around his neck and pressing herself against his chest. He exhaled.

He'd waited two weeks to have her in his arms again, and here she finally was. He wanted to kiss her but held back just in case someone did recognize them. They didn't need it splashed all over the gossip magazines that Deacon Bell was sparking Mary Anderson behind Judah Mitchell's back.

"Welcome home, Princess," he said and breathed her in. She smelled of the same perfume she'd worn at the Christmas party, and he was immediately intoxicated.

"I missed you," she said.

He stepped back and chucked her under the chin. "Missed you too. Ready to get out of here?"

As soon as they were in the Corvette, he leaned over and kissed her. A frisson of excitement shot down his spine as she kissed him back, laying one warm, soft hand on his cheek. When they parted, he stared at her, a smile slowly pulling up the corners of his mouth.

"Come on," he said, his voice husky. "Let's get you home." He fired up the engine and put the car in gear. In minutes, they were sailing down the freeway toward Hollywood.

"How did everyone like Disneyland?" Josie said. "I'm sorry we didn't have enough time for the full story on the phone."

He grinned. "We had a ball. Got there as soon as the park opened and didn't leave until closing. I had to carry Matthew back to the car. Would you believe he rode the Matterhorn three times? Even dragged my parents on the last time."

She giggled. Geez, he'd missed that sound.

"How did they like it?" she said.

"Mom loved it. Dad on the other hand... I'd never heard him scream before in my life. Sounded like he was being murdered." He chuckled. "Matthew already told me that I'm taking him back the next time he visits."

"When will that be? I'd love to see him again." She inhaled sharply. "I mean, if that's all right. I know you don't get to see him much, and I don't want to intrude."

Was she kidding? He immediately imagined the three of them together at Disneyland, Matthew between him and Josie, holding their hands.

Like a little family.

His heart swelled. "I've got to talk to Laura again, but probably over Easter. He gets a week off school then, and we'll be on hiatus. And you're always welcome, Josie. Always." He flashed her a quick grin and then trained his eyes back on the road. "How was *your* visit?"

"I ran into Ethan."

He gripped the steering wheel so hard he was surprised it didn't snap in half.

"How did that go?" he asked through gritted teeth, startled by his sudden surge of anger.

Josie squared her shoulders and smiled smugly. "He tried to suck up to me, and I told him to take a hike, right in front of half the town."

Relieved, he burst out laughing. "Josie, I don't think I've ever been so proud of anybody in my whole life."

She reached out and squeezed his right hand, which rested on the gearshift. Her hand was warm, and her touch sent another shiver down his spine. He took a deep breath that shook a little when he let it out. They were only five minutes or so away from her apartment. He'd never been so eager to get her home.

They had the rest of the day ahead of them. Ed had agreed to check on Sergeant a couple times, so he didn't have to rush back to his house, and since today was Saturday, they didn't have an early morning tomorrow.

As Josie would say, good gravy.

He downshifted on the exit ramp, and his hand left a sweaty shine on the shifter.

When he parked at her apartment building, he helped her out and then went around to the back of the car and pulled her suitcase out of the trunk. They walked in silence to the stairwell, Josie limping in her high heels. Should he offer to carry her? But if he did, what would he do with her suitcase? He supposed he could run it upstairs and come back for Josie. But his heart was already pounding so hard, making two trips up the steps might do him in.

"You coming?" Josie said.

R.J. snapped back into the moment. Josie was already on the fourth step and looking back at him. He muttered an apology and scurried up the stairs.

When they reached Josie's door, Josie's hands trembled as she fumbled with the key in the lock. At last, the door swung open, and they stepped into the dark apartment. After kicking off her shoes, Josie flipped on the kitchen light.

"Musty in here," she said and scurried to the living room window. She drew back the curtains and cracked the window open.

Daylight poured into the room, and R.J. looked around. He'd never been inside Josie's apartment before. A small hallway led away off the kitchen. Her bedroom must be back there. Sweat broke out along his hairline.

Josie's bedroom.

That was probably where he should set the suitcase he was still lugging, but he couldn't just barge in there.

"Would you like it in the bedroom or the living room?" he said.

Josie stared at him, eyes wide and chest heaving. "I'm sorry?"

Oh, God. Was it possible to will yourself to spontaneously combust? Because he'd really love to right about now. He pointed to her suitcase instead.

"Where should I set this?"

Josie closed her eyes and exhaled. "Just there at the beginning of the hall is fine, thank you." She untied her head scarf, tossed it on a saggy armchair, and headed toward the kitchen. He set the suitcase where she'd pointed and followed her to the kitchen.

"Can I get you anything to dr—" She turned around and nearly smacked into him.

"Sorry," he said, his chest only inches from her face. She tilted her head up to look at him.

She smelled amazing. Whatever that perfume was, he hoped she had a big bottle. His mouth watered.

"Can I get you anything to drink?" she said.

He gazed down at her. "No, thanks." He could barely speak above a whisper. "Not thirsty."

They reached for each other at the same time, crushing their bodies together as their lips met. He gently coaxed her lips apart so he could slip his tongue between them. She tasted like Dr. Pepper. Something about that was downright adorable. If his mouth hadn't been occupied by hers, he would have smiled. He slid his hands to her hips and pressed her harder against his pelvis.

She caressed the back of his head as she pulled slowly back. Smiling, she took his hand and led him to the drooping sofa in the living room. It groaned as they sat down, and he raised his eyebrows.

She laughed. "Don't worry. This sofa is all bark and no bite."

He needed to hold her. All of her. He smiled and pulled her crosswise onto his lap and kissed her again, almost dying of sheer happiness when she took the initiative and slipped her tongue into his mouth. He sighed and pulled her a little tighter against him.

Not breaking their kiss, Josie swung around and straddled him, her full pink skirt flaring to each side. Everything from R.J.'s waist down throbbed, begging for more of her. Josie buried her long, delicate fingers in his hair, and he groaned and rocked his hips, rubbing himself against her through their clothes. His hands wandered. First up and down her back, then to the bottom of her sweater, where he played with the hem.

He wanted to rip it off her, but he didn't want to scare her because, damn, he didn't want this to ever end. He slid his hands back to her hips. Hips were safe.

But then Josie slipped her fingers out of his hair and tugged her sweater over her head, revealing a thin blouse underneath. She tossed the sweater onto the armchair, and a few tendrils of hair fell from her updo. He tucked them behind her ears and caressed her left cheek.

All right. She'd made a move by taking off her sweater. Maybe it was safe for him to make one too. Slowly, though. Supporting her head with one hand, he eased her back onto the sofa. He leaned down and took off his shoes, then lowered himself onto her, twining his stocking feet with hers, luxuriating in the feeling of her warm body underneath his.

She stiffened, licked her lips, and gazed up at him, eyes wide.

He smiled, hoping to put her at ease. "This okay? We can sit back up if you want."

Josie relaxed, her body sinking deeper into the cushions, and the sofa squawked a loud reply. They burst out laughing, R.J. never so thankful for a comic relief.

"This is lovely," Josie said.

Thank God.

He caught her gaze again. "If I do anything you don't want me to do, please say so, all right? It's only fun for me if it's fun for you too."

She blinked so rapidly he thought she was going to cry. He stroked her cheek.

"Okay," she said. Then she pulled his face to hers and kissed him.

That was all it took. He rubbed himself against her again, and she moaned, making him throb even harder. Her hands skated from his back to his chest, and she unbuttoned his shirt. He'd dreamed so many times of taking his clothes off for her, but holy smokes, her undressing him was even better. She pushed the shirt off his shoulders and untucked his undershirt. He sat up a little, and she pulled it over his head and tossed it aside.

He'd been shirtless in front of her several times when he was sick, but those had been *very* different circumstances. At last, Josie did what he'd been so desperate for then and ran her hands across his bare torso, her fingers electrifying his skin. He sighed, grabbed one of her hands, and kissed each fingertip. He needed to feel more than just her hands against him. He reached for the buttons on her blouse, his eyebrows raised in a question.

She didn't stiffen this time. Body perfectly relaxed, she nodded. He silently begged his fingers not to tremble, and one by one, he unfastened each delicate white button. She pulled the hem of the blouse from her skirt and sat up. R.J. slid it from her shoulders and tossed it toward the armchair.

At the sight of the flawless, creamy skin on her belly, he almost lost his mind completely and tore her bra off.

Deep breaths, R.J. Deep breaths.

If he took off her bra, everything else might come off, too, and he wasn't prepared for that. He'd thought about getting a package of condoms while he waited for her plane, just in case, but that would have come off as *really* presumptuous. Josie might have done a lot more than just knock him on his ass for that one. Besides, they should take this slow.

He laid her back down, both of them laughing again at the noisy sofa, and kissed her. First on the lips, then the throat, the collarbone, on her bra between her breasts, then her stomach. When he reached the waistband of her skirt, he trailed the kisses back up her body until he reached her soft lips again.

She groaned, and her hands scrabbled at his belt buckle.

Oh, boy.

He drew back and gulped air, trying to calm his body's silent cry for hers.

"I'm sorry," she said, snatching her hands back. "I should have asked." She looked away.

"No, no, no," he said. He placed a finger on her cheek and turned her face back toward him. "It's not that at all. Believe me, I'm having a *very* good time." He smiled, and thank God, she smiled back—a genuine, nose-wrinkling smile. "I just don't want things to go too far. I don't have any prevention with me, and I know from experience it only takes one time." He chuckled.

"I have a diaphragm," she blurted out and locked eyes with him.

Forget taking things slow.

His whole body pulsated. He needed to say something intelligent, but his brain was a swamp. The world was nothing but the swell of Josie's breasts peeking over her bra, the hollow at the base of her throat, her legs wrapped around his.

"Cassie really wanted one, but she was afraid to do it alone. I never planned to use it."

A bark of laughter tore from deep down in his gut before he could stop it. Only Josie. His beautiful, kind, funny Josie. He wanted to drag her to the bedroom and make love to her for the rest of the day. But it had to be her decision. He leaned forward and nuzzled her neck.

"It's entirely up to you, Princess."

Please say yes, he thought. *Oh, please, please, please say yes.*

She stroked the back of his head, her other hand running idly up and down his bare back. Her breathing sped up and she clutched him tighter. This must be a good sign.

But then she put her hands on his chest and shoved. She wasn't strong enough to push him away, but he took the hint and sprang off. She sat up, clutching her midsection and gasping.

Oh, shit. This wasn't excitement. This was some sort of terrified fit. He'd seen it in New York. One of the best actors he ever worked with had these spells before every show. Ten minutes before curtain, like clockwork, the man would curl up in a ball backstage and tremble, gasping like he was drowning. R.J. racked his brain, trying to figure out what he'd done to scare Josie this badly.

"Whoa, hey," he said. His hands hovered around her. He wanted to touch her but wasn't sure if it was a good idea. "Josie, it's all right. We don't have to. I won't be upset."

She shook her head and then dropped it between her knees, still gasping. Slowly, he reached out and laid one hand on her back, just over her bra strap.

"It's all right, Josie, it's all right," he repeated over and over, gently rubbing her back.

Gradually, her trembling slowed, her breathing leveled out. She raised her head, but stayed leaned forward, her forearms resting on her knees. Her eyes brimmed with tears, and she rubbed the base of the bare ring finger on her left hand with her thumb. All at once, he knew what had scared her, and it wasn't him. Blood pounded in his ears, but he couldn't indulge himself with rage right now.

He grabbed a quilt that was draped over the back of the sofa and put it over her shoulders, wrapping it around her to cover her bare torso. The tears spilled down her cheeks, and she wiped at them with shaking hands. His chest ached watching her. He couldn't hold back any longer.

"Come here," he said, his voice soft. He scooped her up and sat her crosswise in his lap. Tucking the quilt securely around her, he cradled her close to his chest. The last of her trembling faded away, but he didn't let her go. He'd hold her all day if she'd let him. Several minutes passed before she said anything.

"This wasn't your fault," she said, keeping her head down. "I'm so sorry. I thought... I thought I was better."

"Please look at me."

She slowly lifted her head, her eyes red-rimmed and bloodshot. Strings of damp hair stuck to her face. He smoothed them away, wanting to cry himself.

"Don't ever apologize for what he did." His jaw clenched, and he had to take a deep breath before he could speak again. "He forced himself on you, didn't he?"

Josie dropped her gaze to the quilt, fresh tears streaming down her face.

"I don't know," she said. "I mean, we were married. You can't...*violate* someone you're married to, can you?"

He stroked her hair. "I don't know. But you can still be cruel. Do you want to tell me about it?"

"Not really."

But she did anyway.

Chapter Fifty-Four

Tears streamed down R.J.'s face by the time Josie finished her story.

"I've never been so relieved in my life as I was the day Margie showed up on my doorstep with that baby in her arms," Josie said, her voice unsteady.

R.J. clutched her to his chest, feeling her breath fall warm and soft on his bare skin. His shirt was still on the floor halfway across the living room, so he wiped his eyes with a bare forearm, then tilted his head down and kissed her forehead.

"Josie, I'm so sorry." He rested his cheek on the top of her head. "It should never be that way. No one should ever get hurt." He let out a long, shuddering breath. "No wonder you're frightened. I am so, so sorry."

Her silent stream of tears broke into shuddering, bone-racking sobs, and she curled into him. He rocked her in his lap and let her cry until she went nearly limp in his arms. Married or not, Ethan had assaulted Josie, no doubt about it. Several times a week, in fact, starting with when he finally staggered home drunk on their wedding night. Thank God Josie had had the good sense to keep her diaphragm in whenever he was home.

R.J. wanted to fix this for her, but how did you fix something like this? Even killing Ethan, enjoyable as that might be, wouldn't fix it. At a loss for other ideas, he did what he'd done that week she stayed at his house.

"Let me make you some tea," he said. Still holding her, he stood and laid her on the sofa. He kissed her forehead again. "Mind if I poke around the kitchen?" She shook her head, so he picked up his short-sleeved undershirt and Josie's blouse from the floor near the armchair. He pulled on his undershirt and handed her the blouse before heading into the kitchen.

He filled the kettle that sat on the stove, clicked on the burner, and opened what seemed to be the pantry door. A box of Earl Grey sat right in front. He grinned and grabbed it, then turned and opened cabinets and drawers until he found mugs and spoons. In one cabinet, he spotted a familiar-looking tall, slim bottle.

"Hello, Jim," he said, grabbing the nearly full bottle of Jim Beam. He stuck his head through the serving window between the kitchen and the living room, brandishing the bottle.

"Mind if I use this?" he said.

Josie's head popped over the back of the sofa, and she smiled. "Please do."

"All right, hot toddies, here we come." He ducked back into the kitchen.

"There's lemon juice in the fridge," she called.

A couple minutes later, R.J. carried two mugs brimming with steaming amber liquid into the living room. Josie sat up and took one, clutching it in both hands and inhaling before taking a small sip.

"Oh, that's good," she said, settling back against the cushions.

He grinned and sat next to her. He'd been generous with the bourbon. He shifted, chuckled when the sofa creaked, and draped his mug-free arm around her shoulders. She leaned against him and took another sip.

"Mom always says a hot toddy is better than anything the doctor can prescribe," he said.

"Your mother is right." She relaxed against him, and he felt his heartrate tick down. He'd been worked up too. He was upset over what Ethan had done to her and terrified that he'd made it worse and she'd push him away again, this time for good. He never knew he could feel so many things in such a short space of time.

"I'm sorry," she said, staring into her tea. "We were having such a nice time and I ruined it crying about my ex-husband."

R.J.'s spine stiffened. She was not going to feel ashamed for what that son of a bitch had done. "Josie, look at me."

She kept her head lowered but looked up with her eyes.

"Don't ever apologize for having been hurt. That was his mistake, not yours. And I'm honored you trusted me enough to tell me about it." He caressed her cheek. "I love you."

She squeaked out, "I love you too," just as another round of tears rose to her eyes. When she shifted to wipe them away, the obnoxious old sofa protested again, and they both laughed.

"So," he said, "what would you like to do the rest of the day?" Josie broke into a full, nose-wrinkling smile, and his heart soared. He'd spend the rest of the day scrubbing her floors like Cinderella if it kept her smiling like that.

They spent the afternoon playing gin rummy, enjoying a second round of hot toddies partway through the afternoon. Josie didn't have much food in the house, so at suppertime R.J. ran out and brought back Chinese takeout. They ended the evening cuddled up together on the still-squeaking sofa and watched *Bonanza*.

"I feel like such a traitor every time I watch another Western," Josie said.

He chuckled. "You know, they only shoot this one in color to get everyone to buy new television sets." He waved at Josie's black-and-white TV. "Apparently, it hasn't worked."

Josie laughed. "And here I thought it was because the men all had such beautiful eyes."

"Don't let Beau hear you say that. You'll give him an inferiority complex."

Josie's lip curled. "I have to kiss him next week. On the lips, this time."

R.J.'s scalp prickled. Wait a second.

"What do you mean 'this time'?" He'd seen every finished episode of *Gunslingers*. Josie's and Beau's characters had barely touched so far. When was she kissing Beau? And if not on the lips, then *where*?

Josie giggled. "Guess I didn't tell you. Beau and I got recognized at the airport by a bunch of teenage girls. They thought we were dating for real, so I kissed him on the cheek to give them a little thrill."

He let out a long breath and chuckled. He had to admit that was pretty clever. He ruffled Josie's hair. "Well done. Those girls are probably still gushing about it. And don't worry about kissing Beau. Like I said, it'll be fine. I won't even be jealous." That wasn't entirely true, but telling her that wouldn't make her first on-screen kiss any easier for her. He leaned over and kissed her softly on the lips for the first time since this afternoon. She kissed him back but broke it off early when a huge yawn nearly split her jaw.

"I hope you don't think that was a commentary on your kissing," she said when it passed.

"Not at all. I forgot you're still running two hours ahead. You must be exhausted." He was surprised she'd made it all day without a nap. Crying jags like she'd had always left him done in. He should let her get to bed. He grabbed his shoes from next to the sofa and put them on. "You're not back on set until next week, are you?"

She shook her head. "I'm at the hospital later this week. I'll be on set on the eleventh."

"You free next Saturday?"

She shook her head again. "Charlie's taking me car-shopping, and I don't know how long we'll be. But I'm free Sunday."

He frowned. "Ed and Lucy invited me over for dinner next Sunday. Guess we'll just have to wait until the eleventh. But I'll call you." He smiled through his disappointment. A week and two days before he'd see her again. She held his hand as they walked to her front door. He kissed her again and caressed her cheek with the back of one hand.

"I love you," he said. He couldn't fix what had happened to her in the past, but he could give her this now.

"I love you too." She popped up on her tiptoes and kissed him one last time before he turned and stepped out the door.

Chapter Fifty-Five

The following Saturday, Josie waited in her living room for Charlie to arrive to take her car-shopping. She was excited about buying her own car—her *own* car!— but she was disappointed she wouldn't get to see R.J. this weekend. She was so angry at herself for panicking last week. She'd wanted him. Oh, good gravy, how she'd wanted him. Her diaphragm was just a few steps away in the bathroom.

And then she'd gone and gotten all hysterical.

Making love could be incredible. Cassie said so, and Cassie wouldn't lie to her. She just needed the right man. And she'd sure as heck found him.

Peace settled over her as she remembered R.J. pulling her into his lap and cradling her against his chest until she calmed down.

He'll always take care of you, Josie Girl. No need to be scared.

She needed a do-over. Next Saturday should be good. She'd invite him for dinner and let the evening run its course. She grinned.

Someone knocked on the door, and Josie opened it to see Charlie standing there, keys in his hand.

"Ready to go buy a car?" he said.

****

A couple hours later, Josie and Charlie stood next to a cherry-red Impala with a wide white stripe along the back half and matching red interior.

"You sure this is the one you want?" Charlie asked, running a hand along the body of the car.

Josie grinned and nodded. She loved the Corvette, but the price was higher than she was comfortable with, considering she didn't know if she'd have television money after the end of March. Merrill still hadn't said anything about her coming back next season, so she had to plan on just her nursing salary.

And the Impala was gorgeous. She opted for the convertible—she could pay the little bit extra for that, no sweat—but she let Charlie do the haggling. She'd guessed correctly that the salesman would treat her like an idiot, as if she hadn't been helping to repair tractor engines since she was seven. Better to let levelheaded Charlie deal with him so she didn't get so annoyed she slugged the guy. Because she just might. She was done letting men treat her like she was stupid.

Charlie turned out to be a good negotiator. He autographed a photo of himself for the salesman's mother and in return got Josie the four-speed for the price of the three. She'd have to remember that trick.

Josie's nerves soared on the drive to the studio on Monday morning. Not only was she terrified about scratching her new car, but she and Beau were filming their kiss today. But she grinned when she parked outside the soundstage. The Impala looked so much better in the parking lot at the studio than it did in its spot under her dreary apartment building. And driving was a *lot* nicer than taking the bus. The entire cast and crew came out and crowded around the car, congratulating her and popping the hood so, in the time-honored tradition of men, they could stare at the engine and pretend to know what they were looking at.

"It's a shame you didn't get a Corvette," R.J. said, nudging her arm. "You look so good in one."

She met his eyes and felt her pulse quicken. She shook her head to clear it before anyone noticed her staring. "Anyone can drive a Corvette," she said, poking him back. "An Impala driver has *elegance*."

"Speaking of elegance," Merrill said, coming up behind them, "you pulled off the most elegant publicity stunt I think I've ever seen."

Josie turned to him and wrinkled her forehead. "What do you mean?"

Merrill beckoned to Beau and pulled a rolled-up magazine out of his back pocket. "This," he said when Beau had joined them.

Josie peered at the magazine, Beau and R.J. staring over her shoulders. It was a copy of *Celebrity Whispers*, a tabloid she'd often seen at the newsstands but had never paid much attention to. There on the cover of the newest issue was a big photo of her straightening Beau's tie at LAX and a headline that read, "Love in Folsom? *Gunslingers'* Beau Fraser and Josephine Donovan are more than costars."

Her jaw dropped, and she ripped the magazine from Merrill's hands. She rifled the pages until she found the brief article.

"Beau Fraser and Josephine Donovan share a lot more than scenes on television," she read aloud. "The two were spotted saying a tender goodbye at Los Angeles International Airport just before Christmas." Inset was a huge photo of her kissing Beau's cheek and another of her hugging him before she boarded her plane. "While their television characters are still warming up to one another, it seems Mr. Fraser and Miss Donovan are already quite cozy. The pair boarded separate flights, but maybe next year we'll see them depart together."

She caught Beau's gaze and they both burst out laughing.

Merrill frowned. "Why is this so funny?" he said, setting Josie and Beau laughing again. Even R.J. joined in this time.

How could she even begin to explain? Tell him that Beau was sleeping with her best friend and she and R.J. were seconds away from making love last week?"

"It wasn't a planned stunt," she said at last. "Some girls showed up and were fawning over Beau, so we decided to have fun. We had no idea there was any press there."

"Besides, I have a girlfriend," Beau said. Josie beamed. He'd just referred to Cassie as his *girlfriend*. Did Cassie know? She hoped so. She'd have to call her later.

"Well, keep her quiet," Merrill said, taking the magazine back from Josie. "Let's maintain the illusion." He looked at R.J. "I'd tell you to keep your mouth shut, too, but I don't suppose I have to worry about *you* talking to any press." He paused. "And come by to see me later. I have some ideas for Deacon Bell I wanted to run by you." He looked at Josie and Beau again. "Planned or not, that was brilliant." He shook the magazine. "We could beat *The Rifleman*'s ratings with this kind of publicity." He turned and walked away toward the production offices, whistling cheerily as he went.

Beau turned to R.J. with his hands up in surrender. "Robert, I swear it was just an act. You know I wouldn't move in on your girl."

R.J. chuckled and extended his hand to Beau. "It's all right. It's just Hollywood."

Josie wanted to cheer when Beau grinned and shook R.J.'s hand. She hoped Cassie would understand too.

The hood of Josie's new car slammed shut, and Charlie sidled up to them. "Did I miss something?" he said.

The trio burst out laughing again.

****

The giddiness of the morning wore off fast when Josie and Beau had to shoot their kiss. They could pull off the entire scene right up to when they had to lock lips. Josie tried so hard to keep a straight face, but every time Beau moved in to kiss her, she'd think of that tabloid headline and start laughing. By the eighth take, everyone was grumbling, especially R.J. and Charlie, who only needed to shoot the last two minutes of the scene before they could go home for the day.

As they set up for a ninth take, Charlie grabbed her arm.

"I know this is awkward for you, but you are making everyone very grumpy, my dear," he said.

Josie wilted. She could stand to disappoint just about anyone but Papa Bear. She whispered an apology. Charlie cupped her chin and tilted her head up.

"Pretend it isn't Beau," he said. His left eyelid fluttered, and she couldn't tell if it was an involuntary twitch or a quick wink. Either way, Josie thought back to that first scene she shot in Yosemite when she imagined she was sitting next to Daddy again instead of Charlie.

She just had to pretend she was kissing the man she wished she was kissing.

The director hollered "Places!" and Josie scurried

back to her mark.

When she and Beau began their lines again, she pictured R.J. in front of her instead of Beau. R.J. saying how frightened he'd been when she/Mary was kidnapped, R.J. professing his love. When Beau leaned in to kiss her, she threw her arms around him, squeezed their bodies together, and crushed her lips against his. Beau's entire body went rigid, but only briefly—he was a darned good actor. He wrapped his arms around her and kissed her back while she buried her hands in his hair.

His lips were thin and hard, not pillowy like R.J.'s, and he tasted of cigarettes. She almost recoiled, but she *really* didn't want to have to do a tenth take. She focused on pretending that Beau's skinny body was actually R.J.'s broad chest and shoulders.

She wanted R.J. so badly—*all* of him—but here she was, lip-locked with Beau.

Golly, wasn't it time for Charlie and R.J. to bust in yet?

Sheriff Anderson and Deputy Bell finally burst into the sheriff's office, catching them in the act. Josie snapped away from Beau, who started sputtering that he/Judah and Mary weren't up to anything. The sheriff made some vague threat, while Deacon Bell nudged Judah and gave him a knowing wink.

"Cut! That's a wrap," the director called. The entire crew burst into applause.

Beau wiped his brow and tore off toward the water cooler. Josie staggered off set, leaned against a wall, and slid to the floor, where she tried to catch her breath. Her heart was pounding, and the back of her neck was sweaty. Good gravy, thinking of R.J. had worked a little *too* well.

And speak of the devil, if R.J. didn't amble over and sit next to her.

"Josie, that was…convincing," he said, his eyes like saucers.

She shuddered and wiped her mouth with her sleeve, trying to get rid of the bitter flavor of Beau's Lucky Strikes.

"You all right?" R.J. said.

"That was the weirdest thing I've ever done."

His cheek dimpled when he chuckled. "Would you like some mouthwash? I think we have a bottle in the dressing room."

She knew what she'd like, and it wasn't mouthwash. And she wasn't waiting until Saturday.

"Can you come over tonight?" she said.

She wouldn't have thought it possible, but his eyes went even wider.

"What's wrong?"

"Nothing. I would just really like for you to come over tonight." She held his gaze and gave a small nod.

R.J.'s jaw worked up and down. "Of…of course. I'll need to run home first, but yeah, of course."

"Good."

Someone was going to notice the two of them trying to devour each other with their eyes. She jumped to her feet.

"I should check on Beau."

R.J. stood, too, and cleared his throat. "Good idea. I still need to talk to Merrill anyway." He lowered his voice. "See you soon."

If she watched him walk away, she'd start second-guessing herself, so she darted to the water cooler. Beau was half-hidden behind it, chugging cold water like it was the only thing keeping him alive.

"You all right?" she said.

He wiped his forehead with his sleeve. His arm trembled.

"God above, Josie, you could have warned me you were going to do that."

"Sorry. I didn't even know I was going to do that until I did it." She smiled slyly. "Guess you don't get kisses like that from Cassie."

Beau's shoulders dropped a degree. "No one gets kisses like that in real life." He chuckled. "That was a Hollywood kiss if ever there was one. It's gonna look great on television." He opened his arms, and Josie stepped into them and hugged him.

"I am so glad that's over," she said.

Beau chuckled again. "Me too. But you know, I'm sure that's not the only time Mary and Judah are going to kiss."

"No, but at least Josie and Beau know what they're doing now." She mussed his hair and stepped away. "See you tomorrow."

Her body singing with anticipation, she kept her farewells to Charlie and the crew brief, changed out of her costume, and headed for her new car.

She had a guest to prepare for.

Chapter Fifty-Six

R.J. had to hold himself back from running flat-out to Merrill's office. He'd been dying to get some depth for Deacon Bell, but if he'd understood Josie right—and he was pretty damn sure he had this time—he'd be getting something even better this evening. So here he was, stepping into what was possibly the most important meeting of his career to this point, and all he could think of was getting the hell out of here.

"Ah, Coolidge," Merrill said when R.J. stepped into his office. The producer was sitting at his desk, bent over a stack of papers, a cigarette between his lips. He tapped it in a cut-glass bowl and straightened up. "Have a seat."

R.J. took a chair in front of the desk.

"Cigarette?" Merrill held out a pack of Camels. R.J. shook his head. Merrill leaned back in his chair and studied him for a moment. "I've been talking to the network, and they agree it's time we do something with Deacon Bell. Your female following isn't as big as Beau's, but giving you more screen time will still help the ratings."

Coming from Merrill, even a backhanded compliment was monumental. R.J. smiled politely.

"What did you have in mind?" he said.

Merrill took a drag from his cigarette and laid out an episode where the sheriff and Judah would be out of town when a pack of bandits arrived. It would be up to

Deacon Bell alone to save the day.

This sounded too good to be true. "Charlie and Beau won't even appear in the episode?" R.J. asked.

"Maybe the last two or three minutes. We might have a scene at the end where they come home and congratulate Deacon on saving Folsom, but we'll have to see what the run time looks like once the episode's written." He paused for another drag. "I know we don't see eye-to-eye, but you're a damn good actor, Coolidge. Let's show America what you can do."

R.J. laughed and ran a hand through his hair. This was more than he'd ever dared hope for with this role. "I don't know what to say."

"You could start with 'Thank you.'" Merrill smiled. It was more like a grimace, but it was as close to a friendly smile as the producer had. R.J. grinned.

"Thank you. I'll look forward to seeing the script." He placed his hands on the chair's armrests and was about to rise when Merrill spoke again.

"One more thing I wanted to talk to you about."

R.J. settled back in his chair, apprehension rising in his throat. "What's that?"

Merrill pulled on his cigarette again and leaned back in his chair. "Am I right to suspect there's something going on between you and Josie?"

R.J. tensed but kept his face neutral. "What makes you say that?"

"I got a funny feeling after the way you all reacted to the story about Josie and Beau this morning, so I asked around a bit. Seems the two of you were quite the dancing pair at the Christmas party."

R.J. relaxed. He could play this off. He chuckled. "Her friend abandoned her for Beau. What was I supposed to do? Let her sit by herself all night? That wouldn't have been very gentlemanly. You were there. You saw."

"I left before the last dance. And from what I hear, it was memorable."

Damn. He was caught after all. But that didn't mean he'd lost. He crossed his arms over his chest and leaned back in his chair. "What I do with my personal time is my business. You own a lot of me, Merrill, but you don't own that."

"Maybe not, but I'm responsible for the welfare of this show. And right now, that welfare depends on audiences believing the dynamic between Josie and Beau. We can't have her running around with him on camera and you in public. It would ruin the illusion."

"People know the difference between television and reality."

"Do they?" Merrill grabbed *Celebrity Whispers* off his desk and shook it. "Because they're eating this up."

He had a point. *Gunslingers* had been lucky to get renewed for this season, and their ratings had risen steadily since Josie joined the cast. The episode they just shot where Josie and Beau finally kissed was likely to be their highest-rated ever. R.J.'s stomach clenched. He'd finally gotten things on the right track with Josie. Please, God, don't let this wreck it.

"If we can keep this excitement going," Merrill continued, "I might be offering everyone, including Josie, three-year contracts next month."

R.J.'s eyebrows shot skyward. A contract that long would probably come with a decent raise. And three more seasons meant more residuals. His head spun trying to imagine so much money. He could buy Matthew anything he wanted. And a full-time contract for Josie? She'd be over the moon.

"So, I'm not *telling* you what you can and can't do with your personal life," Merrill said, "but I am *asking* you, just like I asked Beau, to keep it quiet. Protect the illusion. Protect your paycheck. Protect *her* paycheck."

R.J. frowned. He would have kept the relationship quiet anyway. His private life wasn't the public's business. But three years was a long time to sneak around—longer if there was another contract renewal. Surely he and Josie could manage it, though. They'd find a way. Besides, he'd been ignoring interview requests for so long now, the press was beginning to ignore *him*. They could do this.

Merrill stabbed a finger at him. "And for the love of God, don't get her pregnant."

R.J. bristled and squared his shoulders. "Watch it."

The producer spread his hands. "You know how it is. She gets pregnant out of wedlock, and her career could be over."

R.J. narrowed his eyes. Merrill wasn't worried about anyone's career but his own.

Now's not the time for that argument, R.J.

He unclenched his teeth just enough to speak. "You don't have anything to worry about."

Merrill nodded. "Good man. See you tomorrow."

****

R.J.'s mind churned on the drive home. He'd been hoping to take Josie out for a nice dinner for Valentine's Day next month, but if they got recognized together in public, Merrill would be livid. Oh, God, Merrill wouldn't make her go on sham dates with Beau, would he? She'd hardly be the first actress set up like that. He knew it was innocent between her and Beau but seeing her out on another man's arm would still hurt. Cassie probably wouldn't like it much either. He shook his head. He couldn't worry about this right now. Josie was waiting for him.

When he got home, he flung some food in Sergeant's bowl and dived into the shower. The stage lights made him so sweaty, and he couldn't show up at Josie's smelling like the swamp in July. Especially not if they were about to do what he hoped they were about to do.

Should he stop for condoms? There was a late-night drugstore on the way to Josie's. Maybe he should. But what if he was wrong and Josie just needed to cuddle? Besides, she said she had a diaphragm. He should probably let her take control of this. If he wanted her to trust him, he needed to show he trusted her too.

He shaved after he got out of the shower, the sting of the aftershave making his eyes water. He checked the clock—7:30. Time to get scooting. He dashed to his bedroom and pulled on a pair of jeans and a white T-shirt, hoping against hope his clothes would end up on the floor of Josie's bedroom. The thought made it hard to zip his jeans.

He scratched Sergeant's head before he left. "All right, boy, behave yourself," he said. The dog whined, clearly upset that R.J. was leaving so soon after getting home. "I'll make it up to you this weekend. We'll go to the beach or something." He checked that Sergeant had plenty of water and that the dog door was unlocked—thank God he'd put that in. He ruffled the boxer's uncropped ears one last time and headed for the car.

The twenty-minute cruise along Santa Monica

Boulevard felt like an eternity. When he finally reached Josie's apartment building, he sprinted up the stairs. His chest was heaving and his heart pounding by the time he reached her door, and he didn't think it was just from climbing the stairs. He leaned against the doorframe for a moment, gulping air.

Here went nothing.

Chapter Fifty-Seven

Josie's stomach started fluttering the minute she got home from the studio. R.J.'s conversation with Merrill would give her a little time before he arrived. No idea how much, but some. She took a quick shower and, hair dripping, towel wrapped around her body, stared into her closet.

What in the world should she wear? Did it even matter if her outfit was going to come right back off? What would R.J. be wearing? She imagined undressing him bit by bit, slowly uncovering that last part of his body she hadn't yet seen, and her lower half throbbed.

She decided it didn't matter what she wore. She pulled on her underthings and a light cotton dress with a simple zipper in the back. No use bothering with a slip. The less she had to remove, the better. She brushed her hair, left it loose to dry, and went into the kitchen to find something to eat.

She gave up trying to eat after half a cold chicken leg left over from last night. She was too nervous. Not only nervous, she realized, but excited. Any time the old panic tried to well up, she imagined R.J. shirtless, wrapping her in a quilt, cradling her in his lap. He loved her. He would never hurt her. The thought calmed her right back down.

But for Pete's sake, he needed to hurry up.

She went to the bathroom for at least the fifth time

since she'd gotten home—being anxious always made her have to pee—and put in her diaphragm while she was there. She was ready.

A knock sounded on the front door as she headed back toward the living room, and she jumped.

This is it, Josie Girl. Go get him.

She threw open the door, and there he stood, in jeans and a white T-shirt with the sleeves rolled. She thought at first that he'd gelled his hair, but realized that, like hers, it was damp. He must have showered before he came over. He smelled of soap and aftershave. The fluttering in her stomach disappeared, replaced by an ache deep in her belly.

Good gravy, she loved him.

She couldn't stand not having her hands on him any longer. She grabbed his elbow and yanked him inside.

She slammed and bolted the door, then threw her arms around him and kissed him. He moaned and pressed against her. Even through his jeans, she could tell he was already hard, and she pressed back. He broke off the kiss and stepped back, panting.

"I just want to make sure I haven't misunderstood," he said. "Did you want to—"

She placed a finger over his lips to silence him.

"I already have my diaphragm in," she said.

His cheek got the deepest dimple she'd ever seen, and he scooped her up. As he carried her to the bedroom, she rested her head against his chest and closed her eyes.

This was what it was supposed to be like. Safe in a good man's strong arms.

When they reached the bedroom—a short walk in her tiny apartment—he set her down and kissed her softly. Then he leaned in close and whispered in her ear,

"Remember what I said last time. If I do anything you don't like, just say so, and I'll stop."

She nodded, and he reached behind her and slowly unzipped her dress. He slid it off her shoulders, and she let it drop to the floor and kicked it aside, glad she hadn't bothered to put on shoes. She stood there in nothing but her bra and panties, surprised by her lack of fear. She should have started shaking ages ago, but R.J.'s soft smile and his eyes sweeping languidly up and down her body were a tonic for her nerves. When he stepped toward her, she didn't even think about backing away.

"Maybe you should take your shoes off," she said. He chuckled, sat on the bed, and pulled off his shoes and socks.

"And get rid of this," she said, tugging on his T-shirt. He'd stood again, and she was too short to pull it over his head.

"Yes, ma'am." He pulled it off and tossed it on the floor. She ran her hands over his bare chest and down to his waist.

This time, he didn't draw back when she reached for his belt buckle. She unbuckled it and unfastened his jeans. She grabbed the waistbands of both his jeans and his boxer shorts and started to tug them down, but R.J. smiled and took hold of her hands.

"Let's take our time." He uncurled her fingers from his boxers and let her pull down his jeans. He stepped out of them and kicked them aside near her dress. Then he pulled back the blankets on the bed, picked her up again, and laid her down.

When he slid onto the mattress next to her, she thanked her stars she'd bought the bed new and not secondhand like the rest of her furniture. The squawking sofa was funny, but she would have died of embarrassment if the bed gave a blow-by-blow commentary of what was about to happen. She focused her eyes on R.J., grateful to be able to give him all her attention.

Not breaking eye contact, he trailed the fingers of his right hand down her body, over her breasts, and along her stomach to her panty line, his touch leaving fire trails on her skin. Her breath caught as he traced her outline through her underwear.

"This okay?" he said.

"Oh, God, yes," she said. She reached out and stroked him through his shorts. He closed his eyes and sighed.

This was what true desire felt like. Warm and throbbing and urgent. A desperation to feel him inside of her. She needed to be naked. Now. She reached behind her back, struggling to unfasten her bra.

"Let me help you with that," R.J. said. He put his arms around her, fumbled for a moment, and popped her bra free. Pulling it away, he buried his face in her bosom, kissing first one breast, then the other. His skin was smooth, missing his usual five o'clock shadow. She dissolved under his soft touch as he circled her nipples with his tongue. Whichever one he wasn't kissing, he kneaded softly, every caress like an act of gratitude.

She reached again for his boxers, and this time, he didn't stop her. She slid them off his legs and drank him in. The solid chest that gave way to a hard, flat stomach. The long, tanned legs.

And in between?

Good gravy.

The sight of his arousal made her core throb even

harder, almost painfully. If he didn't take her soon, she might burst. He trailed kisses from her lips to her throat, her collarbone, each breast, and down her stomach until he reached her underwear. He cast his eyes up to her, eyebrows raised, and she nodded. Her panties were wet with her desire and nothing more than a barrier she didn't want. She shivered as he hooked his index fingers around the waistband and slowly pulled them off.

She lay there, stretched out full length on the bed, perfectly relaxed. He stared at her body and sighed, then met her gaze. His eyes asked her another question, and once again, she nodded. He settled himself between her legs and studied her a bit longer. She groaned. What was he waiting for? She grabbed his waist and tried to pull him to her. He chuckled and trailed his fingers down the length of her body. When he reached the thatch of hair below her belly button, he paused. She willed him to keep going and moaned when he did, gasping as he passed over her sensitive little mound of flesh to the folds around her entrance. He traced a circle, his finger slipping in her slickness. He smiled.

Bless him, he was checking to see if she was ready. Ethan had never checked, let alone cared. Tears rose to her eyes.

R.J. lowered himself onto her, their chests pressed together, and their lips meeting. The head of him pressed against her opening, and she went rigid.

No, she wouldn't panic. Not now. Not when they'd come this far. She gulped air.

He propped himself on his forearms, his eyes brimming with concern.

"Josie, we don't have to. If you're scared, we can wait."

She stared into those hazel eyes she'd come to know so well, the beautiful gold flecks like stardust brushed across the brown base. Calm washed over her. Calm, and a determination to banish the last of the ghosts Ethan had left behind. "I want this with you. Tonight."

R.J. nodded, that stubborn lock of hair falling over his brow. "If at any point you've had enough, just say so, and we'll stop. Okay? Doesn't matter how far along we are." His pupils were wide, reducing his irises to a thin ring, and he gnawed his lower lip.

He was nervous too.

A surge of love coursed through her so strong that if she spoke, she'd cry. She caressed his cheek, slid her hand to the back of his head, and pulled him down for a kiss.

"Don't worry," he said when he pulled back, "I'm going to take good care of you. I love you so much."

With one hand, he guided himself back to her entrance and gently nudged inside her. She was so wet he slid in smoothly, praising her softness as he settled into her. When he'd sunk to his root and their pelvises met, she gasped. He filled her perfectly, her body stretching easily to accommodate his. Nothing painful, nothing frightening. Just blissful connection.

"You okay?" he said. His breathing was rapid and shallow.

She nodded, needing to swallow before she could speak. "You feel amazing."

His dimple appeared, and he caressed her cheek before wrapping both arms around her.

Their bodies needed no introduction, rocking together as if they'd been meant for nothing else. Thrills shot up Josie's spine with each thrust, a ball of heat building deep in her core. A sound somewhere between a purr and a growl escaped from her throat, and R.J. moved faster, gasping out the occasional word.

Sweet.

Beautiful.

Love.

His sighs in her ear turned to throaty groans, and he clutched her tighter as if he could meld their bodies together. She knotted his hair around her fingers, ran her hands down his back, clutched his hips, begged for more of him, all of him.

He complied with harder thrusts, not painful but urgent. He must be getting close. The thought of him spilling out inside her turned the heat in her core to fire. She bucked her hips as he moved faster still, building a pressure that nearly drove her mad until all at once the fire broke loose. Everything disappeared except this astonishing man inside her. Wave after wave of joy coursed through her body until she forgot what it had been like to feel anything else.

When at last her release receded and her senses returned, she whispered into R.J.'s ear, "Let go, sweetheart."

With a strangled half-sob, R.J. buried his face in her neck and called her name as he held himself deep inside her.

Chapter Fifty-Eight

Even as the last wave of his orgasm drained away and he softened, R.J. couldn't bring himself to pull out of her. Josie's arms were still wrapped around him, and he clung to her a long time. He couldn't stop trembling. He'd slept with a few women over the past couple years, but this was the first time since things went bad with Laura that he'd made love. And he almost hated to admit it, since Laura was the mother of his child, but he'd never felt anything this passionate with her. Josie breathed life into him.

He kissed her forehead and slowly, reluctantly, withdrew and collapsed onto the bed. He pulled her into his arms, and she snuggled against his chest. A lump rose in his throat. He'd forgotten what it felt like to be loved so completely—if he'd ever known it at all.

He stroked her hair. "I didn't hurt you, did I?"

She propped herself on one elbow and traced lazy circles in his chest hair with her other index finger.

"That was perfect." She kissed him. "I came."

R.J. chuckled at the surprise in her voice. He was damn proud of himself for that. He kissed the tip of her nose. "I noticed. So did I."

She giggled and nuzzled her head back onto his chest. "I love you so much," she said.

Peace coursed through him. "I love you too." He ran a hand idly across her hip. In the dim light of the bedside lamp, he could make out the peaks and valleys of her body under the blankets. She must be strong from handling patients, but she seemed so small, so vulnerable. How could anyone abuse such a perfect creature? He clutched her a little more tightly and closed his eyes. He'd be damned if anyone ever hurt her again.

He could have lain there forever, but after a minute or two, his stomach let out a loud growl. Josie snickered and propped herself up again.

"Are you hungry?"

He stretched and rubbed his stomach. "I'm fine." He didn't ever want to leave this bed, even if it meant starving to death.

His stomach grumbled again, and Josie gave him a skeptical look. "You're hungry," she said.

Dammit. He sighed and rubbed his temples.

"I skipped dinner so I could get over here sooner."

She laughed and sat up. "No need to starve when I have a kitchen full of food. You want an omelet?"

An omelet sounded amazing. He could get up for that. He grinned. "Only if you let me cook."

Fifteen minutes later, they sat at Josie's little table eating omelets he'd stuffed full of chopped vegetables and cheese. Josie pulled out a bottle of wine she said she'd gotten as a Christmas gift at the hospital. She was naked under her bathrobe, and all he'd thrown back on were his boxer shorts, but the meal felt even more elegant than the one they'd had at the Christmas party. And the thin fabric of Josie's bathrobe left so little to the imagination he liked it even more than the gown she'd worn to the party.

"How did your conversation with Merrill go?" she said, topping off their wine glasses.

He hesitated. He should tell her Merrill was on to them, but he hated to spoil the mood. He decided to go with just the good news for now. He beamed and told her about Deacon Bell's big episode. Josie squealed and planted a big kiss on him.

"It's such a relief," he said and rubbed the back of his neck. "I was seriously considering not re-signing for next season. It's no secret I haven't been happy. I wouldn't have even stayed on this season if the money weren't so good."

Better not to mention the possibility of three-year contracts, either. Wouldn't be good to get her hopes up in case Merrill couldn't work it out with the network.

Josie reached across the table and grabbed his hand. "I'm really glad you stayed." She winked.

He smiled and squeezed her hand. "Me too. And now I can stay, make a pile of money, *and* be happy. And not just happy with work either." He squeezed her hand again. "I've hit the jackpot."

"Me too." She grinned mischievously. "Because you're a good cook." He laughed, and she stretched one leg under the table and tickled the undersides of his feet with her toes. "I don't know about you, but I'm ready for some dessert."

His head snapped up. God above, he really had hit the jackpot. He must have grinned like a fool because Josie laughed, grabbed his hand, and dragged him back to the bedroom.

When they got there, he untied her bathrobe sash and slid the robe off her shoulders, letting it puddle on the floor around her feet. He'd never get tired of seeing her naked. She was lean but not skinny, and her toned arms and abs spoke to her years of hard work. She pressed her mouth hungrily against his and shoved his boxers off his hips. He kicked out of them and led her to the bed.

He lay down first and pulled her on top of him. Her eyes widened, and he froze. Oh, no, was he scaring her? Then her brow wrinkled, and it hit him: She was confused. From what she'd told him, she'd never done it from this position and probably had no idea what she was supposed to do. He smiled and playfully tweaked her nose.

"Don't think," he said. "Just do."

Holy smoke, did she ever.

She sat up, bracing her hands on his chest, and lowered herself onto him. He groaned as her warm, silky body embraced him again. He wanted to live inside her. She settled him as deeply as possible, and it was all he could do not to go off like a shot right then. He was damn glad he didn't. Josie rolled her hips, slowly at first, then faster, her moans turning to gasps. Within only a minute or two, she threw back her head and shrieked.

He watched her as she came, dark hair sticking to the sheen of sweat on her forehead, eyes scrunched shut, and a huge smile on her face.

He'd never seen anything so beautiful.

But he didn't get to watch her long because she brought him then, too, harder than he'd ever come, and the whole world exploded in bursts of white light.

He couldn't move. He didn't want to move. Josie collapsed onto his chest, trembling and sweaty, and peppered his face with kisses before slowly pulling off him and rolling onto the mattress.

"Good gravy!" she said.

"Good gravy nothing," he said, wiping his brow.

"Holy *shit*."

They laughed and snuggled up together. A couple minutes later, the clock in the living room struck 11:00, and his heart broke. He groaned and sat up.

"What's wrong?"

"Seven a.m. call tomorrow. We both need to get to bed." Stupid responsibilities. He started to swing his legs out of bed, but Josie caught him around the waist.

"We're already in bed, silly." She sat up and nibbled his earlobe. "Stay," she whispered.

His mind spun. He looked at his discarded clothes on the floor. He could wear those to work tomorrow. He'd be changing into his costume as soon as he arrived anyway. Was there anything at home he'd need for work? Dammit, what about the dog? He sighed.

"I can't leave Sergeant home alone that long."

Josie's face fell. "Right. I didn't think about that."

Her frown was going to be the death of him. There had to be something he could do. He racked his brain.

Josie is portable, R.J.

He grinned. "Come home with me."

Her nose wrinkled.

Thirty minutes later, they were at his house, washing up for bed. It was past midnight when he set his alarm clock for 6:00 and they slid beneath the sheets naked and cuddled up, Sergeant at their feet. They'd both probably have dark circles under their eyes in the morning, but Betty could work wonders with foundation. Feeling happier than he'd felt in years, R.J. twined his legs around Josie's and closed his eyes.

Chapter Fifty-Nine

When R.J.'s alarm clock rang far too soon, Josie groaned and buried her face in his chest. She heard him slapping around on the nightstand until the clock shut up.

"Good morning, Princess," he said and kissed her forehead.

She dragged a pillow over her head.

"I don't wanna go to school today."

He chuckled. "Me either. We'll have to start doing this on weekends instead. You want a shower?"

She shook her head, realized he couldn't see it from under the pillow, and said, "I'm all right. I showered last night." She didn't want to show up at the studio with wet hair. Betty was a wizard, but she pulled hard when she used a blow dryer. Besides, Josie didn't want to rinse away last night.

"Same here. I'll put some coffee on." R.J. patted her head through the pillow. "Come on, Sarge," he said, and she heard him open the door and walk into the hall.

Josie pulled the pillow off her head, rolled onto her back, and giggled. She'd just spent the night with Robert Coolidge. Who loved her.

She swung out of bed, pulled on the T-shirt R.J. had abandoned on the floor last night, and crossed the hall to the bathroom. She took out her diaphragm, rinsed it, and left it to dry on the counter with a whispered, "Thank you." Her stomach rumbled, so she headed for the

335

kitchen.

R.J. got a hungry look in his eyes when she trotted into the kitchen wearing nothing but his T-shirt. All he wore were his boxer shorts, and when he pulled her into his arms and pressed against her, there was no question that he was ready for a third go-round. She laughed and playfully swatted his behind.

"You'll make us late," she said.

He growled and let her go.

They didn't have time for much breakfast, just toast and coffee, but craft services never let the cast starve before lunch. There would be pastries partway through the morning. They sat at the table in the breakfast nook and played footsie while they ate. When the clock in the living room struck the half-hour, R.J. leaned back in his chair.

"Hey, listen," he said, an edge in his voice. "Merrill knows there's something going on between us."

Josie's heart leapt into her mouth. With the tension between R.J. and Merrill, this couldn't be good. "Did he say something to you last night?"

R.J. nodded. "He asked me to keep it quiet."

She laughed. "He felt he needed to ask *you*, of all people, to keep your private life private?"

R.J. chuckled. "I guess since he asked Beau the same thing, it was only fair. He wants to protect this illusion that you and Beau are a real-life item."

Her toes curled. "I am not going out with him."

R.J.'s face did a funny twitch, but then he smiled. "I don't think you need to. Merrill just doesn't want you seen out with me."

They couldn't go out? No dinners, no movies, no Disneyland? She felt like someone had just dunked her in cold water. Her giddiness drained away.

"Can he do that?" she said. "I thought that sort of control died with the studio system." The strict, long-term contracts the movie studios used to keep actors under had been gone for a decade. She'd checked into it before her *Gunslingers* audition because she wanted to make sure the network couldn't tell her she had to quit nursing altogether.

R.J.'s eyebrows shot up. "You've been doing your homework."

Josie shrugged. "Wanted to know what I was getting myself into."

"Contractually, no, he can't. But he and the tabloids could still be a huge pain in the neck if we don't toe the line." He reached across the table and took her hands. "All this means is we need to be careful, especially around the crew on set. You'd be amazed how much those guys love to gossip."

The corners of her mouth pulled up ever so slightly. If R.J. wasn't too worried, maybe she shouldn't be either.

"I never get recognized in public," R.J. continued, "and with a scarf and sunglasses on, you won't either. Especially if we take your car instead of mine."

That was a good point. The Impala was less conspicuous than the Corvette.

"This doesn't change a thing, Princess. Besides..." He grinned. "I like staying in with you."

Chapter Sixty

"What's got you so cocky this morning?" Charlie asked when R.J. strutted into the dressing room one morning in mid-February.

R.J. smirked. "I bought Josie's Valentine's gift last night."

Charlie's fingers paused on the shirt buttons he was doing up. "Oh, yeah? What did you get her?"

R.J. reached into his jacket pocket and pulled out a long, thin jewelry box. He popped it open to show off a strand of glittering pearls. Charlie ambled over and took a closer look.

"These are beautiful," he said. "She'll love them."

R.J. grinned. Like Merrill, Charlie had figured out pretty quickly that he and Josie were an item. Unlike Merrill, Charlie seemed pleased.

Beau moaned. He'd come over and looked at the necklace, too, and now his face was awfully pale.

"What's the matter with you?" Charlie said.

Beau ran his hands down his face. "All I got Cassie was a box of chocolates."

R.J. chomped hard on his lower lip to keep from laughing. He hadn't been trying to show Beau up—he'd just thought how stunning the pearls would look against Josie's black hair—but this was a great side effect. Josie and Cassie were sure to compare gifts. Beau was toast.

"If we get done early enough tonight, I'll take you

over to the jeweler's that Nancy loves," Charlie said. "I'm sure he has plenty of pretty little baubles that will make Cassie very happy."

R.J. chuckled at the relief on Beau's face and slipped the necklace box back in his jacket pocket. He couldn't wait to see the pearls on Josie. It was just a shame he couldn't take her out someplace fancy for dinner. But he was picking up a nice meal from a steakhouse Ed had recommended, and he and Josie had decided to get dressed up anyway, even if they'd just be sitting at his dining room table. He'd even bought a bow tie for Sergeant.

He glanced at his wristwatch. Josie might already be on set. He hustled into his costume and hurried over to the soundstage.

At lunch in the commissary, Charlie had everyone laughing at a story about his and Nancy's disastrous first Valentine's Day together when Merrill approached their table. R.J. straightened. Things had been better between him and Merrill lately, but the producer still made him antsy.

"Josie," Merrill said, wearing that grimace-smile. "The network's had an interview request for you."

Josie looked around at him, Charlie, and Beau, her eyes wide. R.J. grinned. He knew she'd done several interviews at the beginning of the season, but she hadn't mentioned any since then. He hoped it was *TV Week*.

"Why did it come to you instead of her agent?" Beau asked.

"I haven't got one," Josie said. She looked at Merrill. "Who is it?"

Merrill snickered. "*Celebrity Whispers*."

Josie's lip curled, and the men laughed. Beau

squeezed her shoulder.

"It's all right, Josie," he said. "My agent just got a request from them too."

"Mine too," R.J. said. He'd been annoyed Larry had even called him about it. He knew to turn down nearly every request that came in, especially if they were from rags like *Celebrity Whispers*.

"Mine didn't," Charlie said and shrugged. "Guess I'm too old to be interesting."

"Did you take it?" Josie said to Beau.

Beau shook his head so hard his combed-back curls sprang free and bounced over his brow. Josie looked to R.J.

He laughed. "What do you think?"

She snickered.

"Don't feel obligated," Merrill said. "I like what they've done for our ratings, but the gossip magazines know better than to expect stars to talk to them directly. I'm happy to tell them you're too busy."

"Thank you," Josie said.

Merrill patted her shoulder. "Anytime, kid. Hoping to have some news for you soon about next season."

She looked at R.J., her green eyes shining with excitement. His heart soared.

Merrill turned to the men. "Come see me later, gentlemen. I've already got specifics for you all."

Josie squeezed R.J.'s hand under the table.

****

"It's a forty-percent raise," R.J. said, still hardly able to believe it. He'd spent the past few days completely boggled by the amount of money in the three-year contracts Merrill offered him and Beau. He ran a hand across his mouth. "I was so stunned when Merrill said the number I couldn't even do the math. Beau had to work it out for me." In fact, when Merrill had said "six thousand per episode," he'd nearly swallowed his tongue. And Charlie would make even more. R.J. could hardly imagine it.

Josie laughed, reached across the table, and squeezed his hand. She looked stunning in her new string of pearls. He'd given it to her when he picked her up, and for a second, he thought she was going to burst into tears. They were perfect with the sapphire gown she had on. He was pretty sure it was the same dress Cassie had worn to the Christmas party, but Josie wore it better. He wanted to peel it off her right here in the middle of the dining room.

"I assume you're going to sign it?" she said.

He grinned. "Already did. All three of us signed on the spot."

"What are you going to do with it all?" Josie's eyes were gigantic. Probably imagining the raise she might be in store for. He hoped it was huge.

He chuckled. "No idea. I'm still too stunned. Save most of it, probably, though Laura could use a new car. She and Matthew are rattling around in her dad's '38 Buick. Thing's gonna disintegrate underneath them any day now." Josie giggled. "Right now, though, how about some champagne?" He ducked into the kitchen and returned with a bottle of Dom Perignon.

This is the life, R.J.

He was still relieved dinner hadn't been cold by the time they'd gotten back to his house. Josie usually drove to his place for the weekends, but he'd decided to pick her up tonight after he grabbed the food so it felt more like a date. When he arrived, Mrs. Pullman had come out of her apartment next door and struck up a conversation. She went on and on about Josie's beautiful new necklace and what a handsome couple Josie and R.J. were. Though she never could remember R.J.'s name. To be safe, Josie introduced him by his middle name, Jeremy, and Mrs. Pullman called him just about every "J" name but. In ten minutes, she called him John, Jerry, Joe, Jeffrey, and Jacob. He couldn't be rude to such a sweet and confused old lady, but as the minutes ticked by, he'd started to sweat. Thank God Josie finally cut in and said they had to get going.

And thank God they were staying at his place. Josie said the walls in her apartment were thin, and he didn't want to keep Mrs. Pullman up all night.

Chapter Sixty-One

Josie's hands shook as she turned the knob on Merrill's office door the following Friday. She'd guessed this conversation was coming since he'd dropped that hint last week about next season, but now it was here. She was sure he was keeping her on part time, but was she getting a raise like the guys were? Much as she loved nursing, she'd love even more to have just one job. And she'd prefer that job be *Gunslingers*. Even a small raise would give her enough of a cushion in her savings account that she'd feel comfortable leaving the hospital.

Merrill stood and smiled when she stepped into his office. He gestured to a chair in front of his desk, and she smoothed her skirt and sat. They were done shooting for the day, but she hadn't changed out of her costume yet. She was too anxious to change first. Her eyes went straight to a photograph that hadn't been on Merrill's desk the last time she was in the office. It was the whole gang at the Christmas party, including Cassie, Merrill, and Merrill's and Charlie's wives. She smiled, remembering how R.J. had put his hand on her back while they posed.

"Cigarette?" Merrill said, holding out a pack of Camels. Josie shook her head. "Drink?" He gestured to a small shelf with a few bottles behind him. She was about to decline again when she spotted a familiar label.

"I can never say no to Mr. Beam."

Merrill smiled again. Good gravy, he had an odd smile, like someone was pinching him. But he grabbed two lowballs and the bottle of Jim Beam and poured them each two fingers, neat. They clinked glasses, and she let her first long sip linger on her tongue, relaxing into the familiar burn.

The producer folded his cube-shaped body into his tall leather chair and sipped his whiskey. One corner of his mouth turned up.

"I never would have guessed you were a bourbon girl," he said.

She grinned. "I have—"

"Five older brothers," he finished and chuckled. "You need to bring them out here sometime. I think we'd all be interested to meet them."

"Be careful what you wish for."

He chuckled again and leaned forward on his desk. "I just got our ratings for last month, and *Gunslingers* is still gaining ground. The network is so happy that they've renewed us for three more seasons. And just like I thought, it was that episode with Mary and Judah's first kiss that really turned the tide in our favor. Our audience loves your character so much I've told the writers to start working on long-term storylines for her."

A squeak of joy slipped out. "Thank you," she said, almost breathless. "I'd love nothing more than to return next season."

Merrill smiled back. "It's not just a return next season. We're bringing you on full time for the next three years at three thousand per episode. We'll add your name to the main title alongside Beau's and Coolidge's. I'll have the contract ready in a couple weeks."

She almost dropped her Jim Beam. She was now a full-time actress. She could move somewhere with a swimming pool. She could replace her sofa! And she'd get to be with R.J. and Beau and Charlie every day. She had to get out of here and call R.J. No, forget calling him. She wanted to tell him in person so they could celebrate. They usually spent weeknights apart, but today called for an exception. But she did need to call Cassie. And Leighton. And maybe the *Hays Daily News*, just to rub it in.

Then she realized Merrill was staring at her.

Good gravy, Josie Girl, say something.

She stammered several times before she managed a "Thank you!"

Merrill laughed. "You're quite welcome. And deserving. You and me, kid, we're gonna make the viewers forget all about Miss Kitty and the Long Branch Saloon."

"You bet we will. I've been to Dodge City. It ain't such a much."

Merrill laughed and pulled *Celebrity Whispers* from under a stack of papers on his desk. "Just don't get caught out in public with Coolidge. You keep up this illusion with Beau, and we'll go straight to the top."

Heat shot through her cheeks. She supposed she shouldn't be surprised that Merrill was finally saying something to her about her relationship with R.J. He had to look out for the show. Besides, this would be easy. She and R.J. were already staying in. If *Gunslingers'* ratings needed another boost, she and Beau could go grocery shopping together. Let the photographers snap a few photos of them picking out fruit. She smiled.

Merrill smiled back and extended his hand across

his desk. Josie leaned forward and shook it. He raised his glass and said, "Your good health, my dear." Josie clinked her glass against his and downed the rest of her bourbon.

Chapter Sixty-Two

R.J. could tell by the huge smile on Josie's face that something great had happened. As soon as he opened his front door, she jumped at him, threw her arms around his neck, and kissed him, Sergeant bouncing around their feet.

"What is it?" he said when she finally let him pull back.

"Guess who's joining the cast full time for the next three seasons?"

He let out a whoop, grabbed her around the waist, and spun her in a circle. She laughed and hugged him around the neck again. Full time. Josie would be on set with him every day. And he'd never seen her so happy.

"Please tell me you already have your diaphragm in," he murmured in her ear.

"I do."

The chicken he was making for dinner would be all right in the oven a bit longer. He carried her to the bedroom to celebrate.

Later, as they ate a slightly dry chicken, Josie gushed about her conversation with Merrill.

"I was tempted to go straight to the hospital and resign, but I'm waiting until I actually sign the contract. Merrill said he should have it ready in a couple weeks."

He grinned. "I bet you told Cassie already."

She ducked her head. "May have." She rolled her

eyes. "Merrill did remind me that I need to keep up the illusion that I'm with Beau. Told me not to get caught out in public with you."

R.J. tightened his grip on his fork. Merrill talking to Josie about her love life was inappropriate. "He shouldn't have brought it up," he said, "especially since he already talked to me."

Josie waved a hand dismissively. "He's just basking in his glory over that dumb tabloid article. Let him bask."

Something about it still left him unsettled, but he didn't want to burst Josie's bubble. She was so excited about her new contract.

She sighed. "I can't believe I only have two more episodes to shoot. You've got, what? One more week after I'm done?"

He nodded.

"You know," Josie said, flashing a coy smile, "I'll have resigned from the hospital by then. We'll both be off for those two months of hiatus." She winked. "Any idea how we can fill the time?"

R.J. grinned, leaned across the table, and kissed the tip of her nose. They'd been spending their weeknights separately so they could see their friends and get enough sleep to function. He knew it was good for them to spend time apart, but he still spent most of the week begging the weekend to hurry up so Josie would be back in his arms. Sometimes, especially on Sunday nights after she went home, he'd wake in the middle of the night, startled that she wasn't in bed beside him.

He wanted her in bed with him every night, and not just for lovemaking. The sex was fantastic, but he craved her company. Snuggling on the sofa and watching television or getting a little tipsy off Jim Beam while playing cards. A couple weeks ago, they'd had dinner at Ed and Lucy's, and the two couples had sat up long after the kids went to bed, drinking wine and swapping stories. She fit seamlessly into his world. He knew it was fast, but when her apartment lease was up in June, he planned to ask her to move in. Even Ed, who he'd expected would try to talk him out of it, had said it was a good idea. R.J. had never been more certain of anything in his life.

"Of course, Matthew will be here that week of Easter," he said. "Laura and I got it all set up. I bought his plane ticket last week. I promised to take him back to Disneyland." He caught her eye. "He asked if you could go with us. You still wanna come along?"

She pressed a hand to her heart. "I'd love to." She paused. "Do you think it's safe?"

He wasn't sure, but he desperately wanted the three of them to go together. He squeezed Josie's hand and let go, leaning back in his chair. "Just keep your sunglasses on. Besides, having a child with us will throw people off."

If anyone wanted to dig deeply enough, they could find out about Matthew, but R.J. was glad he'd been able to keep his son out of the press. He hadn't mentioned him in any of the few interviews he gave when *Gunslingers* premiered. He'd chosen this life; Matthew hadn't. Maybe someday Matthew would choose it, but for now, he'd keep his little guy to himself.

Chapter Sixty-Three

Josie arrived at the studio Monday morning still exhilarated and pink-cheeked, both from the promise of her contract and her weekend with R.J. Her heart had never felt as full as when he told her Matthew asked her to come along to Disneyland. That little boy was such a beautiful gift. She skipped onto the soundstage and patted Sugar, happy that she'd get to ride the little mare today. When Beau arrived a couple minutes later, she greeted him with a big hug and a kiss on the cheek.

"You're in an awfully good mood," he said, laughing. "Have a nice weekend?" He winked.

"Of course," she said, winking back. "But it's more than just that. I'm coming back full time next season."

Beau whooped like R.J. had and hugged her a second time.

"I'm so happy for you," he said. "And for me! Work's always more fun with you here." He glanced around. "Where's Robert?"

"I don't know. He and Charlie both should have been here by now."

Charlie's horse, a big blue roan gelding named Outlaw, nickered from the hitching rail on set, and Josie turned around. That horse loved Charlie. If Outlaw were happy, it could mean only one thing. A big smile broke across her face as Papa Bear stepped into the soundstage, but her smile fell as fast as it appeared. Charlie's face, usually so bright and friendly, was dark, his mouth a thin line. Behind him was R.J., his face ashen and stunned.

Josie's mouth went sour. She exchanged a glance with Beau, and they darted over to Charlie and R.J.

Charlie didn't waste time on greetings. "We have a problem," he said and held out a magazine. "My wife found this at the newsstand yesterday."

Josie recognized the banner of *Celebrity Whispers* and snatched it. Her breath stuck in her throat.

"*Gunslingers* Love Triangle!" the front cover screamed in bold type underneath publicity headshots of her, Beau, and R.J.

Oh, dear Lord.

She glanced up at R.J. He looked like he was about to vomit.

"It's bad, Josie," he said. He wouldn't meet her eye.

With Beau hanging over her shoulder, she flipped to the story.

"*Gunslingers*' Josephine Donovan has certainly ingratiated herself with her castmates. While in public she kisses Beau Fraser, in private, it would seem she's canoodling with Robert Coolidge.

"Sources tell us that just a few nights before being spotted with Mr. Fraser at Los Angeles International Airport, Miss Donovan and Mr. Coolidge heated up the dance floor at the WBC Christmas party at the Los Angeles Biltmore. They left together in Mr. Coolidge's car at the end of the night."

Inset, next to the photo of her kissing Beau at the airport, was a larger photo of R.J. dipping her at the end of the last dance. His lips were a hairsbreadth from her throat, and her hand rested low on his hip.

She gasped. She hadn't realized at the time how

close her hand was to his rear end. She looked like she was about to goose him. "Who took that photo?" she said. She couldn't bear to look at R.J. He must be mortified. She looked at Charlie instead.

Charlie shrugged. "There were a couple hundred people there. Could have been anyone." He pointed to the magazine. "It gets worse."

Josie kept reading.

"A neighbor in Miss Donovan's building said she's often seen Miss Donovan kissing a tall, dark-haired man outside her apartment, but early one morning just before Christmas, she saw a man matching Mr. Fraser's description arrive at Miss Donovan's door instead."

Josie felt like all the air had been sucked out of her lungs. Sweet, confused Mrs. Pullman. Some unscrupulous reporter took advantage of the poor old woman. The butterflies in Josie's stomach turned to burbling lava. She gripped the magazine so tightly the edges of the pages crumpled.

"We were sharing a cab to the airport," she said. If she ground her teeth any harder, she'd turn her molars to sand. "It was innocent."

Charlie laid a hand on her shoulder. "I know, sweetheart."

Behind her, Beau moaned. "Josie, there's more."

She looked back at the article.

"But this isn't the first time Miss Donovan hasn't been able to make up her mind where men are concerned. We found a divorce record from April 1957 for one Josephine Donovan from an Ethan Winchester of Hays, Kansas, after less than a year of marriage. Miss Donovan refused to speak with us, but in interviews with other publications, she has said she moved to Los Angeles in

May that same year.

"Whatever her reasons for leaving her husband, Miss Donovan would do well to investigate her paramours more closely. Mr. Coolidge has quite the past himself. In 1958, his then-wife sued for divorce on the grounds he'd abandoned her and their then-five-year-old son, leaving them behind in South Carolina while he moved to Los Angeles to pursue his acting career. According to court documents, Mr. Coolidge did not deny the charge. Mr. Coolidge also refused our request for an interview.

"Caught in the middle is poor, bamboozled Mr. Fraser. A favorite among female *Gunslingers* fans, the young Canadian could not be reached for comment. He may have been too busy nursing his broken heart."

The eggs and toast Josie ate for breakfast threatened to make a second appearance. In front of her, R.J.'s stricken face went hazy. She gripped Charlie's arm, digging her fingers in, and he guided her to a chair and told her to sit down. Beau plopped on the floor next to her chair. R.J. stayed put a few feet away.

"I guess now we know why they wanted interviews," Beau said, dropping his head in his hands.

Josie's mind raced. They made it sound like she was some floozy who'd gotten sick of her husband and just decided to split. They hadn't even reported the reason for her divorce. Surely it was in the court records. R.J.'s was.

Oh, R.J.

Her mind swam with the memory of his tear-filled eyes when he told her he hadn't abandoned his family. That he and Laura realized they were no good for each other, and he still took care of them. He'd swallowed his pride and asked Merrill for a week off so he could visit

353

his boy. He flew Matthew out at every opportunity. He planned to buy Laura a new car, for crying out loud. He'd done everything right by her and Matthew, including not fighting the divorce because she deserved her freedom, and now he was paying for it anyway. That reporter had done just about the worst thing anyone could do to Robert Coolidge: Waved his personal life around for everyone to see. Worse still, they'd included his child in it.

And it was all her fault.

If she hadn't kissed Beau in the airport, none of this would have happened.

A sob tore from her aching throat, and she wrapped her arms around her stomach and cried.

Three hands landed on her at once. Two on her back, and one very familiar one on her shoulder. She looked up. R.J. had finally closed the gap between them and stood looking down at her, his face tight, like a post-surgical patient whose morphine just wore off.

"R.J., I'm so, so sorry," she choked out. "This is my fault."

His face crumpled, and he pulled her out of the chair and into his arms. Right there, in front of the entire cast and crew, he held her to him and stroked her hair.

"This is not your fault," he said. "It's theirs, and theirs alone."

"And mine," Beau said from behind them, his voice trembling. "Josie, I'm sorry. I never should have encouraged you to flirt with me at the airport."

"No one could have known how this would play out," Charlie said. "Besides, these things blow over. Two weeks from now, everyone will be so caught up in the next fabricated scandal they won't even remember this."

****

Josie went through the motions that morning, never missing a mark or a line, but with her stomach in knots the whole time. Despite what the men said, this still felt like her fault. Adding to the dread was knowing she had to call Leighton tonight. She had to warn the family this was coming. The Winchesters were going to be unbearable.

Merrill appeared just before lunch. He'd been working on a late-season pilot for a new show, so he'd missed seeing her burst into tears this morning, thank goodness. But his face was pinched when he arrived at the soundstage, clutching a magazine in his hand. Josie had a terrible feeling she knew which magazine it was.

"Josie, could I have a word, please?" he said. His voice was calm, but the tone rang false. She wrapped her arms around her midsection.

"We're about to go to lunch, Merrill," Charlie said. "Could it wait?"

Tears sprang to Josie's eyes. Good old Papa Bear. But she'd much rather get this conversation over with, and she didn't have any appetite anyway.

"It's all right, Charlie," she said. She caught R.J.'s eye and gave him a tight smile. Then she turned and followed Merrill to his office.

As soon as the door closed behind them, Merrill motioned for her to sit, tossed *Celebrity Whispers* on his desk, and dropped into his leather-backed chair. He steepled his fingers under his chin and studied her. This probably should have made her nervous, but she was already so wrung out she couldn't muster any more emotions. She stared blankly back.

"I take it you've seen this," he said at last, pointing

to the magazine.

She nodded.

He exhaled loudly through his nose, but his face stayed steady, contemplative, even. "You told me you weren't married."

"I'm not."

He studied her a bit longer, and that lava burbled in her gut again. She was beginning to understand why R.J. hated questions about his personal life so much. People were awfully nosy about things that didn't concern them.

"You asked me the question in the present tense," she said. "'*Are* you married?' You did not ask 'Have you ever been married?' I answered you truthfully."

Merrill's eyes turned flinty. "You had an obligation to tell me."

She stifled a growl. She was not going to let another man push her around. She narrowed her eyes and stared right back at him.

"I most certainly did not. Besides, my divorce is public record." She pointed to the magazine. "Apparently it doesn't take a genius to look me up."

Merrill's nostrils flared, and Josie was certain he was about to start shouting, but instead, he spun his chair toward his liquor shelf. When he turned back around, he held two lowballs of Jim Beam. He handed her one. She downed it in a single gulp, the bourbon trailing fire down her throat. Merrill sipped his.

"You've had an upsetting morning, so I'll ignore that sass," he said, "but we still need to talk about this. I'm prepared to make a statement in your defense, but before I can do that, I need all the facts. Specifically, why did you leave your husband?"

God above, she was so sick of Ethan Winchester.

Three years later, and he was still haunting her. Well, she wasn't giving him any more screen time. She crossed her arms over her chest to keep them from shaking with rage, leaned back in her chair, and stared Merrill dead in the eye.

"None of your goddamn business."

Goodness, the bourbon made her bold.

Merrill thumped his fist on his desk and jumped to his feet. "Listen, young lady," he said, shouting now, "I'm trying to protect you here. This kind of scandal can wreck an actress's career. Now you either tell me why you left your husband, or I can recast your part."

His words were a slap across the face. Recast her part? *Replace* her? He couldn't. She loved this job. Her throat tightened, and she had to take several gulping breaths before she could speak.

"He raped me," she said, in barely more than a whisper.

Merrill choked on his bourbon.

"Repeatedly," she added, her voice stronger.

She couldn't believe how good it felt to say it aloud. Because it was true. Ethan had taken her violently against her will, marriage certificate be damned. She lifted her chin, her jaw set.

Merrill cleared his throat, then scoffed. "You can't rape your wife."

"I beg to differ." Josie stared him down, silently daring him to contradict her again. He didn't, and she sat up a little taller and continued. "He also fathered two children with another woman. One while we were engaged, the second shortly after our marriage. I divorced him for adultery. He didn't fight it. Convenient how *Whispers* left that out of the article."

"That's what they do," Merrill said, sitting back down. He suddenly looked very tired. "I'll issue that statement."

"What about Robert?" Josie said. "The article went after him, too, and you know damn well he didn't abandon his child."

Merrill sighed and pinched the bridge of his nose. "This kind of thing doesn't affect men the way it affects women. Look at Liberace, Frank Sinatra, Desi Arnaz. They can do whatever they want. Notice how the magazine talked to your neighbor and not his or Beau's. We don't have to worry about Coolidge's image like we do yours."

She narrowed her eyes. "So you're not defending me. You're defending my image."

"It's the same thing."

It wasn't. But she was tired of arguing with men. She thanked Merrill and stormed out of the office.

Chapter Sixty-Four

R.J. couldn't believe he didn't get dragged into Merrill's office, too, but that photo of him and Josie dancing had been taken months before the producer asked them to keep their relationship quiet. Maybe even Merrill realized he couldn't have done anything about it. But he wished Merrill had brought him and Josie in together. He hadn't been able to eat a bite at lunch while Josie was back in the office, and she wouldn't tell him much about the conversation except that Merrill was going to issue a statement explaining why she left Ethan.

He practically begged her to come over that night. He didn't want her to sit alone in her apartment, stewing in her embarrassment. And he wanted to hold her. To pull her into his lap, wrap his arms around her, and tell her everything would be all right. Because he was going to fix this somehow.

"I can't tonight," she said. "I need to call my family and warn them about the gossip they're going to hear." She shook her head. "The town's gonna eat this up. My nieces and nephews will hear about it at school…" A tear slid down her cheek, and he wiped it away. They were in the middle of the parking lot with some of the crew still milling around, but who cared? Thanks to *Celebrity Whispers*, everyone now knew they were an item.

"It's not your fault," he said.

She nodded but kept her eyes on her shoes. He could

tell that now wasn't the time to push her.

He placed a finger under her chin and tilted her head up. "All right. I should probably call Laura anyway, just in case Matthew hears something at school."

Her eyes filled with fresh tears. "I'm so sorry they wrote about him."

He was too. If he ever met the asshole who wrote this garbage, he'd drag him to Hell Hole and throw him to the alligators. But anger didn't solve anything right now. He shrugged.

"It's public record. Someone was bound to dig it up sooner or later. I'm just glad they didn't print his or Laura's names." He kissed her forehead, letting his lips linger on her soft skin. "I love you, Josie."

He was so relieved when she said, "I love you," back that his knees almost buckled. They still had each other. This would blow over, like Charlie said. Everything would be fine.

****

Things seemed better the next morning. Merrill had issued the press release regarding Josie's divorce, painting her—accurately—as an innocent young girl done wrong by a cruel adulterer. Part of R.J. wished Merrill had included a line for him, too, but part of him was glad he didn't. The less Matthew appeared in the press, even unnamed, the better.

He was surprised how well Laura had taken the news last night. She wasn't angry at him, just a little worried what Matthew might hear at school. But she pointed out that everyone in Hell Hole already knew the whole truth: That Will Coolidge's son was a good boy who took care of his family.

"They're probably gonna send that reporter hate

mail," she said.

He'd laughed at that. If Laura could joke about this, it really must be okay.

The cast ate lunch together as usual, and Josie seemed all right too. Relieved, even. As she should be, he thought. Merrill's press release had vindicated her. And they all had a good time teasing Beau about his poor, broken Canadian heart.

By Wednesday, everything was back to normal. R.J. was just about to slide into the Corvette at the end of the day when Merrill sidled up to the car. The little man was red-faced and puffing, like he'd been chasing after him. R.J. was surprised. They hadn't seen him on set today. Everybody had figured he was off working on that new pilot.

"Coolidge," Merrill said between gasps. "Can I have a word with you in my office?"

R.J. sighed. It was already almost 7:00 p.m., and he wanted to go home and call Josie. Maybe he could persuade her to come over tonight now that Monday's shock had worn off.

"Can it wait until tomorrow? I'm really tired."

Merrill's face was stone. "We need to talk now." His tone made R.J.'s stomach twist. This had to have something to do with that dumb magazine article. Oh, no. Was he rescinding Josie's offer?

Don't be ridiculous, R.J. Why would he tell you that instead of Josie?

Whatever it was, he wouldn't find out unless he went to the office. He shut the car door and followed Merrill.

When the producer's office door closed behind them, Merrill pointed R.J. to a chair and offered him a drink. R.J. shook his head. Whatever Merrill was about to say wasn't good, and he wanted his head clear. Merrill sat behind his desk and lit a cigarette. He took a long drag and blew it out slowly, the stale odor wafting over R.J.

"I was in meetings all morning with the network," he said. "They're not happy about this exposé on Josie."

R.J. ran a hand across his mouth. "And?"

"We have to fix her image. Quick. You know why they fired Frances Moore from *Front Desk* last year?"

R.J. shook his head. He'd heard an actress got fired, but he hadn't caught all the details. He didn't follow studio gossip.

"One of these rags caught her cheating on her husband. With multiple men. Mothers flooded the network with letters saying they wouldn't let their husbands and children watch the show so long as that bimbo was still on it. WBC prides itself on being a wholesome network, so they had to let her go."

R.J. knit his brow. "But you sent out that press release about Josie's divorce. She was the victim. She never cheated on anyone."

Merrill grabbed the copy of *Celebrity Whispers* on his desk, almost knocking over a photo of the cast from the Christmas party. The magazine fell open right to the page with the story about Josie, as if he'd turned to it a lot. He tapped the photos of R.J. and Josie dancing and of Josie kissing Beau's cheek, ash from his cigarette sprinkling on Josie's face.

"It sure looks like she has. The network isn't convinced the press release will be enough. They're already getting too many interview requests from other rags. Not to mention messages from outraged wives and mothers."

This was absurd. And it felt like someone had turned the heat up in this room about twenty degrees. Sweat broke out along R.J.'s hairline.

"So have Beau issue a statement saying the airport was all an act. Just a couple of kids having a laugh."

Merrill shook his head. "No good. Beau's squeaky-clean, and the press hasn't found out about his girlfriend. Our best shot at keeping Josie wholesome is to keep her close to him. Clinging to you is just going to tarnish her further. She'll look like she's man-hopping." He paused. "You have to break things off with her."

R.J. let out a shout of laughter. "You can't make me do that."

Merrill took another long drag on his cigarette. "No, but I'm sure you want to fix this, and breaking up with her is the only way Josie comes through this with her reputation intact."

R.J. waved a hand dismissively. "Her lease is up in a couple months. We'll move her somewhere more private. Somewhere without an addled old woman next door." Like his house, he thought but sure as hell wasn't going to say.

Merrill shook his head again. "The press is gunning for you now. They will tail you. They will send detectives to stake out your house and follow you around. You know how they figured out how late Frances Moore was staying at her lovers' houses? They put a wristwatch on the back tire of her car, so when she backed out she crushed it and stopped the time at the exact moment she left. These guys know every trick in the book, and they're inventing new ones every day. You cannot sneak around them."

"Then I'll marry her." The words were out of R.J.'s

mouth before his brain had any idea what was going on. But they were true. He would marry her. Deep down, he'd been hoping for it someday. And if it would fix this, he wouldn't wait. He'd do it now.

Merrill's head jerked back. "Shit, Coolidge, I didn't know it was that serious." The skin around his eyes softened, but then hardened again. "But I'm afraid that won't help either. Josie marries you, and she looks like a gullible little idiot." He tapped the magazine article again. "Because you've already deserted one wife, remember?"

R.J.'s hands curled into fists in his lap. He ought to give this sneering little troll a knuckle sandwich. But that wouldn't help. Well, it would help *him*, but it wouldn't help the situation.

"That's not true," he said between gritted teeth, "and you know it."

Merrill stubbed out his cigarette and leaned back in his chair, his chin disappearing behind the cast photo on his desk. "It's not about what I know, it's about what the public thinks. And right now, they think you're a cad and Josie's easy stuff. You're a man. Your career won't suffer. But Josie's…" He shrugged. "Mary Anderson saved our asses this season, and she's the main reason we're coming back for three more. To protect this show, I have to protect the character, and I see only two ways to do that. Either we fix Josie's image, or I recast her part."

R.J. scoffed. Merrill couldn't be serious. "Recast the part? You spent months looking for the perfect girl."

"Who I needed to make us stand out and get the audience invested in the character. That's done now."

Merrill had him backed against a wall with no exits.

He dug his fingernails into his palms.

"So, what you're saying is if I don't break up with Josie, you're gonna fire her."

The producer spread his hands. The son of a bitch had the nerve to try to look innocent.

"It's just the position I'm in," Merrill said. "It's nothing personal."

"And what's to stop me from marching straight to Josie's and telling her all about this conversation?"

Merrill lowered his head, a gator slinking in for a kill. "Because you know how much she loves this job, and you don't want her to lose it. You already hurt one woman—and a child—with your selfishness. Could you live with yourself if you did that again?"

The words punched him in the chest. He couldn't breathe. There was no air in his lungs. There was no air in this entire room.

Storm out of here, R.J. Go straight to Josie's and tell her everything. She'll choose you. You know she'll choose you.

His feet twitched, but he couldn't make himself stand. Because Merrill was right. Josie adored everything about this job. And he *had* hurt Laura with his selfishness. Dragging her to New York so he could follow his dreams even though it made her miserable. Insisting that the only way he could provide for her was by having everything his way.

He couldn't do that to Josie too.

He closed his eyes and let out a long, shuddering breath. He could have sworn he felt his soul rushing out too.

"I'll break it off."

Chapter Sixty-Five

Josie bustled around the kitchen, fixing herself a sandwich for dinner. After the rollercoaster of the last couple days, she didn't have the energy for anything more.

Thank heavens her phone call Monday night went all right. She'd planned to call Leighton but decided to cut out the middleman and phone Jimmy instead. He and the rest of the Hays crew were more likely to have to deal with the backlash. Jimmy had been so angry at first that she thought he might march to LA and lead an invasion of the *Celebrity Whispers* office, but once she told him about Merrill's press release, he simmered down.

And everything on set had been back to normal since then. There would probably still be some fallout from that dumb story, but Merrill would take care of it.

She was carrying her sandwich to the table when someone knocked on the door. She narrowed her eyes. She wasn't expecting anyone, and the only person who ever dropped by unannounced was Mrs. Pullman. She felt bad the poor old lady had been taken advantage of, but she wasn't ready to talk to her either.

She held her breath and didn't move, hoping Mrs. Pullman would decide she wasn't home and move on.

Another knock.

"Josie?" a familiar baritone called through the door. R.J.

She grinned, dropped her sandwich on the table, and dashed to the door. She'd been dying to go to his place, but she had a different brother calling each night to check on her, and she didn't want to worry them by not being home. And R.J. had said he thought it best if he didn't put himself in Mrs. Pullman's batty crosshairs by coming here.

Looks like he changed his mind, Josie Girl.

She giggled, ripped open the door, and flung her arms around his neck.

He didn't return the embrace. Ice shot down her spine, and she stepped back.

R.J.'s eyes were red-rimmed and puffy, and he hunched forward like his stomach hurt. Josie's entire body went cold. Something truly awful had to have happened to make him look like that. Her stomach dropped. Oh, sweet Lord, please don't let it be Matthew.

"Can I talk to you for a minute?" His voice was raw, like when he'd had the flu.

"Of course." She grabbed his hand and led him inside, hoping her fear didn't show on her face. She directed him to the couch. "You want something to drink?"

He shook his head. "I can't stay."

Why wouldn't he look at her? Her chest tightened. She sat next to him, and for once, the creaking sofa didn't make them laugh.

"What is it?" She reached for his hand, but he kept his curled together in his lap.

He stared at the floor. "I need to break things off between us."

She suddenly felt dizzy. If she hadn't been sitting down, she might have fallen over.

"What?"

At last, he looked up at her, his beautiful hazel eyes brimming. "I can't see you anymore, Josie. I'm no good for you."

Her jaw clenched. "Is this because of that stupid magazine?"

R.J. jumped to his feet and paced the tiny living room. "No, but yes, I guess, in a way." He scrubbed his hands through his hair, making it stick up in sheaves.

Josie stood, too, but didn't step close. He was pacing so fast he might run her over. "But Merrill fixed that. The press release." She reached a hand toward him, but it hung lonely in the empty space between them. Her stomach lurched, and she swallowed bile.

R.J. shook his head and kept pacing. "The press release won't be enough. The other gossip magazines are going to pick this up. They're going to tail our every move. They're going to eviscerate your reputation, and it will all be because of my dirty laundry."

She started trembling so hard she could barely stand, but she wasn't about to sit down. Sitting down felt like giving up, and she couldn't give up on R.J.

"I don't care about any of that," she said. Her voice shook even worse than her body. She could hardly speak around the choking lump knotted up in her throat. "I'll quit acting. I'll go back to nursing full time. Please. I love you."

He stopped pacing and looked at her, tears spilling down his cheeks. "I love you, too, Josie. That's why I can't do this to you. I can't ask you to make that sacrifice for me. I'm not worth it." He rubbed an arm across his eyes. "I'm sorry. I have to go."

Tears poured from her eyes in sheets so thick she

could barely see him turn and walk out her door. "R.J., wait!" She ran into the hall, but he was already halfway to the stairwell. She called his name again, but he didn't turn around. He kept walking, the stairwell door banging behind him like a gunshot.

Josie stumbled back into her apartment, slammed the door, and collapsed on the floor, sobbing.

****

Cassie's voice pulled her out of sleep. "Come on, Josie. You need to get up."

Josie pulled a pillow over her head. She'd rather die than go to the studio today. She felt like she was dying anyway. There was a giant hole somewhere in her middle, and the pain was going to kill her. What was the point of getting out of bed when she was never going to be happy again?

"I know how hard this must be, honey, but you've only got two days left. Just get through these two days, and then you'll have two whole months away from everything. Away from him."

A fresh round of tears spilled from Josie's eyes. She didn't want to be away from R.J. That was the problem. She curled her knees up to her chest and wept.

Cassie pulled the pillow off Josie's head and hauled her half onto her lap. Josie buried her face in her best friend's bosom until she ran out of tears, her throat and eyes burning.

She didn't know how long she'd sobbed on the floor last night after R.J. left, but eventually she dragged herself to the phone and dialed Cassie's number. As soon as she heard her friend's voice, she burst into tears again. Cassie had hung up and made it to Josie's place in record time.

"I called Beau last night after you fell asleep," Cassie said now. "I told him what happened. He wanted to come over, but I asked him to call Charlie and fill him in instead. They'll look after you today. Just stick close to them."

"I'm never going to be happy again," Josie said, her face muffled by Cassie's bathrobe. She didn't know what she would have done if Cassie hadn't stayed over last night. Probably cried herself to sleep on the living room floor.

"I know, honey," Cassie said, "but we still need to get you ready for work. Come on. You'll feel better once you wash your face."

Annoyingly, Josie did feel a smidge better after she washed her face and got the salt off her skin. But her stomach churned at the thought of having to see R.J. She'd never known she could be heartbroken and angry at the same time. And she wasn't sure if, when she saw him, she'd burst into tears or punch him in the nose for being an idiot about that stupid article. She supposed she could do both.

Charlie and Beau were waiting in the parking lot when Cassie pulled the Impala up. Josie hadn't felt up to driving, and Cassie said no way in hell was Josie taking the bus. She'd called the hospital, told them she'd be late, and grabbed the car keys.

As soon as they parked, Charlie pulled Josie out of the car and into his arms. He held her a long time before he and Beau escorted her to the soundstage. Beau and Cassie shared a quick smile, but didn't speak to each other, and while it shouldn't have been possible, Josie's heart broke a little more. Beau and Cassie had to keep their relationship quiet, too, and all because Josie had to show off at the airport. Tears trickled down her cheeks as she, Charlie, and Beau crossed the parking lot. She cringed when she spotted R.J.'s Corvette, but he must have still been in the dressing room, because she didn't see him anywhere.

R.J. didn't appear on set until just a couple minutes before they started shooting. Even with his stage makeup, his face was pale and haggard. He didn't look at her all morning, even when they played the same scene, which neither of them did well. They both caused third and fourth takes. Between scenes, he retreated to a corner and hid his face behind a book. It was like those first few months after Yosemite, only this time, Josie wasn't relieved. Now his distance ripped her to shreds. How was she supposed to survive two days of this? He was right there, but he'd never been farther away.

Sitting with Beau and Charlie in the commissary later, she barely picked at her lunch. She hadn't wanted any. She'd sat at their usual table without getting in line for food, but Charlie brought her a bowl of macaroni and cheese and a bottle of Coke. She ate a few bites, but she was too tired to eat. All she wanted to do was go home, crawl into bed, and sleep for a week. At least R.J. wasn't anywhere in sight.

"Good news, Josie," Merrill said, sidling up to their table. She looked dully up at him.

Good gravy, this man was an idiot, thinking there was still anything good in the world. She wanted to dump her macaroni and cheese all over his lumpy bald head.

Her face must not have betrayed her, though, because the producer continued talking with that same ugly pinched smile. If they ever needed a donkey on set, they had one.

"Your contract is done," he said. "I have it in my office, ready to sign. Come by when you're done eating."

Right. Her contract. Her three-year, full-time contract. The contract that was going to make her see R.J. every single day.

Beau smiled. "Well, that's some good news, isn't it, Josie?"

She looked at Charlie, who patted her knee under the table.

"Can I have a couple days to think about it?" she said.

Merrill's face puckered. "What's there to think about? You were thrilled when we talked about this."

Josie swallowed. "It's just, the hospital's really short on nurses, and—"

He sneered, and his voice turned sharp. "And they can't pay you anything close to what I can. Stop being foolish and come sign your contract like a good girl."

The sound of Charlie's chair scraping on the tile echoed across the commissary, and everyone in the dining room fell silent. Charlie stepped between Merrill and the table, drawing himself up to his full height. He towered over the producer.

"The lady asked for some time, Reynolds."

Startled, Josie reached across the table and grabbed Beau's hand.

Please just let it go, Charlie, she thought. She'd been on display more than enough this week already.

Merrill shrank down even smaller than usual. He peered around Charlie's broad frame at Josie. "You can have until tomorrow. I want it signed before we leave for the weekend." He scurried out of the commissary, passing a surprised-looking R.J., who had just come in.

372

Josie watched him go, careful not to look directly at R.J. As soon as Merrill was out the door, she turned to Beau and Charlie. "I'm not signing it."

Beau's mouth dropped open. "But you have to. It's what you've been hoping for all season."

She closed her eyes and shook her head, wrapping her arms around her stomach. "I can't."

"But—"

She opened her eyes and met his gaze. "Imagine if Cassie broke up with you. How would it be having to work with her every single day? Maybe if we were a bigger ensemble—" She choked off a sob, making a strangled sound.

Charlie put an arm around her. "It's all right, sweetheart. We don't want to lose you, but we understand." He kissed her temple. "You'll always be a part of the family."

Chapter Sixty-Six

R.J. came into the commissary several minutes after the rest of the cast so they wouldn't wind up near each other in line. Not that he was hungry. He hadn't eaten since lunch yesterday, and his stomach was so knotted he was beginning to think he might never want to eat again. But he didn't want to pass out on set twice in one season, so he forced himself to go to the commissary for a bowl of soup.

When he'd gotten home from Josie's last night, he'd collapsed onto his bed fully dressed and sobbed into his pillow like a child. He'd felt eyes on him and looked across the room at Jack and Matthew's smiling photos. He sprang up and turned them face down on his dresser, unable to bear looking at these reminders of how alone he was.

He didn't even have a photo of him and Josie. He'd never be able to stand looking at it if he did, but at least it would have been proof that, for one fleeting moment, he'd been whole.

He dropped back on his bed, trying futilely to forget the sound of Josie screaming "R.J., wait!" as he walked away. He could only drown it out by sobbing again. Sergeant jumped up next to him and whined, nudging him with his cold, wet nose. R.J. slung an arm around him, pulled him close, and cried into the dog's fur.

He didn't know when he fell asleep, but he woke this

morning stiff and sore from sleeping sideways across his bed with no pillow. Sergeant was still there, curled up next to him. He thought about bringing the dog to work today so he'd have someone there on his side, but Sergeant loved Josie. He'd run to her as soon as he saw her, and R.J. would have to fetch him back. And if he got close to Josie, he'd break in half.

He took a book instead and hid behind it during every break. Thank God for Beau and Charlie. Whenever they weren't filming, they turned their backs to him, forming a wall around Josie. Seeing them turn away from him hurt like hell, but he was grateful they were protecting Josie. They'd make sure she was okay.

He guessed correctly that they'd sit at their usual table in the commissary at lunch. He tried not to glance over when he went in, but he couldn't stop himself. Seeing his empty chair there made his eyes sting.

Don't look at them again, R.J. Just get your soup and get out.

But then Charlie's chair scraped across the floor, and R.J.'s head turned on reflex.

Charlie loomed over Merrill like he was about to lay him out.

Holy mackerel, Charlie was threatening Merrill. Why was Charlie threatening *anyone*? He got along with everybody. R.J. looked at Josie. He was too far away to see her expression, but he saw her reach across the table and grab Beau's hand, and it clicked.

Merrill must have upset Josie. That's the only reason Charlie would rear up like that. Adrenaline sang through R.J.'s veins. He should tear over there and tackle Merrill, smack his knobby head on the tile floor. Let *him* feel some pain for once.

But this was Charlie's job now. Josie didn't belong to him anymore.

"Hit him, Charlie," he muttered. He groaned when Charlie let Merrill slither away. He should quit staring, but now that he'd started, he couldn't stop. Charlie sat back down. Beau said something, and Josie shook her head. Then Charlie put his arm around her and kissed her forehead.

Forget the soup. He just wanted out of here.

****

The afternoon was just as agonizing as the morning. R.J. knew he wasn't playing his scenes well, but he couldn't help it. He couldn't act around the hole in his chest where Josie used to be. And he was getting lightheaded from not eating. Thank God they were done by 5:00 today. He never could have lasted longer. As soon as the director called a wrap on the last scene, he tore off to the dressing room to change.

He was buttoning his shirt when the door creaked, and Charlie stepped inside. R.J. nodded a hello. Surely Charlie wouldn't want to talk to him after what he'd done to Josie, but being rude and ignoring him wouldn't help. He almost fell over when Charlie came over and laid a hand on his shoulder.

"How are you doing, Robert?" Charlie's deep voice was gentle.

R.J. wanted to tell him that he was horrible. That he'd shattered the heart of the woman he loved more than life itself and he wasn't sure he could live with it. That he had no idea how he was going to manage the next three minutes, let alone the next three seasons.

He shrugged instead. Charlie patted his shoulder and grabbed his own clothes off the rack. He sat down on the sofa and started tugging off his boots.

It wasn't any of his business, but R.J. couldn't help asking, "What happened at lunch today?"

Charlie's eyebrows lifted. "I didn't think you were at lunch today."

"I came in for a minute. Saw you step between Merrill and Josie."

"Oh, Merrill just stopped by to tell Josie her contract was ready."

"And you threatened him for that?"

Charlie sighed and studied him for a moment. "I guess you'll hear it through the grapevine anyway. She asked for a day or two to think about it, but Merrill was pushing her to sign it right then. I let him know it was in his best interests to give her the time. Young lady's had a rough few days."

R.J. stared at him. Why did Josie need to think about it? If the contract had been ready the day Merrill first told her about it, she would have signed on the spot, he was sure of it.

A finger of ice trailed down his spine. *Oh, shit.*

"She's not going to sign it, is she?"

Charlie was buckling his belt and didn't look up. "I expect she will. Just needs to catch her breath."

Charlie Lyon was an excellent actor, but that was the least believable line R.J. had ever heard.

Josie wasn't going to sign her contract. He'd hurt her so badly she was going to leave the show. He felt dizzy, and it wasn't from hunger. He broke up with Josie so Merrill wouldn't fire her. He couldn't let her lose the show anyway just because she couldn't bear to be around him. He'd messed up so many things in his life. He had to fix this one.

****

R.J. shot out of the dressing room without saying goodbye to Charlie and sprinted all the way to the production office. He barged into Merrill's office.

Merrill was standing behind his desk, putting some papers in his briefcase. He looked up and scowled.

"Don't you know how to knock?"

"I quit."

"What?"

R.J. panted, trying to catch his breath. "I quit."

Merrill squinted and pointed to a chair. "Sit down before you fall down." R.J. sat. His head was spinning anyway. Merrill sat, too, and steepled his fingers under his chin. "Let me guess. Being on set with Josie is too painful to bear, so you're running."

R.J. shook his head so hard his brain rattled. "Being on set with me is too painful for her, so she's not going to sign her contract."

Merrill's left eyebrow pricked up. "She told you that?"

R.J. shook his head again, gentler this time. "I just know Josie. She doesn't stick around to let the same man hurt her twice. She's not going to sign."

Merrill's nose whistled with a long exhalation. "To be honest, I got the same impression." He rubbed his temples. "You've really messed this up for everyone, Coolidge."

"And I'm trying to fix it."

Merrill looked up. "You already signed on for the next three seasons."

"Release me. You can do that."

"What would you do instead?"

"My agent will find me something." Larry knew

he'd been unhappy on *Gunslingers* and had suggested auditioning for a few pilots this season. It might not be too late to pick one up. And Ed was a director. He might have some leads too. R.J. could even return to theater in New York if he had to, but Josie didn't have any of those connections.

Merrill snickered. "You haven't thought this through, have you?"

R.J. rubbed his hands through his hair. "Why are you toying with me? We've been stones in each other's shoes for two years. I'm offering to leave. Just let me go."

A muscle jumped in Merrill's jaw. "So you can badmouth me to the press? Tell them I broke you and Josie apart? I don't think so."

"You *did* break us apart!" R.J. slammed his fist on Merrill's desk. Shockwaves screamed up his arm, and he watched through blurry eyes as the cast photo from the Christmas party jumped and fell off the desk. The glass smashed on the floor.

Merrill scooted his chair back and bumped into his little shelf of liquor bottles. "Fine." His voice trembled, and R.J. felt a surge of triumph. "You want out. Here." He yanked open a desk drawer and ripped out a file with R.J.'s name on it. He pulled out the contract R.J. had signed just a few weeks before, grabbed the cigarette lighter off his desk, and lit the corner of the contract. Flames licked up the document, and he flung it into the metal trashcan next to the desk.

"You're out," he said. He jabbed a finger at R.J. "But if I hear so much as a whisper about any of this, Josie is fired. If I catch wind of the two of you seeing each other again, Josie is fired. I still have to protect the character."

R.J. cradled his hand and gritted his teeth against the piercing bolts of pain shooting up his arm. "Fine," he said between panting breaths.

"You finish out this week, and you're done. I'll have fun killing off your character."

Chapter Sixty-Seven

The last thing Josie wanted to do first thing the next morning was "gather 'round for a quick meeting," as Merrill said. She didn't mind gathering with Charlie and Beau, but Merrill called for the whole cast, which meant R.J. too.

Cassie had stayed over again last night and forced Josie to eat dinner before she'd let her collapse in bed. She'd slept better, but she still felt so heavy and numb. Thank goodness today was her last day. She had to tell Merrill tonight that she wasn't signing the new contract, but after that, she could go back to being Nurse Donovan and forget that this whole ridiculous year ever happened.

At least she'd made good money. Her savings account was healthier than it had ever been.

When the cast and Merrill gathered in a lopsided circle, she tucked in between Charlie and Beau, and Charlie put an arm around her shoulders. R.J. was directly across from her. She flicked her eyes down so she wouldn't have to look at him, but she wasn't fast enough to miss noticing something was wrong. Keeping her head low, she raised her eyes for another look.

R.J. held his right hand close to his body. It was swollen, puffed up to almost twice its usual size, and the edge from his pinky to his wrist was blanketed by a nasty purple bruise. She sucked in a breath.

Good gravy, what had happened? His Corvette was

in the parking lot when she arrived this morning, as pristine as ever, so he couldn't have been in a wreck. She ached to rush over to him, to ask what happened, to examine his hand. But she couldn't. She'd made it twelve whole hours without crying. If she got close to him, she'd wreck her streak.

He's a big boy, Josie Girl. He can take care of himself.

She looked away and focused on Merrill.

"I've got some news for everyone about next season," he said. "Or rather, Coolidge does." He looked at R.J. "They should hear it from you."

Josie's stomach fluttered, and she clutched her midsection. What news could he have about next season? She leaned in closer to Charlie.

R.J. took a small step forward and cleared his throat. He kept his eyes on the ground and tucked his injured hand behind his back.

"I'm not coming back next season."

Josie's face stung like she'd been slapped. How was this possible? He'd already signed his contract. He'd been thrilled about it.

"But you already signed the new contract," Beau said, mirroring Josie's thoughts. His eyes were as big as Josie imagined hers must be.

R.J. shifted and looked to Merrill.

"I agreed to release him," the producer said, "so he'd be free to pursue other opportunities."

"You have something lined up?" Charlie said. He pulled Josie a tiny bit closer to his side.

R.J. shook his head. "Nothing set in stone yet, but my agent has some promising leads."

Promising leads? R.J. was leaving a sure thing for a

possibility? That didn't sound right. Especially not when he was planning to buy Laura and Matthew a new car. He wouldn't do anything to shortchange his son.

But then again, he'd never liked this job. Maybe these leads were more than just promising and he didn't want to say more. He'd always played his cards close to his vest.

"We'll certainly miss you," Charlie said. "You've been an asset to the cast."

R.J. nodded and muttered a thank you.

"We'll have to throw you a sending-off party next week," Beau said.

Josie almost laughed. R.J. would rather die than have a party thrown in his honor.

"Actually, today is my last day," R.J. said.

Josie's head snapped back. Next to her, Beau sucked in air. Those leads had to be more than merely promising.

"But you're in next week's episode," Charlie said.

Merrill shook his head. "I'll have revised scripts for you and Beau by the end of the day. In the meantime, let's wrap up this episode. I'm sure everyone's eager to start their weekend." He clapped his hands once and smiled like he'd just delivered good news.

Josie glanced to each side of her. On her right, Charlie stood staring at R.J., the arm around her shoulders limp. To her left, Beau stood wide-eyed and slack-jawed. Still in the middle of their little circle, R.J. stared at the ground, his puffy hand pressed to his abdomen. Charlie took his arm off Josie's shoulders and stepped forward.

"In case I don't get a chance to say it later, good luck to you," he told R.J. "I'd shake your hand, but..." He pointed to R.J.'s damaged hand.

"Yeah, what did you do?" Beau said.

"Just an accident. It's fine."

Beau clapped him on the back. "We'll miss you," he said.

All four men looked at Josie.

She couldn't bring herself to meet R.J.'s gaze, so she simply pointed to his hand.

"You should get that x-rayed," she said. Then she turned and strode away without looking back.

****

"I've changed my mind," Josie told Beau and Charlie at lunch. "I'm going to sign the contract."

Beau whooped, and Charlie hugged her.

"I'm so glad to hear that," Charlie said. "I hate to see Robert go, but I'd be lying if I said I wasn't hoping that would change your mind."

"Same here," Beau said, hugging her too.

Josie smiled for the first time in two days. "Seems foolish to pass it up now."

R.J. leaving the show so abruptly had niggled her all morning. It seemed like an awfully big coincidence that his agent found promising leads in the thirty-six hours since they'd broken up. Things could happen fast in Hollywood—she, of all people, knew that—but R.J. hadn't mentioned having Larry look for other opportunities over the past few weeks. He'd been excited about the promise of Deacon Bell's solo episode next season and the big pay raise.

She was certain he was leaving so she would stay. Charlie and Beau wouldn't have told him she wasn't planning to sign her contract, but he could have guessed. Except for that night in Yosemite, he'd always read her well.

Her heart broke thinking about it. Sweet little Matthew was going to lose out so she could keep a job she didn't need.

And to top it all off, R.J. was injured. What in the world had he done to his hand?

He'd had to fire his gun during a scene this morning, and when it went off, he turned so pale she thought he'd pass out. The blanks in the prop guns didn't kick much but pulling that trigger still must have hurt like crazy.

But there was nothing she could do about any of it. Even if she quit the show now, Merrill had released R.J. from his contract. Regardless of what she did, he had to find a new job. The best thing she could do now was sign her contract so Matthew's loss wasn't a complete waste.

****

As soon as the director called a wrap that afternoon, Josie darted to the production office. She didn't want to stick around for R.J.'s goodbyes to everyone. His goodbye to her two nights ago had been more than enough.

Halfway to Merrill's office, though, she realized she might never see R.J. again. He'd never be back on set, and she certainly wouldn't see him off set. She ducked into the ladies' restroom just before she came apart. She locked herself in a stall and sobbed. The thought of having to see him on set every day had been bad, but knowing she might never see him again at all—in person, anyway—was so much worse. She'd never smell his aftershave, feel his breath on her neck, rest her head on his chest and fall asleep... She couldn't stop the flood of memories, every little moment with R.J. Taking his temperature when he was sick, his arm around her at Disneyland, his hand on her back during the photo at the

Christmas party. And all those moments they'd been planning to have.

Maybe she shouldn't sign the contract after all. Maybe she should just pack up everything and run back to Kansas with her tail between her legs. She wouldn't have to go back to Hays. Leighton could get her a job at his hospital in Wichita. She could fade into the world like everyone else. At least she'd still have the Impala.

She smiled a little at that, remembering the way Charlie had dickered the salesman down on the price.

Oh, Papa Bear.

Charlie and his wife had been so kind, practically adopting her as their fourth child. Well, fifth, if you counted Beau.

And Beau.

Never seeing R.J. again will be bad enough, Josie Girl. Can you give up Charlie and Beau too?

She couldn't. She dried her eyes, splashed some cold water on her face, and headed toward Merrill's office again.

"You're making the right decision," the producer said, sliding her contract and a pen across his desk. There was a small chip in the wood on the edge of the desk that she was sure hadn't been there before. It was a fresh wound, too, with a couple little splinters hanging off it, not smooth with age. "I would have hated to see you throw everything away too."

She looked up from the damaged desk, her brow knit. "What do you mean 'too'?"

"Coolidge, obviously." He turned and grabbed the Jim Beam and two lowballs off his shelf.

"He said he has promising leads."

Merrill snorted. "Sure he does." He opened the

whiskey and began to pour.

Her stomach rolled. Merrill had just confirmed her suspicions. R.J. didn't have a thing lined up. He'd launched himself off the trapeze with no safety net.

"I always thought he was too emotional for this business," Merrill said, handing her a glass of Jim Beam. "Running away from a pile of money just because the job broke his little heart." He shook his head.

Josie's own heart thumped, and her hand stopped halfway to the glass Merrill extended. "What do you mean the *job* broke his heart?"

Merrill's lips puckered and relaxed so fast that if Josie had blinked, she would have missed it. But years of observing patients had made her quick. Her nostrils flared.

Son of a bitch.

"You made him break up with me, didn't you?"

He thrust the whiskey toward her. "Why would I do that?"

"Because you're protecting the show, which means you're protecting yourself." Good gravy, how had she never realized what a selfish person he was? Merrill Reynolds didn't care about her. He'd proved that with all his talk about protecting her "image," not with protecting her. All he cared about were the ratings, because ratings meant more money in his pocket. And he didn't care how many hearts he stomped on to get that money. He was using her for his own gain, just like Ethan had.

That same white-hot anger she'd felt when she saw Ethan at the diner over Christmas flared through her veins. She'd come to California for a new start, and here she was in the same situation.

But this time, she wasn't letting the pathetic little

man win.

She smacked the glass out of Merrill's hand. It dropped on his desk with a clank, the bourbon creeping like an amber snake across her unsigned contract.

"That was uncalled for," Merrill said, pushing his glasses up the bridge of his nose.

"So was threatening Robert." Josie jumped to her feet and leaned across the desk, putting her nose only inches from his. "Because that's what you did, isn't it? You threatened to fire him if he didn't break up with me."

Merrill leaned back. "What good would that have done? He left anyway." Sweat beaded where his hairline should have been. He was hiding something.

Icy realization stabbed Josie through the heart. "You threatened to fire *me*, didn't you?" Her chest constricted. R.J. had tried to protect her job. This job he knew she loved. This job Merrill would have ripped away from her if R.J. hadn't broken things off. Her hands balled into fists on the desktop. Merrill had used those emotions R.J. carried so much closer to the surface than most people realized against him. She wanted to grab the producer by his shirt collar and shake him until his teeth rattled.

Merrill smirked. "Don't let Coolidge lose the best job he'll ever get for nothing. Sign your contract, Josie."

She narrowed her eyes and feinted toward him, smiling when he flinched. "Not on your life."

She turned and strode for the door.

"Josie!" Merrill called, his voice acid. "If you walk out of here, you'll be making a big mistake."

Josie turned, her hand on the doorknob. "Maybe so, but at least it won't be as big as the mistake you already made."

Merrill scowled. "Oh? And what's that?"

"Thinking I needed you."

She wrenched the door open and stalked out. She needed to find R.J.

Chapter Sixty-Eight

R.J. tore out of the studio as soon as the director called a wrap that afternoon. He didn't want to stick around for drawn-out goodbyes with people he'd barely ever spoken to anyway. But he would have liked to talk to Josie one more time. Apologized to her or tried to say something that would explain why he had to leave her and the show without tipping off Merrill. But she'd darted away right at the end of shooting too.

And he'd likely never see her again. Not in person, anyway.

He suddenly couldn't breathe. He gasped, trying to suck in air, but the harder he fought, the tighter his throat cinched. He was suffocating right here in his car. He yanked on the steering wheel, pain screaming through his injured hand, and parked in front of a gas station. He was fourteen years old again, sitting high up in a cypress tree, sobbing for his dead brother—the only other person he'd ever lost so completely.

What he'd give to talk to Jack right now. Jack always knew how to fix whatever fiasco R.J. found himself in. He always understood, and he never ratted to Mom and Dad.

Oh, God, Mom and Dad. They always asked about Josie when he called on Sundays. He was going to have to tell them. Strangely, the thought soothed him enough that he could inhale. Mom would fuss over him, probably offer to fly out, and Dad would have something wise to say.

He didn't want to wait until Sunday. Ignoring the stabbing pain in his hand, he slammed the car into gear and took off for home.

As soon as he got home, he threw some food into Sergeant's bowl and grabbed the phone. Even his index finger on his right hand was so swollen now that he couldn't manage the rotary, and he had to dial with his left.

"Hello?"

R.J. sank into a chair.

"Dad." His voice cracked on the single syllable.

"R.J.?"

"Dad, I messed up."

"What happened? Are you all right?"

R.J. blurted out the entire story from the article breaking over the weekend to Merrill threatening to fire Josie if he didn't break up with her to his quitting the show so Josie would stay. Dad listened quietly through the whole saga.

"God above, son," he said when R.J. ran out of story. "Why didn't you just tell Josie everything and let her decide what she wanted to do?"

"I couldn't be selfish again."

"What are you talkin' about?"

R.J. took a deep breath. Thank God they were talking on the phone and he didn't have to look his father in the eye right now. He stared at the puffy, bruised hand in his lap. "I made Laura miserable dragging her to New York City. I robbed her of the life she wanted in Hell Hole. I couldn't wreck Josie's life by robbing her of acting. She loves it."

"Laura *is* in Hell Hole, son. With a beautiful little boy she adores and a good job at the post office. When she realized how unhappy she was, she did something about it. Doesn't seem to me like you robbed her of anything."

R.J. sat on that for moment. Dad had a point. "But Josie—"

For the first time in R.J.'s memory, Dad interrupted someone. "R.J., let me ask you this. What are you planning to do now that *you* don't have that job anymore?"

R.J. frowned. "I called my agent last night. And Ed. They both have some good leads. Pilot season isn't quite over, and there's always movies being shot. I'm better known than I used to be. I'll land something."

He could almost hear Dad nodding over the phone. He imagined his father adjusting his glasses and leaning back in his chair. "And did it never occur to you, my boy, that a good agent or your friend Ed could find Josie other parts too? Seems to me this whole issue with her image is only attached to her role on *Gunslingers*."

Dear God. R.J.'s stomach lurched. If this had been an episode of the show, they would have dubbed in the sound of a cricket chirping.

Dad chuckled. "Apparently, you didn't. It's all right. He had you cornered. I'm sure you couldn't think straight." His voice grew serious again. "But you've gotta fix this, son. Do not lose her."

****

R.J. ripped down Santa Monica Boulevard toward Josie's apartment. He had no idea what he was going to say beyond, "I'm sorry," but he had to at least say that much. His hand screamed with every gear shift. He probably should have it looked at, like Josie said, but it would have to wait.

He parked crooked outside Josie's building and tore up the stairs to the second floor. He banged on the door with his left hand and waited for an eternity. At last, he heard footsteps on the other side. Between his pounding heart and the pain shooting through his hand, there was a good chance he was going to throw up all over Josie as soon as she answered the door. He took a deep breath, trying to settle himself.

The door creaked open, and he swallowed bile.

"Robert!" Cassie said, one hand flying to her chest. "What are you doing here?"

His knees wobbled. Why was Cassie here? Please, God, don't let her be about to chase him off. He'd die right on the spot.

"I need to talk to Josie. Please."

Cassie blinked. "She's supposed to be with you. She called from the studio a little bit ago babbling something about Merrill being a snake in the grass and how she had to find you right away. I only caught about half of it. She was talking a mile a minute."

R.J. rested his hand on the doorframe to lean against it and regretted it as soon as his swollen hand brushed the wood. He sucked in air between his teeth and told himself to man up. His hand didn't matter right now. Josie was looking for him.

Cassie's gaze shifted to his hand, and her lips parted. "Oh, my goodness, what happened?" She reached for his hand, but R.J. stepped back.

"When did she call?"

Cassie looked skyward. "Five, ten minutes ago maybe. I figured she was going straight to your house from the studio."

He turned and leaned his back against the doorframe. Five or ten minutes ago. They probably passed each other on Santa Monica Boulevard and he didn't even notice. He ran his good hand through his hair.

"She's probably nearly at my house," he said. A spurt of laughter popped out of him. He straightened and turned to Cassie. "If I miss her, if she comes back here, please tell her to call me."

Cassie smiled. "I will. I promise."

He grinned. "Thank you, Cassie." He turned and sprinted back down the hall.

"Good luck!" Cassie called after him. "And have a doctor look at that hand!"

Chapter Sixty-Nine

Sergeant barked inside the house, but R.J. didn't come to the door. Josie had no idea if his car was in the garage—it was too dark to see through the windows—but there didn't seem to be any lights on inside the house. If he was home, he was doing a good job of looking like he wasn't.

Where was he? He wouldn't have left Sergeant home alone if he left town, and he couldn't have left town this quickly anyway. They only wrapped shooting an hour ago. After her chat with Merrill, she'd stopped at the studio gates and asked the guard to use his phone. She called Cassie and tried to explain what happened, but she was still shaking, and she didn't think she made a whole lot of sense. Hopefully Cassie got the gist of what she meant.

She knocked on R.J.'s door one more time and waited. Still nothing. Tears rose in her eyes. She wasn't going to be able to fix this tonight after all. She trudged back to the Impala and was just about to back out of the driveway when a car whipped around the corner and screeched to a stop in front of the house.

A very familiar black Corvette with white swoops on the side panels.

She set the Impala's brake, slumped in her seat, and pressed her hands to her eyes. She took a deep breath and blew it out slowly, then opened her door.

R.J. was already there, offering his hand to help her out of the car. His left hand, she noticed. Even in the dim light from the streetlamp, she could see his right hand was still a mess. She looked up at his face, and he swallowed hard. She thought she saw his chin tremble. She took his hand, and as soon as her skin touched his, that familiar surge of energy traveled through her. The tears spilled from her eyes, and she wrapped her arms around his waist and buried her face in his chest, breathing in his familiar musky scent. He made a choked sort of sound and gathered her in his arms.

They held onto each other silently for a long time until another car came down the street, slowing as it passed. They both watched it.

R.J. cleared his throat. "We should talk inside."

Josie nodded, closed her car door, and held his hand as they mounted the steps and went into the house. Sergeant danced around her, and she grinned and scratched his head. R.J. clicked on a lamp and turned to her. He opened his mouth, but she reached up and pressed a finger to his lips. Those soft, warm lips.

"I know he threatened to fire me if you didn't break things off."

R.J. closed his eyes and nodded, the anguish on his face tearing her heart into little pieces. She slid her hand to his cheek, and he opened his eyes again.

"Why didn't you just tell me?"

He sighed, took her hand, and led her to the couch. They sat, R.J. still clinging to her hand with his good one. She got a better look at his right hand. He had to have broken it. No wonder he'd been in so much pain on set.

He wouldn't meet her gaze. "I couldn't stand to see you lose the part. You love it." He drew in a shaky breath. "I was afraid telling you would be selfish of me."

Josie wrinkled her brow. "Selfish? Why in the world would you think that?" R.J. kept his eyes down, and a fresh wave of anger swept over her. That bald little bastard. She should have shaken him. "What did Merrill say to you?"

"He said I'd already wrecked Laura and Matthew's lives by insisting on having my way, and he didn't figure I could live with it if I did it again." He swallowed. "I realize now he was wrong, but at the time..."

Josie seethed. How fast could her brothers get here? They'd fix Merrill's flint.

Focus, Josie Girl. Revenge later. R.J. now.

"I'm so sorry, Josie," he said. "I should have told you everything."

"Yes, you should have," she said. At last, his eyes snapped up, and he met her gaze. She melted into those gold-flecked irises. "But I understand why you didn't. He pulled the same trick on you that Ethan used to pull on me. Covering up his own bad behavior by making you think you were the one who'd done something wrong."

R.J.'s eyes widened. "If you'd been a better wife, he wouldn't have had to cheat."

"Exactly."

He rubbed his face with both hands and yelped, snapping the injured one back to his chest. She wasn't giving him a choice anymore. She gently grasped his wrist and drew his hand toward her. The bruising had spread from the outer edge halfway across his hand. Her eyes swam.

"Oh, R.J., what happened?" She raised her eyes from his hand to his face.

He ducked his head. "Slammed it on Merrill's desk

yesterday."

She remembered the splintered edge on Merrill's desk. Good gravy, R.J. had done that?

"On purpose?" she said.

He shrugged. "I was yelling at him for splitting us up." He looked up, a smile playing at the corners of his mouth. "He's lucky I hit his desk and not his face."

Josie snickered. She'd have paid good money to see the look on Merrill's face when R.J. lost it. She ran a finger lightly down his hand from the base of his pinky toward his wrist, and he gasped and drew back. She looked up. His face had gone pale. "Can you bend your pinky?"

He shook his head.

She frowned. "I'm betting you broke this fifth metacarpal. Come on. I'll drive you to the ER."

"I can drive myself."

"Yeah, I'm sure shifting with that hand is real comfortable." She grinned at his sheepish expression. "Besides, I know some of the doctors."

He took her chin with his good hand, and she closed her eyes, soaking in the moment. Goodness gracious, how she'd missed his touch. Two days had felt like forever.

"He'll still fire you if we're spotted together," R.J. said.

She laughed, and he snatched his hand away. She took it in hers.

"I'm off the show anyway. I didn't sign the new contract." She smirked. "In fact, I dumped Jim Beam on it."

A wave of horror crossed his face. "But—"

"After Ethan, I promised myself I'd never let

another man treat me like that. I wasn't about to go back on that promise, no matter how much money was involved."

R.J. groaned and closed his eyes. "After everything we've been through, you're unemployed anyway."

"Speak for yourself. I work for Hollywood Presbyterian."

He laughed, dimpling his cheek, and Josie's heart soared.

"I'll ask Nurse Fletcher on Monday to schedule me back full time. She'll say yes. Hospitals are always short on nurses. But what about you?" Typical R.J. Worried about her even when his own world was collapsing around him. She squeezed his hand, and he squeezed back.

"Larry really does have some good leads for me. I wasn't making that up. I'll find something. And I've got enough savings to carry me through a dry spell."

He studied her, and she smiled. She knew that look on his face. He wanted to ask a question but wasn't sure if he should. She raised her eyebrows expectantly, and he chuckled.

"If you'd like," he said, "I'm sure Larry could look out for roles for you too. I can put you in touch with him."

An acting role besides *Gunslingers*? Golly, she'd never even thought of that. Now she felt kind of stupid. Of course there were other parts out there. She had a little recognition now. R.J.'s agent might be able to scare up something she'd love just as much. And if he came up empty-handed, she still had a good job at the hospital.

She smiled. "I'd like that, thank you."

R.J. grinned, then grew serious. He dropped his eyes

to his lap and ran his thumb across the back of her hand. "So now what? About us, I mean." He swallowed hard. "Would you ever take me back?"

Tears stung her eyes, and her heart nearly burst with love for him. How could he think she wouldn't take him back? She had to swallow hard, too, before she could speak.

"Oh, R.J. I never let you go in the first place."

He looked up, the single tear trickling down his cheek mirroring the one she felt escape from her own eye. His voice shook when he spoke.

"I love you so much, Josie."

"I love you too."

She crawled into his lap—carefully, so she didn't bump his bad hand—and wrapped her arms around his neck. She buried her face in the space where his shoulder and neck met and breathed him in. He threaded his arms around her and pressed her to his chest. She gave up trying not to cry. His chest hitched, and she knew he had too. She felt a hand press to the back of her head, and then R.J. sucked in a sharp breath. He must have used his right hand without thinking. She lifted her head and pulled back. His eyes were red, and she was sure hers matched.

She was about to say they should head to the hospital, but reunited and with their faces so close together, there was only one thing she could do. She leaned forward and crushed her lips against his. He groaned and kissed her back. His good hand slid to the small of her back, and he pressed her hips against his. She felt him stir beneath her, and her hands reached automatically for his shirt buttons. She'd unfastened the top three before she remembered something.

"Darn it," she said, pulling back.

"What's wrong?"

"My diaphragm's at home."

R.J. let out a theatrical groan, buried his face in her bosom, and laughed. She giggled and played with the tiny hairs on the back of his neck.

He lifted his head. "Can we go get it?"

"Absolutely."

He grinned.

"Just as soon as we get you that x-ray."

He laughed again, and this time, she planted a kiss right on his dimple.

Epilogue

From *TV Week* magazine, week of September 10-16, 1960. Listings for Sunday, September 11:

Former *Gunslingers* co-stars Robert "R.J." Coolidge and Josephine Donovan sizzle as a husband-and-wife detective team on *Cracking the Case*. Our critics smell a hit. Debuting tonight, 8:00 p.m., CBS.

Author's Note

No U.S. state recognized marital rape as the crime it is until 1976 when Nebraska eliminated the spousal exception in its definition of rape. Prior to that, the law was that the marriage contract itself provided permanent consent, so a man had a right to sex with his wife. This spousal exception was not eliminated nationwide until 1993.

No-fault divorce didn't arrive until 1969, when California Governor Ronald Reagan signed the nation's first no-fault divorce bill. By 1977, all but three states allowed for no-fault divorce. New York was the final holdout, not passing a no-fault statute until 2010. Until then, a spouse wishing to end a marriage had to make a charge against the other, most commonly adultery, cruelty, or abandonment. However, as is too often the case, these charges favored men. A man whose wife refused him sex could sue for divorce on the grounds of abandonment, but because of the spousal exceptions in rape laws, a woman whose husband raped her could not claim that rape as a form of cruelty.

Celebrity Whispers is the product of my imagination, but it is based on Robert Harrison's magazine *Confidential*, which during its run from 1952-1958 claimed to tell the facts and name the names. *Confidential* focused on A-list celebrities and politicians, but it inspired many other gossip magazines that spread rumors and half-truths about lesser celebrities. Placing a wristwatch on a back tire to record the time someone left was a trick used by *Confidential*'s reporters. By 1959-1960, most producers would have been a bit less worried about actresses' images than they were in the 1940s and early 1950s, but as with every cultural shift, there were conservative holdouts.

If you need help escaping an abusive relationship, please call the National Domestic Violence Hotline at 800.799.SAFE (7233).

A word about the author...

Sarah Hendess is a teacher, runner, and cross-stitcher who grew up in Hutchinson, KS, and Pittsburgh, PA. She now lives in Lake Mary, FL, with her husband, son, two cats, one miniature dachshund, and a 21-year-old turtle.

Follow her on Facebook at:

http://www.facebook.com/sarahhendessauthor

Follow her on Instagram at:

@thewritehendess

Or on Twitter at:

@SarahHendess

Thank you for purchasing
this publication of The Wild Rose Press, Inc.

For questions or more information
contact us at
info@thewildrosepress.com.

The Wild Rose Press, Inc.